# MUTATION

## Also by Robin Cook

# MUTATION

## Robin Cook

MACMILLAN
LONDON

First published in the United States of America 1989
by G. P. Putnam's Sons

First published in the United Kingdom 1989 by
MACMILLAN LONDON LIMITED
4 Little Essex Street London WC2R 3LF
and Basingstoke

Associated companies in Auckland, Delhi, Dublin, Gaborone,
Hamburg, Harare, Hong Kong, Johannesburg, Kuala Lumpur,
Lagos, Manzini, Melbourne, Mexico City, Nairobi, New York,
Singapore and Tokyo

A CIP catalogue record for this book is available from the
British Library.

ISBN 0-333-49656-6

Printed in England

*Thanks to Jean, who provided lots of literal and figurative nourishment.*

## To Grandparents

*For Mae and Ed, whom I wish I had known better*
*For Esther and John, who welcomed me into their family*
*For Louise and Bill, who adopted me out of pure*
*generosity.*

"HOW DARE YOU SPORT THUS WITH LIFE."

Mary Wollstonecraft Shelley
*Frankenstein* (1818)

ENERGY *had been building within the millions of neurons since they'd first formed six months previously. The nerve cells were sizzling with electrical energy steadily galvanizing toward a voltaic threshold. The arborization of the nerve cells' dendrites and the supporting microglia cells had been increasing at an exponential rate, with hundreds of thousands of new synaptic connections arising every hour. It was like a nuclear reactor on the brink of hypercriticality.*

*At last it happened! The threshold was reached and surpassed. Microbolts of electric charges spread like wildfire through the complicated plexus of synaptic connections, energizing the whole mass. Intracellular vesicles poured forth their neurotransmitters and neuromodulators, increasing the level of excitation to another critical point.*

*Out of this complex microscopic cellular activity emerged one of the mysteries of the universe: consciousness! Mind had once more been born of matter.*

*Consciousness was the faculty that provided founda-*

*tion for memory and meaning; and also terror and dread. With consciousness came the burden of knowledge of eventual death. But at that moment, the consciousness created was consciousness without awareness. Awareness was next and soon to come.*

# Prologue

"Oh, God!" Mary Millman said, gripping the sheets with both hands. The agony was starting again in her lower abdomen, spreading rapidly into her groin and into her lower back like a shaft of molten steel.

"Give me something for the pain! Please! I can't stand it!" Then she screamed.

"Mary, you're doing fine," Dr. Stedman said calmly. "Just take deep breaths." He was putting on a pair of rubber gloves, snapping the fingers into place.

"I can't take it," Mary cried hoarsely. She twisted herself into a different position, but it didn't provide any relief. Each second the pain intensified. She held her breath and, by reflex, contracted every muscle in her body.

"Mary!" Dr. Stedman said firmly, grabbing Mary's arm. "Don't push! It won't help until your cervix is dilated. And it might hurt the baby!"

Mary opened her eyes and tried to relax her body. Her breath came out in an agonized groan. "I can't help it," she whimpered through tears. "Please—I

13

can't take it. *Help me!"* Her words were lost in another shriek.

Mary Millman was a twenty-two-year-old secretary who worked for a department store in downtown Detroit. When she'd seen the advertisement to be a surrogate mother, the idea of the money had seemed like a godsend—a perfect way for her to finally settle the seemingly endless debts left from her mother's long illness. But never having been pregnant or seen a birth, except in movies, she'd had no idea what it would be like. At the moment she couldn't think about the thirty thousand dollars she was to receive when it was all over, a figure much higher than the "going" fee for surrogacy in Michigan, the one state where an infant could be adopted before birth. She thought she was going to die.

The pain peaked, then leveled off. Mary was able to snatch a few shallow breaths. "I need a pain shot," she said with some difficulty." Her mouth was dry.

"You've already had two," Dr. Stedman answered. He was preoccupied with removing the pair of gloves he'd contaminated by grabbing her arm, replacing them with a new and sterile pair.

"I don't feel them," Mary moaned.

"Maybe not at the height of a contraction," Dr. Stedman said, "but just a few moments ago you were asleep."

"I was?" Mary looked up for confirmation into the face of Marsha Frank, one of the adoptive parents, who was gently wiping her forehead with a cool, damp washcloth. Marsha nodded. She had a warm, empathetic smile. Mary liked her and was thankful Marsha had insisted on being present at the birth.

Both Franks had made that a condition of the agreement, though Mary was less enthusiastic about the prospective father, who was constantly barking orders at her.

"Remember, the baby gets whatever medications you get," he was now saying sharply. "We can't jeopardize his life just to ease your pain."

Dr. Stedman gave Victor Frank a quick look. The man was getting on his nerves. As far as Dr. Stedman was concerned, Frank was the worst prospective father he'd ever allowed in the labor room. What made it particularly astounding was that Frank was a physician himself and had had obstetric training before going into research. If he had had such experience, it certainly didn't show in his bedside manner. A long sigh from Mary brought Dr. Stedman's attention back to his patient.

The grimace that had distorted Mary's face slowly faded. The contraction was obviously over. "Okay," Dr. Stedman said, motioning for the nurse to lift the sheet covering Mary's legs. "Let's see what's going on." He bent over and positioned Mary's legs.

"Maybe we should do an ultrasound?" Victor suggested. "I don't think we're making much progress."

Dr. Stedman straightened up. "Dr. Frank! If you don't mind . . ." He let his sentence trail off, hoping that his tone conveyed his irritation.

Victor Frank looked up at Dr. Stedman, and Stedman suddenly realized the man was terrified. Frank's face was porcelain white, with beads of perspiration along his hairline. Perhaps using a surrogate was a unique strain even for a doctor.

"Oh!" exclaimed Mary. There was a sudden gush of

fluid onto the bed, drawing Dr. Stedman's attention back to his patient. For the moment he forgot about Frank.

"That's the rupture of the membranes," Dr. Stedman said. "It's entirely normal, as I explained before. Let's see where we are with this baby."

Mary closed her eyes. She felt fingers going back inside of her. Lying in sheets drenched with her own fluid, she felt humiliated and vulnerable. She'd told herself she was doing this not just for the money but to bring happiness to a couple who couldn't have another baby. Marsha had been so sweet and persuasive. Now she wondered if she'd done the right thing. Then another contraction forced all thought from her head.

"Well, well!" Dr. Stedman exclaimed. "Very good, Mary. Very good indeed." He snapped off the rubber gloves and tossed them aside. "The baby's head is now engaged and your cervix is almost entirely dilated. Good girl!" He turned to the nurse. "Let's move the show into the delivery room."

"Can I have some pain medicine now?" Mary asked.

"Just as soon as we get in the delivery room," Dr. Stedman said cheerfully. He was relieved. Then he felt a hand on his arm.

"Are you sure the head isn't too big?" asked Victor abruptly, pulling Dr. Stedman aside.

Dr. Stedman could feel a tremor in the hand that gripped his arm. He reached up and peeled away the fingers. "I said the head was engaged. That means the head has passed through the pelvic inlet. I'm certain you remember that!"

"Are you sure the head is engaged?" asked Victor.

A wave of resentment wafted through Dr. Stedman. He was about to lose his temper, but he saw that Frank

16

was trembling with anxiety. Holding his anger in check, Stedman just said, "The head is engaged. I'm certain." Then he added: "If this is upsetting you, perhaps it would be best if you went to the waiting room."

"I couldn't!" Victor said with emphasis. "I've got to see this thing through."

Dr. Stedman gazed at Dr. Frank. From the first meeting, he'd had a strange feeling about this man. For a while, he'd attributed Frank's uneasiness to the surrogacy situation, but it was more than that. And Dr. Frank was more than the worried father. "I've got to see this thing through" was a strange comment for a father-to-be, even a surrogate one. He made it sound as if this was some kind of mission, not a joyous—if traumatic—experience involving human beings.

Marsha was vaguely aware of her husband's curious behavior as she followed Mary's bed down the hall to the delivery room. But she was so absorbed in the birth itself she didn't focus on it. With all her heart she wished it were she in the hospital bed. She would have welcomed the pain, even though the birth of their son, David, five years earlier had ended in such a violent hemorrhage her doctor had had to perform an emergency hysterectomy to save her life. She and Victor had so desperately wanted a second child. Since she could not bear one, they had weighed the options. After some deliberation, they settled on surrogacy as the preferable one. Marsha had been happy about the arrangement, and glad that even before birth, the child was legally theirs, but she still would have given anything to have carried this much-longed-for baby herself. For a moment she wondered how Mary could bear to part with him. For that reason she was particularly pleased about Michigan law.

17

Watching the nurses move Mary to the delivery table, Marsha said softly, "You're doing just fine. It's almost over."

"Let's get her on her side," said Dr. Whitehead, the anesthesiologist, to the nurses. Then, gripping Mary's arm, she said: "I'm going to give you that epidural block we discussed."

"I don't think I want epidural," said Victor, moving to the opposite side of the delivery table. "Especially not if you're planning on using a caudal approach."

"Dr. Frank!" Dr. Stedman said sternly. "You have a choice: either stop interfering or leave the delivery room. Take your pick." Dr. Stedman had had enough. He'd already put up with a number of Frank's orders, such as performing every known prenatal test, including amniocentesis and chorionic villus biopsy. He'd even permitted Mary to take an antibiotic called cephaloclor for three weeks in the early part of the pregnancy. Professionally, he'd felt none of these things were indicated, but he'd gone along with them because Dr. Frank had insisted and because the surrogacy status made the situation unique. Since Mary did not object, saying it was all part of the deal she'd struck with the Franks, he didn't mind complying. But that was during the pregnancy. The delivery was a different story, and Dr. Stedman was not about to compromise his methodology for a neurotic colleague. Just what kind of medical training had Frank gone through? he wondered. Surely he could abide by standard operating procedures. But here he was questioning each of Stedman's orders, second-guessing every step.

For a few tense seconds, Victor and Dr. Stedman stood glaring at each other. Victor's fists were clenched, and for a brief moment Dr. Stedman thought that the man was about to strike him. But the moment passed, and Victor slouched away to stand nervously in the corner.

Victor's heart was racing and he felt an unpleasant sensation in his abdomen. "Please make the baby normal," he prayed to himself. He looked over at his wife as his eyes clouded with tears. She had wanted another baby so much. He felt himself begin to tremble again. He chided himself inwardly. "I shouldn't have done it. But please, God—let this baby be all right." He looked up at the clock. The second hand seemed to drag slowly around the face. He wondered how much longer he could stand the tension.

Dr. Whitehead's skilled hands had the caudal analgesic in place in seconds. Marsha held Mary's hand, smiling encouragement as the pain began to ease. The next thing Mary knew was that someone was waking her, telling her it was time to push. The second stage of labor went quickly and smoothly, and at 6:04 P.M. a vigorous Victor Frank Jr. was born.

Victor was standing directly behind Dr. Stedman at the moment of birth, holding his breath, trying to see as best he could. As the child came into view, he rapidly scanned the infant as Dr. Stedman clamped and cut the cord. Stedman handed the infant to the waiting resident pediatrician, whom Victor followed to the thermostatically controlled infant care unit. The resident put the silent infant down and began to examine him. Victor felt a rush of relief. The child appeared normal.

"Apgar of ten," the resident called out, indicating that Victor Jr. had the highest possible rating.

"Wonderful," said Dr. Stedman, who was busy with Mary and the imminent delivery of the afterbirth.

"But he's not crying," questioned Victor. Doubt clouded his euphoria.

The resident lightly slapped the soles of Victor Jr.'s feet, then rubbed his back. Still the infant stayed quiet. "But he's breathing fine."

The resident picked up the bulb syringe and tried to suction Victor Jr.'s nose once again. To the doctor's astonishment, the newborn's hand came up and yanked the bulb away from the fingers of the resident and dropped it over the side of the infant care unit.

"Well that settles that," said the resident with a chuckle. "He just doesn't want to cry."

"Can I?" asked Victor, motioning toward the baby.

"As long as he doesn't get cold."

Gingerly, Victor reached into the unit and scooped up Victor Jr. He held the infant in front of him with both hands around his torso. He was a beautiful baby with strikingly blond hair. His chubby, rosy cheeks gave his face a picturesquely cherubic quality, but by far the most distinctive aspect of his appearance was his bright blue eyes. As Victor gazed into their depths he realized with a shock that the baby was looking back at him.

"Beautiful, isn't he?" said Marsha over Victor's shoulder.

"Gorgeous," Victor agreed. "But where did the blond hair come from? Ours is brown."

"I was blond until I was five," Marsha said, reaching up to touch the baby's pink skin.

Victor glanced at his wife as she lovingly gazed at the child. She had dark brown hair peppered with just a few strands of gray. Her eyes were a sultry gray-blue; her features quite sculptured: they contrasted with the rounded, full features of the infant.

"Look at his eyes," Marsha said.

Victor turned his attention back to the baby. "They are incredible, aren't they? A minute ago I'd have sworn they were looking right back at me."

"They are like jewels," Marsha said.

Victor turned the baby to face Marsha. As he did so he noticed the baby's eyes remained locked on his! Their turquoise depths were as cold and bright as ice. Unbidden, Victor felt a thrill of fear.

The Franks felt triumphant as Victor pulled his Oldsmobile Cutlass into the crushed stone driveway leading to their clapboard farmhouse. All the planning and anguish of the in-vitro fertilization process had paid off. The search for an appropriate surrogate mother, the dreary trips to Detroit had worked. They had a child, and Marsha cradled the infant in her arms, thanking God for His gift.

Marsha watched as the car rounded the final bend. Lifting the child up and pulling aside the edge of the blanket, she showed the boy his home. As if comprehending, Victor Jr. stared out of the car windshield at the pleasant but modest house. He blinked, then turned to smile at Victor.

"You like it, huh, Tiger?" said Victor playfully. "He's only three days old but I'd swear he'd talk to me if he could."

"What would you have him say?" Marsha asked as he lowered VJ into her lap. They had nicknamed him that to help distinguish him from his father, Victor Sr.

"I don't know," said Victor, bringing the car to a

stop at the front door. "Maybe say he wanted to grow up and become a doctor like his old man."

"Oh, for goodness' sake," said Marsha, opening the passenger-side door.

Victor jumped out to help her. It was a beautiful, crystal-clear October day, filled with bright sunshine. Behind the house the trees had turned a brilliant profusion of fall colors; scarlet maples, orange oaks and yellow birches all competed with their beauty. As they came up the walk the front door opened and Janice Fay, their live-in nanny, ran down the front steps.

"Let me see him," she begged, stopping short in front of Marsha. Her hand went to her mouth in admiration.

"What do you think?" Victor asked.

"He's angelic!" Janice said. "He's gorgeous, and I don't think I've ever seen such blue eyes." She held out her arms. "Let me hold him." Gently she took the child from Marsha and rocked him back and forth. "I certainly didn't expect blond hair."

"We didn't either," Marsha said. "We thought we'd surprise you like he surprised us. But it comes from my side of the family."

"Oh sure," kidded Victor. "There were a lot of blonds with Genghis Khan."

"Where's David?" asked Marsha.

"Back in the house," said Janice without taking her eyes from VJ's face.

"David!" Marsha called.

The little boy appeared at the doorway, holding one of his previously discarded teddy bears. He was a slight child of five with dark, curly hair.

"Come out here and see your new brother."

Dutifully David walked out to the cooing group.

Janice bent down and showed the newborn to his brother. David looked at the infant and wrinkled his nose. "He smells bad."

Victor chuckled, but Marsha kissed him, saying that when VJ was a little older he'd smell nice like David.

Marsha took VJ back from the nanny and started into the house. Janice sighed. It was such a happy day. She loved newborn babies. She felt David take her hand. She looked down at the boy. He had his head tilted up toward hers.

"I wish the baby hadn't come," he said.

"Shush now," said Janice gently, hugging David to her side. "That's not a nice way to act. He's just a tiny baby and you are a big boy."

Hand in hand, they entered the house just as Marsha and Victor were disappearing into the newly decorated baby's room at the top of the stairs. Janice took David into the kitchen where she had started dinner preparation. He climbed up onto one of the kitchen chairs, placing the teddy bear on the one just opposite. Janice went back to the sink.

"Do you love me more or the baby?"

Janice quickly put down the vegetables she was rinsing and picked David up in her arms. She leaned her forehead on his and said: "I love you more than anybody in the whole world." Then she hugged him forcefully. David hugged her back.

Neither realized that they only had a few more years to live.

# 1

Long, lacy shadows from the leafless maple trees lining the driveway inched across the broad cobblestone courtyard that separated the sprawling white colonial mansion from the barn. A wind had sprung up as the dusk approached, moving the shadows in undulating patterns and making them look like giant spiderwebs. Despite the fact it was almost officially spring, winter still gripped the land in North Andover, Massachusetts.

Marsha stood at the sink in the large country kitchen, staring out at the garden and the fading light. A movement by the driveway caught her eye, and she turned to see VJ peddling home on his bicycle.

For a second, she felt her breath catch in her throat. Since David's death nearly five years ago, she never took her family for granted. She would never forget the terrible day the doctor told her that the boy's jaundice was due to cancer. His face, yellow and wizened from the disease, was etched on her heart. She could still feel his small body clinging to her just before he died. She had been certain he had been trying to tell her something, but all she'd heard was his uneasy gasps as he tried to hold on to life.

Nothing had really been the same since then. And things got even worse just a year later. Marsha's extreme concern for VJ stemmed partly from the loss of David, and partly from the terrible circumstances surrounding Janice's death only a year after his. Both had contracted an extremely rare form of liver cancer, and despite assurances that the two cancers were in no way contagious, Marsha couldn't shake the fear that lightning, having struck twice, might flash a third time.

Janice's death was all the more memorable because it had been so gruesome.

It had been in the fall, just after VJ's birthday. Leaves were falling from the trees, an autumn chill was in the air. Even before she got sick, Janice had been behaving strangely for some time, only willing to eat food that she prepared herself and which came from unopened containers. She'd become fiercely religious, embracing a particularly fanatic strain of born-again Christianity. Marsha and Victor might not have put up with her had she not become practically one of the family in the many years she'd worked for them.

During David's final, critical months, she'd been a godsend. But soon after David's passing, Janice started carrying her Bible everywhere, pressing it to her chest as if it might shield her from unspeakable ills. She'd only put it aside to do her chores, and then reluctantly. On top of that, she'd become sullen and withdrawn, and would lock herself in her room at night.

What was worse was the attitude that she'd developed toward VJ. Suddenly she'd refused to have anything to do with the boy, who was five at the time. Even though VJ was an exceptionally independent child, there were still times when Janice's cooperation was needed, but she refused to help. Marsha had had several talks with her, but to no avail. Janice persisted in shunning him. When pressed, she'd rave about the devil in their midst and other religious nonsense.

Marsha was at her wits' end when Janice got sick. Victor had been the first to notice how yellow her eyes had become. He brought it to Marsha's attention. With horror, Marsha realized Janice's eyes had the same jaundiced cast that David's had had. Victor rushed Janice to Boston so that her condition could be evaluated. Even with her yellow eyes, the diagnosis had come as a tremendous shock: she had liver cancer of the same particularly virulent type that David had died of.

Having two cases of such a rare form of liver cancer in the same household within a year prompted extensive epidemiological investigations. But the results had all been negative. There was no environmental hazard present. The computers determined that the two cases were simply rare chance occurrences.

At least the diagnosis of liver cancer helped explain Janice's bizarre behavior. The doctors felt she might have already suffered brain metastasis. Once she was diagnosed, her downhill course proved swift and merciless. She'd rapidly lost weight despite therapy, became skin and bones within two weeks. But it had been the last day before she'd gone to the hospital to die that had been most traumatic.

Victor had just arrived home and was in the bathroom off the family room. Marsha was in the kitchen preparing dinner, when the house had reverberated with a blood-chilling scream.

Victor shot out of the bathroom. "What in God's name was that?" he yelled.

"It came from Janice's room," said Marsha, who'd turned very pale.

Marsha and Victor exchanged a knowing, fateful glance. Then they dashed out to the garage and up the narrow stairs to Janice's separate studio apartment.

Before they reached her room, a second scream shattered the silence. Its primeval force seemed to rattle the windows.

Victor reached the room first with Marsha on his heels.

Janice was standing in the middle of her bed, clutching her Bible. She was a sorry sight. Her hair, which had become brittle, stood straight out from her head, giving her a demonic appearance. Her face was hollow, her jaundiced skin stretched tautly across her all-too-visible bones. Her eyes were like yellow neon lights and they were transfixed.

For an instant, Marsha was mesmerized by this vision of Janice as a harpy. Then she followed the woman's line of sight. Standing in the doorway to Janice's rear entry was VJ. He didn't even blink but calmly returned Janice's stare with one of his own.

Marsha immediately surmised what had happened: VJ had innocently come up Janice's back stairs, apparently frightening her. In her illness-induced psychosis, Janice had screamed her terrible scream.

"He is the devil!" Janice snarled through clenched teeth. "He is a murderer! Get him away from me!"

"You try to calm Janice," Marsha shouted, running for VJ. She scooped the six-year-old up into her arms, and retreated down the stairs, rushing him into the family room and kicking the door shut behind her. She pressed VJ's head against her chest, thinking how stupid she'd been to keep the crazed woman at home.

Finally Marsha released VJ from her bear hug. VJ pushed away from her and looked up at her with his crystal eyes.

"Janice doesn't mean what she said," Marsha told him. She hoped this awful moment would have no lasting effect.

"I know," VJ said with amazingly adult maturity. "She's very sick. She doesn't know what she's saying."

Since that day, Marsha could never relax and enjoy her life as she had before. If she did she was afraid God might strike again and if anything happened to VJ, she didn't think she could bear the loss.

As a child psychiatrist, she knew she could not expect her child to develop in a certain way, but she often found herself wishing VJ were a more openly affectionate child. Since he had been an infant he had been unnaturally independent. He would occasionally let her hug him, but sometimes she longed for him to climb onto her lap and cuddle the way David had.

Now, watching him get off his bike, she wondered if VJ was as self-absorbed as he sometimes appeared. She waved to get his attention but he didn't look up as he snapped off the saddlebags, letting them fall to the cobblestones. Then he pushed open the barn door and disappeared from sight as he parked his bike for the night. When he reappeared he picked up the saddlebags and started toward the house. Marsha waved again, but although he was walking directly toward her he did not respond. He had his chin pressed down against the cold wind that constantly funneled through the courtyard.

She started to knock on the window, then dropped her hand. Lately she had this terrible premonition there was something wrong with the boy. God knows she couldn't have loved him more if she'd delivered him herself, but sometimes she feared he was unnaturally cold and unfeeling. Genetically he was her own son, but he had none of the warmth and carefree ways she remembered in herself as a child. Before going to sleep she was often obsessed with the thought that being conceived in a petri dish had somehow frozen his emotions. She knew it was a ridiculous idea, but it kept returning.

Shaking off her thoughts, she called, "VJ's home," to Victor, who was reading in front of a crackling fire in the family room next to the kitchen. Victor grunted but didn't look up.

The sound of the back door slamming heralded VJ's entrance into the house. Marsha could hear him taking off his coat and boots in the mud room. Within minutes he appeared at the doorway to the kitchen. He was a handsome boy, about five feet tall, somewhat large for a ten-year-old. His golden blond hair had not darkened like Marsha's had, and his face had retained its angelic character. And just like the day he was born, his most distinctive feature remained his ice-blue eyes. For as cherubic as he seemed, those intense eyes hinted at an intelligence wiser than his years.

"All right, young man," Marsha scolded in mock irritation. "You know you are not supposed to be out on your bike after dark."

"But it's not dark yet," VJ said defensively in his clear, soprano voice. Then he realized his mother was joking. "I've been at Richie's," he added. He put his saddlebags down and came over to the sink.

"That's nice," Marsha said, obviously pleased. "Why didn't you call? Then you could have stayed as long as you liked. I'd have been happy to come and get you."

"I wanted to come home anyway," VJ said as he picked up one of the carrots Marsha had just cleaned. He took a noisy bite.

Marsha put her arms around VJ and gave him a squeeze, aware of the strength in his wiry young body. "Since you have no school this week I'd have thought you would have wanted to stay with Richie and have some fun."

"Nah," VJ said as he wormed his way out of his mother's grasp.

"Are you worrying your mother again?" Victor asked in a teasing tone. He appeared at the doorway to the family room, holding an open scientific journal, his reading glasses perched precariously on the end of his nose.

Ignoring Victor, Marsha asked, "What about this week? Did you make some plans with Richie?"

"Nope. I'm planning on spending the week with Dad at the lab. If that's okay, Dad?" VJ moved his eyes to his father.

"Fine by me as usual," Victor said with a shrug.

"Why in heaven's name do you want to go to the lab?" Marsha asked. But it was a rhetorical question. She didn't expect an answer. VJ had been going to the lab with his father since he'd been an infant. First to take advantage of the superb day-care services offered at Chimera, Inc., and later to play in the lab itself. It

30

had become a routine, even more so after Janice Fay had died.

"Why don't you call up some of your friends from school, and you and Richie and a whole group do something exciting?"

"Let him be," Victor said, coming to VJ's assistance. "If VJ wants to come with me, that's fine."

"Okay, okay," Marsha said, knowing when she was outnumbered. "Dinner will be around eight," she said to VJ, giving his bottom a playful slap.

VJ picked up the saddlebags he'd parked on the chair next to the phone and headed up the back stairs. The old wooden risers creaked under his seventy-four-pound frame. VJ went directly to the second-floor den. It was a cozy room paneled in mahogany. Sitting down at his father's computer, he booted up the machine. He listened intently for a moment to make sure his parents were still talking in the kitchen and then went through an involved procedure to call up a file he'd named STATUS. The screen blinked, then filled with data. Zipping open each saddlebag in turn, VJ stared at the contents and made some rapid calculations, then entered a series of numbers into the computer. It took him only a few moments.

After completing the entry, VJ exited from STATUS, zipped up the saddlebags, and called up Pac-Man. A smile spread across his face as the yellow ball moved through the maze, gobbling up its prey.

Marsha shook the water from her hands, then dried them on the towel hanging from the refrigerator handle. She couldn't get her growing concern for VJ out of her mind. He wasn't a difficult child; there certainly weren't any complaints from teachers at school, yet tough as it was to put her finger on it, Marsha was increasingly certain something was wrong. It was time she brought it up. Picking up Kissa, their Russian Blue cat who'd been doing figure eights around her legs, Marsha walked into the family room where Victor was sprawled on the gingham couch, perusing the latest journals as was his habit after work.

"Can I talk to you for a moment?" Marsha asked.

Victor lowered his magazine cautiously, peering at Marsha over the tops of his reading glasses. At forty-three, he was a slightly built, wiry man with dark wavy, academically unkempt hair and sharp features. He'd been a reasonably good squash player in college and still played three times a week. Chimera, Inc., had its own squash courts, thanks to Victor.

"I'm worried about VJ," Marsha said as she sat down on the wing chair next to the couch, still petting Kissa, who was momentarily content to remain on her lap.

"Oh?" said Victor, somewhat surprised. "Something wrong?"

"Not exactly," Marsha admitted. "It's a number of little things. Like it bothers me that he has so few friends. A few moments ago when he said he'd been with this Richie boy, I was so pleased, like it was an accomplishment. But now he says he doesn't want to spend any time with him over his spring break. A child VJ's age needs to be with other kids. It's an important part of normal latency development."

Victor gave Marsha one of his looks. She knew he hated this kind of psychological discussion, even if psychiatry was her field. He didn't have the patience for it. Besides, talk of any problems related to VJ's development had always seemed to fuel anxieties

Victor preferred not to fire. He sighed, but didn't speak.

"Doesn't it worry you?" Marsha persisted when it was apparent Victor wasn't about to say anything. She stroked the cat, who took the attention as if it were a burden.

Victor shook his head. "Nope. I think VJ is one of the best-adapted kids I've ever met. What's for dinner?"

"Victor!" Marsha said sharply. "This is important."

"All right, all right!" Victor said, closing his magazine.

"I mean, he gets along fine with adults," Marsha continued, "but he never seems to spend time with kids his own age."

"He's with kids his own age at school," Victor said.

"I know," Marsha admitted. "But that's so highly structured."

"To tell the truth," Victor said, knowing he was being deliberately cruel, but given his own anxiety about VJ—anxiety very different from his wife's—he couldn't bear to stay on the subject, "I think you're just being neurotic. VJ's a great kid. There's nothing wrong with him. I think you're still reacting to David's death." He winced inwardly as he said this, but there was no getting around it: the best defense was an offense.

The comment hit Marsha like an open-hand slap. Emotion bubbled up instantly. Blinking back tears, she forced herself to continue. "There are other things besides his apparent lack of friends. He never seems to need anyone or anything. When we bought Kissa we told VJ it was to be his cat, but he's never given her a second glance. And since you've brought up David's

33

death, do you think it normal that VJ has never mentioned his name? When we told him about David he acted as if we'd been talking about a stranger."

"Marsha, he was only five years old. I think you're the one who's disturbed. Five years is a long time to grieve. Maybe you should see a psychiatrist."

Marsha bit her lip. Victor was usually such a kind man, but any time she wanted to discuss VJ, he just cut her off.

"Well, I just wanted to tell you what was on my mind," she said, getting up. It was time to go back into the kitchen and finish dinner. Hearing the familiar sounds of Pac-Man from the upstairs den, she felt slightly reassured.

Victor got up, stretched, and followed her into the kitchen.

# 2

*March 19, 1989*
*Sunday, Early Evening*

Dr. William Hobbs was looking across the chessboard at his son, marveling over him as he did most every day, when the boy's intensely blue eyes rolled back into his head, and the child fell backward off his seat. William didn't see his son hit the floor, but he heard the sickening thud.

"Sheila!" he screamed, jumping up and rushing around the table. To his horror, he saw that Maurice's arms and legs were flailing wildly. He was in the throes of a grand mal seizure.

As a Ph.D., not an M.D., William was not certain what to do. He vaguely remembered something about protecting the victim's tongue by putting something between his teeth, but he had nothing appropriate.

Kneeling over the boy, who was just days short of his third birthday, William yelled again for his wife. Maurice's body contorted with surprising force; it was hard for William to keep the child from injuring himself.

Sheila froze at the sight of her husband juggling the

wildly thrashing child. By this time Maurice had bit-
ten his tongue badly, and as his head snapped up and
down, a spray of frothy blood arched onto the rug.

"Call an ambulance!" shouted William.

Sheila broke free of the paralyzing spell and rushed
back to the kitchen phone. Maurice hadn't felt well
from the moment she'd picked him up from Chimera
Day Care. He'd complained of a headache—one of a
pounding variety, like a migraine. Of course most
three-year-olds wouldn't describe a headache that
way, but Maurice wasn't most three-year-olds. He was
a true child prodigy, a genius. He'd learned to talk at
eight months, read at thirteen months, and now could
beat his father at their nightly chess game.

"We need an ambulance!" shouted Sheila into the
phone when a voice finally answered. She gave their
address, pleading with the operator to hurry. Then she
rushed back into the living room.

Maurice had stopped convulsing. He was lying quite
still on the couch where William had placed him. He'd
vomited his dinner along with a fair amount of bright
red blood. The awful mess had become matted in his
blond hair and drooled from the corners of his mouth.
He'd also lost control of his bladder and bowels.

"What should I do?" William pleaded in frustration.
At least the child was breathing and his color, which
had turned a dusky blue, was returning to normal.

"What happened?" Sheila asked.

"Nothing," William answered. "He was winning as
usual. Then his eyes rolled up and back and he fell
over. I'm afraid he hit his head pretty hard on the
floor."

"Oh, God!" Sheila said, wiping Maurice's mouth
with the corner of her apron. "Maybe you shouldn't

have insisted he play chess tonight with his headache and everything."

"He wanted to," William said defensively. But that wasn't quite true. Maurice had been lukewarm to the idea. But William couldn't resist an opportunity to watch the child use his phenomenal brain. Maurice was William's pride and joy.

He and Sheila had been married for eight years before they finally were willing to admit they were unable to conceive. Since Chimera had its own fertility center, Fertility, Inc., and since William was an employee of Chimera, he and Sheila had gone there free of charge. It hadn't been easy. They had to face the fact that both of them were infertile, but eventually, via a surrogate and gamete-donation plans, they got their long-awaited child: Maurice, their miracle baby with an IQ right off the charts.

"I'll get a towel and clean him up," Sheila said, starting for the kitchen. But William grabbed her arm.

"Maybe we shouldn't move him around."

The couple sat watching the child helplessly, until they heard the ambulance scream down their street. Sheila rushed to let the medics in.

A few moments later, William found himself balancing on a seat in the back of the lurching vehicle with Sheila following behind in the family car.

When they reached Lowell General Hospital, the couple waited anxiously while Maurice was examined and evaluated, then declared stable enough for transfer. William wanted the child to go to Children's Hospital in Boston, about a half hour's drive. Something told him that his child was deathly ill. Maybe they had been too proud of his phenomenal brilliance. Maybe God was making them pay.

\* \* \*

"Hey, VJ!" Victor shouted up the back stairs. "How about a swim!" He could hear his voice carom off the walls of their spacious house. It had been built in the eighteenth century by the local landowner. Victor had bought and renovated it shortly after David's death. Business at Chimera had begun to boom after the company had gone public, and Victor felt Marsha would be better off if she didn't have to face the same rooms where David had grown up. She'd taken David's passing even harder than he had.

"Want to go in the pool?" Victor shouted again. It was at times like this that he wished they'd put in an intercom system.

"No, thanks," came VJ's answer echoing down the stairwell.

Victor remained where he was for a moment, one hand on the handrail, one foot on the first step. His earlier conversation with Marsha had reawakened all his initial fears about his son. The early unusual development, the incredible intelligence which had made him a chess master at three years of age, the precipitous drop in intelligence before he was four; VJ's was by no means a standard maturation. Victor had been so guilt-ridden since the moment of the child's birth that he had been almost relieved at the disappearance of the little boy's extraordinary powers. But now he wondered if a normal kid wouldn't jump at the chance to swim in the family's new pool. Victor had decided to add a pool for exercise. They'd built it off the back of the house in a type of greenhouse affair. Construction had just been completed the previous month.

Making up his mind not to take no for an answer, Victor bounded up the stairs two at a time in his stocking feet. Silently, he whisked down the long hall to VJ's bedroom, which was located in the front of the house overlooking the driveway. As always, the room was neat and orderly, with a set of the *Encyclopaedia Britannica* lining one wall and a chemical chart of the elements on the wall opposite. VJ was lying on his stomach on his bed, totally absorbed in a thick book.

Advancing toward the bed, Victor tried to see what VJ was reading. Peering over the top of the book, all he could make out was a mass of equations, hardly what he expected.

"Gotcha!" he said, playfully grabbing the boy's leg.

At his touch, VJ leaped up, his hands ready to defend himself.

"Whoa! Were you concentrating or what?" Victor said with a laugh.

VJ's turquoise eyes bore into his father. "Don't ever do that again!" he said.

For a second, Victor felt a familiar surge of fear at what he had created. Then VJ let out a sigh and dropped back onto the bed.

"What on earth are you reading?" Victor asked.

VJ closed the book as if it had been pornography. "Just something I picked up on black holes."

"Heavy!" Victor said, trying to sound hip.

"Actually, it's not very good," VJ said. "Lots of errors."

Again, Victor felt a cold chill. Lately he had wondered if his son's precocious intelligence wasn't returning. Attempting to shrug off his worries, Victor said firmly, "Listen, VJ, we're going for a swim."

He went over to VJ's bureau and extracted a pair of bathing trunks and tossed them at his son. "Come on, I'll race you."

Victor walked down to his own bedroom, where he pulled on a bathing suit, then called for VJ. VJ appeared and came down the hall toward his father. Victor noted with pride that his son was well built for a ten-year-old. For the first time Victor thought that VJ could be an athlete if he were so inclined.

The pool had that typical humid chlorine smell. The glass that comprised the ceiling and walls of its enclosure reflected back the image of the pool; the wintry scene outside was not in view. Victor tossed his towel over the back of an aluminum deck chair as Marsha appeared at the door to the family room.

"How about swimming with us?" Victor asked.

Marsha shook her head. "You boys enjoy yourself. It's too cold for me."

"We're going to race," Victor said. "How about officiating?"

"Dad," VJ said plaintively. "I don't want to race."

"Sure you do," Victor said. "Two laps. The loser has to take out the garbage."

Marsha came out onto the deck and took VJ's towel, rolling her eyes at the boy in commiseration.

"You want the inside lane or the outside one?" Victor asked him, hoping to draw him in.

"It doesn't matter," VJ said as he lined up next to his father, facing down the length of the pool. The surface swirled gently from the circulator.

"You start us," Victor said to Marsha.

"On your mark, get set," Marsha said, pausing, watching her husband and her son teeter on the side of the pool. "Go!"

After backing up to avoid the initial splash, Marsha sat down in one of the deck chairs and watched. Victor was not a good swimmer, but even so she was surprised to see that VJ was leading through the first lap and the turn. Then, on the second lap, VJ seemed to hold back and Victor won by half a length.

"Good try," Victor said, sputtering and triumphant. "Welcome to the garbage detail!"

Perplexed at what she thought she had witnessed, Marsha eyed VJ curiously as he hoisted himself from the water. As their eyes met, VJ winked, confusing her even more.

VJ took his towel and dried himself briskly. He really would have liked to be the sort of son his mother longed for, the kind David had been. But it just wasn't in him. Even times he tried to fake it, he knew he didn't get it quite right. Still, if moments like this one at the pool gave his parents a sense of family happiness, who was he to deny them?

"Mother, it hurts even more," Mark Murray said to Colette. He was in his bedroom on the third floor of the Murray townhouse on Beacon Hill. "Whenever I move I feel pressure behind my eyes and in my sinuses." The precise terms were a startling contrast to the tiny toddler's palms with which the child clutched his head.

"It's worse than before dinner?" Colette asked, smoothing back his tightly curled blond hair. She was no longer startled by her toddler's exceptional vocabulary. The boy was lying in a standard-size bed, even though he was only two and a half years old. At thirteen months he'd demanded that the crib be put in the basement.

"It's much worse," Mark said.

"Let's take your temperature once more," Colette said, slipping a thermometer into his mouth. Colette

41

was becoming progressively alarmed even though she tried to reassure herself it was just the beginning of a cold or flu. It had started about an hour after her husband, Horace, had brought Mark home from the day-care center at Chimera. Mark told her he wasn't hungry, and for Mark that was distinctly abnormal.

The next symptom was sweating. It started just as they were about to sit down to eat. Although he told his parents that he didn't feel hot, the sweat poured out of him. A few minutes later he vomited. That was when Colette put him to bed.

As an accountant who'd been too queasy even to take biology in college, Horace was happy to leave the sickroom chores to Colette, not that she had any real experience. She was a lawyer and her busy practice had forced her to start Mark at day care when he was only a year old. She adored their brilliant only child, but getting him had been an ordeal the likes of which she had never anticipated.

After three years of marriage, she and Horace had decided to start a family. But after nearly a year of trying with no luck, they'd both gone in for fertility consultation. It was then they learned the hard truth: Colette was infertile. Mark resulted from their last resort: in-vitro fertilization and the use of a surrogate mother. It had been a nightmare, especially with all the controversy generated by the Baby M case.

Colette slipped the thermometer from Mark's lips, then rotated the cylinder, looking for the column of mercury. Normal. Colette sighed. She was at a loss. "Are you hungry or thirsty?" she asked.

Mark shook his head. "I'm starting not to see very well," he said.

"What do you mean, not see very well?" she asked,

alarmed. She covered Mark's eyes alternately. "Can you see out of both eyes?"

"Yes," Mark responded. "But things are getting blurry. Out of focus."

"Okay, you stay here and rest," Colette said. "I'm going to talk with your father."

Leaving the child, Colette went downstairs and found Horace hiding in the study, watching a basketball game on the miniature TV.

When Horace saw his wife in the doorway, he guiltily switched it off. "The Celtics," he said as an explanation.

Colette dismissed a fleeting sense of irritation. "He's much worse," she said hoarsely. "I'm worried. He says he can't see well. I think we should call the doctor."

"Are you sure?" Horace asked. "It is Sunday night."

"I can't help that!" Colette said sharply.

Just then an earsplitting shriek made them rush for the stairs.

To their horror, Mark was writhing around in the bed, clutching his head as if in terrible agony, and screaming at the top of his lungs. Horace grabbed the child by the shoulders and tried to restrain him as Colette went for the phone.

Horace was surprised at the boy's strength. It was all he could do to keep the child from hurling himself off the bed.

Then, as suddenly as it had begun, the screaming stopped. For a moment, Mark lay still, his small hands still pressed against his temples, his eyes squeezed shut.

"Mark?" Horace whispered.

Mark's arms relaxed. He opened his blue eyes and

looked up at his father. But recognition failed to register in them and when he opened his mouth he spouted pure gibberish.

Sitting at her vanity, brushing her long hair, Marsha studied Victor in the mirror. He was at the sink, brushing his teeth with rapid, forceful strokes. VJ had long since gone to bed. Marsha had checked him when she'd come upstairs fifteen minutes earlier. Looking at his angelic face, she again considered his apparent ploy in the pool.

"Victor!" she called suddenly.

Victor spun around, toothpaste foaming out of his mouth like a mad dog. She'd startled him.

"Do you realize VJ let you win that race?"

Victor spat noisily into the sink. "Now just a second. It might have been close, but I won that contest fair and square."

"VJ had the lead through most of the race," said Marsha. "He deliberately slowed down to let you win."

"That's absurd," Victor said indignantly.

"No it's not. He does things that just don't make sense for a ten-year-old. It's like when he was two and a half and started playing chess. You loved it, but it bothered me. In fact, it scared me. I was relieved when his intelligence dropped, at least after it stabilized at its high normal. I just want a happy, normal kid." Tears suddenly welled up in her eyes. "Like David," she added, turning away.

Victor dried his face quickly, tossed the towel aside, and came over to Marsha. He put his arms around her. "You're worrying about nothing. VJ's a fine boy."

"Maybe he acts strange because I left him with Janice so much when he was a baby," Marsha said, fighting her tears. "I was never home enough. I should have taken a leave from the office."

"You certainly are intent on blaming yourself," Victor said, "even if there's nothing wrong."

"Well," Marsha said, "there is something odd about his behavior. If it were one episode, it would be okay. But it's not. The boy just isn't a normal ten-year-old. He's too secretive, too adult." She began to weep. "Sometimes he just frightens me."

Leaning over to comfort his wife, Victor remembered the terror he'd felt when VJ had been born. He'd wanted his son to be exceptional, not abnormal in any kind of deviant way.

# 3

Breakfast was always casual at the Franks'. Fruit, cereal, coffee, and juice on the run. The major difference on this particular morning was that it wasn't a school day for VJ so he wasn't in his usual rush to catch the bus. Marsha was the first to leave, around eight, in order to give her time to see her hospital patients before starting office hours. As she went out the door she passed Ramona Juarez, the cleaning lady who came on Mondays and Thursdays.

Victor watched his wife get into her Volvo station wagon. Each exhale produced a transient cloud of vapor in the crisp morning air. Even though spring was supposed to arrive the next day, the thermometer registered a chilly 28 degrees.

Upending his coffee mug in the sink, Victor turned his attention to VJ, who was alternately watching TV and leafing through one of Victor's scientific journals. Victor frowned. Maybe Marsha was right. Maybe the boy's initial brilliance was returning. The articles in that journal were fairly sophisticated. Victor wondered just how much his son might be gleaning.

He debated saying something, then decided to leave it alone. The kid was fine, normal. "You sure you want to come to the lab today?" he asked. "Maybe you could find something more exciting to do with your friends."

"It's exciting to come to the lab," said VJ.

"Your mother thinks you ought to spend more time with kids your own age," Victor said. "That's the way you learn to cooperate and share and all that kind of stuff."

"Oh, please!" VJ said. "I'm with kids my own age every day at school."

"At least we think alike," Victor said. "I told your mother the same thing. Well, now that we have that cleared up, how do you want to get to the lab—ride with me or bike?"

"Bike," VJ answered.

Despite the chill in the air, Victor had the sunroof open on his car and the wind tousled his hair. With the radio tuned to the only classical station he could get, he thundered over an ancient bridge spanning the swollen Merrimack River. The river was a torrent of eddies and white water, and it was rising daily thanks to winter snow melting in the White Mountains of New Hampshire, a hundred miles to the north.

On the street before Chimera, Inc., Victor turned left and drove the length of a long brick building that crowded the side of the road. At the end of the building, he took another left, then slowed as he drove past a manned security checkpoint. Recognizing the car, the uniformed man waved as Victor passed under the raised black and white gate onto the grounds of a vast private biotechnology firm.

Entering the nineteenth-century red-brick mill complex, Victor always felt a rush of pride that came with ownership. It was an impressive place, especially since many of the buildings had had their exteriors restored rather than renovated.

The tallest buildings of the compound were five stories high, but most were three, and they stretched off in both directions like studies in perspective. Rectangular in shape, they enclosed a huge inner court which was spotted with newer buildings in a variety of shapes and sizes.

At the western corner of the property and dominating the site was an eight-story clock tower designed as a replica of Big Ben in London. It soared above the other buildings from the top of a three-story structure built partially over a concrete dam across the Merrimack. With the river as swollen as it was, the millpond behind the dam was filled to overflowing. A thunderous waterfall at the spillway in the center of the dam filled the air with a fine mist.

Back in the old days when the mill turned out textiles from southern cotton, the clock tower building had been the power station. The entire complex had been run by waterpower until electrification had shut the main sluice and quieted the huge paddle wheels and gears in the basement of the building. The Big Ben replica had chimed its last years before, but Victor was thinking of having it restored.

When Chimera had purchased the abandoned complex in 1976, it had renovated less than half of the available square feet, leaving the rest for future expansion. In anticipation of growth, however, all the buildings had been equipped with water, sanitation, and power. There was no doubt in Victor's mind that it would be easy to get old Big Ben going again. He made a mental note to bring it up at the next development meeting.

As Victor pulled into his assigned parking spot in front of the administration building and pulled the sunroof shut, he paused to review his day. Despite the pride the expansive site evoked, he recognized he had some mixed feelings about the success of Chimera. In his heart Victor was a scientist, yet as one of the three founding partners of Chimera, he was required to assume his share of the administrative responsibilities. Unfortunately, these obligations were increasingly taking more time.

Victor entered the building through the elaborate Georgian entranceway, replete with columns and pediments. The architects had paid painstaking attention to detail in the restoration. Even the furnishings were from the early nineteenth century. The lobby was a fair cry from the utilitarian halls of MIT where Victor was teaching back in 1973 when he first started talking with a fellow academician, Ronald Beekman, about the opportunities afforded by the explosion of biotechnology. Technically, it was a good marriage, since Victor was in biology and Ronald was in biochemistry. They had combined forces with a businessman by the name of Clark Fitzsimmons Foster, and in 1975 founded Chimera. The result was better than their wildest expectations. In 1983, under the guidance of Clark, the company went public and they'd all become enormously wealthy.

But with success came responsibilities that kept Victor away from his first love: the lab. As a founding partner, he was a member of the Board of Directors of the parent company, Chimera. He was also senior vice president of the same company in charge of research. At the same time he was acting director of the Department of Developmental Biology. In addition to those duties he was the president and managing director of the enormously lucrative subsidiary, Fertility, Inc., which owned an expanding chain of infertility clinics.

Victor paused at the top of the main stairs and gazed out of the multipaned arched window at the sprawling factory complex that had been brought back to life. There was no doubt about the satisfaction he felt. In the nineteenth century the factory had been a huge success, but it had been based on exploitation of an immigrant working class. Now its success rested on firmer ground. Chimera's foundation stood on the laws of science and the ingenuity of the human mind in its endeavor to unlock the mysteries of life. Victor knew that science in the form of biotechnology was the wave of the future, and he gloated that he was at the epicenter. In his hands was a lever that could move the world, maybe the universe.

VJ whistled as he freewheeled down Stanhope Street. He had his down parka zipped up to keep out the cold wind, and his hands were crammed into mittens filled with the same insulation the astronauts used.

Switching his bike into the highest gear possible, he caught up to the pedals. With the swish of the wind and the whine from the tires, he felt like he was going a hundred miles an hour. He was free. No more school for a week. No more need to pretend in front of the teachers and those kids. He could spend his time doing what he'd been born to accomplish. He smiled a strange, unchildlike grin. His blue eyes blazed and he was happy his mother was nowhere near to see him. He had a mission, just like his father. And he could not let anything interfere.

VJ had to slow when he reached the small town of North Andover. He pedaled up the center of the main shopping street and stopped in front of the local bank, where he parked his bike in a metal rack and locked it with his Kryptonite lock. Slinging his saddlebags over his shoulder, he climbed the three brownstone steps and went inside.

"Good morning, Mr. Frank," the manager said, twisting around in his swivel desk chair. His name was Harold Scott and VJ generally tried to avoid him, but since his desk was just to the right of the entrance, it was difficult. "May I talk with you, young man?"

VJ paused, considered his options, then reluctantly detoured to the man's desk.

"I know you are a good customer of the bank," Harold said, "so I thought it would be appropriate if I discussed with you some of the benefits of banking here. Do you understand the concept of interest, young man?"

"I believe so," VJ answered.

"If so, then I wanted to ask why you don't have a savings account for your paper route money?"

"Paper route?" VJ questioned.

"Yes," Harold answered. "You told me some time ago that you had a paper route. I assume you still have it since you are still coming into the bank on a fairly regular basis."

"Of course I still have it," VJ answered. Now he

51

remembered having been previously cornered by the same man. It must have been a year ago.

"Once your money is in savings account, it begins to work for you. In fact your money grows. Let me give you an example."

"Mr. Scott," VJ said as the manager got some paper from a drawer at his desk. "I don't have a lot of time. My father expects me at his lab."

"This won't take long," Harold said. He then proceeded to show Victor what happened to twenty dollars left in The North Andover National Bank for twenty years. When he was finished, he asked: "What do you say? Does this convince you."

"Absolutely," VJ said.

"Well then," Harold said. He took some forms from another drawer and quickly filled them in. Then he pushed them in front of VJ and pointed to a dotted line near the bottom. "Sign here."

Dutifully VJ took the pen and signed his name.

"Now then," Harold repeated. "How much would you like to deposit?"

VJ chewed his cheek, then extracted his wallet. He had three dollars in it. He took them out and gave them to Harold.

"Is this all?" Harold questioned. "How much do you make a week with your paper route? You have to start a habit of savings early in your life."

"I'll add to it," VJ said.

Taking the forms and the bills, Harold went behind the teller's window. He had to be buzzed in through the plexiglass door. When he returned, he handed VJ a deposit slip. "This is an important day in your life," Harold said.

VJ nodded, pocketed the slip, then went to the rear

of the bank. He watched Mr. Scott. Thankfully a customer came in and sat down at his desk.

VJ buzzed for the attendant for the safe deposit vault. A few minutes later he was safely in one of the privacy cubicles with his large safe deposit box. Putting his saddlebags carefully on the floor, he unzipped them. They were filled with tightly bound stacks of hundred-dollar bills. When he was finished adding them to those already there, he had to use both hands to heave the box back up and into its slot in the vault.

Back on his bike, VJ left North Andover, heading west. He pedaled steadily and was soon in Lawrence. Crossing the Merrimack, he eventually entered the grounds of Chimera. The security man at the gate waved with the same kind of respect he reserved for Dr. Frank.

As soon as Victor reached his office, his very pretty and very efficient secretary, Colleen, cornered him with a stack of phone messages.

Victor silently groaned. Mondays were all too frequently like this, keeping him from the lab, sometimes for the entire day. Victor's current and primary research interest involved the mysteries of how a fertilized egg got implanted in a uterus. No one knew how it worked and what were the factors necessary to facilitate it. Victor had picked the project many years ago because its solution would have major academic and major commercial importance. But with his current rate of progress he would be working on it for many years to come.

"This is probably the most important message," Colleen said, handing over a pink slip.

Victor took the paper, which said for him to call

Ronald Beekman ASAP. "Oh, wonderful," Victor thought. Although he and Ronald had been the best of friends during the initial phases of the founding of Chimera, Inc., their relationship was now strained over their differing views about the future of the company. Currently they were arguing about a proposed stock offering that was being championed by Clark Foster as a means of raising additional capital for expansion.

Ronald was adamantly opposed to any dilution of the stock, fearing a hostile takeover in the future. It was his belief that expansion should be tied directly to current revenues and current profits. Once again, Victor's vote was to be the swing vote, just as it had been back in 1983 over the question of going public. Victor had voted against Ronald then, siding with Clark. Despite the incontrovertible success of going public, Ronald still felt Victor had sold out his academic integrity.

Victor put Ronald's message in the center of his blotter. "What else?" he asked.

Before Colleen could respond, the door opened and VJ stuck his head in, asking if anybody had seen Philip.

"I saw him earlier at the cafeteria," Colleen said.

"If anybody sees him," VJ said, "tell him that I'm here."

"Certainly," Colleen said.

"I'll be around," VJ said.

Victor waved absently, still wondering what he would say to Ronald. Victor was certain they needed capital now, not next year.

VJ closed the door behind him.

"No school?" Colleen questioned.

"Spring vacation," Victor said.

"Such an exceptional child," Colleen said. "So undemanding. If my son were here, he'd be underfoot the entire time."

"My wife thinks differently," Victor said. "She thinks VJ has some kind of problem."

"That's hard to believe," Colleen said. "VJ is so polite, so grown up."

"Maybe you should talk to Marsha," Victor said. Then he stuck his hand out, anxious to move on. "What's the next message?"

"Sorry," Colleen said. "This is the phone number for Jonathan Marronetti, Gephardt's attorney."

"Lovely!" Victor said. George Gephardt was the director of personnel for Fertility, Inc., and had been supervisor of purchasing for Chimera until three years ago. Currently, he was on a leave of absence, pending an investigation regarding the disappearance of over one hundred thousand dollars from Fertility, Inc. Embarrassingly enough, it had been the IRS that had first discovered that Gephardt was banking the paychecks of a deceased employee. As soon as he had heard, Victor ordered an audit of the man's purchasing bills for Chimera from 1980 to 1986. Sighing, Victor put the attorney's number behind Ronald's.

"What's next?" Victor asked.

Colleen shuffled through the remaining messages. "That's about all the important ones. The rest of these I can handle."

"That's it?" Victor questioned with obvious disbelief.

Colleen stood up and stretched. "That's all the messages, but Sharon Carver is waiting to see you."

"Can't you handle her?" Victor asked.

"She's demanded to see you," Colleen said. "Here's her file."

Victor didn't need the file, but he took it and placed it on his desk. He knew all about Sharon Carver. She'd been an animal handler in Developmental Biology before she'd been "terminated because of dereliction of duty." "Let her wait," Victor said, standing up. "I'll see her after I see Ronald."

Using the rear entrance to his office, Victor started off for his partner's office. Maybe Ronald would be reasonable face to face.

Rounding a corner, Victor spotted a familiar figure backing out of a doorway and pulling a cart. It was Philip Cartwright, one of the retarded persons whom Chimera had hired to work to the extent of their abilities; they were all valuable employees. Philip did custodial and messenger work, and had been popular from his first day on. In addition, he'd taken a particular liking to VJ over the years and had spent lots of time with him, particularly before VJ started school. They made an improbable pair. Philip was a big, powerfully built man with scant hair, closely set eyes, and a broad neck that sloped from just behind his ears to the tip of his shoulders. His long arms ended in spadelike hands, with all the fingers the same length.

As soon as Philip saw Dr. Frank, there was a wide smile of recognition, displaying a mouthful of square teeth. The man could have been frightening, but he had such a pleasant personality, his demeanor overcame his appearance.

"Good morning, Mr. Frank," Philip said. He had a surprisingly childlike voice despite his size.

"Good morning, Philip," Victor said. "VJ is here

someplace and was looking for you. He'll be here all week."

"That makes me happy," Philip said with sincerity. "I'll find him right away. Thank you."

Victor watched him hurry off with his cart, wishing all the Chimera employees were as dependable as Philip.

Reaching Ronald's office, which was a mirror image of his, Victor said hello to Ronald's private secretary and asked if her boss was available. She kept Victor waiting for a few minutes before ushering him in.

"Does Brutus come to praise Caesar?" Ronald asked, looking up at Victor from under bushy brows. He was a heavyset man with a thick mat of unkempt hair.

"I thought we could discuss the stock offering," Victor suggested. From Ronald's manner and tone, it was clear he was in no mood for conversation.

"What's there to talk about?" Ronald said with thinly disguised resentment. "I've heard you're for a dilution of stock."

"I'm for raising more capital," Victor said.

"It's the same thing," Ronald said.

"Are you interested in my reasons?" Victor asked.

"I think your reasons are very clear," Ronald said. "You and Clark have been plotting against me since we went public!"

"Oh, really?" Victor questioned, unable to keep the sarcasm from his voice. Such ridiculous paranoia began to give him the idea the man was cracking under the strain of his administrative duties. He certainly had as much if not more than Victor and neither one of them was trained for such work.

"Don't 'oh, really' me!" Ronald said, heaving his

bulk to his feet. He leaned forward on his desk. "I'm warning you, Frank. I'll get even with you."

"What on earth are you talking about?" Victor said with disbelief. "What are you going to do to me, let the air out of my tires? Ronald, it's me, Victor. Remember?" Victor waved his hand in front of Ronald's face.

"I can make your life just as miserable as you're making mine," Ronald snapped. "If you continue to press me to sell more stock, I promise I'll get even with you."

"Please!" Victor said, backing up. "Ronald, when you wake up, call me. I'm not going to stand here and be threatened."

Victor turned and left the office. He could hear Ronald start to say something else, but Victor didn't stop to hear it. He was disgusted. For a moment he considered throwing in the towel, cashing in his stock, and going back to academia. But by the time he got back to his desk, he felt differently. He wasn't about to let Ronald's personality problems deny him access to the excitement of the biotechnology industry. After all, there were limitations in academia as well; they were just of a different sort.

Staring up at Victor from his desk blotter was the telephone number for Jonathan Marronetti, Gephardt's attorney. Resigned, Victor dialed the number and got the lawyer on the phone. The man had a distinctive New York accent that grated on Victor's nerves.

"Got good news for you people," Jonathan said.

"We can use some," Victor said.

"My client, Mr. Gephardt, is willing to return all the funds that mysteriously ended up in his checking account, plus interest. This is not to imply guilt; he just wants the matter to be closed."

"I will discuss the offer with our attorneys," Victor said.

"Wait, there's more," Jonathan said. "In return for transferring these funds, my client wants to be reinstated, and he wants all further harassment ceased, including any current investigation of his affairs."

"That's out of the question," Victor said. "Mr. Gephardt can hardly expect reinstatement without our completing the investigation."

"Well," Jonathan said, pausing, "I suppose I can reason with my client and talk him out of the reinstatement proviso."

"I'm afraid that wouldn't make much difference," Victor said.

"Listen, we're trying to be reasonable."

"The investigation will proceed as scheduled," Victor said.

"I'm sure there is some way—" Jonathan began.

"I'm sorry," Victor interrupted. "When we have all the facts, we can talk again."

"If you're not willing to be reasonable," Jonathan said, "I'll be forced to take action you may regret. You are hardly in a position to play holier than thou."

"Good-bye, Mr. Marronetti," Victor said, slamming down the phone.

Slumping back in his chair, Victor buzzed Colleen and told her to send in the Carver woman. Even though he was familiar with the case, he opened up her folder. She'd been a problem practically from the first day on the job. She had been undependable, with frequent absences. The folder contained five letters

ROBIN COOK

from various people complaining about her poor performance.

Victor looked up. Sharon Carver came into the room wearing a skin-tight mini with a silk top. She oozed into the chair opposite Victor, showing a lot of leg.

"Thank you for seeing me," she whispered.

Victor glanced at the Polaroid shot in her file. She'd been dressed in baggy jeans and a flannel shirt.

"What can I do for you?" Victor asked, looking her directly in the eye.

"I'm sure you could do a lot of things," Sharon said coyly. "But what I'm most interested in right now is having my job back. I want to be rehired."

"That's not possible," Victor said.

"I believe it is," Sharon persisted.

"Miss Carver," Victor began, "I must remind you that you were fired for failing to perform your job."

"How come the man I was with when we were caught in the stockroom wasn't fired?" Sharon asked, uncrossing her legs and leaning forward defiantly. "Answer me that!"

"Your amorous activities on your last day were not the sole basis for your termination," Victor explained. "If that had been the only problem, you would not have been fired. And the man you mentioned had never neglected his responsibilities. Even on the day in question he was on his official break. You were not. At any rate, what is done is done. I'm confident you will find employment elsewhere, so if you will excuse me . . ." Victor rose from his seat and motioned toward the door.

Sharon Carver did not move. She looked up at Victor with cold eyes. "If you refuse to give me my job back I'll serve you with a sex-discrimination suit that will make your head spin. I'll make you suffer."

"You're already doing a pretty good job," Victor said. "Now if you'll excuse me."

Like a cat about to attack, Sharon rose slowly from the chair, glaring at Victor out of the corner of her eye. "You've not seen the last of me!" she spat.

Victor waited until the door closed before buzzing Colleen to tell her that he was heading over to his lab and that she shouldn't call him for anybody less than the Pope.

"Too late," said Colleen. "Dr. Hurst is in the waiting room. He wants to see you and he's quite upset."

William Hurst was the acting chief of the Department of Medical Oncology. He, too, was the subject of a newly ordered investigation. But contrary to Gephardt's, Hurst's involved possible research fraud, a growing menace in the scientific world. "Send him in," Victor said reluctantly. There was no place to hide.

Hurst came through the door as if he planned to assault Victor, and rushed up to the desk. "I just heard that you ordered an independent lab to verify the results on the last paper I published in the journal."

"I don't think that's surprising in light of the article in Friday's *Boston Globe*," Victor said. He wondered what he'd do if this maniac came around behind the desk.

"Damn the *Boston Globe!*" Hurst shouted. "They based that cockamamie story on the remarks of one disgruntled lab tech. You don't believe it, do you?"

"My beliefs are immaterial at this point," Victor said. "The *Globe* reported that data in your paper were deliberately falsified. That kind of allegation can be detrimental to you and Chimera. We have to nip such a rumor before it gets out of hand. I don't understand your anger."

"Well then, I'll explain," Hurst snapped. "I expected support from you, not suspicion. The mere ordering of a verification of my work is tantamount to ascribing guilt. Besides, some insignificant graphite statistics can sneak into any collaborative paper. Even Isaac Newton himself was later known to have improved some planetary observations. I want that verification request canceled."

"Look, I'm sorry you're upset," Victor said. "But Isaac Newton notwithstanding, there is no relativity when it comes to research ethics. The public's confidence in research—"

"I didn't come in here to get a lecture!" Hurst yelled. "I tell you I want that investigation stopped."

"You make yourself very clear," Victor said. "But the fact remains that if there is no fraud, you have nothing to fear and everything to gain."

"Are you telling me that you will not cancel the verification?"

"That's what I'm telling you," Victor said. He'd had enough of trying to appease this man's ego.

"I'm shocked by your lack of academic loyalty," Hurst said finally. "Now I know why Ronald feels as he does."

"Dr. Beekman advocates the same ethics of research as I do," said Victor, finally letting his anger show. "Good-bye, Dr. Hurst. This conversation is over."

"Let me tell you something, Frank," said Hurst, leaning over the desk. "If you persist in dragging my name through the mud, I'll do the same to you. Do you hear me? I know you're not the 'white knight' scientific savior you pretend to be."

"I'm afraid I've never published falsified data," Victor said sarcastically.

"The point is," Hurst said, "you're not the white knight you want us to believe."

"Get out of my office."

"Gladly," Hurst said. He walked to the door, opened it and said: "Just remember what I've told you. You're not immune!" Then he slammed the door behind him with such force that Victor's medical school diploma tilted on its hanger.

Victor sat at his desk for a few moments, trying to regain a sense of emotional equilibrium. He'd certainly had enough threats for one day. He wondered what Hurst was referring to when he said that Victor was not a "white knight." What a circus!

Pushing back his chair, Victor got up and pulled on his white lab coat. He opened the door, expecting to lean out and tell Colleen he was heading over to the lab. Instead he practically bumped into her as she was on her way in to see him.

"Dr. William Hobbs is here and he's an emotional wreck," Colleen said quickly.

Victor tried to see around Colleen. He spotted a man sitting in the chair next to her desk, hunched over, holding his head.

"What's the problem?" Victor whispered.

"Something about his son," Colleen said. "I think something has happened to the boy and he wants to take some time off."

Victor felt perspiration appear in the palms of his hands and a constriction in his throat. "Send him in," he managed.

He couldn't help but feel a twinge of empathy, having gone through the same extraordinary measures to get a child himself. The thought that something might now be wrong with the Hobbs boy revived all of his apprehensions concerning VJ.

"Maurice . . ." Hobbs began, but he had to stop while he choked back tears. "My boy was about to turn three. You never met him. He was such a joy. The center of our life. He was a genius."

"What happened?" Victor asked, almost afraid to hear.

"He died!" Hobbs said with sudden anger breaking through his sadness.

Victor swallowed hard. His throat was as dry as sandpaper. "An accident?" he asked.

Hobbs shook his head. "They don't know exactly what happened. It started with a seizure. When we got him to the Children's Hospital, they decided he had edema of the brain: brain swelling. There was nothing they could do. He never regained consciousness. Then his heart stopped."

A heavy silence hung over the office. Finally, Hobbs said, "I'd like to take some time off."

"Of course," said Victor.

Hobbs slowly got up and went out.

Victor sat staring after him for a good ten minutes. For once the last place in the world he wanted to go was the lab.

# 4

## *Later Monday Morning*

The small alarm on Marsha's desk went off, signaling the end of the fifty-minute session with Jasper Lewis, an angry fifteen-year-old boy with a smudge of whiskers along his chin line. He was slouched in the chair opposite Marsha's, acting bored. The fact of the matter was that the kid was heading for real trouble.

"What we haven't discussed yet is your hospitalization," Marsha said. She had the boy's file open on her lap.

Jasper hooked a thumb over his shoulder toward Marsha's desk. "I thought that bell means the session is over."

"It means it is almost over," Marsha said. "How do you feel about your three months in the hospital now that you are back home?" Marsha's impression was that the boy had benefited from the hospital's structured environment, but she wanted to learn his opinion.

"It was okay," Jasper said.

"Just okay?" asked Marsha encouragingly. It was so tough to draw this boy out.

"It was like fine," Jasper said, shrugging. "You know, no big deal."

Obviously it was going to take a bit more effort to extract the boy's opinion, and Marsha made a note of reminder to herself in the margin of the boy's file. She'd start the next session with that issue. Marsha closed the file and made eye contact with Jasper. "It's been good to see you," Marsha said. "See you next week."

"Sure," Jasper said, avoiding Marsha's eyes as he got up and awkwardly left the room.

Marsha went back to her desk to dictate her notes. Flipping open the chart, she looked at her preadmission summary. Jasper had had a conduct disorder since early childhood. Once he hit age eighteen, the diagnosis would change to an antisocial personality disorder. On top of that, he also had what appeared to Marsha as a schizoid personality disorder.

Reviewing the salient features of the boy's history, Marsha noted the frequent lying, the fights at school, the record of truancy, the vindictive behavior and fantasies. Her eye stopped at the statement: *cannot experience affection or show emotion.* She suddenly pictured VJ pulling away from her embrace, looking at her coldly, his blue eyes frigid as mountain lakes. She forced her eyes back down on the chart. *Chooses solitary activities, does not desire close relationships, has no close friends.*

Marsha's pulse quickened. Was she reading a summary of her own son? With trepidation, she reread the review of Jasper's personality. There were a number of uncomfortable correlations. She was happy when her train of thought was interrupted by her nurse and secretary, Jean Colbert, a prim and proper New Englander with auburn hair. As she looked up, her eye caught a sentence that she had underlined in red: *Jasper was essentially reared by an aunt, since his mother worked two jobs to support the family.*

"You ready for your next patient?" Jean asked.

Marsha took a deep breath. "Remember those articles I saved on day care and its psychological effects?" she asked.

"Sure do," Jean said. "I filed them in the storage room."

"How about pulling them for me," Marsha said, trying to mask her concern.

"Sure," Jean said. She paused, then asked: "Are you okay?"

"I'm fine," Marsha said, picking up the next chart. As she scanned her recent notes, twelve-year-old Nancy Traverse slunk into the room and tried to disappear into one of the chairs. She pulled her head low into her shoulders like a turtle.

Marsha moved over to the therapy area, taking the seat opposite Nancy. She tried to remember where the girl had left off at the previous visit, describing her forays into sex.

The session began and dragged on. Marsha tried to concentrate, but fears for VJ floated at the back of her mind along with guilt for having worked when he had been little. Not that he'd ever minded when she'd left. But as Marsha well knew, that in itself could be a symptom of psychopathology.

After Hobbs left, Victor tried to busy himself with correspondence, partly to avoid the lab, partly to take his mind off the terrible news that Hobbs had told him. But his thoughts soon drifted back to the circumstances of the boy's death. Edema of the brain, meaning acute brain swelling, had been the immediate cause. But what could have been the cause of the edema? He wished Hobbs had been able to give him more details. It was the lack of a specific diagnosis that fed Victor's fears.

"Damn!" Victor yelled as he slammed his open palm on the top of his desk. He stood up abruptly and stared out the window. He had a good view of the clock tower from his office. The hands had been frozen in the distant past at quarter past two.

"I should have known better!" Victor said to himself, pounding his right fist into his left palm with enough strength to make them both tingle. The Hobbs child's death brought back all the concern Victor had had for VJ—concern he had finally put to rest. While Marsha fretted over the boy's psychological state, Victor's worries had more to do with the boy's physical being. When VJ's IQ dropped, then stabilized at what was still an exceptional level, Victor had felt terror. It had taken years for him to overcome his fear and relax. But the Hobbs boy's sudden death raised his fears again. Victor was particularly concerned since the parallels between VJ and the Hobbs boy did not stop with their conception. Victor understood that, like VJ, the Hobbs boy was something of a child prodigy. Victor had been keeping surreptitious tabs on the child's progress. He was curious to see if the boy would suffer as precipitous a drop in IQ as VJ had. But now, Victor only wanted to learn the circumstances of the child's tragic death.

Victor went to his computer terminal and cleared

the screen. He called up his personal file on Baby Hobbs. He wasn't looking for anything in particular, he just thought that if he scanned the data, some explanation for the child's death might occur to him. The screen stayed dark past the usual access time. Confused, Victor hit the Execute button again. Answering him, the word SEARCHING blinked in the screen's lower-right-hand corner. Then, to Victor's surprise, the computer told him there was no such file.

"What the devil?" Victor said. Thinking he might have made an entry error, Victor tried again, typing BABY-HOBBS very deliberately. He pressed execute and after a pause during which the computer searched all its storage banks, he got the exact same response: NO FILE FOUND.

Victor turned off the computer, wondering what could have happened to the information. It was true that he hadn't accessed it for some time, but that shouldn't have made a difference. Drumming his fingers on the desk in front of the keyboard, Victor thought for a moment, then accessed the computer again. This time he typed in the words BABY-MURRAY.

There was the same pause as with the Hobbs file and ultimately the same response appeared: NO FILE FOUND.

The door to the office opened and Victor twisted around. Colleen was standing in the doorway. "This is not a day for fathers," she said, gripping the edge of the door. "You have a phone call from a Mr. Murray from accounting. Apparently his baby isn't doing well either and he's crying too."

"I don't believe it," Victor blurted. The timing was so coincidental.

"Trust me," Colleen said. "Line two."

Dazed, Victor turned to his phone. The light was blinking insistently, each flash causing a ringing sensation in Victor's head. This couldn't be happening, not after everything had gone so well for so long. He had to force himself to pick up the receiver.

"I'm sorry to bother you," Murray managed, "but you've been so understanding when we were trying to get a baby. I thought you'd want to know. We brought Mark to the Children's Hospital and he is dying. The doctors tell me there is nothing they can do."

"What happened?" Victor asked, barely able to speak.

"Nobody seems to know," Horace said. "It started with a headache."

"He didn't hit his head or anything?" Victor questioned.

"Not that we know of," Horace said.

"Would you mind if I came over?" Victor asked.

A half hour later, Victor was parking his car in the garage opposite the hospital. He went inside and stopped at the information desk. The receptionist told him Mark Murray was in the surgical intensive-care unit, and gave him directions to the waiting room. Victor found Horace and Colette distraught with worry and lack of sleep. Horace got to his feet when he saw Victor.

"Any change?" Victor asked hopefully.

Horace shook his head. "He's on a respirator now."

Victor conveyed his condolences as best he could. The Murrays seemed touched that Victor had taken the time to come to the hospital, especially since they never socialized.

"He was such a special child," Horace said. "So exceptional, so intelligent . . ." He shook his head. Colette hid her face in her hands. Her shoulders began to quiver. Horace sat back down and put an arm around his wife.

"What's the name of the doctor taking care of Mark?" Victor asked.

"Nakano," Horace answered. "Dr. Nakano."

Victor excused himself, left his coat with the Murrays, and departed the waiting room with its anxious parents. He walked toward Pediatric Surgical Intensive Care, which was at the end of the corridor, behind a pair of electronic doors. As Victor stepped on the rubberized area in front of the doors, they automatically opened.

The room inside was familiar to Victor from his days as a resident. There was the usual profusion of electronic gear and scurrying nurses. The constant hiss of the respirators and bleeps of the cardiac monitors gave the room an aura of tension. Life here was in the balance.

Since Victor acted at ease in the environment, no one questioned his presence, despite the fact that he was not wearing an ID. Victor went to the desk and asked if Dr. Nakano was available.

"He was just here," a pert young woman replied. She half stood and leaned over the counter to see if she could spot him. Then she sat down and picked up the phone. A moment later the page system added Dr. Nakano's name to the incessant list that issued from speakers in the ceiling.

Walking about the room, Victor tried to locate Mark, but too many of the kids were on respirators that distorted their faces. He returned to the desk just as the ward clerk was hanging up the phone. Seeing

Victor, she told him that Dr. Nakano was on his way
back to the unit.

Five minutes later, Victor was introduced to the
handsome, deeply tanned Japanese-American. Victor
explained that he was a physician and friend of the
Murray family, and that he hoped to get some idea of
what was happening to Mark.

"It's not good," Dr. Nakano said candidly. "The child
is dying. It's not often we can say that, but in this case
the problem is unresponsive to any treatment."

"Do you have any idea of what's going on?" Victor
asked.

"We know what's happening," Dr. Nakano said,
"what we don't know is what's causing it. Come on, I'll
show you."

With the hurried step of a busy doctor, Dr. Nakano
took off toward the rear of the ICU. He stopped outside a cubicle separated from the main portion of the
ICU.

"The child's on precautions," Dr. Nakano explained.
"There's been no evidence of infection, but we thought
just in case . . ." He handed Victor a gown, hat, and
mask. Both men donned the protective gear and entered the small room.

Mark Murray was in the center of a large crib with
high side rails. His head was swathed in a gauze band-
age. Dr. Nakano explained that they'd tried a decompression and a shunt, hoping that might help, but it
hadn't.

"Take a look," Dr. Nakano said, handing Victor an
ophthalmoscope. Leaning over the stricken two-year-
old, Victor lifted Mark's eyelid and peered through the
dilated, fixed pupil. Despite his inexperience with the

instrument, he saw the pathology immediately. The optic nerve was bulging forward as if being pushed from behind.

Victor straightened up.

"Pretty impressive, no?" Dr. Nakano said. He took the scope from Victor and peered himself. He was quiet for a moment, then straightened up. "The disappointing thing is that it is getting progressively worse. The kid's brain is still swelling. I'm surprised it's not coming out his ears. Nothing has helped; not the decompression, not the shunt, not massive steroids, not mannitol. I'm afraid we've just about given up."

Victor had noticed there was no nurse in attendance. "Any hemorrhage or signs of trauma?" he asked.

"Nope," Dr. Nakano said simply. "Other than the swelling, the kid's clean. No meningitis as I said earlier. We just don't understand. The man upstairs is in control." He pointed skyward.

As if responding to Dr. Nakano's morbid prediction, the cardiac monitor let out a brief alarm, indicating that Mark's heart had paused. Mark's heart rate was becoming irregular. The alarm sounded briefly again. Dr. Nakano didn't move. "This happened earlier," he said. "But at this point it's a 'no-code' status." Then, as an explanation, he added: "The parents see no sense in keeping him alive if his brain is gone."

Victor nodded, and as he did so, the cardiac monitor alarm came on and stayed on. Mark's heart went into fibrillation. Victor looked over his shoulder toward the unit desk. No one responded.

Within a short time the erratic tracing on the CRT screen flattened out to a straight line. "That's the ball game," Dr. Nakano said. It seemed like such a heart-

73

less comment, but Victor knew that it was born more of frustration than callousness. Victor remembered being a resident too well.

Dr. Nakano and Victor returned to the desk where Dr. Nakano informed the secretary that the Murray baby had died. Matter-of-factly the secretary lifted the phone and initiated the required paperwork. Victor understood you couldn't work here if you let yourself become upset by the frequent deaths.

"There was a similar case last night," Victor said. "The name was Hobbs. The child was about the same age, maybe a little older. Are you familiar with it?"

"I heard about it," Dr. Nakano said vaguely. "But it wasn't my case. I understand many of the symptoms were the same."

"Seems so," Victor said. Then he asked: "You'll get an autopsy?"

"Absolutely," Dr. Nakano said. "It will be a medical examiner's case, but they turn most over to us. They're too busy downtown, especially for this kind of esoteric stuff. Will you tell the parents or do you want me to do it?"

Dr. Nakano's rapid change of direction in his conversation jarred Victor. "I'll tell them," he said after a pause. "And thanks for your time."

"No problem," Dr. Nakano said, but he didn't look at Victor. He was already involved with another crisis.

Stunned, Victor walked out of the ICU, appreciating the quiet as the electronic doors closed behind him. He returned to the waiting room where the Murrays guessed the bad news before he could tell them. Gripping each other, they again thanked Victor for coming. Victor murmured a few words of condolence. But even as he spoke a frightful image gripped his heart.

He saw VJ white and hooked up to a respirator in the bed where Mark had lain.

Cold with terror, Victor went to Pathology and introduced himself to the chief of the department, Dr. Warren Burghofen. The man assured Victor that they would do everything in their power to get the two autopsies, and get them as soon as possible.

"We certainly want to know what's going on here," Burghofen said. "We don't want any epidemic of idiopathic cerebral edema ravaging this city."

Victor slowly returned to his car. He knew there was little likelihood of an epidemic. He was only too conscious of the number of children at risk. It was three.

As soon as Victor got back to his office he asked Colleen to contact Louis Kaspwicz, the head of Chimera's data processing, and have him come up immediately.

Louis was a short, stocky man with a shiny bald head, who had a habit of sudden unpredictable movements. He was extremely shy and rarely looked anyone in the eye, but despite his quirky personality, he was superb at what he did. Chimera depended upon his computer expertise for almost every area, from research to production to billing.

"I have a problem," Victor said, leaning back against his desk, his arms folded across his chest. "I can't find two of my personal files. Any idea how that could be?"

"Can be a number of reasons," Louis said. "Usually it's because the user forgets the assigned name."

"I checked my directory," Victor said. "They weren't there."

"Maybe they got in someone else's directory," Louis said.

"I never thought of that," Victor admitted. "But I can remember using them, and I never had to designate another path to call them up."

"Well, I can't say unless I look into it," Louis said. "What were the names you gave the files?"

"I want this to remain confidential," Victor emphasized.

"Of course."

Victor gave Louis the names and Louis sat down at the terminal himself.

"No luck?" asked Victor after a few minutes when the screen remained blank.

"Doesn't seem so. But back in my office I can look into it by using the computer to search through the logs. Are you sure these were the designated file names?"

"Quite sure," Victor said.

"I'll get right on it if it's important," Louis said.

"It's important."

After Louis left, Victor stayed by the computer terminal. He had an idea. Carefully he typed onto the screen the name of another file: BABY-FRANK. For a moment he hesitated, afraid of what might turn up—or what might not. Finally he pushed Execute and held his breath. Unfortunately his fears were answered: VJ's file was gone!

Sitting back in his chair, Victor began to sweat. Three related but uncrossreferenced files could not disappear by coincidence. Suddenly Victor saw Hurst's engorged face and remembered his threat: "You're not the white knight you want us to believe.... You're not immune."

Victor got up from the terminal and went to the window. Clouds were blowing in from the east. It was either going to rain or snow. He stood there for a few moments, wondering if Hurst had anything to do with the missing files. Could he possibly suspect? If he did, that might have been the basis for his vague threat. Victor shook his head. There was no way Hurst could have known about the files. No one knew about them. No one!

# 5

*Monday Evening*

Marsha looked across the dinner table at her husband and son. VJ was absorbed in reading a book on black holes, barely looking up to eat. She would have told him to put the book away, but Victor had come home in such a bad mood she didn't want to say anything that would make it worse. And she herself was still troubled about VJ. She loved him so much she couldn't bear the thought that he might be disturbed, but she also knew she couldn't help him if she didn't face the truth. Apparently he'd spent the whole day at Chimera, seemingly by himself because Victor admitted, when she'd specifically asked, that he'd not seen VJ since morning.

As if sensing her gaze, VJ abruptly put down his book and took his plate over to the dishwasher. As he rose, his intense blue eyes caught Marsha's. There was no warmth, no feeling, just a brilliant turquoise light that made Marsha feel as if she were under a microscope. "Thank you for the dinner," VJ said mechanically.

Marsha listened to the sound of VJ's footsteps as he ran up the back stairs. Outside the wind suddenly whistled, and she looked out the window. In the beam of light from over the garage she could see that the rain had changed to snow. She shivered, but it wasn't from the wintry landscape.

"I guess I'm not too hungry tonight," Victor offered. As far as Marsha remembered, it was the first time he'd initiated conversation since she'd gotten home from making her hospital rounds.

"Something troubling you?" Marsha asked. "Want to talk about it?"

"I don't need you to play psychiatrist," Victor said harshly.

Marsha knew that she could have taken offense. She wasn't playing psychiatrist. But she thought that she'd play the adult, and not push things. Victor would tell her soon enough what was on his mind.

"Well, something is troubling me," Marsha said. She decided that at least she'd be honest. Victor looked at her. Knowing him as well as she did, she imagined that he already felt guilty at having spoken so harshly.

"I read a series of articles today," Marsha continued. "They talked about some of the possible effects of parental deprivation on children being reared by nannies and or spending inordinate amounts of time in day care. Some of the findings may apply to VJ. I'm concerned that maybe I should have taken time off when VJ was an infant to spend more time with him."

Victor's face immediately reflected irritation. "Hold it," he said just as harshly, holding up both hands. "I don't think I want to hear the rest of this. As far as I'm concerned, VJ is just fine and I don't want to listen to a bunch of psychiatric nonsense to the contrary."

"Well, isn't that inappropriate," Marsha stated, losing some of her patience.

"Oh, save me!" Victor intoned, picking up his unfinished dinner and discarding it in the trash. "I'm in no mood for this."

"Well, what *are* you in the mood for?" Marsha questioned.

Victor took a deep breath, looking out the kitchen window. "I think I'll go for a walk."

"In this weather?" Marsha questioned. "Wet snow, soggy ground. I think something is troubling you and you're unable to talk about it."

Victor turned to his wife. "Am I that obvious?"

Marsha laughed. "It's painful to watch you struggle. Please tell me what's on your mind. I'm your wife."

Victor shrugged and came back to the table. He sat down and intertwined his fingers, resting his elbows on his place mat. "There is something on my mind," he admitted.

"I'm glad my patients don't have this much trouble talking," Marsha said. She reached across to lovingly touch Victor's arm.

Victor got up and went to the bottom of the back stairs. He listened for a moment, then closed the door and returned to the table. He sat down, and he leaned toward Marsha: "I want VJ to have a full neuro-medical work-up just like he did seven years ago when his intelligence fell."

Marsha didn't respond. Worrying about VJ's personality development was one thing, but worrying about his general health was something else entirely. The mere suggestion of such a work-up was a shock, as was the reference to VJ's change in intelligence.

"You remember when his IQ fell so dramatically around age three and a half?" Victor said.

"Of course I remember," Marsha said. She studied Victor intently. Why was he doing this to her? He had to know this would only make her concerns worse.

"I want the same kind of work-up as we did then," Victor repeated.

"You know something that you are keeping from me," Marsha said with alarm. "What is it? Is there something wrong with VJ?"

"No!" Victor said. "VJ is fine, like I said before. I just want to be sure and I'd feel sure if he had a repeat work-up. That's all there is to it."

"I want to know why you suddenly want a work-up now," Marsha demanded.

"I told you why," Victor said, his voice rising with anger.

"You want me to agree to allow our son to have a full neuro-medical work-up without telling me the indications?" Marsha questioned. "No way! I'm not going to let the boy have all those X-rays etcetera without some explanation."

"Damn it, Marsha!" Victor said gritting his teeth.

"Damn it yourself," Marsha returned. "You're keeping something from me, Victor, and I don't like it. You're trying to bulldoze right over my feelings. Unless you tell me what this is all about, VJ is not having any tests, and believe me, I have something to say about it. So either you tell me what's on your mind or we just drop it."

Marsha leaned back in her chair and and inhaled deeply, holding her breath for a moment before letting it out. Victor, obviously irritated, stared at Marsha, but her strength began to wear him down. Her position was clear, and by experience he knew she'd not be apt to change her mind. After sixty seconds of silence, his stare began to waver. Finally he looked down at his hands. The grandfather clock in the living room chimed eight times.

"All right," he said finally as if exhausted. "I'll tell you the whole story." He sat back and ran his fingers through his hair. He established eye contact with Marsha for a second, then looked up at the ceiling like a young boy caught in a forbidden act.

Marsha felt a growing sense of impatience and concern about what she was about to hear.

"The trouble is I don't know where to begin," Victor said.

"How about at the beginning," Marsha suggested, her impatience showing again.

Victor's eyes met hers. He'd kept the secret surrounding VJ's conception for over ten years. Looking at Marsha's open, honest face, he wondered if she would ever forgive him when she learned the truth.

"Please," Marsha said. "Why can't you just tell me?"

Victor lowered his eyes. "Lots of reasons," he said. "One is you might not believe me. In fact, for me to tell you we have to go to my lab."

"Right now?" questioned Marsha. "Are you serious?"

"If you want to hear."

There was a pause. Kissa surprised Marsha by jumping up on her lap. She'd forgotten to feed him. "All right," she said. "Let me feed the cat and say something to VJ. I can be ready in fifteen minutes."

VJ heard footsteps coming down the hall toward his bedroom. Without hurrying, he closed the cover of his Scott stamp album and slipped it onto the shelf. His parents knew nothing about philately, so they wouldn't know what they were looking at. But there was no reason to take any chances. He didn't want them to discover just how large and valuable his collection had become. They had thought his request for a bank vault more childish conceit than anything else and VJ saw no reason to make them think otherwise.

"What are you doing, dear?" Marsha asked as she appeared in his doorway.

VJ pursed his lips. "Nothing really." He knew she was upset, but there was nothing he could do about it. Ever since he was a baby he realized there was something she wanted from him, something other mothers got from their children that he couldn't give her. Sometimes, like now, he felt sorry.

"Why don't you invite Richie over one night this week?" she was saying.

"Maybe I will."

"I think it would be nice," Marsha said. "I'd like to meet him."

VJ nodded.

Marsha smiled, shifted her weight. "Your father and I are going out for a little while. Is that okay with you?"

"Sure."

"We won't be gone long."

"I'll be fine."

Five minutes later VJ watched from his bedroom window as Victor's car descended the drive. VJ stood for a while looking out. He wondered if he should be concerned. After all, it was not usual for his parents to go out on a weekday night. He shrugged his shoul-

83

ders. If there was something to worry about, he'd hear about it soon enough.

Turning back into his room, he took his stamp album from the shelf and went back to putting in the mint set of early American stamps he'd recently received.

The phone rang a long time before he heard it. Finally, remembering that his parents were out, he got up and went down the hall to the study. He picked up the receiver and said hello.

"Dr. Victor Frank, please," the caller said. The voice sounded muffled, as if it was far away from the receiver.

"Dr. Frank is not at home," VJ said politely. "Would you care to leave a message?"

"What time will Dr. Frank be back?"

"In about an hour," VJ answered.

"Are you his son?"

"That's right."

"Maybe it will be more effective if you give him the message. Tell your father that life will be getting progressively unpleasant unless he reconsiders and is reasonable. You got that?"

"Who is this?" VJ demanded.

"Just give your father the message. He'll know."

"Who is this?" VJ repeated, feeling the initial stirrings of fear. But the caller had hung up.

VJ slowly replaced the receiver. All at once he was acutely aware that he was all alone in the house. He stood for a moment listening. He'd never realized all the creaking sounds of an empty house. The radiator in the corner quietly hissed. From somewhere else a dull clunking sounded, probably a heating pipe. Outside the wind blew snow against the window.

Picking up the phone again, VJ made a call of his own. When a man answered he told the person that he was scared. After being reassured that everything would be taken care of, VJ put down the phone. He felt better, but to be on the safe side, he hurried down-stairs and methodically checked every window and every door to make sure they were all securely locked. He didn't go down into the basement but bolted the door instead.

Back in his room he turned on the computer. He wished the cat would stay in his room, but he knew better than to bother looking for her. Kissa was afraid of him, though he tried to keep his mother from realiz-ing the fact. There were so many things he had to keep his mother from noticing. It was a strain. But then he hadn't chosen to be what he was, either.

Booting up the computer, VJ loaded Pac-Man and tried to concentrate.

The fluorescent lights blinked, then filled the room with their rude light. Victor stepped aside and let Mar-sha precede him into the lab. She'd been there on a few occasions, but it had always been during the day. She was surprised how sinister the place looked at night with no people to relieve its sterile appearance. The room was about fifty feet by thirty with lab benches and hoods along each wall. In the center was a large island comprised of scientific equipment, each instrument more exotic than the next. There was a profusion of dials, cathode ray tubes, computers, glass tubing, and mazes of electronic connectors.

A number of doors led from the main room. Victor led Marsha through one to an L-shaped area filled with dissecting tables. Marsha glanced at the scalpels and other horrid instruments and shuddered. Beyond that room and through a glass door with embedded wire was the animal room, and from where Marsha was standing she could see dogs and apes pacing behind the bars of their cages. She looked away. That was a part of research that she preferred not to think about.

"This way," Victor said, guiding her to the very back of the L, where the wall was clear glass.

Flipping a switch, Victor turned on the light behind the glass. Marsha was surprised to see a series of large aquariums, each containing dozens of strange-looking sea creatures. They resembled snails but without their shells.

Victor pulled over a stepladder. After searching through a number of the tanks, he took a dissecting pan from one of the tables and climbed the ladder. With a net, he caught two creatures from separate tanks.

"Is this necessary?" asked Marsha, wondering what these hideous creatures had to do with Victor's concern about VJ's health.

Victor didn't answer. He came down the stepladder, balancing the tray. Marsha took a long look at the creatures. They were about ten inches long, brownish in color, with a slimy, gelatinous skin. She choked down a wave of nausea. She hated this sort of thing. It was one of the reasons she'd gone into psychiatry: therapy was clean, neat, and very human.

"Victor!" Marsha said as she watched him impale the creatures into the wax-bottomed dissecting pan, spreading out their fins, or whatever they were. "Why can't you just tell me?"

"Because you wouldn't believe me," Victor said. "Be

patient for a few moments more." He took a scalpel and inserted a fresh, razor-sharp blade.

Marsha looked away as he quickly slit open each of the animals.

"These are Aplasia," Victor said, trying to cover his own nervousness with a strictly scientific approach. "They have been used widely for nerve cell research." He picked up a scissor and began snipping quickly and deliberately.

"There," he said. "I've removed the abdominal ganglion from each of the Aplasia."

Marsha looked. Victor was holding a small flat dish filled with clear fluid. Within, floating on the surface of the liquid, were two minute pieces of tissue.

"Now come over to the microscope," Victor said.

"What about those poor creatures?" Marsha asked, forcing herself to look into the dissecting pan. The animals seemed to be struggling against the pins that held them on the bottom of the tray.

"The techs will clean up in the morning," Victor said, missing her meaning. He turned on the light of the microscope.

With one last look at the Aplasia, Marsha went over to Victor, who was already busily peering down and adjusting the focus on the two-man dissecting scope.

She bent over and looked. The ganglia were in the shape of the letter H with the swollen crosspiece resembling a transparent bag of clear marbles. The arms of the H were undoubtedly transsected nerve fibers. Victor was moving a pointer, and he told Marsha to count the nerve cells or neurons as he indicated them.

Marsha did as she was told.

ROBIN COOK

"Okay," Victor said. "Let's look at the other ganglion."

The visual field rushed by, then stopped. There was another H like the first. "Count again," Victor said.

"This one has more than twice as many neurons as the other."

"Precisely!" Victor said, straightening up and getting to his feet. He began to pace. His face had an odd, excited sheen, and Marsh began to feel the beginnings of fear. "I got very interested in the number of nerve cells of normal Aplasia about twelve years ago. At that time I knew, like everyone else, that nerve cells differentiated and proliferated during early embryological development. Since these Aplasia were relatively less complicated than higher animals, I was able to isolate the protein which was responsible for the process which I called nerve growth factor, or NGF. You follow me?" Victor stopped his pacing to look directly at Marsha.

"Yes," Marsha said, watching her husband. He seemed to be changing in front of her eyes. He'd developed a disturbing messianic appearance. She suddenly felt queasy, with the awful thought that she knew where this seemingly irrelevant lecture was heading.

Victor recommenced his pacing as his excitement grew. "I used genetic engineering to reproduce the protein and isolate the responsible gene. Then, for the brilliant part . . ." He stopped again in front of Marsha. His eyes sparkled. "I took a fertilized Aplasia egg or zygote and after causing a point mutation in its DNA, I inserted the new NGF gene along with a promoter. The result?"

"More ganglionic neurons," Marsha answered.

88

"Exactly," Victor said excitedly. "And, equally as important, the ability to pass the trait on to its offspring. Now, come back into the main room." He gave Marsha a hand, and pulled her to her feet.

Dumbly she followed him to a light box, where he displayed some large transparencies of microscopic sections of rat brains. Even without counting, Marsha was able to appreciate that there were many more nerve cells in one photograph than the other. Still speechless, she let him herd her into the animal room itself. Just inside the door he slipped on a pair of heavy leather gloves.

Marsha tried not to breathe. It smelled like a badly run zoo. There were hundreds of cages housing apes, dogs, cats, and rats. They stopped by the rats.

Marsha shuddered at the innumerable pink twitching noses and hairless pink tails.

Victor stopped by a specific cage and unhooked the door. Reaching in, he pulled out a large rat that responded by biting repeatedly at Victor's gloved fingers.

"Easy, Charlie!" Victor said. He carried the rat over to a table with a glass top, raised a portion of the glass, and dropped the rat into what appeared to be a miniature maze. The rat was trapped just in front of the starting gate.

"Watch!" Victor said, raising the gate.

After a moment's pause, the rat entered the maze. With only a few wrong turns the animal reached the exit and got its reward.

"Quick, huh?" Victor said with a satisfied smile. "This is one of my 'smart' rats. They are rats in which I inserted the NGF gene. Now watch this."

Victor adjusted the apparatus so that the rat was returned to the start position, but in a section that did not have access to the maze. Victor then went back to the cages and got a second rat. He dropped it inside the table so the two rats faced each other through a wire mesh.

After a moment or two he opened the gate and the second rat went through the maze without a single mistake.

"Do you know what you just witnessed?" Victor asked.

Marsha shook her head.

"Rat communication," Victor said. "I've been able to train these rats to explain the maze to each other. It's incredible."

"I'm certain it is," Marsha said with less enthusiasm than Victor.

"I've done this 'neuronal proliferation' study on hundreds of rats," Victor said.

Marsha nodded uncertainly.

"I did it on fifty dogs, six cows, and one sheep," Victor added. "I was afraid to try it on the monkeys. I was afraid of success. I kept seeing that old movie *Planet of the Apes* play in my mind." He laughed, and the sound of his laughter echoed hollowly off the animal-room walls.

Marsha didn't laugh. Instead she shivered. "Exactly what are you telling me?" she asked, although her imagination had already begun to provide disturbing answers.

Victor couldn't look her in the eye.

"Please!" Marsha cried, almost in tears.

"I'm only trying to give you the background so you'll understand," Victor said, knowing that she never would. "Believe me, I didn't plan what happened next. I'd just finished the successful trial with the sheep when you started talking of having another child. Remember when we decided to go to Fertility, Inc.?

Marsha nodded, tears beginning to roll down her cheeks.

"Well, you gave them a very successful harvest of ova. We got eight."

Marsha felt herself swaying. She steadied herself, grabbing on to the edge of the maze.

"I personally did the in-vitro fertilization with my sperm," Victor continued. "You knew that. What I didn't tell you is that I brought the fertilized eggs back here to the lab."

Marsha let go of the table and staggered over to one of the benches. She wanted to faint. She sat down heavily. She didn't think she could stand hearing the rest of Victor's story. But now that he had begun she realized he was going to tell her whether she liked it or not. He seemed to feel he could minimize the enormity of his sin if he confined himself to a purely scientific description. Could this be the man she married?

"When I got the zygotes back here," he said, "I chose a nonsense sequence of DNA on chromosome 6 and did a point mutation. Then, with micro-injection techniques and a retro viral vector, I inserted the NGF gene along with several promoters, including one from a bacterial plasmid that coded for resistance to the cephalosporin antibiotic called cephaloclor."

Victor paused for a moment, but he didn't look up. "That's why I insisted that Mary Millman take the cephaloclor from the second to the eighth week of her pregnancy. It was the cephaloclor that kept the gene turned on, producing the nerve growth factor."

Victor finally looked up. "God help me, when I did

it, it seemed like a good idea. But later I knew it was wrong. I lived in terror until VJ was born."

Marsha suddenly was overcome with rage. She leaped up and began striking Victor with her fists. He made no attempt to protect himself, waiting until she lowered her hands and stood before him, weeping silently. Then he tried to take her in his arms, but she wouldn't let him touch her. She went out to the main lab and sat down. Victor followed, but she refused to look at him.

"I'm sorry," Victor said again. "Believe me, I never would have done it unless I was certain it would work. There's never been a problem with any of the animals. And the idea of having a super-smart child was so seductive . . ." His voice trailed off.

"I can't believe you did something so dreadful," she sobbed.

"Researchers have experimented on themselves in the past," he said, realizing it was no excuse.

"On themselves!" cried Marsha. "Not on innocent children." She wept uncontrollably. But even in the depths of her emotion, fear reasserted itself. With difficulty, she struggled to control herself. Victor had done something terrible. But what was done, was done. She couldn't undo it. The problem now was to deal with reality, and her thoughts turned to VJ, someone she loved dearly. "All right," she managed, choking back additional tears. "Now you've told me. But what you haven't told me is why you want VJ to have another neuro-medical work up. What are you afraid of? Do you think his intelligence has dropped again?"

As she spoke, her mind took her back six and a half years. They were still living in the small farmhouse and both David and Janice were alive and well. It had been a happy time, filled with wonder at VJ's unbelievable mind. As a three-year-old, he could read anything and retain almost everything. As far as she could determine at the time, his IQ was somewhere around two hundred and fifty.

Then one day, everything changed. She'd gone by Chimera to pick VJ up from the day-care center, where he was taken after spending the morning at the Crocker Preschool. She knew something was wrong the moment she saw the director's face.

Pauline Spaulding was a wonderful woman, a forty-two-year-old, ex–elementary-school teacher and ex-aerobics instructor who had found her calling in day-care management. She loved her job and loved the children, who in return adored her for her boundless enthusiasm. But today she seemed upset.

"Something is wrong with VJ," she said, not mincing any words.

"Is he sick? Where is he?"

"He's here," Pauline said. "He's not sick. His health is fine. It's something else."

"Tell me!" Marsha cried.

"It started just after lunch," Pauline explained. "When the other kids take their rest, VJ generally goes into the workroom and plays chess on the computer. He's been doing that for some time."

"I know," Marsha said. She had given VJ permission to miss the rest period after he told her he did not need the rest and he hated to waste the time.

"No one was in the workroom at the time," Pauline said. "But suddenly there was a big crash. When I got in there VJ was smashing the computer with a chair."

"My word!" Marsha exclaimed. Temper tantrums

were not part of VJ's behavioral repertoire. "Did he explain himself?" she asked.

"He was crying, Dr. Frank."

"VJ, crying?" Marsha was astounded. VJ never cried.

"He was crying like a normal three-and-a-half-year-old child," Pauline said.

"What are you trying to tell me?" Marsha asked.

"Apparently VJ smashed the computer because he suddenly didn't know how to use it."

"That's absurd," Marsha said. VJ had been using the computer at home since he'd been two and a half.

"Wait," Pauline said. "To calm him, I offered him a book that he'd been reading about dinosaurs. He tore it up."

Marsha ran into the workroom. There were only three children there. VJ was sitting at a table, coloring in a coloring book like any other preschooler. When he saw her, he dropped his crayon and ran into her arms. He started to cry, saying that his head hurt.

Marsha hugged him. "Did you tear your dinosaur book?" she asked.

He averted his eyes. "Yes."

"But why?" Marsha asked.

VJ looked back at Marsha and said: "Because I can't read anymore."

Over the next several days VJ had a neuro-medical work-up to rule out any acute neurological problems. The results came back negative, but when Marsha repeated a series of IQ tests the boy had taken the previous year, the results were shockingly different. VJ's IQ had dropped to 130. Still high, but certainly not in the genius range.

Victor brought Marsha back to the present by

swearing that there was nothing wrong with VJ's intelligence.

"Then why the work-up?" Marsha asked again.

"I . . . I just think it would be a good idea," Victor stammered.

"I've been married to you for sixteen years," Marsha said after a pause. "And I know you are not telling me the truth." It was hard for her to believe she had anything worse to discover than what Victor had already told her.

Victor ran a hand through his thick hair. "It's because of what has happened to the Hobbs' and the Murrays' babies."

"Who are they?"

"William Hobbs and Horace Murray work here," Victor answered.

"Don't tell me you created chimeras out of their children, too."

"Worse," Victor admitted. "Both of those couples had true infertility. They needed donor gametes. Since I'd frozen the other seven of our zygotes, and since they could provide uniquely qualified homes, I used two of ours."

"Are you saying that these babies are genetically mine?" Marsha asked with renewed disbelief.

"Ours," Victor corrected.

"My God!" Marsha said, staggered by this new revelation. For the moment she was beyond emotion.

"It's no different than donating sperm or eggs," Victor said. "It's just more efficient, since they have already united."

"Maybe it's no different to you," Marsha said. "Considering what you did to VJ. But it is to me. I can't even comprehend the idea of someone else bringing up my children. What about the other five zygotes? Where are they?"

Exhaustedly, Victor stood up and walked across the room to the central island. He stopped next to a circular metal appliance, about the size of a clothes washer. Rubber hoses connected the machine to a large cylinder of liquefied nitrogen.

"They're in here," Victor said. "Frozen in suspended animation. Want to see?"

Marsha shook her head. She was appalled. As a physician she knew that such technology existed, but the few times she even thought about it, she considered it in the abstract. She never thought that it would involve her personally.

"I wasn't planning on telling you all this at once," Victor said. "But now you have it: the whole story. I want VJ to have a neuro-medical work-up so that I can be sure that he has no remedial problems."

"Why?" said Marsha bitterly. "Has something happened to the other children?"

"They got sick," Victor said.

"How sick?" Marsha asked. "And sick with what?"

"Very sick," Victor answered. "They died of acute cerebral edema. No one knows why yet."

Marsha felt a wave of dizziness sweep over her. This time she had to put her head down to keep from passing out. Every time she got herself under control, Victor unveiled a further outrage.

"Was it sudden?" she asked, looking up. "Or had they been ill for a long time?"

"It was sudden," Victor admitted.

"How old were they?" Marsha asked.

"About three years old."

One of the computer print-out devices suddenly

came to life and furiously printed out a mass of data. Then a refrigeration unit kicked in, emitting a low hum and vibration. It seemed to Marsha that the lab was running itself. It didn't need humans.

"Did the children who died have the same NGF gene as VJ?" Marsha asked.

Victor nodded.

"And they are about the same age as VJ when his intelligence fell," Marsha said.

"Close!" Victor said. "That's why I want to do the work-up, to make sure that VJ isn't brewing any further problem. But I'm sure he's fine. If it hadn't been for the Hobbs' and the Murrays' babies, I wouldn't have thought about having VJ examined. Trust me."

If Marsha could have laughed, she would have. Victor had just about destroyed her life, and he was asking her to trust him. How he could have experimented on his own baby was beyond her comprehension. But that couldn't be changed. Now she had to worry about the present. "Do you think the same thing that happened to the others could happen to VJ?" she asked hesitantly.

"I doubt it. Especially with the seven-year difference in ages. It would seem VJ already survived the critical point back when his IQ dropped. Perhaps what happened to the other children was a function of their being frozen in zygote form," he said, but then broke off, seeing the expression on his wife's face. She wasn't about to take a scientific interest in the tragedy.

"What about VJ's fall in intelligence?" Marsha asked. "Could that have been the same problem in some arrested form, since he was nearly the same age when it happened?"

"It's possible," Victor said, "but I don't know."

Marsha let her eyes slowly sweep around the lab, seeing all the futuristic equipment in a different light. Research could provide hope for the future by curing disease, but it had another far more disturbing potential.

"I want to get out of here!" Marsha said suddenly, getting to her feet. Her abrupt movement sent her chair spinning to the center of the room where it hit the freezer containing the frozen zygotes. Victor retrieved it and returned it to its place at the lab bench. By that time Marsha was already out the door, heading down the corridor. Victor quickly locked up, then hurried after her. The elevator doors had almost closed when he squeezed in beside her. She moved away from him, hurt, disgusted, and angry. But most of all she was worried. She wanted to get home to VJ.

They left the building in silence. Victor was smart enough not to try to make her talk. The snow had started to stick, and they had to walk carefully to keep from slipping. Marsha was aware Victor was watching her intently as they got into the car. Still she didn't say anything. It wasn't until they crossed the Merrimack River that she finally spoke.

"I thought that experimenting on human embryos was against the law." She knew Victor's real crime was a moral one, but for the moment she couldn't face the complete truth.

"Policy has never been clear," Victor said, pleased not to have to deal with the ethical issue. "There was a notice published in the Federal Register forbidding such experimentation, but it only covered institutions getting federal grant money. It didn't cover private institutions like Chimera." Victor didn't elaborate further. He knew his actions were indefensible. They drove in silence again until he said, "The reason I didn't tell you years ago was because I didn't want you to treat VJ any differently."

Marsha looked across at her husband, watching the play of light flickering on his face from the oncoming cars. "You didn't tell me because you knew what a terrible thing it was," Marsha said evenly.

As they turned on Windsor Street, he said, "Maybe you're right. I suppose I did feel guilty. Before VJ was born, I thought I'd have a nervous breakdown. Then, after his intelligence fell, I was again a basket case. It's only been during the last five years that I've been able to relax."

"Then why did you use the zygotes again?" Marsha asked.

"By that time the experiment seemed like a big success," Victor said. "And also because the families in question were uniquely qualified to have an exceptional child. But I shouldn't have done it. I know that now."

"Do you mean that?" Marsha asked.

"Oh God, yes!"

As they pulled into their driveway, Marsha felt for the first time since he'd shown her the rats that she might someday be able to forgive him. Then maybe— if VJ was truly all right, if her concern about his development was groundless—maybe they might be able to continue as a family. A lot of ifs. Marsha closed her eyes and prayed. Having lost one child, she asked God to spare the other. She didn't think she could suffer such a loss again.

The light in VJ's room was still on. Every night he

was up there reading or studying. For however aloof he seemed, he was essentially a good kid.

Victor used the automatic button to raise the garage door. As soon as the car came to a stop, Marsha dashed out, anxious to reassure herself VJ was fine. Without waiting for Victor, she used her own key on the door to the back hall. But when she tried to push it open, the door wouldn't budge. Victor came up behind her and tried it himself.

"The dead bolt's been thrown," Victor said.

"VJ must have locked it after we left." She raised a fist and pounded on the door. It sounded loud in the garage but there was no response from VJ. "Do you think he's all right?" she asked.

"I'm sure he's fine," Victor said. "There is no way he could hear you knocking out here unless he was in the family room. Come on! We'll go to the front."

Victor led the way out through the garage and around to the front of the house. He tried his key. But that door had been deadbolted as well. He tried the bell. There was still no response. He rang again, beginning to feel a little of Marsha's anxiety. Just when they were about to try another door, they heard VJ's clear voice asking who was there.

As soon as the front door was opened, Marsha tried to hug VJ, but he eluded her grasp. "Where you have been?" he demanded.

Victor looked at his watch. It was a quarter to ten. They'd been gone about an hour and a half.

"Just been over to the lab," Marsha said. It wasn't like VJ to notice one way or the other when they weren't around. He was so self-sufficient.

VJ looked at Victor. "You got a phone call. I'm supposed to give you the message that things will be getting unpleasant unless you reconsider and are reasonable."

"Who was it?" Victor demanded.

"The caller didn't leave a name," VJ said.

"Was it male or female?" Victor asked.

"I couldn't tell," VJ said. "Whoever it was didn't speak into the receiver, or at least that's what it sounded like."

Looking from husband to son, Marsha said, "Victor, what is this all about?"

"Office politics," he said. "It's nothing to worry about."

Marsha turned to VJ. "Did the caller frighten you? We noticed the doors were all bolted."

"A little," VJ admitted. "Then I realized they wouldn't have called with that kind of message if they intended to come over."

"I suppose you're right," Marsha said. VJ had an impressive way of intellectualizing situations. "Why don't we all go into the kitchen. I could use some herbal tea."

"Not for me, thanks," VJ said. He turned to head up the stairs.

"Son!" Victor called.

VJ hesitated on the first step.

"I just wanted to let you know that we will be going to Children's Hospital in Boston tomorrow morning. I want you to have a physical."

"I don't need a physical," VJ complained. "I hate hospitals."

"I understand your feelings," Victor said. "Nonetheless, you will have a physical, just like I do and your mother does."

VJ looked toward Marsha. She wanted to hold him

and make sure that he didn't have a headache or any symptoms whatsoever. But she didn't move, intimidated by her own son.

"Nothing is wrong with me," VJ persisted.

"The matter is closed," Victor said. "Discussion over."

His cupid's mouth set, VJ glared at his father, then turned and disappeared upstairs.

Back in the kitchen, Marsha put on the kettle. She knew it would take days before she could sort out all her feelings about what she'd learned that evening. Sixteen years of marriage and she wondered if she knew her husband at all.

Wind whipped snow against the window, causing the sash to rattle against the frame. Rolling over, Marsha squinted at the face of the digital radio-alarm clock. It was half past midnight, and she was a long way from sleep. Next to her she could hear Victor's rhythmic breathing.

Swinging her feet from under the covers, Marsha searched for her slippers. Getting up, she picked up her robe from the chair in the corner, opened the door, and stepped into the hall.

A sudden gust of wind hit the house and the old timbers groaned. She thought of going down to her study on the floor below, but instead continued down the long corridor, to VJ's room. She pushed open the door. VJ had left his window open a crack and the lace curtains were snapping in the snowy breeze. Marsha slipped through the door and silently pushed the window shut.

Marsha looked down at her sleeping son. With his blond curls and high coloring, he looked perfectly angelic. She had to restrain herself from touching him. His aversion to affection was so strong; sometimes it was difficult to think of him and David as brothers. She wondered if his disinclination to hug or cuddle had anything to do with Victor's injection of foreign genes. She'd probably never know. But she realized her earlier concern about VJ had some basis in reality.

Moving the clothes from the chair next to VJ's bed, Marsha sat down. As an infant, he'd been almost too good to be true. He rarely cried, and he slept almost every night the whole night through. To her astonishment, he began to talk when he was only a few months old.

Marsha realized that her excitement and pride of VJ's accomplishments had been the reason she'd never questioned them. And she'd certainly never suspected any artificial enhancement. Now she realized she'd been naive. VJ's brilliance was more than genius. She remembered when a French scientist and his wife had come to Chimera for a six-month stay when VJ was just three. Their daughter, Michelle, had been brought to the day-care center. She was five, and within a week she could say a number of sentences in English. But what was more astounding was that during the same period of time, VJ had become fluent in French.

And then there was VJ's third birthday. To celebrate, Marsha had planned a surprise birthday party, inviting most of the children his age from the day-care center. When he came downstairs Saturday for lunch, he'd found a roomful of mothers and kids shouting "Happy Birthday." It was not a success. VJ pulled Marsha aside and said, "Why did you ask these kids? I have to put up with them every day. I hate them. They drive me crazy!"

Marsha was shocked, but at the time she told herself that he was so much brighter than the other children that being forced to socialize was a punishment. VJ much preferred the company of adults, even at age three.

VJ suddenly turned over, muttering in his sleep, bringing Marsha back to the present and all the problems she wanted to forget. He was such a beautiful boy. It was hard to reconcile his innocent face in slumber with the monstrous truth revealed at the lab. At least now she felt she had some understanding of why he was so cold and unaffectionate. Maybe that was why he shared so many of the personality disorders displayed by Jasper Lewis. Ruefully, she reflected that at least her absences from home in VJ's early years were not to blame.

Well, as long as Victor was insisting on a neuro-medical work-up, Marsha decided that she would give VJ a battery of psychological tests. It certainly wouldn't hurt.

# 6

## *Tuesday Morning*

They took separate cars to drive to Boston since Victor wanted to return directly to Chimera. VJ chose to ride with Marsha.

The ride itself was uneventful. Marsha tried to get VJ to talk, but he answered all her questions with a curt yes or no. She gave up until they were a few minutes away from Children's Hospital.

"Have you been having any headaches?" she asked, breaking the long silence.

"No," VJ said. "I told you I'm fine. Why the sudden concern about my health?"

"It's your father's idea," Marsha said. She couldn't think of any reason not to tell the truth. "He calls it preventive medicine."

"I think it's a waste of time," VJ said.

"Have you had any change in your memory?" Marsha asked.

"I'm telling you," VJ snapped, "I'm entirely normal!"

"All right, VJ," Marsha said. "There is no reason to get angry. We're glad that you're healthy and we want

105

you to stay that way." She wondered what the boy would think if he were told he was a chimera, and that he had animal genes fused into his chromosomes.

"Do you remember back when you were three and suddenly couldn't read?" Marsha asked.

"Of course," VJ said.

"We've never talked much about that period," Marsha said.

VJ turned away from Marsha and looked out the window.

"Were you very upset?" Marsha asked.

VJ turned to her and said, "Mother, please don't play psychiatrist with me. Of course it bothered me. It was frustrating not being able to do things that I'd been able to do. But I relearned them and I'm fine."

"If you ever want to talk about it, I'm available," Marsha said. "Just because I've never brought it up doesn't mean I don't care. You have to understand that it was a stressful time for me too. As a mother I was terrified that you were ill. Once it was clear you were all right, I guess I tried not to think about it."

VJ just nodded.

They all met in the waiting room of Dr. Clifford Ruddock, Chief of the Department of Neurology. Victor had beat them by fifteen minutes. As soon as VJ sat down with a magazine, Victor took Marsha aside. "I spoke with Dr. Ruddock as soon as I arrived. He's agreed to compare VJ's current neurological status with what he found at the time VJ's IQ dropped. But he is a little suspicious about why we brought him in today. Obviously, he knows nothing about the NGF gene, and I do not plan to tell him."

"Naturally," said Marsha.

Victor shot her a look. "I hope you are planning to be cooperative."

"I'm going to be more than cooperative," Marsha said. "As soon as VJ is finished here, I'm planning to take him to my office and have him go through a battery of psychological tests."

"What on earth for?" Victor asked.

"The fact that you have to ask means that I probably couldn't explain it to you."

Dr. Ruddock, a tall, slender man with salt and pepper hair, called all the Franks into his office for a few minutes before the examination. He asked if the boy remembered him. VJ told the man that he did, particularly his smell.

Victor and Marsha chuckled nervously.

"It was your cologne," VJ said. "You were wearing Hermès after-shave."

Somewhat taken aback by this personal reference, Dr. Ruddock introduced everyone to Dr. Chris Stevens, his current fellow in pediatric neurology.

It was Dr. Stevens who examined VJ. In deference to the fact that both parents were physicians, Dr. Stevens allowed Victor and Marsha to remain in the room. It was as complete a neurological exam as either had ever witnessed. After an hour just about every facet of VJ's nervous system had been evaluated and found to be entirely normal.

Then Stevens started the lab work. He drew blood for routine chemistries, and Victor had several tubes iced and put aside for him to take back to Chimera. Afterward, VJ was subjected to both PET and NMR scanning.

The PET scanning involved injecting harmless radioactive substances which emitted positrons into

VJ's arm while his head was positioned inside a large doughnut-shaped apparatus. The positrons collided with electrons in VJ's brain, releasing a burst of energy with each collision in the form of two gamma rays. Crystals in the PET scanner recorded the gamma rays, and a computer tracked the course of the radiation, creating an image.

For the second test, the NMR scanning, VJ was placed inside a six-foot-long cylinder surrounded by huge magnets supercooled with liquid helium. The resultant magnetic field, which was sixty thousand times greater than the earth's magnetic field, aligned the nuclei of the hydrogen atoms in the water molecules of VJ's body. When a radio wave of a specific frequency knocked these nuclei out of alignment, they sprang back, emitting a faint radio signal of their own which was picked up in radio sensors in the scanner and transformed by computer into an image.

When all the tests were done, Dr. Ruddock summoned Victor and Marsha back to his office. VJ was left outside in the waiting room. Victor was plainly nervous, crossing and uncrossing his legs and running his hand through his hair. Throughout the testing neither Dr. Stevens nor the technician made any comment. By the end, Victor was almost paralyzed with tension.

"Well," Dr. Ruddock began, fingering some of the print-outs and images from the tests, "not all the results are back, specifically the blood work, but we do have several positive findings here."

Marsha's heart sank.

"Both the PET and the NMR scans are abnormal," Dr. Ruddock explained. He held up one of the multicolored PET scan images with his left hand. In his right hand he held a Mont Blanc pen. Carefully pointing to different areas, he said, "There is a markedly elevated but diffuse uptake of glucose in the cerebral hemispheres." He dropped the paper and picked up another colored image. "In this NMR scan we can see the ventricles quite clearly."

With her heart pounding, Marsha leaned forward to get a better look.

"It's quite obvious," Dr. Ruddock continued, "that these ventricles are significantly smaller than normal."

"What does this mean?" Marsha asked hesitantly.

Dr. Ruddock shrugged. "Probably nothing. The child's neurological exam is entirely normal according to Dr. Stevens. And these findings, although interesting, most likely have no effect on function. The only thing I can think of is that if his brain is using that much glucose, maybe you should feed him candy whenever he's doing much thinking." Dr. Ruddock laughed heartily at his own attempt at humor.

For a moment both Victor and Marsha sat there numbly, trying to make the transition from the bad news they'd expected to the good news they'd received. Victor was the first to recover. "We'll certainly take your advice," he said with a chuckle. "Any candy in particular?"

Dr. Ruddock laughed anew, enjoying that his humor was so well received. "Peter Paul Mounds is the therapy I recommend!"

Marsha thanked the doctor and ran out the door. Catching VJ unaware, she had him in a bear hug before he could move away. "Everything is fine," she whispered in his ear. "You're okay."

VJ extracted himself from her grasp. "I knew I was fine before we came. Can we go now?"

Victor tapped Marsha on the shoulder. "I've got some other business here and then I'll go directly to work. I'll see you at home, okay?" Victor said.

"We'll have a special dinner," Marsha said, turning back to VJ. "We can leave but you, young man, are not finished. We are going to my office. I have a few more tests for you."

"Oh, Mom!" whined VJ.

Marsha smiled. He sounded just like any other ten-year-old.

"Humor your mother," Victor said. "I'll see you both later." He gave Marsha a peck on the cheek and tousled VJ's hair.

Victor crossed from the professional building to the hospital proper and took the elevator to Pathology. He found Dr. Burghofen's office. The man's secretary was nowhere to be seen so Victor looked inside. Burghofen was typing with his two index fingers. Victor knocked on the doorjamb.

"Come in, come in!" Burghofen said with a wave. He continued to peck at the typewriter for a few moments, then gave up. "I don't know why I'm doing this except my secretary calls in sick every other day, and I'm constrained from firing her. Administering this department is going to be the death of me."

Victor smiled, reminding himself to remember that academia had its own limitations the next time he got fed up with office problems at Chimera.

"I was wondering if you had finished the autopsies on the two children who died of cerebral edema," Victor said.

Dr. Burghofen scanned the surface of his cluttered desk. "Where's that clipboard?" he asked rhetorically. He spun around in his chair, finding what he was searching for on the shelf directly behind him. "Let's see," he said, flipping over the pages. "Here we are: Maurice Hobbs and Mark Murray. Are those the ones?"

"Yup," Victor said.

"They were assigned to Dr. Shryack. He's probably doing them now."

"All right if I go look?" asked Victor.

"Suit yourself," he said, checking the clipboard. "It's amphitheater three." Then as Victor was about to leave, he asked, "You did say you were a medical doctor, didn't you?"

Victor nodded.

"Enjoy yourself," Dr. Burghofen said, returning to the typewriter.

The pathology department, like the rest of the hospital, was new, with state-of-the-art equipment. Everything was steel, glass or Formica.

The four autopsy rooms looked like operating rooms. Only one was in use and Victor went directly inside. The autopsy table was shining stainless steel, as were the other implements in sight. Two men standing on either side of the table looked up as Victor entered. In front of them was a young child whose body was splayed open like a gutted fish. Behind them on a gurney was the small, covered body of another.

Victor shuddered. It had been a long time since he'd seen an autopsy and he'd forgotten the impact. Particularly when viewing a child.

"Can we help you?" the doctor on the right asked. He

was masked like a surgeon, but instead of a gown, he wore a rubberized apron.

"I'm Dr. Frank," Victor said, struggling to suppress nausea. Besides the visual assault, there was the fetid odor that even the room's modern air conditioning could not handle. "I'm interested in the Hobbs baby and the Murray baby. Dr. Burghofen sent me down."

"You can watch over here if you like," the pathologist said, motioning Victor over with his scalpel.

Tentatively, Victor advanced into the room. He tried not to look at the tiny eviscerated body.

"Are you Dr. Shryack?" asked Victor.

"That's me." The pathologist had a pleasant, youthful voice and bright eyes. "And this is Samuel Harkinson," he said, introducing his assistant. "These children your patients?"

"Not really," Victor said. "But I'm terribly interested in the cause of their deaths."

"Join the group," Dr. Shryack said. "Strange story! Come over here and look at this brain."

Victor swallowed. The child's scalp had been cut and pulled down over the face. Then the skull had been sawed around the circumference of the head, and the crown lifted off. Victor found himself looking at the child's brain, which had risen out of its confinement, giving the child the appearance of some sort of alien being. Most of the gyri of the cerebral cortices had been flattened where they had pressed against the inside of the skull.

"This has to be the worst case of cerebral edema I've ever seen," Dr. Shryack said. "It makes getting the brain out a chore and a half. Took me half an hour with the other one." He pointed toward the shrouded body.

"Till you figured out how to do it," Harkinson said with a faint Cockney accent.

"Right you are, Samuel."

With Harkinson holding the head and pushing the swollen brain to the side, Dr. Shryack was able to get his knife between the brain and the base of the skull to cut the upper part of the spinal cord.

Then, with a dull, ripping sound, the brain pulled free. Harkinson cut the cranial nerves, and Dr. Shryack quickly hoisted the brain and placed it in the pan of the overhead scale. The pointer swung wildly back and forth, then settled on 3.2.

"It's a full pound more than normal," Dr. Shryack said, scooping the brain back up with his gloved hands and carrying it over to a sink that had continuous running water. He rinsed the clotted blood and other debris from the brain, then put it on a wooden chopping block.

With experienced hands, Dr. Shryack carefully examined the brain for gross pathology. "Other than its size, it looks normal."

He selected a carving knife from a group in a drawer, and began slicing off half-inch sections. "No hemorrhage, no tumors, no infection. The NMR scanner was right again."

"I was wondering if I could ask a favor," Victor said. "Would it be at all possible for me to take a sample back to my own lab to have it processed?"

Dr. Shryack shrugged. "I suppose, but I wouldn't want it to become common knowledge. It would be a great thing to get into the *Boston Globe* that we're giving out brain tissue. I wonder what that would do to our autopsy percentage?"

"I won't tell a soul."

"You want this case, which I think is the Hobbs kid, or do you want the other one?" Dr. Shryack asked.

"Both, if you wouldn't mind."

"I suppose giving you two specimens is no different than giving you one," said Dr. Shryack.

"Have you done the gross on the internal organs yet?" asked Victor.

"Not yet," Shryack said. "That's next on the agenda. Want to watch?"

Victor shrugged. "Why not. I'm here."

VJ was even less communicative on the ride back to Lawrence than he'd been on the ride into Boston that morning. He was obviously mad about the whole situation, and Marsha wondered if he would be cooperative enough to make psychological testing worthwhile.

She parked across from her office. They waited for the elevator even though they were going up only one floor because the stairwell door was locked from the inside. "I know you're angry," Marsha said. "But I do want you to take some psychological tests, yet it's not worth your time or Jean's unless you cooperate. Do I make myself clear?"

"Perfectly," VJ said crisply, fixing Marsha with his dazzlingly blue eyes.

"Well, will you cooperate?" she asked as the elevator doors opened.

VJ nodded coldly.

Jean was overjoyed to see them. She'd had a terrible time juggling Marsha's patients, but she'd managed in her usual efficient way.

As for VJ, she was really happy to see him, even

though he greeted her without much enthusiasm, then excused himself to use the bathroom.

"He's a bit out of sorts," Marsha explained. She went on to tell Jean about the neuro work-up and her desire to have him take their basic battery of psychological tests.

"It will be hard for me to do it today," Jean said. "With you out all morning the phone has been ringing off the hook."

"Let the service handle the phone," Marsha advised. "It's important I get VJ tested."

Jean nodded and immediately began getting out the forms and preparing their computer to grade and correlate the results.

When VJ returned from the bathroom, Jean had him sit right down at the keyboard. Since he was familiar with some of the tests, she asked him which kind he wanted to take first.

"Let's start with the intelligence tests," VJ said agreeably.

For the next hour and a half, Jean administered the WAIS-R intelligence test, which included six verbal and five performance subtests. From her experience she knew that VJ was doing well, but nowhere near what he'd done seven years previously. She also noted that VJ tended to hesitate before he answered a question or performed a task. It was like he wanted to be doubly sure of his choice.

"Very good!" Jean said when they'd reached the completion. "Now how about the personality test?"

"Is that the MMPI?" VJ asked. "Or the MCMI?"

"I'm impressed," Jean said. "Sounds like you have been doing a little reading."

"It's easy when one of your parents is a psychiatrist," VJ said.

"We use both, but let's start with the MMPI," Jean said. "You don't need me for this. It's all multiple choice. If you have any problems, just yell."

Jean left VJ in the testing room, and went back to the reception desk. She called the service and got the pile of messages that had accumulated. She attended to the ones that she could and when Marsha's patient left, gave her the messages she had to handle herself.

"How's VJ doing?" Marsha asked.

"Couldn't be better," Jean reported.

"He's being cooperative?" Marsha asked.

"Like a lamb," Jean said. "In fact, he seems to be enjoying himself."

Marsha shook her head in amazement. "Must be you. He was in an awful mood with me."

Jean took it as a compliment. "He's had a WAIS-R and he's in the middle of an MMPI. What other tests do you want? A Rorschach and a Thematic Apperception Test or what?"

Marsha chewed on her thumbnail for a moment, thinking. "Why don't we do the TAT and let the Rorschach go for now. We can always do it later."

"I'll be happy to do both," Jean said.

"Let's just do the TAT," Marsha said as she picked up the next chart. "VJ's in a good mood but why push it? Besides, it might be interesting to cross check the TAT and the Rorschach if they are taken on different days." She called the patient whose chart she was holding and disappeared for another session.

After Jean finished as much paperwork as she could, she returned to the testing room. VJ was absorbed in the personality test.

116

"Any problems?" Jean asked.

"Some of these questions are too much," VJ said with a laugh. "A couple of them have no appropriate answers."

"The idea is to select the best one possible," Jean said.

"I know," VJ said. "That's what I'm doing."

At noon, they broke for lunch and walked to the hospital. They ate in the coffee shop. Marsha and Jean had tuna salad sandwiches while VJ had a hamburger and a shake. Marsha noted with contentment that VJ's attitude had indeed changed. She began to think she had worried for nothing; the tests he was taking would probably result in a healthy psychological portrait. She was dying to ask Jean about the results so far, but she knew she couldn't in front of VJ. Within thirty minutes they were all back at their respective tasks.

An hour later, Jean put the phone back on service and returned to the testing room. Just as she closed the door behind her, VJ spoke up: "There," he said, clicking the last question. "All done."

"Very good," Jean said, impressed. VJ had gone through the five hundred and fifty questions in half the usual time. "Would you like to rest before the next test?" she asked.

"Let's get it over with," VJ said.

For ninety minutes, Jean showed the TAT cards to VJ. Each contained a black and white picture of people in circumstances that elicited responses having psychological overtones. VJ was asked to describe what he thought was going on in each picture and how the people felt. The idea was for VJ to project his fantasies, feelings, patterns of relationships, needs, and conflicts.

117

With some patients the TAT was no easy test to administer. But with VJ, Jean found herself enjoying the process. The boy had no trouble coming up with interesting explanations and his responses were both logical and normal. By the end of the test Jean felt that VJ was emotionally stable, well adjusted, and mature for his age.

When Marsha was finished with her last patient, Jean went into the office and gave her the computer print-outs. The MMPI would be sent off to be evaluated by a program with a larger data base, but their PC gave them an initial report.

Marsha glanced through the papers, as Jean gave her own positive clinical impression. "I think he is a model child. I truly can't see how you can be concerned about him."

"That's reassuring," Marsha said, studying the IQ test results. The overall score was 128. That was only a two-point variation from the last time that Marsha had had VJ tested several years previously. So VJ's IQ had not changed, and it was a good, solid, healthy score, certainly well above average. But there was one discrepancy that bothered Marsha: a fifteen-point difference between the verbal and the performance IQ, with the verbal lower than the performance, which suggested a cognitive problem relating to language disabilities. Given VJ's facility in French, it didn't seem to make sense.

"I noticed that," Jean said when Marsha queried it, "but since the overall score was so good I didn't give it much significance. Do you?"

"I don't know," Marsha said. "I don't think I've ever seen a result like this before. Oh well, let's go on to the MMPI."

Marsha put the personality inventory results in front of her. The first part was called the validity scales. Again something immediately aroused her attention. The F and K scales were mildly elevated and at the upper limit of what would be considered normal. Marsha pointed that out to Jean as well.

"But they are in the normal range," Jean insisted.

"True," Marsha said, "but you have to remember that all this is relative. Why would VJ's validity scales be nearly abnormal?"

"He did the test quickly," Jean said. "Maybe he got a little careless."

"VJ is never careless," Marsha said. "Well, I can't explain this, but let's go on."

The second part of the report was the clinical scales, and Marsha noted that none were in the abnormal range. She was particularly happy to see that scale four and scale eight were well within normal limits. Those two scales referred to psychopathic deviation and schizophrenic behavior respectively. Marsha breathed a sigh of relief because these scales had a high degree of correlation with clinical reality, and she'd been afraid they would be elevated, given VJ's history.

But then Marsha noted that scale three was "high normal". That would mean VJ tended toward hysteria, constantly seeking affection and attention. That certainly did not correlate with Marsha's experience.

"Was it your impression that VJ was cooperating when he took this test?" Marsha asked Jean.

"Absolutely," Jean said.

"I suppose I should be happy with these results," Marsha said, as she gathered the papers together, then stood them on end, tapping them against the desk until they were lined up.

"I think so," Jean said encouragingly.

Marsha stapled the papers together, then tossed them into her briefcase. "Yet both the Wechsler and the MMPI are a little abnormal. Well, maybe unexpected is a better word. I'd have preferred they be unqualifyingly normal. By the way, how did VJ respond to the TAT with the man standing over the child with his arm raised?"

"VJ said he was giving a lecture."

"The man or the child?" Marsha asked with a laugh.

"Definitely the man."

"Any hostility involved?" Marsha asked.

"None."

"Why was the man's arm raised?"

"Because the man was talking about tennis, and he was showing the boy how to serve," Jean said.

"Tennis? VJ has never played tennis."

As Victor drove onto the grounds of Chimera, he noted that none of the previous night's snow remained. It was still cloudy but the temperature had risen into the high forties.

He parked his car in the usual spot, but instead of heading directly into the administration building, he took the brown paper bag from the front seat of the car and went directly to his lab.

"Got some extra rush work for you," he said to his head technician, Robert Grimes.

Robert was a painfully thin, intense man, who wore shirts with necks much too large for him, emphasizing his thinness. His eyes had a bulging look of continual surprise.

Victor pulled out the iced vials of VJ's blood and sample bottles containing pieces of the dead children's brains. "I want chromosome studies done on these."

Robert picked up the blood vials, shook them, then examined the brain samples. "You want me to let other things go and do this?"

"That's right," Victor said. "I want it done as soon as possible. Plus I want some standard neural stains on the brain slices."

"I'll have to let the uterine implant work slide," Robert said.

"You have my permission."

Leaving the lab, Victor went to the next building, which housed the central computer. It was situated in the geometric center of the courtyard, an ideal location since the building had easy access to all other facilities. The main office was on the first floor, and Victor had no trouble locating Louis Kaspwicz. There was some problem with a piece of hardware, and Louis was supervising several technicians who had the massive machine open as if it were undergoing surgery.

"Have any information for me?" Victor asked.

Louis nodded, told the technicians to keep searching, and led Victor back to his office where he produced a loose-leaf notebook containing the computer logs. "I've figured out why you couldn't call up those files on your terminal," Louis said. He began to flip the pages of the computer log.

"Why?" Victor asked, as Louis kept searching through the book.

Not finding what he was looking for, he straightened up and glanced around his office. "Ah," he said, spying a loose sheet of paper and snatching it from the desk top.

"You couldn't call up the files on Baby Hobbs or Baby Murray because they'd been deleted on November 18," he said, waving the paper under Victor's nose.

"Deleted?"

"I'm afraid so," Louis said. "This is the computer log for November 18, and it clearly shows that the files were deleted."

"That's strange," Victor said. "I don't suppose you can determine who deleted them, can you?"

"Sure," Louis said. "By matching the password of the user."

"Did you do that?"

"Yes," Louis said.

"Well, who was it?" Victor asked irritably. It seemed like Louis was deliberately making this difficult.

Louis glanced at Victor, then looked away. "You, Dr. Frank."

"Me?" Victor said with surprise. That was the last thing he expected to hear. Yet he did remember thinking about deleting the files, maybe even planning on doing it at some time, but he could not remember actually having done it.

"Sorry," Louis said, shifting his weight. He was plainly uncomfortable.

"It's quite all right," Victor said, embarrassed himself. "Thank you for looking into it for me."

"Any time," Louis said.

Victor left the computer center, perplexed at this new information. It was true that he'd become somewhat forgetful of late, but could he have actually deleted the files and forgotten about it? Could it have been an accident? He wondered what he'd been doing November 18. Victor went back to the administration building and slowly climbed the back stairs. As he walked down the second-floor corridor toward the rear entrance of his office, he decided to check back over his calendar. He took off his coat, hung it up, and then went to talk to Colleen.

"Dr. Frank, you frightened me!" she exclaimed when Victor tapped her on the shoulder. She'd been concentrating on typing with dictation headphones on. "I had no idea you were here."

Victor apologized, saying that he'd come in the back way.

"How was the visit to the hospital?" Colleen asked. Victor had called her early that morning to explain why he wouldn't be in until afternoon. "I hope to God VJ is okay."

"He's fine," Victor said with a smile. "The tests were normal. Of course, we are waiting on a group of blood tests. But I feel confident they'll be fine as well."

"Thank God!" Colleen said. "You scared me when you called this morning: a full neuro work-up sounded pretty serious."

"I was a little worried myself," Victor admitted.

"I suppose you want your phone messages," Colleen said as she peeked under some papers on her otherwise neat desk. "I've got a ton of them for you somewhere here."

"Hold the messages a minute," Victor said. "Would you haul out the calendar for 1988? I'm particularly interested in November 18."

"Certainly," Colleen said. She detached herself from her dictation machine and headed for the files.

Victor went back into his office. While he waited, he thought about the harassing phone call that VJ had unfortunately received, and he debated what to do about it. Reluctantly, he realized there was little he could do. If he asked any of the people he was having a problem with, they'd obviously deny it.

Colleen came into his office carrying the calendar already opened to November 18, and stuck it under Victor's nose. It had been a fairly busy day. But there was nothing that had anything even slightly to do with the missing files. The last entry noted that Victor had taken Marsha into Boston to eat at Another Season and go to the Boston Symphony.

Removing her robe, Marsha slid into the deliciously warm bed. She turned down the controls of the electric blanket from high to three. Victor had edged as far away from the heat as possible. His side of the electric blanket was never used. He'd been in bed for over a half hour and was busy reading from a stack of professional journals.

Marsha rolled on her side, studying Victor's profile. The sharp line of his nose, the slightly hollow cheeks, the thin lips were as familiar to Marsha as her own. Yet he seemed like a stranger. She still hadn't fully accepted what he'd done to VJ, vacillating between disbelief, anger, and fear, with fear being paramount.

"Do you think those tests mean VJ's really all right?" she asked.

"I'm reassured," Victor said without looking up from his magazine. "And you acted pretty happy in Dr. Ruddock's office."

Marsha rolled over on her back. "That was immediate relief that nothing obvious showed up, like a brain tumor." She looked back at Victor. "But there still is no explanation for his dramatic drop in intelligence."

"But that was six and a half years ago."

"I'm still worried that the process will start again."

124

"Suit yourself," Victor said.

"Victor!" Marsha said. "Can't you put whatever it is you're reading aside for a moment to talk with me?"

Letting the open journal drop, he said, "I am talking to you."

"Thank you," Marsha said. "Of course I'm glad VJ's physical exam was normal. But his psychological exams weren't. They were unexpected, and a little contradictory." Marsha then went on to explain her findings, finishing with VJ's relatively high score on the hysteria scale.

"VJ's not emotional," Victor said.

"That's the point," Marsha said.

"Seems to me the result says more about psychological tests than anything else. They probably aren't accurate."

"On the contrary," Marsha said. "These tests are considered very reliable. But I don't know what to make of them. Unfortunately they just add to my uneasiness. I can't help feeling that something terrible is going to happen."

"Listen," Victor said. "I took some of VJ's blood back to the lab. I'm going to have chromosome six isolated. If it hasn't changed, I'll be perfectly satisfied. And you should be as well." He reached out as if to pat her thigh but she moved her leg away. Victor let his hand fall back to the bed. "If VJ has some mild psychological problems, well that's something else and we can get him some therapy, okay?" He wanted to reassure her further, but he didn't know what else to say. He certainly wasn't about to mention the missing files.

Marsha took a deep breath. "Okay," she said. "I'll try to relax. You'll tell me about the DNA study as soon as you look at it?"

"Absolutely," Victor said. He smiled at her. She managed to smile back weakly.

Victor raised his journal and tried to read. But he kept thinking about the missing files. Victor wondered again if he could have deleted them. It was a possibility. Since they weren't cross-referenced, it was unlikely someone else could have deleted all three.

"Did you find out what caused the death of those poor babies?" Marsha asked.

Victor let the journal drop once more. "Not yet. The autopsies aren't complete. The microscopic hasn't been done."

"Could it have been cancer?" Marsha asked nervously, remembering the day David got sick. That was another date that Marsha would never forget: June 17, 1984. David was ten, VJ five. School had been out for several weeks and Janice was planning to take the children to Castle Beach.

Marsha was in her study, getting her things ready to take to the office when David appeared in the doorway, his thin arms hanging limply at his sides.

"Mommy, something is wrong with me," he said.

Marsha didn't look up immediately. She was trying to find a folder she'd brought from the office the day before.

"What seems to be the trouble?" she asked, closing one drawer and opening another. David had gone to bed the night before complaining of some abdominal discomfort, but Pepto-Bismol had taken care of that.

"I look funny," David said.

"I think you are a handsome boy," Marsha said, turning to scan the built-in shelves behind her desk.

"I'm getting yellow," David said.

Marsha stopped what she was doing and turned to

face her son, who ran to her and buried his face in her bosom. He was an affectionate child.

"What makes you think you're turning yellow?" she asked, feeling the first stirrings of fear. "Let me see your face," she said, gently trying to pull the boy away from her. She was hoping that he was wrong and there would be some silly explanation for his impression.

David would not let go. "It's my eyes," he said, his voice muffled against her. "And my tongue."

"Your tongue can get yellow from a lemon candy," Marsha said. "Come, now. Let me see."

The light in her study was poor, so she walked him into the hall where she looked at David's eyes in the light streaming through the window. Marsha caught her breath. There was no doubt. The boy was severely jaundiced.

Later that day a CAT scan showed a diffuse tumor of the liver. It was an enormously aggressive cancer that destroyed the child's liver within days of making the diagnosis.

"Neither baby seemed to have cancer," Victor was saying, rousing Marsha from her reverie. "The gross studies showed no signs of malignancy."

Marsha tried to shake away the haunting image of David's yellow eyes looking at her from his gaunt face. Even his skin had rapidly turned yellow. She cleared her throat. "What do you think the chances are that the babies' deaths were caused by the foreign genes you inserted?"

Victor didn't answer immediately. "I'd like to think the problem was unrelated. After all, none of the hundreds of animal experiments resulted in any health problems."

"But you can't be sure?" Marsha asked.

"I can't be sure," Victor agreed.

"What about the other five zygotes?" Marsha asked.

"What do you mean?" Victor asked. "They are stored in the freezer."

"Are they normal or did you mutate them too?" Marsha asked.

"All of them have the NGF gene," Victor said.

"I want you to destroy them," Marsha said.

"Why?" Victor asked.

"You said you were sorry for what you'd done," Marsha said angrily. "And now you are asking why you should destroy them?"

"I'm not going to implant them," Victor said. "I can promise you that. But I might need them to help figure out what went wrong with the Hobbs and Murray babies. Remember, their zygotes had both been frozen. That was the only difference between them and VJ."

Marsha studied Victor's face. It was a horrible feeling to realize that she didn't know if she believed him or not. She did not like the idea of those zygotes being potentially viable.

Before she could argue further, a crash shattered the night. Even before the sound of the broken glass faded, a high-pitched scream reverberated from VJ's room. Marsha and Victor leaped from the bed and ran headlong down the hall.

# 7

VJ was curled up in a ball at the head of his bed, cradling his head in both hands. In the center of the room, resting on the rug, was a brick. A length of red ribbon was tied around it, securing a piece of paper, making the package appear like a gift. VJ's window had been smashed and shards of glass littered the room. Obviously the brick had been thrown from the driveway.

Victor put out his hand to restrain Marsha from coming into the room and rushing to VJ's side.

"Watch the glass!" Victor yelled.

"VJ, are you all right?" Marsha shouted.

VJ nodded.

Reaching around Marsha, Victor grabbed the Oriental runner that extended down the hall. Pulling it into VJ's room, he let it roll out toward the window. Then he ran across it to look down at the driveway. He saw no one.

"I'm going out," Victor said, running past Marsha.

"Don't be a hero," Marsha yelled, but Victor was

129

already halfway down the stairs. "And don't you move," she said to VJ. "There's so much glass, you're sure to be cut. I'll be right back."

Marsha ran back to the master bedroom and hastily pulled on her slippers and her robe. Returning to VJ's room, she finally got to the bed. VJ allowed her to hug him. "Hold on," she said, as she strained to lift him up. He was heavier than she'd anticipated. Staggering to the hallway, she was glad to set him down.

"A few months from now I won't be able to do that," she said with a groan. "You're getting too big for me."

"I'm going to find out who did that," VJ snarled, finding his voice.

"Did it frighten you, dear?" Marsha asked, stroking his head.

VJ parried Marsha's hand. "I'm going to find out who threw that brick and I'm going to kill him."

"You're safe now," Marsha said soothingly. "You can calm down. I know you're upset, but everything is all right. No one got hurt."

"I'll kill him," VJ persisted. "You'll see. I'll kill him."

"Okay," Marsha said. She tried to draw him to her but he resisted. For a moment she looked at him. His blazing eyes held a piercing, unchildlike intensity. "Let's go down to the study," she said. "I want to call the police."

Victor ran the length of the driveway and stood in the street, looking both ways. Two driveways down, he heard a car being started. Just as he was debating sprinting in that direction, he saw the headlights come on and the car accelerate away. He couldn't tell the make.

In frustration, he threw a rock after it, but there was no way he could have hit it. Turning around, he hurried back to the house. He found Marsha and VJ in the study. It was apparent they'd been talking, but as Victor arrived they stopped.

"Where's the brick?" Victor asked, out of breath.

"Still in VJ's room," Marsha said. "We've been too busy talking about how VJ is planning on killing whoever threw it."

"I will!" VJ promised.

Victor groaned, knowing how Marsha's mind would take this as further evidence that VJ was disturbed. He went back to his son's room. The brick was still where it had fallen after crashing through VJ's window. Bending down, he extracted the paper from beneath the ribbon. "Remember our deal" said the typed message. Victor made an expression of disgust. Who the hell had done this?

Bringing the brick and the note with him, Victor returned to the study. He showed both to Marsha, who took them in her hands. She was about to say something when the downstairs doorbell sounded.

"Now what?" Victor questioned.

"Must be the police," Marsha said, getting to her feet. "I called them while you were outside running around." She left the room, heading down the stairs.

Victor looked at VJ. "Scared you, huh, Tiger?"

"I think that's obvious," VJ said. "It would have scared anyone."

"I know," Victor said. "I'm sorry you're getting the brunt of all this, what with the phone call last night and the brick tonight. I'm sure you don't understand, but I've some personnel problems at the lab. I'll try to do something to keep this kind of thing from happening."

"It doesn't matter," VJ said.

"I appreciate you being a good sport about it," Victor said. "Come on, let's talk to the police."

"The police won't do anything," VJ said. But he got up and started downstairs.

Victor followed. He agreed, but he was surprised that at age ten, VJ knew it too.

The North Andover police were polite and solicitous. A Sergeant Widdicomb and Patrolman O'Connor had responded to the call. Widdicomb was at least sixty-five, with florid skin and a huge beer belly. O'-Connor was just the opposite: he was in his twenties and looked like an athlete. Widdicomb did all the talking.

When Victor and VJ arrived in the foyer, Widdicomb was reading the note while O'Connor fingered the brick. Widdicomb handed the note back to Marsha. "What a dadblasted awful thing," he said. "Used to be that this kinda stuff only happened in Boston, not out here." Widdicomb took out a pad, licked the end of a pencil and started taking notes. He asked the expected questions, like the time it happened, if they saw anyone, whether the lights had been on in the boy's room. VJ quickly lost interest and disappeared into the kitchen.

After he ran out of questions, Widdicomb asked if they could take a gander around the yard.

"Please," Marsha said, motioning toward the door.

After the police left, Marsha turned to Victor. "Last night you told me not to worry about the threatening call, that you would look into it."

"I know . . ." Victor said guiltily. She waited for Victor to continue. But he didn't.

"A threatening phone call is one thing," Marsha said. "A brick through our child's window is quite another. I told you I couldn't handle any more surprises. I think you better give me some idea of these office problems you mentioned."

"Fair enough," Victor said. "But let me get a drink. I think I could use one."

VJ had the Johnny Carson show on in the family room and was watching, his head propped up against his arm. His eyes had a glazed look.

"Are you okay?" Marsha called from the doorway to the kitchen.

"Fine," VJ said without turning his head.

"I think we should let him unwind," Marsha said, directing her attention to Victor, who was busy making them a hot rum drink.

Mugs in hand, they sat down at the kitchen table. In capsule form, Victor highlighted the controversy with Ronald, the negotiations with Gephardt's attorney, Sharon Carver's threats, and the unfortunate situation with Hurst. "So there you have it," he concluded. "A normal week at the office."

Marsha mulled over the four troublemakers. Aside from Ronald, she guessed any of the other three could be guilty of acting out.

"What about this note?" she asked. "What deal is it referring to?"

Victor took a drink, put the mug on the table, then reached across and took the note. He studied it for a moment, then said, "I haven't the slightest idea. I haven't made any deals with anyone." He tossed the paper onto the table.

"Somebody must have thought you had," Marsha said.

"Look, anyone capable of throwing a rock through our window is capable of fantasizing some mythical deal. But I'll get in touch with each of them and make sure they know that we are not going to sit idly by and allow them to throw bricks through our windows."

"What about hiring some security?" Marsha asked.

"It's an idea," Victor said. "But let me make these calls tomorrow. I have a feeling that it will solve this problem."

The doorbell sounded again.

"I'll get it," said Victor. He put his mug on the table and left the kitchen.

Marsha got up and went into the family room. The TV was still on but Johnny Carson had changed to *David Letterman.* It was that late. VJ was fast asleep. Turning off the TV, Marsha looked at her son. He looked so peaceful. There was no hint of the intense hostility that he'd displayed earlier. Oh God, she thought, what had Victor's experiment done to her darling baby?

The front door banged shut, and Victor came in saying, "The police didn't find anything. They just said they'd try to watch the house best they could over the next week or so." Then he looked down at VJ. "I see he has recovered."

"I wish," Marsha said wistfully.

"Oh, come on now," Victor said. "I don't want a lecture about his hostility and all that bull."

"Maybe he was really upset when his IQ fell," she said, following her own train of thought. "Can you imagine what kind of self-esteem loss the boy probably suffered when his special abilities evaporated?"

"The kid was only three and a half," Victor pleaded.

"I know you don't agree with me," Marsha said, looking back at the sleeping boy. "But I'm terrified. I can't believe your genetic experiment didn't affect his future."

The following morning the temperature had climbed to nearly sixty degrees by nine o'clock. The sun was out and Victor had both front windows open in the car as well as the sunroof. The air was fragrant with the earthy aroma that presaged spring. Victor pressed the accelerator and let the car loose on the short straightaways.

He glanced over at VJ, who seemed fully recovered from the previous night. He had his arm out the window and was playing with the wind with his open hand. It was a simple gesture, but so normal. Victor could remember doing it many times when he was VJ's age.

Looking at his son, Victor couldn't rid himself of Marsha's fears. He seemed fine, but could the implant have affected his development? VJ was a loner. In that regard he certainly didn't take after anyone else in the family.

"What's your friend Richie like?" Victor asked suddenly.

VJ shot him a look that was midway between vexation and disbelief. "You sound like Mother," he said.

Victor laughed. "I suppose I do. But really, what kinda kid is this Richie? How come we haven't met him?"

"He's okay," VJ said. "I see him every day at school. I don't know, we have different interests when we're at home. He watches a lot of TV."

"If you two want to go into Boston this week, I'll have someone from the office drive you."

"Thanks, Dad," VJ said. "I'll see what Richie says."

Victor settled back into his seat. Obviously the kid had friends. He made a mental note to remind Marsha about Richie that evening.

The moment Victor pulled into his parking space, Philip's hulking form appeared in front of the car as if by magic. Seeing VJ, a smile broke across his face. He grabbed the front of the car and gave it a shake.

"Good gravy," Victor said.

VJ jumped out of the car and gave the man a punch on the arm. Philip pretended to fall, backing up a few steps, clutching his arm. VJ laughed and the two started off.

"Wait a second, VJ," Victor called. "Where are you going?"

VJ turned and shrugged. "I don't know. The cafeteria or the library. Why? You want me to do something?"

"No," Victor said. "I just want to be sure you stay away from the river. This warm weather is only going to make it rise higher."

In the background Victor could hear the roar of the water going over the spillway.

"Don't worry," VJ said. "See you later."

Victor watched as they rounded the building, heading in the direction of the cafeteria. They certainly made an improbable pair.

In the office, Victor got right to work. Colleen gave him an update on all the issues that had to be addressed that day. Victor delegated what he could, the things he had to do himself he put in an orderly stack in the center of his desk. That done, he took out the note that had been wrapped around the brick.

"Remember our deal," Victor repeated. "What the

hell does that mean?" Suddenly furious, he picked up the phone and called Gephardt's attorney, William Hurst, and Sharon Carver. He didn't give any of them a chance to talk. As soon as they were on the phone he shouted that there were no deals and that he'd put the police onto anyone who'd harassed his family.

Afterward he felt a little silly, but he hoped the guilty party would think twice before trying again. He did not call Ronald because he couldn't imagine his old friend stooping to violence.

With that taken care of, Victor picked up the first of Colleen's notes and started on the day's administrative duties.

Marsha's day was a seemingly endless stream of difficult patients until a cancellation just before lunch gave her an hour to review VJ's tests. Taking them out, she remembered the intensity of his anger over the thrown brick. She looked at clinical scale four that was supposed to reflect such suppressed hostility. VJ had scored well below what she would have expected with such behavior.

Marsha got up, stretched and stared out her office window. Unfortunately she looked over a parking lot, but beyond that there were some fields and rolling hills. All the trees in view still had that midwinter look of death, their branches like skeletons against the pale blue sky.

So much for psychological testing, she thought. She wished that she could have talked with Janice Fay. The woman had lived with them until her death in 1985. If anyone would have had insight into VJ's change in intelligence, it would have been Janice. The only other adult who had been close to VJ during that period was Martha Gillespie at the preschool. VJ had started before his second birthday.

On impulse, Marsha called to Jean: "I think I'll be skipping lunch; you go whenever you want. Just don't forget to put the phone on service."

Busy with the typewriter, Jean waved understanding.

Five minutes later, Marsha was going sixty-five miles an hour on the interstate. She only had to go one exit and was soon back to small country roads.

The Crocker Preschool was a charming ensemble of yellow cottages with white trim and white shutters on the grounds of a much larger estate house. Marsha wondered how the school made ends meet, but rumor had it that it was more of a hobby for Martha Gillespie. Martha had been widowed at a young age and left a fortune.

"Of course I remember VJ," Martha said with feigned indignation. Marsha had found her in the administrative cottage. She was about sixty, with snow white hair and cheery, rosy cheeks. "I remember him vividly right from his first day with us. He was a most extraordinary boy."

Marsha recalled the first day also. She'd brought VJ in early, worried about his response since he had not been away from home except when accompanied by Janice or herself. This was to be his first brush with such independence. But the adaptation had proved to be harder for Marsha than for her son, who ran into the middle of a group of children without even one backward glance.

"In fact," Martha said, "I remember that by the end of his first day he had all the other children doing exactly what he wanted. And he wasn't even two!"

"Then you remember when VJ's intelligence fell?" Marsha asked.

Martha paused while she studied Marsha. "Yes, I remember," she said.

"What do you remember about him after this occurred?" Marsha asked.

"How is the boy today?"

"He's fine, I hope," Marsha said.

"Is there some reason you want to upset yourself by going through this?" Martha asked. "I remember how devastated you were back then."

"To be honest," Marsha said, "I'm terrified the same problem might happen again. I thought that if I learned more about the first episode, I might be able to prevent another."

"I don't know if I can help that much," Martha said. "There certainly was a big change, and it occurred so quickly. VJ went from being a confident child whose mind seemed infinite in its capability, to a withdrawn child who had few friends. But it wasn't as if he was autistic. Even though he stayed by himself, he was always uncannily aware of everything going on around him."

"Did he continue to relate to children his own age?" Marsha asked.

"Not very much," Martha said. "When we made him participate, he was always willing to go along, but left to his own devices, he'd just watch. You know, there was one thing that was curious. Every time we insisted that VJ participate in some kind of game, like musical chairs, he would always let the other children win. That was strange because prior to this, VJ won most of the games no matter what the age of the children involved."

"That is curious," Marsha said.

Later, when Marsha was driving back to her office, she kept seeing a three-and-a-half-year-old VJ letting other children win. It brought back the episode in the pool Sunday evening. In all her experience with young children, Marsha had never come across such a trait.

"Perfect!" Victor said as he held one of the microscope slides up to the overhead light. He could see the paper-thin section of brain sealed with a cover slip.

"That's the Golgi stain," Robert said. "You also have Cajal's and Bielschowsky's. If you want any others you'll have to let me know."

"Fine," Victor said. As usual, Robert had accomplished in less than twenty-four hours what would have taken a lesser technician several days.

"And here are the chromosome preparations," Robert said, handing Victor a tray. "Everything is labeled."

"Fine," Victor repeated.

Taking the preparations in his hands, Victor headed across the main room of the lab to the light microscopes. Seating himself before one, he placed the first slide under the instrument. It was labeled *Hobbs, right frontal lobe.*

Victor ran the scope down so that the objective was just touching the cover slip. Then, looking through the eyepieces, he corrected the focus.

"Good God!" he exclaimed as the image became clear. There was no sign of malignancy, but the effect was the same as if a tumor had been present. The children didn't die of cerebral edema, or an accumulation of fluid. Instead, what Victor saw was evidence of diffuse mitotic activity. The nerve cells of the brain were multiplying just as they did in the first two months of fetal development.

Victor quickly scanned slides of other areas of the Hobbs brain and then studied the Murray child's tissue. All of them were the same. The nerve cells were actively reproducing themselves at a furious rate. Since the children's skulls were fused, the new cells had nowhere to go other than to push the brain down into the spinal canal, with fatal results.

Horrified yet astounded at the same time, Victor snatched up the tray of slides and left the light microscope. He hurried across the lab and entered the room which housed the scanning electron microscope. The place had the appearance of a command center of a modern electronic weapons system.

The instrument itself looked very different from a normal microscope. It was about the size of a standard refrigerator. Its business portion was a cylinder approximately a foot in diameter and about three feet tall. A large electrical trunk entered the top of this cylinder and served as the source of electrons. The electrons were then focused by magnets which acted like glass lenses in a light microscope. Next to the scope was a good-sized computer. It was the computer that analyzed multiple-plano images of the electron microscope and constructed the three-dimensional pictures.

Robert had made extremely thin preparations of the chromatin material from some of the brain cells that were in the initial process of dividing. Victor placed one of these preparations within the scope and searched for chromosome six. What he was looking for was the area of mutation where he'd inserted the foreign genes. It took him over an hour, but at last he found it.

"Jesus," Victor gulped. The histones that normally enveloped the DNA were either missing or attenuated in the area of the inserted gene. In addition, the DNA, which was usually tightly coiled, had unraveled, suggesting that active transcription was taking place. In other words, the inserted genes were turned on!

Victor tried a preparation from the other child with the same results. The inserted genes were turned on, producing NGF. There was no doubt about it.

Switching to preparations made from VJ's blood, which must have taken much more patience on Robert's part since appropriate cells would have been harder to find, Victor introduced one within the electron microscope. Within thirty minutes he located chromosome six. Then, with painstaking effort, he scanned up and down the chromosome several times. The genes were quiescent. The area of the inserted gene was covered with the histone protein in the usual fashion.

Victor rocked back in the chair. VJ was all right, but the other two children had died as the result of his experiment. How could he ever tell Marsha? She would leave him. In fact, he wasn't sure he could live with himself.

Abruptly he stood up and paced the small room. What could have turned the gene back on? The only thing Victor could imagine was the ingestion of cephaloclor, the same antibiotic that he had used during the early embryological development. But how could these children have gotten the drug? It was not a common prescription, and the parents had been specifically warned that both children were deathly allergic to it. Victor was sure neither the Hobbs nor the Murrays would have permitted anyone to administer cephaloclor to their sons.

With both children dying at once, there was no way it could have been an accident. With a sudden chill of fear, Victor wondered if the area of chromosome six that he'd chosen to insert the manufactured genes was not an area of nonsense DNA as most people thought. Maybe its location in respect to an indigenous promoter caused the gene to turn on by some unknown mechanism. If that were the case, then VJ would indeed be at a risk too. Perhaps his gene had turned on for a short burst of activity back when his intelligence fell.

Victor tried to swallow, but his mouth was too dry. Picking up all the samples, he went to the water fountain and took a drink. There were a number of lab assistants working in the main room, but Victor was in no mood to talk. He hurried into his research office and closed the door behind him. He tried calming himself, but just as the pounding of his heart began to ease he remembered the photomicrographs he'd made of VJ's chromosomes six and a half years ago.

Jumping to his feet, he dashed to the files and frantically searched until he came up with the photos he'd taken when VJ's intelligence fell. Studying them, he let out a sigh of relief. VJ's had not changed at all. His chromosome six looked exactly the same six and a half years ago as it did today. There was not even the slightest uncovering or unraveling of the DNA.

Breathing more easily, Victor left his office to find Robert. The technician was in the animal room, supervising Sharon Carver's replacement. Victor took him aside. "I'm afraid I have some more special work for you."

"You're the boss," Robert answered.

"There is an area on chromosome six in the brain samples where the DNA is exposed and unraveled. I want the DNA sequenced just as soon as you can."

"That is going to take some time," Robert said.

"I know it's tedious," Victor said. "But I have some radioactive probes you can use."

"That's altogether different."

Robert followed Victor back to his office and collected the myriad small bottles. For a few moments after he'd left, Victor stayed in his office, trying to come up with another explanation besides the cephaloclor. Why else would the NGF gene turn on in the two infants? At age two and a half to three, growth was decelerating, and there were no monumental physiological changes such as those that occurred at puberty.

The other curious fact was that the NGF gene had apparently turned on in the two children at the exact same time. That didn't make sense. The only way the two children's lives intersected at all was that both attended the day-care center at Chimera. That was another reason Victor had selected the two couples. He'd wanted an opportunity to view the children during their development. He had also made sure that the Hobbses and the Murrays did not know each other before they became parents. He didn't want them comparing notes and getting suspicious.

Reaching across his desk for the phone, Victor called personnel and got the bereaved families' home addresses. He wrote them down, then went to tell Colleen that he'd be out for several hours.

Victor decided on the Hobbses first because it was closer. They lived in an attractive brick ranch in a town called Haverhill. Victor pulled up to the front of the house and rang the bell.

"Dr. Frank," William Hobbs said with surprise. He opened the door wider, and gestured for Victor to enter. "Sheila!" he called. "We have company!"

Victor stepped inside. Although the house was pleasantly decorated in a contemporary fashion, an oppressive silence hung over the rooms like a shroud.

"Come in, come in," William said, escorting Victor into the living room. "Coffee? Tea?" His voice echoed in the stillness.

Sheila Hobbs came into the room. She was a dynamic woman with bobbed hair. Victor had met her at several of the obligatory Chimera social occasions.

Victor agreed to some coffee, and soon all three were sitting in the living room, balancing tiny Wedgwood cups on their knees.

"I was just thinking about giving you a call," William said. "It's such a coincidence that you stopped by."

"Oh?" Victor said.

"Sheila and I have decided to get back to work," William said, directing his attention at his coffee cup. "At first we thought we'd get away for a while. But now we think we'll feel better with something to do."

"We'll be pleased to have you back, whenever you choose," said Victor.

"We appreciate that," William said.

Victor cleared his throat. "There is something I wanted to ask you," he began. "I believe you'd been warned that your son was allergic to an antibiotic called cephaloclor."

145

"That's right," Sheila said. "We'd been told that
before we even picked him up." She lowered her coffee cup and it rattled against the saucer.

"Is there any chance that your son had been given
cephaloclor?" Victor asked.

The couple looked at each other, then answered in
unison: "No." Then Sheila continued: "Maurice hadn't
been sick or anything. Besides, we'd made sure that
his antibiotic allergy was part of his medical record.
I'm certain he'd not been given any antibiotic. Why do
you ask?"

Victor stood up. "It was just a thought. I didn't
think he would have, but I'd remembered about the
allergy . . ."

Back in his car, Victor headed toward Boston. He
was pretty certain the Murrays would tell him the
same thing the Hobbses had, but he had to be sure.

Since it was the middle of the afternoon, he made
excellent time. His major problem was what to do
with his car when he got there. Eventually he found
a spot on Beacon Hill. A sign said it was a tow zone,
but Victor decided to take the chance.

The Murrays' house was on West Cedar, in the middle of the block. He rang the bell.

The door was opened by a man in his late twenties
or early thirties, sporting a punk hair style.

"Are the Murrays in?" Victor asked.

"They're both at work," the man said. "I work for
their cleaning service."

"I thought they'd taken some time off."

The man laughed. "Those workaholics! They took
one day after their son died and that was it."

Victor returned to his car, irritated with himself for

not having called before coming. It would have saved him a trip.

Back at Chimera, Victor went directly to the accounting department. He found Horace Murray at his desk, bent over computer print-outs. When the man saw Victor he sprang to his feet saying, "Colette and I wanted to thank you again for coming to the hospital."

"I only wish I could have done something to help," Victor said.

"It was in God's hands," Horace said resignedly.

When Victor asked him about the cephaloclor, the man swore that Mark had not been given an antibiotic, especially not cephaloclor.

Leaving the accounting department, Victor was struck by still another fear. What if there was a link between the deaths and the fact that the children's files were missing? That was the most disturbing thought of all because it implied that the genes had been turned on deliberately.

Heart pounding again, Victor ran back to his lab. One of his newer technicians tried to ask a question, but Victor waved the man away, telling him to talk to Grimes if he had a problem.

Inside his office Victor bent down in front of a cabinet at the bottom of his bookcase. He unlocked the heavy door and reached in to grasp the NGF data books that he'd written in code. But his hand met empty space. The entire shelf was empty.

Victor closed the cabinet and carefully locked it even though there was no longer anything to protect.

"Calm down," he told himself, trying to stem a rising tide of paranoia. "You're letting your imagination run away with itself. There has to be an explanation."

Getting up, he went out to find Robert. He tracked him down in the electrophoresis unit, working on the task that Victor had earlier assigned him. "Have you seen my NGF data books?" Victor asked.

"I don't know where they are," Robert said. "I haven't seen them for six months. I thought you'd moved them."

Mumbling his thanks, Victor walked away. This was no longer some fantasy. The evidence was mounting. Someone had interfered in his experiment, with lethal results. Deciding to face his worst apprehensions, Victor went over to the liquid nitrogen freezer. He put his hand on the latch and hesitated. Intuition told him what he would find, but he had to force himself to raise the hood. He kept hearing Marsha telling him that he had to destroy the other five zygotes right away.

Slowly he looked down. At first his view was blocked by the frozen mist as it floated out of the storage container and spilled silently to the floor. Then it cleared, and he saw the plate that contained the embryos. It was empty.

For a moment Victor supported himself by leaning against the freezer, staring at the empty tray, not wanting to believe what his eyes were clearly telling him. Then he let the lid fall shut. The cool nitrogen mist swirled about his legs as if it were alive. He staggered back to his office and fell into the chair. Someone else knew about his NGF work! But who could it be and why had they intentionally brought about the babies' deaths, or had that been an accident? Was someone so intent on destroying Victor that they didn't care who else was hurt? Suddenly Hurst's threats took on a new dimension.

With a wave of apprehension, Victor realized that he had to find out who was behind all these strange events. He rose from the chair and began to pace, remembering with a start that David had died soon after the battle for taking Chimera public. Could his death have been involved as well? Could Ronald be involved? No, that was ridiculous. David had died of liver cancer, not poisoning or an accident that someone could have caused. Even the idea that the Hobbs and Murray children had been intentionally killed was preposterous. Their deaths had to be an intracellular phenomenon. Maybe there had been a second mutation caused by the freezing which he would see when Robert completed the DNA sequencing.

Telling himself to calm down and think logically, he headed over to the computer center to see Louis Kaspwicz. The piece of hardware Louis had been working on had been reduced to an empty metal shell. Surrounding it were hundreds of parts and pieces.

"I hate to bother you again," Victor said, "but I need to know the time of day when my files were deleted," Victor said. "I'm trying to figure out how I did it."

"If it's any consolation," Louis said, "lots of people accidentally delete their files. I wouldn't be too hard on yourself. As for the time, I think it was around nine or ten o'clock."

"Could I look at the log itself?" Victor asked. He thought that if he'd accessed the computer before or after the deletion, it might give him a clue about why he did it.

"Dr. Frank," Louis said with one of his distracting

twitches, "this is your company. You can look at whatever you want."

They went back to Louis's office and he gave the November 18 log to Victor. Victor scanned through the print-out. He couldn't find any entry between eight-thirty and ten-thirty.

"I don't see it," Victor admitted.

Louis came around the desk to look over Victor's shoulder. "That's odd," he said, checking the date on the top of the page. "November 18, all right!" He looked back at the entries. "Oh, for God's sake!" he exclaimed. "No wonder you couldn't find it. You were looking in the A.M. section." Louis handed the print-out back, pointing to the entry in question.

"P.M.?" Victor asked, looking at the correct place on the sheet. "That couldn't be. At 9:45 P.M. I was in Symphony Hall in Boston."

"What can I say?" Louis said with a twitch.

"Are you certain that this is correct?" Victor asked.

"Absolutely." Louis pointed to the entries before and after. "See how it's sequenced? It has to be the right time. Are you sure you were at the symphony?"

"Yes," Victor said.

"You didn't use the phone?"

"What are you talking about?" Victor asked.

"Just that this entry was made off-site. See this access number? That's for your PC at home."

"But I wasn't at home," Victor complained.

Louis's shoulders jerked spasmodically. "In that case, there's only one explanation," he said. "The entry had to have been made by someone who knows your password as well as the unpublished phone number of our computer. Have you ever given your password to anyone?"

"Never," Victor said without hesitation.

"How often do you access the computer from home?" Louis inquired.

"Almost never," Victor said. "I used to do it frequently, but that was years ago when the ·company was just starting."

"Good lord!" Louis said, staring at the print-out.

"What now?" asked Victor.

"I hate to tell you this, but there have been a lot of entries into the computer on a regular basis with your password. And that can only mean that some hacker has found our telephone number."

"Isn't that difficult?" Victor asked.

Louis shook his head. "The phone number is the easy part. Just like the kid did in *War Games.* You can program your computer to make endless calls using permutations. As soon as you stumble on a computer tone, that's when the fun begins."

"And this hacker used the computer frequently?"

"Sure did," Louis said. "I've noticed the entries, but I always thought it was you. Look!"

Louis flipped open the log and pointed to a series of entries using Victor's password. "It's usually Friday nights." He flipped the pages and showed other entries. "Must be when the kid is out of school. What a pain in the ass! Here's another one. Look, the hacker'd logged into Personnel and Purchasing. God, this makes me sick. We've been having some problem with files and I wonder if this kid is the source. I think we'd better change your password right away."

"But then we stand less chance of catching him. I don't use my password much anyway. Why don't we keep watch on Friday evenings and see if we can trace him. You can do that, can't you?"

"It's possible," Louis agreed, "if the kid stays on line long enough and the telephone people are standing by."

"See if you can arrange it," Victor said.

"I'll try. There's only one thing that's worse than a meddlesome hacker and that's a computer virus. But in this case I'll put my money on the hacker."

As Victor left the computer center, he thought he'd better check up on VJ. Given the day's developments he thought he better warn him to stay away from Hurst and even Ronald Beekman.

The first place Victor looked was the lab, but Robert had not seen him or Philip all day. Nor had any of the other technicians. This surprised Victor, since VJ spent most of his time trying out the various microscopes and other equipment. Victor decided to try the cafeteria. Since it was late afternoon there were only a few scattered people having coffee. Victor talked with the manager, who was busy closing out the cash registers. He'd seen VJ around lunchtime, but not since then.

Leaving the cafeteria, Victor stopped in the library, which was in the same building. The circular cement columns that had been added for structural support had been left in plain sight, giving the area a Gothic feeling. The stacks for books and periodicals were shoulder height, affording a view of the entire room. A comfortable reading area to the right looked out over the inner courtyard of the complex.

When Victor asked the librarian if she'd seen VJ or Philip, she shook her head no. With rising concern, Victor checked out the gym and day-care center. No VJ and no Philip.

Returning to his lab prepared to call security, Victor found a message from the manager of the cafeteria, saying VJ and Philip had come in for ice cream.

Victor went to the cafeteria. He found the two sitting at a table near the window.

"All right, you two," Victor said with mock anger. "Where the devil have you been?"

VJ turned to look at his father. He had his spoon in his mouth upside down. Philip, obviously thinking that Victor was angry, stood up, with his large, shovel-like hands not knowing what to do with themselves.

"We've been around," VJ said evasively.

"Where?" Victor challenged. "I've looked high and low for you."

"We were down by the river for a while," VJ admitted.

"I thought I told you to stay away from the river."

"Oh, come on, Dad," VJ said. "We weren't doing anything dangerous."

"I would never let anything bad happen to VJ," Philip said in his childlike voice.

"I don't imagine you would," Victor said, suddenly impressed by what a powerfully built man Philip was. He and VJ were an improbable pair, but Victor certainly appreciated Philip's loyalty to his son. "Sit down," Victor said more kindly. "Finish your ice cream."

Pulling up a chair himself, Victor turned to his son. "I want you to be especially careful around here for a while. After that brick last night, I'm sure you've guessed that there are some problems."

"I'll be all right," VJ said.

"I'm sure you will," Victor agreed. "But a little prudence won't hurt. Don't say anything to anybody, but keep your eyes open when Beekman or Hurst are around, okay?"

"Okay," VJ said.

"And you," Victor said to Philip. "You can act as VJ's unofficial bodyguard. Can you do that?"

"Oh, yes, Dr. Frank," Philip said with alacrity.

"In fact . . ." Victor said, knowing Marsha would appreciate the idea, "why don't you come and spend a few nights with us like you used to when VJ was little. Then you can be with VJ even in the evenings."

"Thank you, Dr. Frank," Philip said with a smile that exposed most of his large teeth. "I'd like that very much."

"Then it's settled," Victor said, getting to his feet. "I've got to get back to the office; I've been running around all day. We'll probably be leaving in a couple of hours. We can stop by Philip's to pick up his things on the way home."

Both VJ and Philip waved at Victor with their ice cream spoons.

Marsha was just taking the groceries out of the bag when she heard Victor's car come up the drive. As Victor waited for the automatic garage door to rise, Marsha noticed a third head in the back seat and groaned. She'd only bought six small lamb chops.

Two minutes later they came into the kitchen. "I've invited Philip to stay with us for a few days," Victor said. "I thought with all the excitement around here it would be good to have some muscle in the house."

"Sounds good," Marsha said, but then she added, "I hope that's not in lieu of professional security."

Victor laughed. "Not quite." Turning to VJ and Philip, he said, "Why don't you two hit the pool?"

VJ and Philip disappeared upstairs to change.

Victor moved as if to kiss Marsha, but she was back to digging in the grocery bag. Then she stepped around him to put some things in the pantry. He could tell she was still angry and, given the previous evening's events, he knew she had good reason to be.

"Sorry about Philip; it was a last-minute idea," he said. "But I don't think we'll have any more bricks or calls, anyway. I phoned the people who might have threatened us and laid it on the line."

"Then how come Philip?" asked Marsha, coming back from the pantry.

"Just an added precaution," Victor said. Then, to change the subject, he added: "What's for dinner?"

"Lamp chops—and we'll have to stretch them," Marsha said, looking at Victor out of the corner of her eye. "Why do I have the feeling that you're still keeping things from me?"

"Must be your suspicious nature," Victor said, even though he knew she was in no mood for teasing. "What else besides lamb chops?" he asked, trying to change the subject.

"Artichokes, rice, and salad." It was obvious that he was covering something, but she let it go.

"What can I do?" Victor asked, washing his hands at the kitchen sink. It was generally their habit to share the preparation of the evening meal since they both worked long hours. Marsha told him to rinse the salad greens.

"I talked with VJ this morning about his friend Richie," Victor said. "He's going to ask him to go to Boston to a day's outing this week so I don't think it's fair to say that VJ doesn't have any friends."

"I hope it happens," Marsha said noncommittally.

As she put the rice and artichokes on to cook, she continued to watch Victor out of the corner of her eye. She was hoping that he'd volunteer some information about the two unfortunate babies, but he fussed over the salad in silence. Exasperated, Marsha asked: "Any news about the cause of death of the children?"

Victor turned to face her. "I looked at the inserted gene in VJ as well as in the Hobbs and Murray kids. In the toddlers it appeared overtly abnormal, like it was actively transcribing, but in VJ it looked absolutely quiet. What's more," he added, "I got out some photos of the same gene back when VJ's intelligence dropped. Even then it didn't look anything like these kids'. So whatever VJ had, it wasn't the same problem."

Marsha gave a sigh of relief. "That's good news. Why didn't you tell me right away?"

"I just got home," Victor said. "And I'm telling you."

"You could have called," Marsha said, convinced he was still hiding something. "Or brought it up without my asking."

"I'm having the dead kids' genes sequenced," Victor said, getting out the oil and vinegar. "Then maybe I'll be able to tell you what turned the gene back on."

Marsha went to the cupboard and got out the dishes to set the table. She tried to control the rage that was beginning to reassert itself. How could he remain so casual about all this? When Victor asked if there were anything else he could do for dinner, she told him he'd done enough. He took her literally and sat on one of the kitchen counter stools, watching her set the table.

"VJ's letting you win that swimming race wasn't a fluke," Marsha said, hoping to goad her husband. "He started doing that when he was three." Marsha went on to tell him what Martha Gillespie had said about his behavior in nursery school.

"How can you be so sure he threw the race?" Victor asked.

"My goodness, that still bothers you," said Marsha, turning down the burner under the rice. "I was pretty sure he did when I was watching Sunday night. Now that I talked with Martha, I'm positive. It's as if VJ doesn't want to draw attention to himself."

"Sometimes by throwing a race you attract more attention," Victor said.

"Maybe," Marsha added, but she wasn't convinced. "The point is I wish to God I knew more about what went on in his mind when his intelligence changed so dramatically. It might give some explanation for his current behavior. Back then we were too concerned with his health to worry about his feelings."

"I think he weathered the episode extremely well," Victor said. He went to the refrigerator and took out a bottle of white wine. "I know you don't agree with me, but I think he's doing great. He's a happy kid. I'm proud of him. I think he's going to make one hell of a researcher one day. He really loves the lab."

"Provided his intelligence doesn't fall again," Marsha snapped. "But I'm not worried about his ability to work. I'm worried your unspeakable experiment has interfered with his human qualities." She turned away to hide new tears as emotion welled up within her. When all this was over she didn't see how she could stay married to Victor. But would VJ ever be willing to leave his precious lab and live with her?

"You psychiatrists . . ." Victor muttered as he got out the corkscrew.

Marsha gave the rice a stir and checked the artichokes. She struggled to control herself. She didn't want more tears. She didn't speak for a few minutes. When she did, she said, "I wish I'd kept a diary of VJ's development. It would really be helpful."

"I kept one," Victor said, pulling out the cork with a resounding pop.

"You did?" Marsha asked. "Why didn't you ever tell me?"

"Because it was for the NGF project."

"Can I see it?" Marsha asked, again swallowing her anger at Victor's arrogance, using her baby as a guinea pig.

Victor tasted the wine. "It's in my study. I'll show it to you later after VJ is in bed."

Marsha was sitting in Victor's study. She'd insisted on reading the diary alone because she knew Victor's presence would only upset her more. Her eyes filled with tears as she relived VJ's birth. Even though much of the record was no more than a standard laboratory account, she was painfully moved by it. She'd forgotten how VJ's eyes had followed her from birth, long before an average baby's had even begun to track.

All the usual milestones had been reached at incredibly early ages, particularly the ability to speak. At seven months, when VJ was supposed to be pronouncing no more than "Mama" and "Dada," he was already composing sentences. By one year he had a whole vocabulary. By eighteen months, when he was supposed to be able to walk reasonably well, he could ride a small bicycle that Victor had had specially made.

Reading the history made Marsha remember how exciting it had been. Every day had been marked by a mastery of some different task and the uncovering of a new and unexpected ability. She realized she had been guilty too of reveling in VJ's unique accomplishments. At the time she had given very little thought to the impact of the child's precociousness on his personal development. As a psychologist, she should have known better.

Victor came in with some flimsy excuse about needing a book as she reached a section labeled "mathematics." Discomforted by her own shortcomings as a caring parent, she let him stay as she continued reading. Math had always been her *bête noire*. In college she'd had to be tutored to get through the required calculus course. When VJ began to demonstrate an exceptional facility with numbers, she had been astounded. At three VJ actually explained in terms she could understand the basis for calculus. For the first time in her life, Marsha properly comprehended the principles.

"What amazed me," Victor was saying, "was his ability to translate mathematical equations into music."

Marsha remembered, thinking they had another Beethoven on their hands. "And I never thought to worry if the burden of genius was more than a toddler could handle," she thought with regret. Sadly, she flipped the next few pages and was surprised to see the diary come to an end.

"I hope this isn't all," she said.

"I'm afraid so."

Marsha read the final pages. The last entry was for

May 6, 1982. It described the experience in the day-care center at Chimera that Marsha remembered so vividly. It then dispassionately summarized VJ's sudden diminution in intelligence. The last sentence read: "VJ appears to have suffered an acute alteration in cerebral function that now appears stable."

"You never made any further entries?" asked Marsha.

"No," Victor admitted. "I thought the experiment was a failure despite its initial success. There didn't seem to be any reason to continue the narrative."

Marsha closed the book. She had hoped to find more clues to what she considered the deficiencies in VJ's personality. "I wish his history pointed to some psychosomatic illness or even a conversion reaction. Then he might be responsive to therapy. I just wish I'd been more sensitive back when all this happened."

"I think VJ's problem was the result of some sort of intracellular phenomenon," Victor offered. "I don't think the history would make much difference anyway."

"That's what terrifies me," said Marsha. "It makes me afraid that VJ is going to die like the Hobbs and Murray children, or of cancer like his brother, or Janice for that matter. I've read enough about your work to know that cancer is a big worry for the future of gene therapy. People are worried that inserted genes might cause proto-onco genes to become oncogenes, turning the involved cell into a cancer."

She broke off. She could feel her emotions taking over. "How can I go on talking about this as if it were simply a scientific problem? It's our son—and for all I know you triggered something inside him that will make him die."

Marsha covered her face with her hands. Despite her attempts to control herself, tears returned. She let herself cry.

Victor tried to put his arm around her, but she leaned away. Frustrated, he stood up. He watched her for a moment, with her shoulders silently shaking. There was nothing he could say in defense. Instead, he left the room and started upstairs. The pain of his own grief was overwhelming. And after what he'd discovered today, he had more reason than his wife to fear for VJ's safety.

# 8

## *Thursday Morning*

Wondering how the other people put up with it on a daily basis, Victor suffered the congested traffic of a normal Boston rush hour.

Once he got on Storrow Drive heading west, traffic improved, only to slow down again near the Fenway. It was after nine when he finally entered the busy Children's Hospital. He went directly to Pathology.

"Dr. Shryack, please?" Victor asked. The secretary glanced up at him and, without removing her dictation headset, pointed down the corridor.

Victor looked at the nameplates as he walked.

"Excuse me. Dr. Shryack?" Victor called as he stepped through the open door. The extraordinarily young-looking man raised his head from a microscope.

"I'm Dr. Frank," Victor said. "Remember when I stopped in while you were autopsying the Hobbs baby?"

"Of course," said Dr. Shryack. He stood up and ex-

162

tended his hand. "Nice to meet you under more pleasant circumstances. The name is Stephen."

Victor shook his hand.

"I'm afraid we haven't any definitive diagnosis yet," Stephen said, "if that is what you've come for. The slides are still being processed."

"I'm interested, of course," Victor said. "But the reason I stopped by was to ask another favor. I was curious if you routinely take fluid samples."

"Absolutely," Stephen answered. "We always do toxicology, at least a screen."

"I was hoping to get some of the fluid myself," Victor said.

"I'm impressed with your interest," Stephen said. "Most internists give us a rather wide berth. Come on, let's see what we have."

Stephen led Victor out of his office, down the hall, and into the extensive laboratory where he stopped to speak to a severely dressed middle-aged woman. The conversation lasted for a minute before she pointed toward the opposite end of the room. Stephen then led Victor down the length of the lab and into a side room.

"I think we're in luck." Stephen opened the doors to a large cooler on the far wall and began searching through the hundreds of stoppered Erlenmeyer flasks. He found one and handed it back to Victor. Soon he found three others.

Victor noticed he had two flasks of blood and two of urine.

"How much do you need?" Stephen asked.

"Just a tiny bit," Victor said.

Stephen carefully poured a little from each flask into test tubes that he got from a nearby counter top.

He capped them, labeled each with a red grease pencil, and handed them to Victor.

"Anything else?" Stephen asked.

"Well, I hate to take advantage of your generosity," Victor said.

"It's quite all right," Stephen said.

"About five years ago, my son died of a very rare liver cancer," Victor began.

"I'm so sorry."

"He was treated here. At the time the doctors said there had only been a couple of similar cases in the literature. The thought was that the cancer had arisen from the Kupffer cells so that it really was a cancer of the reticuloendothelial system."

Stephen nodded. "I think I read about that case. In fact, I'm sure I did."

"Since the tumor was so rare," Victor said, "do you think that any gross material was saved?"

"There's a chance," Stephen said. "Let's go back to my office."

When Stephen was settled in front of his computer terminal, he asked Victor for David's full name and birth date. Entering that, he obtained David's hospital number and located the pathology record. With his finger on the screen, he scanned the information. His finger stopped. "This looks encouraging. Here's a specimen number. Let's check it out."

This time he took Victor down to the subbasement. "We have a crypt where we put things for long-term storage," he explained.

They stepped off the elevator into a dimly lit hall that snaked off in myriad directions. There were pipes and ducts along the ceiling, the floor a bare, stained concrete.

"We don't get to come down here that often," Stephen said as he led the way through the maze. He finally stopped at a heavy metal door. When Victor helped pull it open, Stephen reached in and flipped on a light.

It was a large, poorly lit room with widely spaced bulbs in simple ceiling fixtures. The air was cold and humid. Numerous rows of metal shelves reached almost to the ceiling.

Checking a number that he had written on a scrap of paper, Stephen set off down one of the rows. Victor followed, glancing into the shelves. At one point he stopped, transfixed by the image of an entire head of a child contained in a large glass canister and soaking in some kind of preservative brine. The eyes stared out and the mouth was open as if in some perpetual scream. Victor looked at the other glass containers. Each contained some horrifying preserved testament to past suffering. He shuddered, then realized that Stephen had passed from sight.

Looking nervously around, he heard the resident call. "Over here."

Victor strode forward, no longer looking at the specimens. When he reached the corner, he saw the pathologist reaching into one of the shelves, noisily pushing around the glass containers. "Eureka!" he said, straightening up. He had a modest-sized glass jar in his hands that contained a bulbous liver suspended in clear fluid. "You're in luck," he said.

Later, on the way up in the elevator, he asked Victor why he wanted the tissue.

"Curiosity," Victor said. "When David died my grief was so overwhelming I didn't ask any questions. Now after all these years, I want to know more about why he died."

Marsha drove VJ and Philip through the Chimera gates. During the drive VJ had chatted about a new Pac-Man video just like any other ten-year-old.

"Thanks for the lift, Mom," he said, jumping out.

"Let Colleen know where you're playing," she said. "And I want you to stay away from the river. You saw what it looked like from the bridge."

Philip got out from the back seat. "Nothing's going to happen to VJ," he said.

"Are you sure you wouldn't rather go over to your friend Richie's?" Marsha questioned.

"I'm happy here," VJ said. "Don't worry about me, okay?"

Marsha watched VJ stride off with Philip rushing to catch up. "What a pair," she thought, trying to keep last night's revelation from panicking her.

She parked the car and headed for the day-care center. As she entered the building she could hear the thwack of a racquetball. The courts were on the floor above, in the fitness center.

Marsha found Pauline Spaulding kneeling on the floor, supervising a group of children who were finger-painting. She leaped up when she saw Marsha, her figure giving proof to all those years as an aerobics instructor.

When Marsha asked for a few minutes of her time, Pauline left the kids and went off to find another teacher. After she returned with a younger woman in tow, she led Marsha to another room filled with cribs and folding cots.

"We'll have some privacy here," Pauline said. Her

large oval eyes looked nervously at Marsha, who she assumed had come on official business for her husband.

"I'm not here as the wife of one of the partners," Marsha said, trying to put Pauline at ease.

"I see." Pauline took a deep breath and smiled. "I thought you had some major complaint."

"Quite the contrary," Marsha said. "I wanted to talk to you about my son."

"Wonderful boy," Pauline said. "I suppose you know that he comes in here from time to time and helps out. In fact, he visited us just last weekend."

"I didn't know the center was open on weekends," Marsha said.

"Seven days a week," Pauline said with pride. "A lot of people here at Chimera work every day. I suppose that's called dedication."

Marsha wasn't sure she'd call it dedication, and she wondered what kind of stress such devotion would have on family life that was already suffering. But she didn't say any of this. Instead, she asked Pauline if she remembered the day VJ's IQ dropped.

"Of course I remember. The fact that it happened here has always made me feel responsible somehow."

"Well, that's plainly absurd," Marsha said with a warm smile. "What I wanted to ask about was VJ's behavior afterwards."

Pauline looked down at her feet, thinking. After a minute or so, she raised her head. "I suppose the thing I noticed the most was that he'd changed from a leader of activities to an observer. Before, he was always eager to try anything. Later, he acted bored and had to be forced to participate. And he avoided all competition. It was as if he were a different person. We didn't push him; we were afraid to. Anyway, we saw much less of him after that episode."

"What do you mean?" Marsha asked. "Once he finished his medical work-up, he still came here every afternoon after preschool."

"No, he didn't," Pauline said. "He began to spend most of the time in his father's lab."

"Really? I didn't think that started until he began school. But what do I know, I'm just the mother!"

Pauline smiled.

"What about friends?" Marsha questioned.

"That was never one of VJ's strong points," Pauline said diplomatically. "He always got along better with the staff than the children. After his problem, he tended to stay by himself. Well, I take that back. He did seem to enjoy the company of the retarded employee."

"You mean Philip?" Marsha questioned.

"That's the fellow," Pauline said.

Marsha stood up, thanked Pauline, and together they walked to the entrance.

"VJ may not be quite as smart as he was," Pauline said at the door, "but he is a fine boy. We appreciate him here at the center."

Marsha hurried back to the car. She hadn't learned much, but it seemed VJ had always been even more of a loner than she had suspected.

Victor knew he should go to his office the moment he reached Chimera. Colleen was undoubtedly inundated by emergencies. But instead, carrying his latest samples from Children's Hospital, he headed for his lab. En route he stopped at the computer center.

Victor looked for Louis Kaspwicz around the malfunctioning hardware, but the problem had apparently been solved. The machine was back on line with lights blinking and tape reels running. One of the many white-coated technicians said Louis was in his office trying to figure out a glitch that had occurred in one of the accounting programs.

When Louis saw Victor, he pushed aside the thick program he was working on and took out the log sheets that he was saving to show Victor.

"I've checked over the last six months," Louis said, organizing the papers for Victor to see, "and underlined the times the hacker has logged on. It seems the kid checks in every Friday night around eight. At least fifty percent of the time he stays on long enough to be traced."

"How come you say 'kid'?" Victor asked, straightening up from glancing at the logs.

"It's just an expression," Louis answered. "Somebody who breaks into a private computer system could be any age."

"Like one of our competitors?" Victor said.

"Exactly, but historically there's been a lot of teenagers that do it just for the challenge. It's like some kind of computer game for them."

"When can we try to trace him?" Victor asked.

"As soon as possible," Louis said. "It terrifies me that this has been going on for so long. I have no idea what kind of mischief this guy has been up to. Anyway, I talked the phone company into sending over some technicians to watch tomorrow night, if it's all right with you."

"Fine," Victor said.

That settled, Victor continued on to his lab. He found Robert still absorbed in sequencing the DNA of the inserted genes.

"I've got some more rush work," Victor said hurriedly. "If you need to, pull one of the other techs off a project to help, but I want you to be personally responsible for this work."

"I'll get Harry if it's necessary," Robert said. "What do you have?"

Victor opened the brown paper bag and removed a small jar. He extended it toward Robert. His hand trembled.

"It's a piece of my son's liver."

"VJ's?" Robert's gaunt face looked shocked. His eyes seemed even more prominent.

"No, no, David's. Remember we did DNA fingerprinting on everyone in my family?"

Robert nodded.

"I want that tumor fingerprinted, too," Victor said. "And I want some standard H and E stains and a chromosome study."

"Can I ask why you want all this?"

"Just do it," Victor said sharply.

"All right," Robert said, nervously looking down at his feet. "I wasn't questioning your motives. I just thought that if you were looking for something in particular, I could keep an eye out for it."

Victor ran his hand through his hair. "I'm sorry for snapping at you like that," he said. "I'm under a lot of pressure."

"No need to apologize," Robert said. "I'll start work on it right now."

"Wait, there's more," Victor said. He removed the four stoppered test tubes. "I've got some blood and

urine samples I need assayed for a cephalosporin antibiotic called cephaloclor."

Robert took the samples, tilted them to see their
consistency, then checked the grease-pencil labels.
"I'll put Harry on this. It will be pretty straightforward."

"How is the sequencing coming?" Victor asked.

"Tedious, as usual," Robert said.

"Any mutations pop up?"

"Not a one," Robert said. "And the way the probes
pick up the fragments, I'd guess at this point that the
genes have been perfectly stable."

"That's unfortunate," Victor said.

"I thought you'd be pleased with that information,"
Robert said.

"Normally I would," Victor said. He didn't elaborate. It would have been too hard for him to explain
that he was hoping to find concrete evidence that the
dead children's NGF gene differed from VJ's.

"So here you are!" a voice called, startling both Victor and Robert. They turned to see Colleen standing at
the door, legs apart and arms akimbo. "One of the
secretaries told me she saw you creeping around," she
said with a wink.

"I was just about to come over to the office," Victor
said defensively.

"Sure, and I'm about to win the lottery," Colleen
laughed.

"I suppose the office is bedlam?" Victor asked sheep-
ishly.

"Now he thinks he's indispensable," Colleen joked
to Robert. "Actually, things aren't too bad. I've handled most of what has come up. But there is something
that you should know right away."

"What is it?" said Victor, suddenly concerned.

"Perhaps I could talk to you in private?" Colleen said. She smiled at Robert to indicate she did not mean to be rude.

"Of course," Victor said awkwardly. He moved across the lab to one of the benches. Colleen followed.

"It's about Gephardt," Colleen said. "Darryl Webster, who's in charge of the investigation, has been trying to get you all day. He finally told me what it was all about. Seems that he has uncovered a slew of irregularities. While Gephardt was purchasing supervisor for Chimera a lot of laboratory equipment vanished."

"Like what?" Victor questioned.

"Big-ticket items," Colleen said. "Fast protein liquid chromatography units, DNA sequencers, mass spectrometers, things like that."

"Good God!"

"Darryl thought you should know," Colleen added.

"Did he find bogus orders?"

"No," Colleen said. "That's what makes it so weird. Receiving got the equipment. It just never went to the department that was supposed to have ordered it. And the department in question never said anything because they hadn't placed the order."

"So Gephardt fenced it," Victor said, amazed. "No wonder his attorney was so hot to cut a deal. He knew what we would find."

Angrily, Victor remembered that the note around the brick referred to a deal. In all likelihood, Gephardt had been behind the harassment.

"I assume we have the bastard's telephone number," Victor said with venom.

"I guess," Colleen said. "Should be in his employee record."

"I want to give Gephardt a call. I'm tired of talking through that lawyer of his."

On the way back to the administration building, Colleen had to run to keep up with Victor. She'd never seen him so angry.

He was still fuming as he dialed Gephardt's number, motioning for Colleen to stay in the room so she could be a witness to what was said. But the phone rang interminably. "Damn it!" Victor cursed. "The bastard either is out or he's not answering. What's his address?"

Colleen looked it up and found a street number in Lawrence, not far from Chimera.

"I think I'll stop and pay the man a visit on the way home," Victor said. "I have a feeling he's been to my house. It's time I return the call."


When one of her patients called in sick, Marsha decided to use the hour to visit Pendleton Academy, the private school that VJ had been attending since kindergarten.

The campus was beautiful even though the trees were still bare and the grass a wintry brown. The stone buildings were covered with ivy, giving the appearance of an old college or university.

Marsha pulled up to the administration building and got out. She wasn't as familiar with the school as she might have been. Although she and Victor had made regular Parents' Day visits, she'd met the headmaster, Perry Remington, on only two occasions. She hoped he would see her.

When she entered the building she was pleased to find a number of secretaries busy at their desks. At least it wasn't a vacation week for the staff. Mr. Remington was in his office and was kind enough to see Marsha within a few minutes.

He was a big man with a full, well-trimmed beard. His bushy brows poked over the top of his horn-rimmed glasses.

"We are always delighted to see parents," Mr. Remington said, offering her a chair. He sat down, crossed his legs, and balanced a manila folder on his knee. "What's on your mind?"

"I'm curious about my son, VJ," Marsha said. "I'm a psychiatrist and to be honest with you, I'm a bit worried about him. I know his grades are good, but I wondered how he was doing generally." Marsha paused. She didn't want to put words into Mr. Remington's mouth.

The headmaster cleared his throat. "When they told me you were outside, I quickly reviewed VJ's record," he said. He tapped the folder, then he shifted his position, crossing the other leg. "Actually, if you hadn't stopped I'd have probably given you a ring when school reopened. VJ's teachers are also concerned about him. Despite his excellent grades, your son seems to have an attention problem. His teachers say that he often appears to be daydreaming or off in his own world, though they admit if they call on him he always has the right answer."

"Then why are the teachers concerned?" asked Marsha.

"I guess it's because of the fights."

"Fights!" exclaimed Marsha. "I've never heard a word about fights."

"There have been four or five episodes this year alone."

"Why hasn't this been brought to my attention?" Marsha asked with some indignation.

"We didn't contact you because VJ specifically asked us not to do so."

"That's absurd!" Marsha said, raising her voice. "Why would you take orders from VJ?"

"Just a moment, Dr. Frank," Mr. Remington said. "In each incident it was apparent to the staff member present that your son was severely provoked and that he only used his fists as a last resort. Each incident involved a known bully apparently responding childishly to your son's . . . er, uniqueness. There was nothing equivocal about any of these incidents. VJ was never at fault and never the instigator. Consequently, we respected his wishes not to bother you."

"But he could have been hurt," Marsha said, settling back in her chair.

"That's the other surprising thing," Mr. Remington said. "For a boy who doesn't go out for athletics, VJ handled himself admirably. One of the other boys came away with a broken nose."

"I seem to be learning a lot about my son these days," Marsha said. "What about friends?"

"He's pretty much of a loner," Mr. Remington said. "In fact, he doesn't interact well with the other students. Generally, there is no hostility involved. He just does 'his own thing.'"

That was not what Marsha wanted to hear. She'd hoped her son was more social in school than at home. "Would you describe VJ as a happy child?" she asked.

"That's a tough question," Mr. Remington said. "I

don't feel he is unhappy, but VJ doesn't display much emotion at any time."

Marsha frowned. The flat effect sounded schizoid. The picture was getting worse, not better.

"One of our math instructors, Raymond Cavendish," Mr. Remington offered, "took a particular interest in VJ. He made an enormous effort to penetrate what he called VJ's private world."

Marsha leaned forward. "Really? Was he successful?"

"Unfortunately, no," Mr. Remington said. "But the reason I mentioned it was because Raymond's goal was to get VJ involved in extracurricular activities like sports. VJ was not very interested even though he'd shown an innate talent for basketball and soccer. But I agree with Raymond's opinion: VJ needs to develop other interests."

"What initially interested Mr. Cavendish in my son?"

"Apparently he was impressed by VJ's aptitude for math. He put VJ in a gifted class that included kids from several grades. Each was allowed to proceed at his own pace. One day when he was helping some high school kids with their algebra, he noticed VJ daydreaming. He called his name to tell him to get back to work. VJ thought he was calling on him for an answer and, to everyone's amazement, VJ offered the solution to the high schooler's problem."

"That's incredible!" Marsha said. "Would it be possible for me to talk with Mr. Cavendish?"

Mr. Remington shook his head. "I'm afraid not. Mr. Cavendish died a couple of years ago."

"Oh, I'm sorry," Marsha said.

"It was a great loss to the school," Mr. Remington agreed.

There was a pause in the conversation. Marsha was about to excuse herself when Mr. Remington said, "If you want my opinion, I think it would be to VJ's benefit if he were to spend more time here in school."

"You mean summer session?" Marsha asked.

"No, no, the regular year. Your husband writes frequent notes for VJ to spend time in his research lab. Now, I am all for alternative educational environments, but VJ needs to participate more, particularly in the extracurricular area. I think—"

"Just a second," Marsha interrupted. "Are you telling me that VJ misses school to spend time at the lab?"

"Yes," Mr. Remington said. "Often."

"That's news to me," Marsha admitted. "I know VJ spends a lot of time at the lab, but I never knew he was missing school to do it."

"If I were to guess," Mr. Remington said, "I'd say that VJ spends more time at the lab than he does here."

"Good grief," Marsha said.

"If you feel as I do," Mr. Remington said, "then perhaps you should talk to your husband."

"I will," Marsha said, getting to her feet. "You can count on it."


"I want you to wait in the car," Victor said to VJ and Philip as he leaned forward and looked at Gephardt's house through the windshield. It was a nondescript two-story building with a brick façade and fake shutters.

"Turn the key so we can at least listen to the radio,"

VJ said from the passenger seat; Philip was in the back.

Victor flipped the ignition key. The radio came back on with the raucous rock music VJ had previously selected. It sounded louder with the car engine off.

"I won't be long," he said, getting out of the car. He was having second thoughts about the confrontation now that he was standing on Gephardt's property. The house was set on a fairly large lot, hidden from its neighbors by thick clusters of birches and maples. A bay window stuck out on the building's left, probably indicating the living room. There were no lights on even though daylight was fading, but a Ford van stood idle in the driveway so Victor figured somebody might be home.

Victor leaned back inside the car. "I won't be long."

"You already said that," VJ said, keeping time to the music on the dashboard with the flat of his palm.

Victor nodded, embarrassed. He straightened up and started for the house. As he walked, he wondered if he shouldn't go home and call. But then he remembered the missing laboratory equipment, the embezzlement of some poor dead employee's paychecks, and the brick through VJ's window. That raised Victor's anger and put determination in his step. As he got closer he glanced at the brick façade and wondered if the brick that had crashed into his house was a leftover from the construction of Gephardt's. Eyeing the bay window, Victor had the urge to throw one of the cobblestones lining the walk through it. Then he stopped.

Victor blinked as if he thought his eyes were not telling the truth. He was about twenty feet away from the bay window and he could see that many of the panes were already broken, with sharp shards of glass still in place. It was as if his retribution fantasy had become instant reality.

Glancing back to his car where he could see the silhouettes of VJ and Philip, Victor struggled with an urge to go back and drive away. There was something wrong. He could sense it. He looked back at the broken bay window, then up the front steps at the door. The place was too quiet, too dark. But then Victor wondered what he'd tell VJ: he was too scared? Having come that far, Victor forced himself to continue.

Going up the front steps, he saw that the door was not completely shut.

"Hello!" Victor called. "Anybody home?" He pushed the door open wider and stepped inside.

Victor's scream died on his lips. The bloody scene in Gephardt's living room was worse than anything he'd ever seen, even during his internship at Boston City Hospital. Seven corpses, including Gephardt's, were strewn grotesquely around the living room. The bodies were riddled with bullets and the smell of cordite hung heavily in the air.

The killer must have only just left because blood was still oozing from the wounds. Besides Gephardt, there was a woman about Gephardt's age who Victor guessed was his wife, an older couple, and three children. The youngest looked about five. Gephardt had been shot so many times that the top part of his head was gone.

Victor straightened up from checking the last body for signs of life. Weak and dizzy, he walked to the phone wondering if he should be touching anything. He didn't bother with an ambulance, but dialed the police, who said a car would be there right away.

Victor decided to wait in the car. He was afraid if he stayed in the house any longer he'd be sick.

"We're going to be here for a little while," Victor shouted as he slid in behind the wheel. He turned the radio down. The image of all the dead people was etched in his mind. "There's a little trouble inside the house and the police are on their way."

"How long?" VJ asked.

"I'm not sure. Maybe an hour or so."

"Any fire trucks coming?" Philip asked eagerly.

The police arrived in force with four squad cars, probably the entire Lawrence PD fleet. Victor did not go back inside but hung around on the front steps. After about a half hour one of the plainclothesmen came out to talk to him.

"I'm Lieutenant Mark Scudder," he said. "They got your name and address, I presume."

Victor told him they had.

"Bad business," Scudder said. He lit a cigarette and tossed the match out onto the lawn. "Looks like some drug-related vendetta—the kind of scene you expect to see south of Boston, but not up here."

"Did you find drugs?" Victor asked.

"Not yet," Scudder said, taking a long drag on his cigarette. "But this sure wasn't any crime of passion. Not with the artillery they used. There must have been two or three people shooting in there."

"Are you people going to need me much longer?" Victor asked.

Scudder shook his head. "If they got your name and number, you can go whenever you want."

Upset as she was, Marsha could hardly focus on her afternoon patients and needed all her forbearance to appear interested in the last, a narcissistic twenty-year-old with a borderline personality disorder. The moment the girl left, Marsha picked up her purse and went out to her car, for once letting her correspondence go to the following day.

All the way home she kept going over her conversation with Remington. Either Victor had been lying about the amount of time VJ was spending at the lab or VJ had been forging his excuses. Both possibilities were equally upsetting, and Marsha realized that she couldn't even begin dealing with her feelings about Victor and his unconscionable experiment until she had found out how badly VJ had been harmed. The discovery of his truancy added to her worries; it was such a classic symptom of a conduct disorder that could lead to an antisocial personality.

Marsha turned into their driveway and accelerated up the slight incline. It was almost dark and she had on her headlights. She rounded the house and was reaching for the automatic garage opener when the headlights caught something on the garage door. She couldn't see what it was and as she pulled up to the door, the headlights reflected back off the white surface, creating a glare. Shielding her eyes, Marsha got out of the car and came around the front. Squinting, she looked up at the object, which looked like a ball of rags.

"Oh, my God!" she cried when she saw what it was. Shaking off a wave of nausea, she ventured another look. The cat had been strangled and nailed against the door as if crucified.

Trying not to look at the bulging eyes and protruding tongue, she read the typed note secured to the tail: YOU'D BETTER MAKE THINGS RIGHT.

Leaving her car where it was but turning off the headlights and the engine, Marsha hurried inside the house and bolted the door. Trembling with a mixture of revulsion, anger, and fear, she took off her coat and went to find the maid, Ramona, who was tidying up in the living room. Marsha asked whether she'd heard any strange noises.

"I did hear some pounding around noon," Ramona said. "I opened the front door but nobody was there."

"Any cars or trucks?" Marsha asked.

"No," said Ramona.

Marsha let her go back to her cleaning and went to phone Victor, but once she got through, the office said he'd already left. She debated calling the police, but decided Victor would be home any minute. She decided to pour herself a glass of white wine. As she took a sip she saw headlights play against the barn.

"God damn it!" Victor cursed as he found Marsha's car blocking the garage. "Why does your mother do that? She could at least keep her heap on her side."

Angling the car toward the back door of the house, Victor came to a stop and turned off the lights and the ignition. He was a bundle of nerves following the experience at Gephardt's. VJ and Philip were blithely unaware of what had happened there, and they didn't ask for an explanation despite the fact that they had had to wait in the car for so long.

Victor got out slowly and followed the other two inside. By the time he closed the door he could tell that Marsha was in one of her moods. It was all in her tone as she ordered VJ and Philip to take off their shoes, get upstairs, and wash for dinner.

Victor hung up his coat, then entered the kitchen.

"And you!" said Marsha. "I suppose you didn't see our little present on the garage door?"

"What are you talking about?" Victor said, matching Marsha's testy tone.

"How you could have missed it is beyond me," Marsha said, putting down her wineglass, flipping on the courtyard light and brushing past Victor. "Come with me!"

Victor hesitated for a moment, then followed. She marched him through the family room and out the back door.

"Marsha!" Victor called, hurrying to keep up with her.

She stopped by the front of her car. Victor came up beside her.

"What are you . . ." he began. His words trailed off as he found himself looking at the gruesome sight of Kissa, brutally nailed to the garage door.

Marsha was standing with her hands on her hips, looking at Victor, not at the cat. "I thought you'd be interested to see how well you 'laid it on the line' with the problem people."

Victor turned away. He couldn't bear to look at the dead, tortured animal, and he couldn't face his wife.

"I want to know what you're going to do to see that this is stopped. And don't think you'll get away with a simple 'I'll handle it.' I want you to tell me what steps you're going to take, and now. I just can't take any more of this . . ." Her voice broke.

Victor wasn't sure how much more of it he could take either. Marsha was treating him as if he was to blame, as though he'd brought this down on them.

Maybe he had. But he'd be damned if he knew who was behind this. He was as baffled as Marsha was.

Victor slowly turned back to the garage door. It was only then he saw the note. He didn't know whether to be angry or sick. Who the hell was doing this? If it were Gephardt, at least he wouldn't be bothering them again.

"We've gone from a phone call to a broken window to a dead pet," said Marsha. "What's next?"

"We'll call the police," Victor said.

"They were a big help last time."

"I don't know what you expect from me," Victor said, regaining some composure. "I did call the three people I suspected of being behind this. By the way, the list of suspects has been reduced to two."

"What does that mean?" Marsha asked.

"Tonight on the way home I stopped at George Gephardt's," Victor said. "And the man was—"

"Yuck!" VJ voiced with a disgusted expression.

Both Victor and Marsha were startled by VJ's sudden appearance. Marsha had hoped to spare her son from this. She stepped between VJ and the garage door, trying to block the gruesome sight.

"Look at her tongue," VJ said, glancing around Marsha.

"Inside, young man!" Marsha said, trying to herd VJ back to the house. She really never would forgive Victor for this. But VJ would have none of it. He seemed determined to have a look. His interest struck Marsha as morbid; it was almost clinical. With a sinking feeling she realized there was no sorrow in his reaction— another schizoid symptom.

"VJ!" Marsha said sharply. "I want you in the house *now!*"

"Do you think Kissa was dead before she got nailed to the door?" VJ asked, still calmly, trying to look at the cat as Marsha pushed him toward the door.

Once they were inside, Victor went directly to the phone while Marsha tried to have a talk with VJ. Surely he had some feelings for their cat. Victor got through to the North Andover police station. The operator assured him they'd send a patrol car over right away.

Hanging up the phone, he turned into the room. VJ was going up the back stairs two steps at a time. Marsha was on the couch with arms folded angrily. It was clear she was even more upset now that VJ had seen the cat.

"I'll hire some temporary security until we get to the bottom of this," said Victor. "We'll have them watch the house at night."

"I think we should have done that from the start," Marsha said.

Victor shrugged. He sat down on the couch, suddenly feeling very tired.

"Do you know what VJ told me when I tried to ask him about his feelings?" Marsha asked. "He said we can get another cat."

"That sounds mature," Victor said. "At least VJ can be rational."

"Victor, it's been his cat for years. You'd think he would show a little emotion, grief at the loss." Marsha swallowed hard. "I think it is a cold and detached response." She hoped she could remain composed while they discussed VJ, but as much as she tried to hold them back, tears welled in her eyes.

Victor shrugged again. He really didn't want to get into another psychological chitchat. The boy was fine.

"Inappropriate emotion is not a good sign," Marsha managed, hoping at last Victor would agree. But Victor didn't say anything.

"What do you think?" Marsha asked.

"To tell you the truth," Victor said, "I am a little preoccupied at the moment. A little while ago before VJ appeared I was telling you about Gephardt. On the way home I went to visit the man, and I walked in on a scene—you just can't imagine. Gephardt and his entire family were murdered today. Machine-gunned in their living room in the middle of the afternoon. It was a massacre." He ran his fingers through his hair. "I was the one to call the police."

"How awful!" she cried. "My God, what's going on?" She looked at Victor. He was her husband, after all, the man she'd loved all these years. "Are you all right?" she asked him.

"Oh, I'm hanging in there," Victor said, but his tone lacked conviction.

"Was VJ with you?" she asked.

"He was in the car."

"So he didn't see anything?"

Victor shook his head.

"Thank God," Marsha said. "Do the police have any motive for the killings?"

"They think it's drug-related."

"What a terrible thing!" Marsha exclaimed, still stunned. "Can I get you something to drink? A glass of wine?"

"I think I'll take something a bit stronger, like a Scotch," Victor said.

"You stay put," said Marsha. She went to the wet bar and poured Victor a drink. Maybe she was being too hard on him, but she had to get him to focus on their son. She decided to bring the subject back to VJ. Handing the glass to Victor, she began.

"I had an upsetting experience myself today—not anything like yours. I went to VJ's school to visit the headmaster."

Victor took a sip.

Marsha then told Victor about her visit with Mr. Remington, ending with the question of why Victor hadn't discussed with her his decision to have VJ miss so much school.

"I never made a decision for VJ to miss school," Victor said.

"Haven't you written a number of notes for VJ to spend time at the lab rather than at school?"

"Of course not."

"I was afraid of that," Marsha said. "I think we have a real problem on our hands. Truancy like that is a serious symptom."

"It seemed like he was around a lot, but when I asked him, VJ told me that the school was sending him out to get more practical experience. As long as his grades were fine, I didn't think to question him further."

"Pauline Spaulding also told me that VJ spent most of his time in your lab," Marsha said. "At least after his intelligence dropped."

"VJ has always spent a lot of time in the lab," Victor admitted.

"What does he do?" Marsha asked.

"Lots of things," Victor said. "He started doing basic chemistry stuff, uses the microscopes, plays computer games which I loaded for him. I don't know. He just hangs out. Everybody knows him. He's well-liked. He's always been adept at entertaining himself."

The front door chimes sounded and both Marsha and Victor went to the front foyer and let in the North Andover police.

"Sergeant Cerullo," said a large, uniformed policeman. He had small features that were all bunched together in the center of a pudgy face. "And this here is Patrolman Hood. Sorry about your cat. We've been tryin' to watch your house better since Widdicomb's been here, but it's hard, settin' where it is so far from the road and all."

Sergeant Cerullo got out a pad and pencil as Widdicomb had Tuesday night. Victor led the two of them out the back to the garage. Hood took several photos of Kissa, then both policemen searched the area. Victor was gratified when Hood offered to take the cat down and even helped dig a grave at the edge of a stand of birch trees.

On the way into the house, Victor asked if they knew anybody he could call for the security duty he had in mind. They gave him the names of several local firms.

"As long as we're talkin' names," Sergeant Cerullo said, "do you have any idea of who would want to do this to your cat?"

"Two people come to mind," Victor said. "Sharon Carver and William Hurst."

Cerullo dutifully wrote down the names. Victor didn't mention Gephardt. Nor did he mention Ronald Beekman. There was no way Ronald would stoop to this.

After seeing the police out, Victor called both of the recommended firms. It was apparently after hours; all he got was recordings, so he left his name and number at work.

"I want us both to have a talk with VJ," Marsha said.

Victor knew by the tone of her voice there'd be no putting her off. He merely nodded and followed her up the back stairs. VJ's door was ajar and they entered without a knock.

VJ closed the cover of one of his stamp albums and slipped the heavy book onto the shelf above his desk.

Marsha studied her son. He was looking up at her and Victor expectantly, almost guiltily, as if they'd caught him doing something naughty. Working on a stamp album hardly qualified.

"We want to talk with you," began Marsha.

"Okay," VJ agreed. "About what?"

To Marsha he suddenly looked the ten-year-old child he was. He looked so vulnerable, she had to restrain herself from leaning down and drawing him to her. But it was time to be stern. "I visited Pendleton Academy today and spoke with the headmaster. He told me that you had been producing notes from your father to leave school and spend time at Chimera. Is this true?"

With her professional experience, Marsha expected VJ to deny the allegation initially, and then when denial proved to be impossible, to use some preadolescent externalization of responsibility. But VJ did neither.

"Yes, it is true," VJ said flatly. "I am sorry for the deceit. I apologize for any embarrassment it may have caused you. None was intended."

For a moment Marsha felt like someone had let the air out of her sails. How she would have preferred the standard, childish denial. But even in this instance, VJ varied from the norm. Looking up, she glanced at Victor. He raised his eyebrows but said nothing.

"My only excuse is that I am doing fine at school," VJ said. "I've considered that my main responsibility."

"School is supposed to challenge you," Victor said, suspecting Marsha was stumped by VJ's utter calm. "If school is too easy, you should be advanced. After all, there have been cases where children your age have matriculated into college, even graduated."

"Kids like that are treated like freaks," VJ replied. "Besides, I'm not interested in more structure. I've learned a lot at the lab, much more than at school. I want to be a researcher."

"Why didn't you come and talk to me about this?" Victor said.

"I just thought it would be the easiest way," VJ said. "I was afraid if I asked to spend more time at the lab, you'd say no."

"Thinking you know the outcome of a discussion shouldn't keep you from talking," Victor said.

VJ nodded.

Victor looked at Marsha to see if she was about to say anything else. She was thoughtfully chewing the inside of her cheek. Sensing that Victor was looking at her, she glanced at him. He shrugged. She did the same.

"Well, we'll talk about this again," said Victor. Then he and Marsha left VJ's room and retreated down the back stairs.

"Well," Victor said, "at least he didn't lie."

"I can't get over it," Marsha said. "I was sure he was going to deny it." She retrieved her glass of wine, freshened it, and sat down in one of the chairs around the kitchen table. "He's difficult to anticipate."

"Isn't it a good sign that he didn't lie?" Victor asked, leaning up against the kitchen counter.

"Frankly, no," said Marsha. "Under the circumstances, for a child his age, it's not normal at all. Okay, he didn't lie, but he didn't show the slightest sign of remorse. Did you notice that?"

Victor rolled his eyes. "You really are never satisfied, are you? Well, I'm not convinced this is so important. I skipped a bunch of days back in high school. I think the only real difference was that I was never caught."

"That's not the same thing," Marsha said. "That kind of behavior is typical of adolescent rebellion. That's why you didn't do it until you were in high school. VJ is only in fifth grade."

"I don't think forging a few notes, especially when he is doing okay in school, means the boy is going to grow up to a life of crime. He's a prodigy, for God's sake. He skips school to be in a lab. The way you're acting, you'd think we'd discovered he was on crack."

"I wouldn't be concerned if it were just this. But there's a whole complex of qualities that are just not right about our son. I can't believe you don't see—"

A crashing sound from outside froze Marsha in midsentence.

"Now what?" said Victor.

"It sounded like it came from near the garage," Marsha answered.

Victor ran into the family room and switched off the light. He got a battery-driven spotlight from the closet and went to the window that looked onto the courtyard. Marsha followed.

"Can you see anything?" Marsha asked.

"Not from in here," Victor said, starting for the door.

"You're not going outside?"

"I'm going to see who's out there," Victor said over his shoulder.

"Victor, I don't want you going out there by yourself."

Ignoring her, Victor tiptoed onto the stoop. He felt Marsha right behind him, holding on to his shirt back. There was a scraping sound coming from near the garage door. Victor pointed the spotlight in the direction and turned it on.

Within the bright beam of light, two ringed eyes looked back at Victor and Marsha, then scampered off into the night.

"A raccoon," said Victor with relief.

# 9

## *Friday Morning*

By the time Victor got to work, he had himself worked
up to a minor fury over the killing of the family cat.
With Marsha's concern for VJ deepening, all they
needed was the added problem of harassment. Victor
knew that he had to act, and quickly, to prevent another attack, especially since they were progressively
worsening. After killing the cat, what was next? Victor
shuddered as he considered the possibilities.

He pulled into his parking place and killed the engine. VJ and Philip, who had been riding in the back
seat, piled out of the car and took off toward the cafeteria. Victor watched them go, wondering if Marsha
was right about VJ fitting a potentially dangerous psychiatric pattern. Last night after they'd gotten into
bed, Marsha had told him that Mr. Remington said
that VJ had been involved in a number of fights at
school. Victor had been more shocked by that news
than by anything else. It seemed so unlike VJ. He
could not imagine it was true. And if it was, he didn't
know how he felt about it. In some ways he was proud

of VJ. Was it really so bad to defend yourself? Even Remington seemed to have some admiration for the way the boy handled himself.

"Who the hell knows?" Victor said aloud as he got out of the car and started for the front door. But he didn't get far. Out of nowhere a man dressed in a policeman's uniform appeared.

"Dr. Victor Frank?" the man questioned.

"Yes," Victor responded.

The man handed Victor a packet. "Something for you from the sheriff's office," he said. "Have a good day."

Victor opened up the envelope and saw that he was being summoned to respond to the attached complaint. The first page read: "Sharon Carver vs. Victor Frank and Chimera, Inc."

Victor didn't have to read any further. He knew what he was holding. So Sharon was moving ahead with her threatened sex-discrimination suit. He felt like throwing the papers to the wind. It just made him fume all the more as he climbed the front steps and entered the building.

The office was alive with an almost electric intensity. He noticed that people eyed him as he approached, then murmured among themselves after he passed. When he got into his office and as he was removing his coat, he asked Colleen what was going on.

"You've become a celebrity," she said. "It was on the news that you were the one to discover the Gephardt family murder."

"Just what I need," Victor said. He went over to his desk. Before he sat down he handed the Carver summons over to Colleen and told her to send it to the legal department. Then he sat down. "So what's the good word?"

"Lots of things," Colleen said. She handed a sheet of paper to Victor. "That's a preliminary report concerning Hurst's research. They just started and have already found serious irregularities. They thought you should know."

"You are ever a bearer of good news," Victor said. He fingered the report. Based on Hurst's reaction to his decision to look into the matter, he wasn't surprised, though he hadn't thought the irregularities would show up so quickly. He would have guessed Hurst to be a bit more subtle than that.

"What else?" Victor asked, putting the report aside.

"A board meeting has been scheduled for next Wednesday to vote on the stock offering," Colleen said, handing over a reminder slip for Victor to put in his calendar.

"That's like getting invited to play Russian roulette," Victor said, taking the paper. "What else?"

Colleen went down her list, ticking off myriad problems—mostly minor ones, but ones that had to be dealt with nonetheless. She made notes, depending on Victor's reaction. It took them about half an hour to get through.

"Now it's my turn," Victor said. "Have I gotten any calls from security firms?"

Colleen shook her head.

"All right, next I want you to get on the phone and use your considerable charms to find out where Ronald Beekman, William Hurst, and Sharon Carver were around noon yesterday."

Colleen made a note for herself and waited for more instructions. When she saw that was it, she nodded good-bye and slipped out of the office back to her desk.

Victor started to work through the pile of papers in his in-box.

Thirty minutes later, Colleen returned with her steno pad from which she read: "Both Dr. Beekman and Dr. Hurst were here at Chimera all day, although Dr. Hurst did disappear for lunch. No one saw him at the cafeteria. Heaven only knows where he went. As for Miss Carver, I couldn't find out a thing."

Victor nodded and thanked her. He picked up the phone and tried one of the numbers of the security firms, one called Able Protection. A woman answered. After, he had been put briefly on hold, a deep-voiced man got on the line, and Victor made arrangements to have his home watched from 6 P.M. to 6 A.M.

Colleen returned with a sheet of paper which she slipped under Victor's nose. "Here's an update on the equipment that Gephardt managed to have disappear."

Victor ran down the list: polypeptide synthesizers, scintillation counters, centrifuges, electron microscope . . .

"Electron microscope!" Victor yelled. "How the hell did that vanish? How did this guy get the equipment off-site, much less fence it? I mean the market for a hot electron microscope has to be small." Victor looked at Colleen questioningly. In his mind's eye he saw the van parked in Gephardt's driveway.

"You've got me," was all she could offer.

"It's a disgrace that he was able to get away with it for so long. It certainly says something about our accounting methods and our security."

By eleven-thirty Victor was finally able to slip out

the back of his office and walk over to his lab. The morning's administrative work had only agitated him to an even more exasperated state. But, stepping into his lab, he began to unwind. It was an immediate, almost reflexive response. Research was the reason he'd started Chimera, not fussy paperwork.

Victor was walking to his lab office door when one of the technicians spotted him and hurried over. "Robert was looking for you," she told him. "We were supposed to tell you as soon as we saw you."

Victor thanked her and began to look for Robert. He found him back at the gel electrophoresis unit.

"Dr. Frank!" Robert said happily. "We had a positive on two of your samples."

"You mean—" Victor asked.

"Both blood samples you gave me were positive for trace amounts of cephaloclor."

Victor froze. For a moment he couldn't even breathe. When he handed those samples over to Robert, he'd never expected a positive finding. He was just doing it to be complete, like a medical student doing a standard work-up.

"Are you sure?" Victor voiced with some difficulty.

"That's what Harry said," said Robert. "And Harry's pretty reliable. You didn't expect this?"

"Hardly," said Victor. He was already considering the implications if this were true. Turning to Robert he added, "I want it checked."

Without another word, Victor turned and and went back to his lab office. In one of his desk drawers he had a small bottle of cephaloclor capsules. He took one out and walked back through the main lab, through the dissecting room, and into the animal room. There he selected two compatible smart rats,

197

put them in a cage by themselves, and added the contents of the capsule to their water. He watched as the white powder dissolved, then hooked the water bottle to the side of the cage.

Leaving his Department of Developmental Biology, Victor walked down the long hall and up one flight to the Department of Immunology. He went directly to Hobbs.

"How are you doing now that you're back to work?" Victor asked him.

"My concentration isn't one hundred percent," Hobbs admitted, "but it is much better for me to be here and busy. I was going crazy at home. So was Sheila."

"We're glad to have you back," Victor said. "I wanted to ask once more if there was any chance at all that your boy could have gotten some cephaloclor."

"Absolutely not," Hobbs said. "Why? Do you think that cephaloclor could have triggered the edema?"

"Not if he didn't get any," said Victor in a manner that conveyed case closed. Leaving a somewhat confused Hobbs in his wake, Victor set out for Accounting to question Murray. His response was the same. There was no way that either child had been given cephaloclor.

On the way back to his lab, Victor passed the computer center. Entering, he sought out Louis and inquired about the evening's plans.

"We'll be ready," Louis said. "The phone company representatives will be here around six to start setting up. It's just up to the hacker to log on and stay on. I'll keep my fingers crossed."

"Me too," Victor said. "I'll be in my lab. Have someone get in touch with me if he tries to tap in. I'll come right over."

"Sure thing, Dr. Frank."

Victor continued on to his lab, trying to keep his thoughts steady. It wasn't until he was sitting down at his desk that he allowed himself to consider the significance of cephaloclor in the two unfortunate toddlers' bloodstreams. Clearly the antibiotic had somehow been introduced. There was no doubt it had turned the NGF gene on, which, when activated, would effectively stimulate the brain cells to the point at which they'd begin dividing. With closed skulls unable to expand, the swelling brain could swell only to a certain limit. Unchecked, the swelling would herniate the brainstem down into the spinal canal, as discovered in the children at the autopsy.

Victor shuddered. Since neither child could have gotten the cephaloclor by accident, and since both got it at apparently the same time, Victor had to assume that they'd both received the antibiotic in a deliberate attempt to kill them.

Victor rubbed his face roughly, then ran his fingers through his hair. Why would someone want to kill two extraordinary, prodigiously intelligent babies? And who?

Victor could hardly contain himself. He rose to his feet and paced the length of the room. The only idea that came to mind was a long shot: some rapid, half-baked moralistic reactionary had stumbled onto the details of the NGF experiment. In a vengeful attempt to blot out Victor's efforts, the madman had murdered the Hobbs and Murray kids.

But if this scenario were the case, why hadn't the

smart rats been disposed of? And what about VJ? Besides, so few people had access to the computer and the labs. Victor thought about the hacker who had deleted the files. But how would such a person gain access to the labs, or even the day-care center? All at once, Victor understood that it was only at the day-care center that the Hobbs and Murray babies' lives intersected. They had to have received the cephaloclor at the day-care center!

Victor angrily considered Hurst's threat: "You're not the white knight you want us to believe." Maybe Hurst knew all about the NGF project and this was his way of retaliating.

Victor started pacing again. Even the Hurst idea didn't fit well with the facts. If Hurst or anyone wanted to get back at him, why not old-fashioned blackmail, or just exposure to the newspapers? That made more sense than killing innocent children. No, there had to be another explanation, something more evil, less obvious.

Victor sat down at his desk and took out some results from recent laboratory experiments and tried to do some work. But he couldn't concentrate. His thoughts kept circling back to the NGF project. Considering what he was up against, it was too bad he couldn't go to the authorities with his suspicions. Doing so would require a full disclosure of the NGF project, and Victor understood that he could never do that. It would amount to professional suicide. To say nothing of his family life. If only he had never done this experiment in the first place.

Leaning back in his chair and putting his hands behind his head, Victor stared up at the ceiling. Back when VJ's intelligence had dropped, Victor had never even considered testing him for cephaloclor. Could the antibiotic have been sequestered in his body since birth, only to leach out when he was between two and four years old? "No," Victor voiced to the ceiling, answering his own question. There was no physiological process that could cause such a phenomenon.

Victor marveled at the storm of events whirling around him: Gephardt's murder, the possible purposeful elimination of two genetically engineered children, an escalating series of threats to himself and his family, fraud, and embezzlement. Could these disparate incidents be related in some fantastic, grisly plot?

Victor shook his head. The fact that all these things were happening at once had to be coincidence. But the thought they were related nagged. Victor thought again of VJ. Could he be at risk? How could Victor prevent him from receiving cephaloclor if there was some sinister hand trying to effect just that?

Victor stared blankly ahead. The idea of VJ's being at risk had disturbed him since Wednesday afternoon. He began to wonder if his warnings about Beekman and Hurst had been adequate. He got up from the desk and walked to the door. Suddenly he didn't like the idea of VJ wandering around Chimera on his own.

Starting out in the lab just as he had done on Wednesday, he began asking if anyone had seen VJ. But no one had seen either him or Philip for some time. Victor left the lab building and went to the cafeteria. It was just before lunchtime and the cafeteria staff was in the final countdown in preparation for the noontime rush. A few people who preferred to get a jump on the others were already eating their lunches. Victor went directly to the manager,

Curt Tarkington, who was supervising the stocking of the steam table.

"I'm looking for my son again," Victor said.

"He hasn't been in yet," Curt said. "Maybe you should give him a beeper."

"Not a bad idea," Victor said. "When he shows up, would you ring my secretary?"

"No problem," Curt said.

Victor checked the library, which was in the same building, but there wasn't a soul there. Stepping outside, he debated going to the fitness and day-care centers. Instead, he headed for the security office at the main gate.

Wiping his feet on a straw mat, Victor entered the small office that was built between the entrance and the exit to the Chimera compound. One man was operating the gates, another sat at a small desk. Both wore official-looking brown uniforms with the Chimera insignia patch on the upper sleeves. The man at the desk jumped to his feet as Victor entered.

"Good morning, sir," the guard said. His name tag gave his name: Sheldon Farber.

"Sit down," Victor said in a friendly tone. Sheldon sat. "I have a question about protocol. When a truck or van leaves the compound, does someone take a look inside?"

"Oh, yes," Sheldon said. "Always."

"And if there is equipment on board you make sure it is supposed to be there?" Victor asked.

"Certainly," Sheldon said. "We check the work order or call electronic maintenance. We always check it out."

"What if it is being driven by one of the Chimera employees?"

"Doesn't matter," Sheldon said. "We always check."

"What if it is being driven by one of the management?"

Sheldon hesitated, then spoke. "Well, I suppose that would be different."

"So if a van is driven out of here by one of the executives, you let it go?"

"Well, I'm not sure," Sheldon said nervously.

"From now on I want all trucks, vans, and the like looked into no matter who is driving. Even me. Understand?"

"Oh, yes, sir," Sheldon said.

"One other question," Victor said. "Has anyone seen my son today?"

"I haven't," Sheldon said. Then to the man operating the gates he said, "George, did you see VJ today?"

"Only when he arrived with Dr. Frank."

Sheldon held up a hand for Victor to wait. Turning to a radio set up behind the desk, he put out a call for Hal.

"Hal's been cruising around this morning," Sheldon explained. Some crackles heralded Hal's voice. Sheldon asked if VJ was around.

"I saw him down near the dam earlier this morning," Hal said through a good deal of static.

Victor thanked the security men and left their office. He felt a minor amount of irritation, remembering how willful VJ was. Victor could remember telling him to stay away from the river at least four or five times.

Pulling his lab coat more closely around him, Victor started for the river. He thought about going back to the main building to get his regular coat, but didn't. Although the temperature had dropped from the previous day, it still was not that cold.

Although the day had started clear, it was now cloudy. The prevailing breeze, from the northeast, smelled of the ocean. High above, several sea gulls circled, squawking shrilly.

Directly ahead stood the clock tower building with its Big Ben replica stopped at 2:15. Victor reminded himself to bring up the issue of renovating the structure as well as the clock at next Wednesday's board meeting.

The closer he got to the river, the louder the roar from the waterfall over the spillway of the dam became.

"VJ!" Victor shouted as he approached the river's edge. But his voice was lost in the crash of the water. He continued past the eastern edge of the clock tower building, crossed over a wooden bridge that spanned the sluice exiting from the basement of the building, and arrived at the granite quay built along the river below the dam. He looked down at the white water as it swirled furiously eastward toward the ocean. Glancing left, he gazed at the expanse of the dam spanning the river and at the broad millpond upstream. Water poured over the center of the dam in an imposing arc of emerald green. The force was enough for Victor to feel through his feet, standing on the granite quay. It was an awesome testimony to the power of nature that had started earlier that year with gentle snow-flakes.

Turning around, Victor shouted at the top of his lungs: "VJ!" But he bit off his shout with the shock that VJ was standing directly behind him. Philip was a little farther away.

"There you are," Victor said. "I've been looking all over for you."

"I guessed as much," VJ said. "What do you want?"

"I want . . ." Victor paused. He wasn't sure what he wanted. "What have you been doing?"

"Just having fun."

"I'm not sure I want you wandering around like this, especially down here by the river," Victor said sternly. "In fact, I want you home today. I'll have a driver from the motor pool give you and Philip a lift."

"But I don't want to go home," VJ complained.

"I'll explain more later," Victor said firmly. "But I want you home for now. It's for your own good."

Marsha opened the door to her office that gave out to the hall and Joyce Hendricks slipped out. She'd told Marsha that she was terrified of running into someone she knew while coming out of a psychiatrist's office, and for the time being Marsha indulged her. After a time, Marsha was certain that she could convince the woman that seeking psychiatric help was no longer a social stigma.

After updating the Hendricks file, Marsha poked her head into the office waiting room and told Jean that she was going off to lunch. Jean waved in acknowledgment. As usual, she was tied up on the phone.

Marsha was having lunch with Dr. Valerie Maddox, a fellow psychiatrist whom she admired and respected, whose office was in the same building complex as Marsha's. But more than colleagues, the two women were friends.

"Hungry?" Marsha asked after Valerie herself opened the door.

"Starved." Valerie was in her late fifties and looked every day of it. She'd smoked for many years and had a ring of deep creases that radiated away from her mouth like the lines a child would draw indicating the rays of the sun.

Together they went down in the elevator and crossed to the hospital, using the crossway. In the hospital shop they managed to get a small table in the corner that allowed them to talk. They both ordered tuna salads.

"I appreciate your willingness to have lunch," Marsha said. "I need to talk with you about VJ."

Valerie just smiled encouragement.

"You were such a help back when his intelligence dropped. I've been concerned about him lately, but what can I say? I'm his mother. I can't pretend to have any objectivity whatsoever, where he's concerned."

"What's the problem?" asked Valerie.

"I'm not even sure there is a problem. It certainly isn't one specific thing. Take a look at these psychological test results."

Marsha handed Valerie VJ's folder. Valerie scanned the various test reports with a careful eye. "Nothing appears out of the ordinary," she said. "Curious about that validity scale on the MMPI, but otherwise, there's nothing here to be concerned about."

Marsha had the feeling that Valerie was right. She went on to explain VJ's truancy, the forged notes, and the fights he'd been in in school.

"VJ sounds resourceful," said Valerie with a smile. "How old is he again?"

"Ten," Marsha said. "I'm also concerned that he only seems to have one friend his own age, a boy named Richie Blakemore, and I've never even met him."

"VJ never brings this boy to your home?" Valerie asked.

"Never."

"Maybe it might be worth chatting with Mrs. Blakemore," Valerie said. "Get an idea from her how close the boys are."

"I suppose."

"I'd be happy to see VJ if you think he would be willing," Valerie offered.

"I'd certainly appreciate it," Marsha said. "I really think I'm too close to the situation to evaluate him. At the same time, I'm terrified at the thought he's developing a serious personality disorder right under my nose."

Marsha left Valerie in the elevator, thanking her profusely for taking the time to hear her out, and for offering to see VJ. She promised to call Valerie's secretary to set up an appointment.

"Your husband called," Jean said as Marsha came back in the door. "He wants you to be sure to call back."

"A problem?" Marsha asked.

"I don't think so," Jean said. "He didn't say one way or the other, but he didn't sound upset."

Marsha picked up her mail and went into the inner office, closing the door behind her. Flipping through her mail, she phoned Victor. Colleen patched the call through to the lab, and Victor came on the line.

"What's up?" asked Marsha. Victor didn't often call during the day.

"The usual," Victor said.

"You sound tired," Marsha said. She wanted to say he sounded strange. His voice was toneless, as if he'd

just had an emotional outburst and was forcing himself to remain calm.

"There are always surprises these days," Victor said
without explanation. "The reason I called was to say
that VJ and Philip are at home."

"Something wrong?" asked Marsha.

"No," Victor said. "Nothing is wrong. But I'm going
to be working late so you and the others go ahead and
eat. Oh, by the way, there will be security watching the
house from 6 P.M. until 6 A.M."

"Does the reason you're staying late have anything
to do with the harassment?" Marsha asked.

"Maybe," Victor said. "I'll explain when I get home."

Marsha hung up the phone but her hand remained
on the receiver. Once again she had that uncomfortable feeling that Victor was keeping something from
her, something that she should know. Why couldn't he
confide in her? More and more, she was feeling alone.

A particular stillness hung over the lab when Victor
was there by himself. Various electronic instruments
kicked on at times, but otherwise it was quiet. By
eight-thirty Victor was the only person in the lab.
Closed behind several doors, he couldn't even hear the
sounds of the animals as they paced in their cages or
used their exercise wheels.

Victor was bent over strips of film that bore darkened horizontal stripes. Each stripe represented a portion of DNA that had been cleaved at a specific point.
Victor was comparing his son David's DNA fingerprint—one taken when David was still healthy—and
one of his cancerous liver tumor. What amazed him
was that the two did not entirely match. Victor's first
hunch was that Dr. Shryack had given him the wrong

sample—a piece of tumor from some other patient. But that did not explain the vast homology of the two strips; for whatever differences there were between the two fingerprints, much was the same.

After running the two in a computer that could numerically establish areas of homology versus the areas of heterogeneity, Victor realized that the two samples of DNA differed in only one area.

To make matters more confusing, the sample that Victor had given Robert contained some small areas of normal liver tissue in addition to the tumor. In his habitually compulsive fashion, Robert had carefully fingerprinted both areas of the sample. When Victor compared the normal liver DNA fingerprint with David's previous fingerprint, the match was perfect.

Discovering a cancer with a documented alteration in the DNA was not a usual finding. Victor did not know whether he should be excited about the possibility of an important scientific discovery or fearful that he was about to find something that he either couldn't explain or didn't want to know.

Victor then started the process of isolating the part of the DNA that was unique in the tumor. By initiating the protocol, it would be that much easier for Robert to complete the work in the morning.

Leaving the main lab room, Victor went through the dissecting room and entered the animal room. As he turned on the light there was a lot of sudden activity in each of the occupied cages.

Victor walked over to the cage which housed the two smart rats whose water contained the single capsule of cephaloclor. He was amazed to find one rat already dead and the other semicomatose.

Removing the dead rat, Victor took it back into the

dissecting room and did an autopsy of sorts. When he opened the skull, the brain puffed out as if it was being inflated.

Carefully removing a piece of the brain, he prepared it to be sectioned in the morning. Just then, the telephone rang.

"Dr. Frank, this is Phil Moscone. Louis Kaspwicz asked me to call you to let you know that the hacker has logged onto the computer."

"I'll be right there," said Victor. He put away his rat brain sample, turned out the lights, and dashed out of the lab.

It was only a short jog to the computer center; Victor was there within a few minutes.

Louis came directly to him. "It's looking good for the trace. The guy has been logged on now for seven minutes. I just hope to hell he's not causing any mischief."

"Can you tell where he is in the system?" Victor asked.

"He's in Personnel right now," Louis said. "First he did some sizable number crunching, then he went into Purchasing. It's weird."

"Personnel?" Victor questioned. He'd been thinking the hacker was indeed no kid, but some competitor's hired gun. Biotechnology was an extremely competitive field, and most everybody wanted to compete against the big boys like Chimera. But an industrial agent would want to get into the research files, not Personnel.

"We got a positive trace!" the man with the two-way radio announced with a big smile.

There was a general cheer among all those present.

"Okay," said Louis. "We've got the telephone number. Now we just need the name."

The man with the radio held up his hand, listened, then said, "It's an unpublished number."

Several of the other men who were already busy breaking down their equipment booed at this news.

"Does that mean they can't get the name?" asked Victor.

"Nah," Louis said. "It means it just takes them a little longer."

Victor leaned against one of the covered print-out devices and folded his arms.

"Who's got a piece of paper?" the man with the radio said suddenly, holding the radio up against his left ear. One of the other men handed him a legal-sized pad. He jotted down the name given him over the radio. "Thanks a lot, over and out." He switched off his radio unit, pushed in the antenna, then handed Louis the paper.

Louis read the name and address and turned pale. Without saying anything he handed it to Victor. Victor looked down and read it. Disbelieving, he read it again. What he saw on the paper was his name and address!

"Is this some kind of joke?" Victor said, raising his head and looking at Louis. Victor then glanced at the others. No one said a word.

"Did you program your PC to access the mainframe on a regular basis?" Louis asked, breaking the spell.

Victor looked back at his systems administrator and realized the man was trying to give him an out. After an awkward minute, Victor agreed. "Yeah, that must be it." Victor tried to remain composed. He thanked everyone for their effort and left.

Victor walked out of the computer center, got his coat from the administration building, and walked to his car in a kind of daze. The idea of someone using his computer to break into the Chimera mainframe was simply preposterous. It didn't make any sense. He knew that he had always left the computer telephone number and his password taped to the bottom of his keyboard, but who could have been using it? Marsha? VJ? The cleaning lady? There had to have been some mistake. Could the hacker have been so clever as to divert a trace? Victor hadn't thought of that, and he made a mental note to ask Louis if it were possible. That seemed to make the most sense.

Marsha heard Victor's car before she saw the lights swing into the driveway. She was in her study vainly trying to tackle the stack of professional periodicals that piled up on a regular basis on her desk. Getting to her feet, she saw the headlights silhouetting the leafless trees that lined the driveway. Victor's car came into view, then disappeared behind the house. The automatic garage door rumbled in the distance.

Marsha sat back down on her flower-print chintz couch and let her eyes roam around her study. She'd decorated it with pale pastel striped wallpaper, dusty rose carpet, and mostly white furniture. In the past it had always provided a comforting haven, but not lately. Nothing seemed to be able to relieve her ever-increasing anxiety about the future. The visit with Valerie had helped, but unfortunately even that mild relief had not lasted.

Marsha could hear the TV in the family room where VJ and Philip were watching a horror movie they'd rented. The intermittent screams that punctuated the soundtrack didn't help Marsha's mood either. She'd even closed her door but the screams still penetrated.

She heard the dull thud of the back door slam, then muffled voices from the family room, and finally a knock on her door.

Victor came in and gave her a perfunctory kiss. He looked as tired as his voice had sounded on the phone that afternoon. A constant crease was beginning to develop on his forehead between his eyebrows.

"Did you notice the security man outside?" Victor asked.

Marsha nodded. "Makes me feel much better. Did you eat?" she asked.

"No," Victor said. "But I'm not hungry."

"I'll scramble you some eggs. Maybe some toast," Marsha offered.

Victor restrained her. "Thanks, but I think I'll take a swim and then shower. Maybe that will revive me."

"Something wrong?" Marsha asked.

"No more than usual," Victor said evasively. He left, leaving her door ajar. Ominous music from the soundtrack of the movie crept back into the room. Marsha tried to ignore it as she went back to her reading, but a sharp scream made her jump. Giving up, she reached over and gave the door a shove. It slammed with a resounding click.

Thirty minutes later, Victor reappeared. He looked considerably better, dressed in more casual clothes.

"Maybe I'll take you up on those eggs," he said.

In the kitchen, Marsha went to work while Victor set the table. A series of bloodcurdling gurgles emanated from the family room. Marsha asked Victor to close the connecting door.

"What in heaven's name are they watching in there?" he asked.

*"Sheer Terror,"* Marsha said.

Victor shook his head. "Kids and their horror movies," he said.

Marsha made herself a cup of tea and when Victor sat down to eat his omelet, she sat opposite him.

"There is something I wanted to discuss with you," Marsha said, waiting for her tea to cool.

"Oh?"

Marsha told Victor about her lunch with Valerie Maddox; she also told him about Valerie's offer to see VJ on a professional basis. "How do you feel about that?"

Wiping his mouth with his napkin, Victor said, "That kind of question involves your area of expertise. Anything that you think is appropriate is fine with me."

"Good," Marsha said. "I do think it is appropriate. Now I just have to convince VJ."

"Good luck," Victor said.

There was a short period of silence as Victor mopped up the last of the egg with a wedge of toast. Then he asked, "Did you use the computer upstairs tonight?"

"No, why do you ask?"

"The printer was hot when I went upstairs to swim and shower," Victor said. "How about VJ? Did he use it?"

"I couldn't say."

Victor rocked back in his chair in a way that made Marsha grit her teeth. She was always afraid he was about to go over backward and hit his head on the tile floor.

"I had an interesting evening at the Chimera computer center," Victor said, teetering on his chair. He went on to tell her everything that had happened, including the fact that the trace of the hacker ended up right there in their home.

In spite of herself, Marsha laughed. She quickly apologized. "I'm sorry, but I can just see it," she said. "All this tension and then your name suddenly appearing."

"It wasn't funny," Victor said. "And I'm going to have a serious talk with VJ about this. As ridiculous as it sounds, it must have been him breaking into the Chimera mainframe."

"Is this serious talk going to be something like the one you had with him when you learned he'd been forging notes from you in order to skip school?" Marsha taunted.

"We'll see," Victor said, obviously irritated.

Marsha leaned over and grasped Victor's arm before he could leave the table. "I'm teasing you," she said. "Actually I'd be more concerned about you cornering him or pushing him. I'm afraid there is a side to VJ's personality that we've not seen. That's really why I want him to see Valerie."

Victor nodded, then detached himself from Marsha's grasp. He opened the connecting door. "VJ, would you come in here a minute? I'd like to talk with you."

Marsha could hear VJ complaining, but Victor was insistent. Soon the sound of the movie soundtrack was off. VJ appeared at the door. He looked from Victor to Marsha. His sharp eyes had that glazed look that comes from watching too much television.

"Please sit at the table," Victor said.

With a bored expression, VJ dutifully sat at the table to Marsha's immediate left. Victor sat down across from both of them.

Victor got right to the point. "VJ, did you use the computer upstairs tonight?"

"Yeah," VJ said.

Marsha watched as VJ glared at Victor insolently. She saw Victor hesitate, then avert his eyes, probably to maintain his train of thought. For a moment there was a pause. Then Victor continued: "Did you use the PC to log on to the Chimera mainframe computer?"

"Yes," VJ said without a moment's hesitation.

"Why?" Victor asked. His voice had changed from accusatory to confused. Marsha remembered her own confusion when VJ had so quickly confessed to his truancy.

"The extra storage makes some of the computer games more challenging," VJ said.

Marsha saw Victor roll his eyes. "You mean you are using all that computer power of our giant unit to play Pac-Man and games like that?"

"It's the same as me doing it at the lab," VJ said.

"I suppose," Victor said uncertainly. "Who taught you to use the modem?"

"You did," VJ said.

"I don't remember . . ." Victor began, but then he did. "But that was over seven years ago!"

"Maybe," VJ said. "But the method hasn't changed."

"Do you access the Chimera computer every Friday night?" Victor asked.

"Usually," VJ answered. "I play a few games, then I range around in the files, mostly Personnel and Purchasing, sometimes the research files, but those are harder to crack."

"But why?" asked Victor.

"I just want to learn as much as I can about the company," VJ said. "Someday I want to run it like you. You've always encouraged me to use the computer. I won't do it anymore if you don't want me to."

"In future, I think it would be better if you don't," Victor said.

"Okay," VJ said simply. "Can I go back to my movie?"

"Sure," Victor said.

VJ pushed away from the table and disappeared through the door. Instantly, the soundtrack for *Sheer Terror* was back on.

Marsha looked at Victor. Victor shrugged. Then the doorbell sounded.

"Sorry to bother you folks so late," Sergeant Cerullo said after Victor had opened the door. "This is Sergeant Dempsey from the Lawrence police." The second officer stepped from behind Cerullo and touched the brim of his hat in greeting. He was a freckled fellow with bright red hair.

"We have some information for you and we wanted to ask a few questions," Cerullo said.

Victor invited the men inside. They stepped in and removed their hats.

"Would you like some coffee or anything?" Marsha asked.

"No, thank you, ma'am," Cerullo said. "We'll just say what we come to say and be off. You see, we at the North Andover police station are pretty friendly with the men over in Lawrence, both being neighbors and all. There's a lot of talk that goes back and forth. Anyway, they have been proceeding with the investigation of that mass murder over there involving the

ROBIN COOK

Gephardt family, the one Dr. Frank here discovered. Well, they found some rough drafts of the notes that you people got tied to your cat and around that brick. They were in the Gephardt house. We thought you'd like to know that."

"I should say," Victor said with some relief.

Dempsey coughed to clear his throat. "We also have ascertained by ballistics that the guns used to kill the Gephardts match those used in several battles between some rival South American drug gangs. We got that from Boston. Boston is very interested to find out what the connection is up here in Lawrence. They've some reason to believe something big is going down up here. What they want to know from you, since you employed Gephardt, is how the man was connected to the drug world. Do you people have any idea whatsoever?"

"Absolutely none," Victor said. "I suppose you know the man was under investigation for embezzlement?"

"Yeah, we got that," Dempsey said. "You're sure there's nothing else that you can give us? Boston is really eager to learn anything they can about this."

"We also think the man had been fencing laboratory equipment," Victor said. "That investigation had just started before he was killed. But for however much I suspected him of these sorts of crimes, it never occurred to me he was involved with drugs."

"If anything occurs to you, we'd appreciate it if you'd call us immediately. We sure don't want some drug war breaking out up here."

The policemen left. Victor closed the door and leaned his back on it and looked at Marsha.

"Well, that solves one problem," Victor said. "At

least now we know where the harassment was coming from, and better still, that it isn't going to continue."

"I'm glad they came by to let us know we can stop worrying," Marsha added. "Maybe we should send that security man home."

"I'll cancel in the morning," Victor said. "I'm sure we'll be paying for it one way or another."

Victor sat bolt upright with such suddenness that he inadvertently pulled all the covers from Marsha. The sudden movement awakened her. It was pitch dark outside.

"What's the matter?" Marsha asked, alarmed.

"I'm not sure," Victor said. "I think it was the front doorbell."

They both listened for a moment. All Marsha heard was the wind under the eaves and the rat-a-tat of rain against the windows.

Marsha leaned over and turned the bedside clock so that she could see the face. "It's five-fifteen in the morning," she said. She fell back against the pillow and pulled the covers back over her. "Are you sure you weren't dreaming?"

But just then the doorbell rang. "It was the bell!" Victor said, leaping out of bed. "I knew I wasn't dreaming." He hastily pulled on his robe, but had the wrong arm in the wrong hole. Marsha turned on the light.

"Who on earth could it be?" Marsha asked. "The police again?"

Victor got the robe on properly and tied the belt. "We'll soon find out," he said, opening the door to the hall. He walked quickly to the head of the stairs and started down.

After a moment of indecision, Marsha put her feet out on the cold floor and donned her robe and put on her slippers as well. By the time she got downstairs, a man and woman were standing in the front hall facing Victor. Small pools of water had formed at their feet, and their faces were streaked with moisture. The woman was holding a spray can. The man was holding the woman.

"Marsha!" Victor called, not taking his eyes from the new arrivals. "I think you'd better call the police."

Marsha came up behind Victor, clutching her robe around her. She glanced at the people. The man was wearing an oilcloth hooded cape, although the hood had been pushed back, exposing his head. All in all, he looked dressed for the weather. The woman was dressed in a ski parka that had long since soaked through.

"This is Mr. Peter Norwell," Victor said. "He's from Able Protection."

"Evening, ma'am," Peter said.

"And this is Sharon Carver," Victor said, motioning toward the woman. "An ex-Chimera employee with a sexual-harassment suit lodged against us."

"She was set to paint your garage door," Peter elaborated. "I let her do one short burst so we'd have something on her besides trespassing."

Feeling somewhat embarrassed for the bedraggled woman, Marsha hurried to the nearest phone and called the North Andover police. The operator said they'd send a car right over.

Meanwhile, the whole group went into the kitchen

where Marsha made tea for everyone. Before they'd had more than a few sips, the doorbell sounded again. Victor went to the door. It was Widdicomb and O'Connor.

"You folks are certainly keeping us busy," Sergeant Widdicomb said with a smile. They stepped through the door and took off their wet coats.

Peter Norwell brought Sharon Carver from the kitchen.

"So this is the young lady?" Widdicomb said. He took out a pair of handcuffs.

"You don't have to handcuff me, for Christ's sake!" Sharon snapped.

"Sorry, miss," Widdicomb said. "Standard procedure."

Within a few moments, all was ready. The police then left with their prisoner.

"You are welcome to finish your tea," Marsha said to Peter, who was standing in the foyer.

"Thank you, ma'am, but I already finished. Good night." The security man let himself out the door and pulled it shut behind him. Victor threw the deadbolt and turned into the room.

Marsha looked at him. She smiled and shook her head in disbelief. "If I read this in a book, I wouldn't believe it," she said.

"It's a good thing we kept that security," Victor said. Then, extending his hand, he said, "Come on. We can still get a few more hours of sleep."

But that was not as easy as Victor had thought. An hour later, he was still awake, listening to the howling storm outside. The rain beat against the windows in sudden gusts; he jumped with every buffet. He couldn't get the results of David's DNA fingerprinting out of his mind nor of the cephaloclor being in the blood samples.

"Marsha," he whispered, wondering if she were awake as well. But she didn't answer. He whispered again, but still she didn't answer. Victor slid out of bed, put his robe back on, and went down the hall to the upstairs study.

Sitting down at the desk, he booted up the PC. He logged onto the main Chimera computer with the modem, rediscovering how easy it was. Absently, he wondered if he had ever transferred copies of the Hobbs and Murray files onto the PC's hard disk. To check, he called up the directory of the hard disk and searched. There were no Hobbs or Murray files. In fact, he was surprised to find so few files on the disk at all, other than the operating programs. But then, just before he was about to turn the machine off, he noticed that most of the storage space of the hard disk was used up.

Victor scratched his head. It didn't make sense, knowing the fantastic storage capacity of one hard disk. He tried to pry an explanation of this apparent discrepancy out of the machine, but the machine wouldn't cooperate. Finally, in irritation, he turned the blasted thing off.

He debated going back to bed, but, glancing at the clock, he realized that he might just as well stay up. It was already after seven. Instead of going back to the bedroom, he headed downstairs to make himself some coffee and breakfast.

As he padded down the stairs, he realized that when he'd had his talk with VJ about using the computer, he'd forgotten to quiz the boy about the deletion of the

Hobbs and Murray files. He'd have to remember to do that. Nosing around in files was one thing, deleting them was quite another.

Reaching the kitchen, Victor realized the other thing that was bothering him: namely, the issue about VJ's safety, particularly at Chimera. Philip was fine for watching VJ, but obviously his help could only go so far. Victor decided that he'd call Able Protection, since they'd obviously done such a good job watching the house. He'd get an experienced companion for the boy. It would probably be expensive, but peace of mind was worth the price. Until he got to the bottom of the Hobbs and Murray deaths, he'd feel infinitely better knowing VJ was safe.

Getting out the coffee, Victor was struck by another realization. In the back of his mind the similarities between David's and Janice's cancers had been bothering him, especially in light of the results of DNA fingerprinting of David's tumor. Victor resolved to look into it as best he could.

# 10

*Saturday Morning*

It was still windy and rainy when Victor went out to
the garage and got in his car. He'd breakfasted, show-
ered, shaved, and dressed, and still no one else had
stirred. After leaving a note explaining that he would
be at the lab most of the day, Victor had left.

But he didn't drive straight to the lab. Instead he
headed west and got on Interstate 93 and drove south
to Boston. In Boston he got off Storrow Drive at the
Charles Street and Government Center exit. From
there it was easy to drive onto the Massachusetts General Hospital grounds and park in the multistory parking garage. Ten minutes later he was in the pathology
department.

Since it was early Saturday morning none of the
staff pathologists were available. Victor had to be content with a second-year resident named Angela Ci-
rone.

Victor explained his wish to get a tumor sample
from a patient that had passed away four years previously.

"I'm afraid that is impossible," Angela said. "We don't keep—"

Victor politely interrupted her to tell her of the special nature of the tumor and its rarity.

"That might make things different," she said.

The hardest part was finding Janice Fay's hospital record, since Victor did not know Janice's birthday. Birthdates were the major method of cross-referencing hospital records. But persistence paid off, and Angela was able to find both the hospital record number as well as the pathology record. She was also able to tell Victor that a gross specimen existed.

"But I can't give you any," Angela said after all the effort they'd expended to find it. "One of the staff members is up doing frozens this morning. When he gets through, we can see if he'll give authorization."

But Victor explained about his son David's death of the same rare cancer and his interest in examining Janice's cancerous cells. When he tried to, he could be charming in a winning way. Within the space of a few minutes, he'd persuaded the young resident to help.

"How much do you need?" she asked finally.

"A tiny slice," Victor said.

"I guess it can't hurt," Angela said.

Fifteen minutes later, Victor was on his way down the elevator with another small jar within a paper bag. He knew he could have waited for the staff man, but this way he could get to work more quickly. Climbing into his car, he left the Massachusetts General Hospital grounds and headed north for Lawrence.

Arriving at Chimera, Victor called Able Protection. But he got a recording—it was Saturday, after all— and had to be content to leave his name and number.

With that done, he searched for Robert, finding him already deeply involved with the project that Victor had started the night before, the separation of the section of David's tumor DNA that differed from his normal DNA.

"You are going to hate me," Victor said, "but I have another sample." He took out the sample he had just gotten at Mass. General. "I want this DNA finger-printed as well."

"You don't have to worry about me," Robert said. "I like doing this stuff. You'll just have to realize that I'm letting my regular work slide."

"I understand," Victor said. "For the moment this project takes priority."

Taking the rat specimens that he'd prepared the night before, Victor made slides and stained them. While he was waiting for them to dry, a call came through from Able Protection. It was the same deep-voiced man whom Victor had dealt with earlier.

"First, I'd like to commend Mr. Norwell," Victor said. "He did a great job last night."

"We appreciate the compliment," the man said.

"Second," Victor said, "I need additional temporary security. But it's going to require a very special person. I want someone with my son, VJ, from 6 A.M. until 6 P.M. And when I say I want someone with him, I mean constantly."

"I don't think that will be a problem," the man said. "When do you want it to start?"

"As soon as you can send someone," Victor answered. "This morning, if possible. My son is at home."

"No problem. I have just the person. His name is Pedro Gonzales and I'll send him on his way."

226

Victor hung up and called Marsha at home.

"How did you sneak out without waking me this morning?" she asked.

"I never got to sleep last night after all the excitement," Victor said. "Is VJ there?"

"He and Philip are still sleeping," Marsha said.

"I've just made arrangements to have a security man stay with VJ all day. His name is Pedro Gonzales. He'll be over shortly."

"Why?" Marsha questioned, obviously surprised.

"Just to be one hundred percent sure he is safe," Victor said.

"You're not telling me something," Marsha warned. "I want to know what it is."

"It's just to be sure he's safe," Victor repeated. "We'll talk more about it later when I come home. I promise."

Victor hung up the phone. He wasn't about to confide in Marsha, at least not about his latest suspicions: that the Hobbs and Murray kids might have been deliberately killed. And that VJ could be killed the same way if anyone introduced cephaloclor to his system. With these thoughts in mind, he returned to the slides of the rat brains that he had drying and began to examine them in one of the light microscopes. As he expected, they appeared very similar to the slides of the children's brains. Now there was no doubt in his mind that the children had indeed died from the cephaloclor in their blood. It was how they got the cephaloclor that was the question.

Removing the slides from the microscope, Victor went back to where Robert was working. They'd worked together so long, Victor could join in and help without a single word of direction from Robert.

* * *

After making herself a second cup of coffee, Marsha sat down at the table and looked out at the rainy day with its heavy clouds. It felt good not to have to go to the office, although she still had to make her inpatient rounds. She wondered if she should be more concerned than she was about Victor's arranging for a bodyguard for VJ. That certainly sounded ominous. At the same time, it sounded like a good idea. But she was still sure there were facts that Victor was keeping from her.

Footsteps on the stairs heralded the arrival of both VJ and Philip. They greeted Marsha but were much more interested in the refrigerator, getting out milk and blueberries for their cereal.

"What are you two planning on doing today?" Marsha asked when they'd sat down at the table with her.

"Heading in to the lab," VJ said. "Is Dad there?"

"He is," Marsha said. "What happened about the idea of going to Boston for the day with Richie Blakemore?"

"Didn't pan out," VJ said. He gave the blueberries a shove toward Philip.

"That's too bad," Marsha said.

"Doesn't matter," VJ said.

"There is something I want to talk to you about," Marsha said. "Yesterday I had a conversation with Valerie Maddox. Do you remember her?"

VJ rested his spoon in his dish. "I don't like the sound of this. I remember her. She's the psychiatrist whose office is on the floor above yours. She's the lady with the mouth that looks like she's always getting ready to kiss somebody."

Philip laughed explosively, spraying cereal in the

process. He wiped his mouth self-consciously while trying to control his laughter. VJ laughed himself, watching Philip's antics.

"That's not very nice," Marsha said. "She is a wonderful woman, and very talented. We talked about you."

"This is starting to sound even worse," VJ said.

"She has offered to see you and I think it would be a good idea. Maybe twice a week after school."

"Oh, Mom!" VJ whined, his face contorting into an expression of extreme distaste.

"I want you to think about it," Marsha said. "We'll talk again. It is something that might help you as you get older."

"I'm too busy for that stuff," VJ complained, shaking his head.

Marsha had to laugh to herself at that comment. "You think about it anyway," she said. "One other thing. I just spoke to your father. Has he said anything to you about being concerned about your safety, anything like that?"

"A little," VJ said. "He wanted me to watch out for Beekman and Hurst. But I never see those guys."

"Apparently he's still worried," Marsha said. "He just told me that he has arranged for a man to be with you during the day. The man's name is Pedro and he's on his way over here."

"Oh, no!" VJ complained. "That will drive me nuts."

After finishing her inpatient rounds, Marsha got on Interstate 495 and headed west to Lowell. She got off after only three exits, and with the help of some directions she'd written on a prescription blank, she wound around on little country roads until she found 714

229

Mapleleaf Road, an ill-kept, Victorian-style house painted a drab gray with white trim. At some time in the past it had been converted into a duplex. The Fays lived on the first floor. Marsha rang the bell and waited.

Marsha had called from the hospital so the Fays knew to expect her. Despite the fact that their daughter had worked for her and Victor for eleven years, Marsha had only met the mother and father at Janice's funeral. Janice had been dead for four years. Marsha felt odd standing on her parents' porch, waiting for them to open the door. Knowing Janice so intimately for so many years, Marsha had come to the conclusion that there had been significantly disturbing emotional undercurrents in her family, but she had no idea what they could have been. On that issue, Janice had been completely noncommunicative.

"Please come in," Mrs. Fay said after she'd opened the door. She was a white-haired, pleasant-looking but frail woman who appeared to be in her early sixties. Marsha noted that the woman avoided eye contact.

The inside of the house was much worse than the outside. The furniture was old and threadbare. What made it particularly unpleasant was that the place was dirty. Wastepaper baskets were filled to overflowing with such things as beer cans and McDonald's wrappers. There were even cobwebs in one corner up near the ceiling.

"Let me tell Harry that you're here," Mrs. Fay said.

Marsha could hear the sounds of a televised sporting event somewhere in the background. She sat down, but kept to the very edge of the sofa. She didn't want to touch anything.

"Well, well," said a husky voice. "About time the fancy doctor paid us a visit is all I can say."

Marsha turned to see a large man with a huge belly and wearing a tank-top undershirt come into the room. He walked right up to her and stuck out a calloused hand for her to shake. His hair was cut severely in a military-style crew cut. His face was dominated by a large, swollen nose with red capillaries fanning the side of each nostril.

"Can I offer you a beer or something?" he asked.

"No, thank you," Marsha said.

Harry Fay sank into a La-Z-Boy armchair. "To what do we owe this visit?" he asked. He burped and excused himself.

"I wanted to talk about Janice," Marsha said.

"I hope to God she didn't tell you any lies about me," Harry said. "I've been a hardworking man all my life. Drove sixteen-wheelers back and forth across this country so many times I lost count."

"I'm sure that was hard work," Marsha said, wondering if she should have come.

"Bet your ass," Harry said.

"What I was wondering," Marsha began, "is whether Janice ever talked about my boys, David and VJ."

"Lots of times," Harry said. "Right, Mary?"

Mary nodded but didn't say anything.

"Did she ever remark on anything out of the ordinary about them?" There were specific questions she could have asked, but she preferred not to lead the conversation.

"She sure did," Harry said. "Even before she got nuts about all that religious bunk, she told us that VJ had killed his brother. She even told us that she tried to warn you but you wouldn't listen."

231

"Janice never tried to warn me," Marsha said, color rising in her cheeks. "And I should tell you that my son David died of cancer."

"Well, that's sure different than what Janice told us," Harry said. "She told us the kid was poisoned. Drugged and poisoned."

"That's patently preposterous," Marsha said.

"What the hell does that mean?" Harry said.

Marsha took a deep breath to calm herself down. She realized that she was trying to defend herself and her family before this offensive man. She knew that wasn't the reason that she was there. "I mean to say that there was no way that my son David could have been poisoned. He died of cancer just like your daughter."

"We only know what we've been told. Right, Mary?"

Mary nodded dutifully.

"In fact," Harry said, "Janice told us that she'd been drugged once too. She told us that she didn't tell anybody because she knew no one would believe her. She told us that she got mighty careful about what she ate from then on."

Marsha didn't say anything for a moment. She'd remembered the change in Janice. Overnight, she'd gotten extremely fastidious about what she ate. Marsha had always wondered what had caused the change. Apparently it had been this delusion of being drugged or poisoned.

"Actually, we didn't believe too much of what Janice was telling us," Harry admitted. "Something happened inside her head when she got so religious. She even went so far as to tell us that your boy, VJ, or whatever his name, was evil. Like he had something to do with the devil."

"I can assure you that is not the case," Marsha said. She stood up. She'd had enough.

"It is strange that your son David and our daughter died of the same cancer," Harry said. He rose to his feet, his face reddening with the considerable effort.

"It was a coincidence," Marsha agreed. "In fact, at the time it caused some concern. There was a worry that it had something to do with environment. Our home was studied extensively. I can assure you their both having it was nothing more than a tragic coincidence."

"Tough luck, I guess," Harry admitted.

"Very bad luck," Marsha said. "And we miss Janice as we miss our son."

"She was all right," Harry said. "She was a pretty good kid. But she lied a lot. She lied a lot about me."

"She never said anything to us about you," Marsha said. And after a curt handshake, she was gone.

"You sure you don't mind?" Victor asked Louis Kaspwicz. He'd called the man at home to ask him about the discrepancy regarding his hard disk on the personal computer.

"I don't mind in the slightest," Louis said. "If your hard disk has no storage space available, it means the existing storage is filled with data. There is no other explanation."

"But I looked at the file directory," Victor said. "All there is listed are the operating systems files."

"There have to be more files," Louis said. "Trust me."

"I'd hate to mess up your Saturday afternoon if it is some stupid thing," Victor said.

"Look, Dr. Frank," Louis said, "I don't mind. In fact,

on a rainy day like this I'll enjoy the excuse to get out of the house."

"I'd appreciate it," Victor said.

"Just give me directions and I'll meet you there," Louis said.

Victor gave him directions, then went out into the main lab and told Robert that he was leaving but that he'd probably be back. He asked Robert about what time he'd be calling it a day. Robert said that his wife had told him dinner was to be at six so he'd be leaving about five-thirty.

Louis was already at the house by the time Victor got there.

"Sorry to make you wait," Victor said as he fumbled with his keys.

"No problem," Louis said cheerfully. "You certainly have a beautiful house," he added. He stomped the moisture off his shoes.

"Thank you." Victor led Louis upstairs to his Wang PC. "Here it is," he said. He reached behind the electronics unit and switched the system on.

Louis gave the computer a quick look, then lifted his narrow briefcase onto the counter top, snapping open the latches. Inside, encased in styrofoam, was an impressive array of electronic tools.

Louis sat down in front of the unit and waited for the menu to come up. He quickly went through the same sequence that Victor had early that morning, getting the same result.

"You were right," Louis said. "There's not much space left on this Winchester." He reached over to his briefcase and unsnapped the accordion-like file area built under the lid, pulled out a floppy disk, and loaded it.

"Luckily, I happen to have a special utility for locating hidden files," Louis said.

"What do you mean by hidden files?" Victor asked.

Louis was busy with manipulating information on the screen. He spoke without looking "It is possible to store files so that they don't appear on any directory," he said.

Miraculously, data started to appear on the computer. "Here we are," Louis said. He leaned aside so Victor could have a better view of the screen. "Any of this make sense to you?"

Victor studied the information. "Yeah," he said. "These are contractions for the nucleotide bases of the DNA molecule." The screen was completely filled with vertical columns of the letters AT, TA, GC, and CG. "The A is the adenine, the T is for pyrimidine, the G is for guanine, and the C is for cytosine," Victor explained.

Louis advanced to the next page. The lists continued. He advanced a number of pages. The lists were interminable. "What do you make of this?" Louis asked, flipping through page after page.

"Must be a DNA molecule or gene sequence," Victor said, his eyes following the flashing lists as if he were watching a Ping-Pong game.

"Well, have you seen enough of this file?" Louis asked.

Victor nodded.

Louis punched some information into the keyboard. Another file appeared, but it was similar to the first. "The whole hard disk could be taken up with this stuff," Louis suggested. "You don't remember putting this material in here?"

"I didn't put it in," Victor said without elaborating.

He knew that Louis was probably dying to ask where it could have come from and who was the person logging onto the Chimera mainframe last night. Victor was grateful that the man held his curiosity in check.

For the next half hour, Louis rapidly went from file to file. All looked essentially like the first. It was like a library of DNA molecules. Then suddenly it changed.

"Uh oh," Louis said. He had to hold up hitting the sequence of keys that scrolled through the hidden files. What appeared on the screen was a personnel file. Louis flipped through a couple of pages. "I recognize this because I formatted it. This is a personnel file from Chimera."

Louis looked up at Victor, who didn't say a word. Louis turned back to the computer and went to the next file. It was George Gephardt's. "This stuff was pulled directly out of the mainframe," Louis said. When Victor still did not respond, he went to the next file, then the next. There were eighteen personnel files. Then came a series of accounting files with spread sheets. "I don't recognize these," Louis said. He looked up at Victor again. "Do you?"

Victor shook his head in disbelief.

Louis redirected his attention to the computer screen. "Wherever it came from, it represents a lot of money. It is a clever way to present it, though. I wonder what kind of program was used. I wouldn't mind getting a copy of it."

After going through a number of pages of the accounting data, Louis went on to the next file. It was a stock portfolio of a number of small companies, all of which held Chimera stock. All in all, it represented a large portion of the Chimera stock not held by the three founders and their families.

"What do you think this is?" Louis asked.

"I haven't the slightest idea," Victor said. But there was one thing that he had a good idea about. He was going to have another talk with VJ about using the computer. If the information before him represented actual truths and wasn't part of some elaborate fantasy computer game, the ramifications were very grave. And on top of that was the question of the deleted Hobbs and Murray files.

"Now we're back to more of the DNA stuff," Louis said as the screen filled again with the lists of the nucleotide sequences. "Do you want me to go on?"

"I don't think that's necessary," said Victor. "I think I've seen enough. Would you mind leaving that floppy disk you've used to bring these files up? I'll bring it to Chimera on Monday."

"Not at all," Louis said. "In fact, this is just a copy. You can keep it if you want. I have the original at home."

Victor saw Louis off, holding the front door ajar until the man got in his van and drove off. Victor waved and then shut the door. Going upstairs, he made sure that VJ was not around. Back in the study, he called Marsha's office but got the service. They didn't know where she was, although she'd been at the hospital earlier.

Victor put the phone down. Then he got the idea of contacting Able Protection. Maybe they could get in touch with their operative. If so, then Victor could find out where VJ was.

But a call to Able Protection only yielded the recording. Victor was forced to leave his name and number with the request that he be called as soon as possible.

For the next half hour, Victor paced back and forth in the upstairs study. For the life of him, he could not understand what it was all about.

The phone rang and Victor grabbed it. It was the grating voice of the man from Able Protection. Victor asked if it were possible to contact the man accompanying VJ.

"All our people carry pagers," the man told him.

"I want to know where my son is," Victor said.

"I'll call you right back." With that, the man hung up. Five minutes later, the phone rang again. "Your son is at Chimera, Inc.," the man said. "Pedro is at the security gate this minute if you want to talk to him."

Victor thanked the man. He hung up the phone and went downstairs for his coat. A few minutes later he was cutting his wheels sharply to do a U-turn in front of the house.

After a quick drive, Victor made an acute turn into the entrance to the Chimera compound and came to an abrupt halt inches from the gatehouse barrier. He drummed his fingers expectantly on the steering wheel, waiting for the guard to raise the black and white striped gate. Instead, the man came out of the office in spite of the rain and bent down next to Victor's window. Without hiding his irritation at being detained, Victor lowered his window.

"Afternoon, Dr. Frank!" the guard said. He touched the brim of his hat in some kind of salute. "If you're looking for that special security man, he's here in the guardhouse."

"You mean the man from Able Protection?" Victor asked.

"That I don't know," the guard said. He straightened up. "Hey, Pedro, you from Able Protection?"

A handsome young man came to the door of the guardhouse. His hair was coal black and he sported a narrow mustache. He looked about twenty.

"Who wants to know?" he asked.

"Your boss here, Dr. Frank."

Pedro came out of the guardhouse and over to Victor's car. He stuck out his hand. "Nice to meet you, Dr. Frank. I'm Pedro Gonzales from Able Protection."

Victor shook hands with him. He wasn't happy. "Why aren't you with my boy?" Victor asked brusquely.

"I was," Pedro explained, "but when we got here, he said he was safe inside the compound at Chimera and that I was supposed to wait in the guardhouse."

"I think your orders were pretty clear to stay with the boy at all times," Victor said.

"Yes, sir," Pedro answered, realizing he'd made a mistake. "It won't happen again. Your son was quite convincing. He said you'd wanted it this way. I'm sorry."

"Where is he?" Victor asked.

"That I can't say," Pedro answered. "He and Philip are on the grounds here someplace. They haven't left if that is what you're concerned about."

"That's not what I'm concerned about," Victor snapped. "I'm concerned that I hired Able Protection to watch over him and the job's not being done."

"I understand," Pedro said.

Victor looked up at the gate operator. "Is Sheldon working today?"

"Hey, Sheldon!" the guard yelled.

Sheldon appeared at the doorway. Victor asked if he had any idea where VJ was.

"Nope," Sheldon said, "but when he arrived this morning, he and Philip headed that way." He pointed west.

"Toward the river?" Victor asked.

"Could have been," Sheldon said. "But he could have gone to the cafeteria, too."

"Would you like me to come with you and help find him?" Pedro asked.

Victor shook his head no as he put his car in gear. "You wait here until I find him." Then, to the guard, who was blankly listening to the conversation, he said, "I'd appreciate it if you could raise this gate before I drive through it."

The guard jumped and ran back inside to activate the gate mechanism.

Victor floored the accelerator and sped onto the Chimera lot. Forsaking his reserved parking space, he drove to the building that housed his lab and parked in front of the entrance. It said no parking but he didn't care. He pulled his coat collar up and hunched over, running for the door.

Robert was the only one still there. He was as busy as usual, again working with the gel electrophoresis unit. That was where the bits and pieces of the cleaved DNA were separated.

"Have you seen VJ?" Victor asked, shaking off some of the rainwater.

"Haven't seen him," Robert said. He rubbed his eyes

with the heels of his hands. "But I have something else to show you." He picked up two strips of film which had dark bands in exactly the same location and held them out for Victor to take. "That second tumor sample you gave me had the same extra piece of DNA as your son's. But the sample was from a different person."

"It was from our live-in nanny," Victor said. "Are you positive that the moiety was the same in both samples?"

"Quite sure," Robert said.

"That's astounding," Victor said, forgetting VJ for a moment.

"I thought you'd find it interesting," Robert said with pride. "It's the kind of finding that cancer researchers have been seeking. It could even be the breakthrough that medicine has been waiting for."

"You've got to sequence it," Victor said impatiently. "Immediately."

"That's what I've been doing," Robert said. "I've got a number of other runs with the electrophoresis unit and then I'll let the computer have a go at it."

"If it turns out to be a retro virus or something like that . . ." Victor said, letting his sentence trail off. It was just one more unexpected finding to be added to a growing list.

"If VJ shows up, tell him I'm looking for him," Victor said. Then he turned and left the lab.

In the cafeteria, Victor went straight to the manager. "Have you seen VJ?"

"He was in here for an early lunch. Philip was with him along with one of the guards."

"One of the guards?" Victor questioned. He wondered why Sheldon hadn't told him that. Victor asked the manager to call his lab if VJ showed up. The manager nodded.

There were a handful of people in the library. Most of them were reading, a few were asleep. The librarian told Victor that VJ had not been around.

Victor got the same response at the fitness center and the day-care center. Except at the cafeteria, no one had seen VJ all day.

Getting an umbrella from his car, Victor set off toward the river. He walked north and hit it at about the middle of the Chimera complex. He turned west, walking along the granite quay. None of the buildings lining the river had been renovated by Chimera as yet, but they'd make ideal sites for some of the intended expansion. Victor was considering moving his administrative office down there. After all, if he had to spend all his time doing administrative work, he might as well have a view.

As he walked, Victor gazed down at the river. In the rain the white water appeared even more turbulent than it had on the previous day. Looking upriver toward the dam, he could barely see its outline through the mist rising from the base of the falls.

Passing the line of empty buildings, he realized there were hundreds of nooks here a boy could find entertaining. It could be a paradise for games like hide-and-seek or sardines. But those games required a group of kids. Except for Philip, VJ was always on his own.

Victor continued moving upstream until his path was blocked by the portion of the clock tower building that was cantilevered out over part of the dam and a portion of the millpond. To go beyond,

Victor had to skirt the building, then approach the river on its west side. There, Victor's path was blocked by the ten-foot-wide sluice that separated from the millpond, then ran parallel to it before leading to a tunnel. Back in the days when water-power ran the entire mill, the sluice carried the water into the basement of the clock tower building. There the rushing water turned a series of huge paddle wheels which effectively powered thousands of looms and sewing machines as well as the tower clock.

Standing at the tunnel's edge, Victor inspected the bottom of the sluice. Besides a trickle of water, there was debris mostly made up of broken bottles and empty beer cans. Victor eyed the junction of the sluice and the raging river. Two heavy steel doors had once regulated the water flow. Now the whole unit was horribly corroded with rust. Victor wondered how it could still hold back the horrendous force the water exerted on it. The river was practically at the level of the top of the doors.

Victor skirted the sluice and continued his walk westward. The rain stopped and he lowered his umbrella. Soon he came to the last building of the Chimera complex. It, too, was cantilevered out over the river. Beyond it was a city street. Victor turned around and started back.

He didn't call VJ as he'd done the last time. He just looked around and listened. When he got back to the clock tower building, he headed toward the occupied portion of the complex. Stopping in at his lab, he asked Robert if VJ had appeared, but he hadn't.

At a loss as to what to do, Victor returned to the cafeteria.

"Hasn't shown up yet," the manager said before Victor even asked him.

"I didn't expect so," Victor said. "I came over for some coffee."

Still damp from the rain, Victor had become quite chilled as he'd walked along the river. He could tell that the temperature was dropping again now that the storm was over.

Once he'd finished his coffee and felt sufficiently warm, Victor pulled on his damp coat. He again reminded the manager to call over to the lab if and when VJ showed up. Then he returned to the security office. The warmth in there was welcome even if it was heavy with cigarette smoke. Pedro had been playing solitaire on a small couch in the back of the office. He got up when Victor appeared. Sheldon stood up behind his small desk.

"Anybody seen my son?" Victor asked abruptly.

"I just spoke to Hal not two minutes ago," Sheldon said. "I specifically asked him, but he said he hadn't seen VJ all day."

"The manager at the cafeteria told me that VJ had lunch with one of you guys today," Victor said. "How come you didn't tell me?"

"I didn't eat with VJ!" Sheldon said, pressing his palm against his chest. "I know Hal didn't either. He ate with me. We both brown-bagged it. Hey, Fred!"

Fred stuck his head into the main part of the office from the spot where he operated the entrance and the exit gates. Sheldon asked him if he ate lunch with VJ.

"Sure didn't," he said. "I went off-site for lunch."

Sheldon shrugged. Then he said to Victor, "There's only three of us on duty today."

"But the manager said . . ." Victor started, but he stopped. There was no point getting into an argument over who ate with VJ and who didn't. The point was, where the hell was he now? Victor was getting curious and a little concerned. Marsha had wondered, and now he did too, just what did VJ do at Chimera to keep himself occupied. Up until that moment Victor had never given it much thought.

Leaving the security office, Victor went back to his lab. He was running out of ideas of where to search.

"The manager over at the cafeteria just called," Robert said as soon as Victor appeared. "VJ's turned up."

Victor went to the nearest phone and called the manager.

"He's here right now," the manager said.

"Is he alone?" Victor asked.

"Nope. Philip is with him."

"Did you tell him I was looking for him?" Victor asked.

"No, I didn't. You just told me to call. You didn't tell me to say anything to VJ."

"That's fine," Victor said. "Don't say anything. I'm on my way."

Crossing to the building that housed both the cafeteria and the library, Victor chose not to enter through the main cafeteria entrance. He went in a side entrance instead, climbed to the second floor, and only then entered the cafeteria on the balcony level. Going to the railing and looking down, he saw VJ and Philip eating ice cream.

Keeping back out of sight, Victor allowed VJ and Philip to finish their afternoon snack. Before long they got up and disposed of their trays. As they were leaving, Victor came down the stairs, staying out of sight close to the wall. He could hear the door close behind them as they left.

Quickening his step, he got to the door in time to see them turn west on the walkway.

"Something wrong?" the manager asked.

"No, nothing is wrong," Victor said, straightening up and trying to appear nonchalant. The last thing he wanted was office gossip. "Just curious about my son's whereabouts," he said. "I've told him time and time again not to go near the river when it's raging like it is now. But I'm afraid he's not minding me at all."

"Boys will be boys," said the manager.

Victor exited the cafeteria in time to see VJ and Philip in the distance, turning to the right beyond the building housing Victor's lab. Clearly they were heading toward the river. Moving to a slow jog, Victor followed as far as the point where VJ and Philip had turned right. About fifty yards ahead he could still see them. He waited until they veered left just before the river and disappeared from sight. Victor ran down the alleyway.

When he arrived at the point VJ and Philip had gone left, he caught sight of them nearing the clock tower building. As he watched, the two mounted the few steps in front of the deserted building and entered through the doorless entranceway.

"What on earth can they be doing in there?" Victor asked himself. Keeping out of sight as much as possible, he went as far as the entranceway, then paused to listen. But all he could hear was the sound of the falls.

Perplexed, Victor entered. He waited a moment until his eyes adjusted to the dim light. Once they had, he found just the kind of mess he'd expected to find in the abandoned building. The floor was littered with rubble and trash.

The first floor was dominated by a large room with window openings over the millpond. Any glass had long since been broken. Not even the sashes remained. In the center of the room was a pile of debris giving evidence of squatters who had probably occupied the place before Chimera purchased the complex and fenced it in. Over the whole scene hung a pervasive smell of rotting wood, fabric, and cardboard.

Stealthily moving toward the center of the room, Victor tried to listen again, but the noise of the falls was even more dominating inside than it had been outside. He could make out no other sounds.

Along the side opposite the river was a series of small rooms that opened onto the main room. Victor started at the first and worked his way down. Each was filled with trash, to varying degrees. At either end and in the center of the building were stairwells that led to the two floors above. Victor went to the center staircase and slowly climbed up. On each floor he searched the warren of little rooms on both sides of a long hallway. Each room had its complement of rubble, litter, and dirt.

Mystified, Victor returned to the first floor. He walked to one of the front window openings and gazed out at the river, the dam, the pond, and then at the empty sluice, closed from the river with its rusted doors.

It was then that Victor remembered that the clock tower building was connected to the other buildings by elaborate tunnel systems to distribute the rotary mechanical power of the paddle wheels. It was obvious VJ was not in the clock tower building now. Victor wondered if it was this system his son had stumbled onto.

Victor whirled about, his hair standing on edge. He thought he'd heard something over the roar of the falls, or felt something; he wasn't sure which. His eyes rapidly scanned the room but no one was there, and when he strained to listen, all he heard was the sound of the river.

Going from one stairwell to the other, Victor searched for the entrance to the basement. But he couldn't find it. He looked again, still to no avail. There were no steps leading down. Stepping over to a window opening on the south side of the building, he looked to see if there might be a basement entrance from the outside, but there wasn't. There seemed no way to get into the basement.

Victor left the building and walked back to the occupied section of the Chimera complex to visit the office of Buildings and Grounds. Using his master key, he let himself in and turned on the lights. He immediately went to the file room. From a huge metal cabinet he retrieved the architectural drawings of all the existing structures on the Chimera property. Referencing the clock tower building on the master site plan, he found the drawings for it and pulled them out.

The first drawing was of the basement. It showed where the water tunnel entered the edifice. Within the basement the water flowed through a heavily planked trough where it turned a series of paddle wheels that were mounted both horizontally and vertically. The basement itself was divided into one central room with all the power wheels and a number of side rooms. The tunnel system emanated from one of the side rooms on the east end.

Victor then looked at the plan for the first floor. He found the stairway that led down to the basement easily enough. It was immediately to the right of the central stairwell. He could not imagine how he had missed it.

To be doubly sure, he made a copy of the basement and first-floor plans, using the special copy machine that Chimera had for that purpose. He reduced the copies to legal-paper size. With these in hand, he returned to the clock tower building, determined to explore below.

Victor made his way through the trash on the floor and approached the central stairwell. Standing in front of it, he looked to the immediate right. He even took the copy of the existing floor plan and held it up to make sure he'd read it right.

Victor couldn't understand what he was doing wrong. There were no basement stairs. He even walked around the other side of the stairwell just in case the blueprints were in error. But there were no stairs going down on that side either.

Walking back to the location where the plans said the stairway was supposed to be, Victor noticed that the area was devoid of the debris that was scattered over the rest of the floor. Finding that odd, he bent down and noticed something else: the floor planking was wider than it was in the rest of the building. And it was newer wood.

Victor started at a sound from behind. He turned, but it seemed there was nothing there. Still, he felt there was someone there in the semidarkness. Someone very near. Terrified, Victor tried to scan the surrounding cavernous room. Again from behind he heard or felt a second sound or vibration. No doubt about it: a footfall. Victor turned, but too late. He could just make out the shadowy silhouette of a figure raising some sort of object over his head. He tried to lift his hands to protect himself from the blow, but could not save himself from its power. His mind collapsed into a black abyss.

After leaving Lowell, Marsha stopped at a roadside concession and used the phone and called the Blakemores. She felt mildly awkward, but managed to get herself invited over for a short visit. It took her about half an hour to get to their home in West Boxford at 479 Plum Island Road.

As she pulled in, Marsha was glad it had stopped raining. But as she opened the door to her car, she wished she'd taken one of her down coats. The temperature was dropping rapidly.

The Blakemore house was a cozy structure reminiscent of the kind of houses seen on Cape Cod. The windows were mullioned and painted white. Arching over the entranceway was a latticed wood arbor. Marsha climbed the front steps and rang the bell.

Mrs. Blakemore opened the door. She was a stocky woman about Marsha's age, with short hair turned up at the ends. "Come in," she said, eyeing Marsha curiously. "I'm Edith Blakemore."

Marsha felt the woman's stare and wondered if there was something amiss with her appearance, like a dark spot between her front teeth from the fruit she'd just eaten. She ran her tongue over her teeth just to be sure.

Inside the house was every bit as charming as the exterior. The furniture was early American antique with chintz-covered couches and wing chairs. On the wide-planked pine floor were rag rugs.

"May I take your coat?" Edith asked. "How about some coffee or tea?"

"Tea would be nice," Marsha said. She followed Edith into the living room.

Mr. Blakemore, who had been sitting by the fire with the newspaper, got to his feet as Marsha entered. "I'm Carl Blakemore," he said, extending his hand. He was a big man with leathery skin and dark features.

Marsha shook his hand.

"Sit down, make yourself at home," Carl said, motioning to the couch. After Marsha sat down, he returned to his own seat, placing the paper on the floor next to his chair. He smiled pleasantly. Edith disappeared into the kitchen.

"Interesting weather," Carl said, attempting to make conversation.

Marsha could not rid herself of the uncomfortable feeling she'd gotten when Edith had first looked at her. There was something stiff and unnatural about these people but Marsha couldn't put her finger on it.

A boy came down the stairs and into the room. He was just about VJ's age but larger and stockier, with sandy-colored hair and dark brown eyes. There was a tough look about him, and the resemblance to Mr. Blakemore was striking. "Hello," he said, extending his hand in a gentlemanly fashion.

"You must be Richie," Marsha said, shaking hands with the boy. "I'm VJ's mother. I've heard a lot about you." Marsha felt an exaggeration was in order.

"You have?" Richie asked uncertainly.

251

"Yes," Marsha said. "And the more I heard, the more I wanted to meet you. Why don't you come over to our house sometime? I suppose VJ has told you we have a swimming pool."

"VJ never told me you have a swimming pool," Richie said. He sat on the hearth and stared up at Marsha to the point that she felt even more uncomfortable.

"I don't know why he didn't," Marsha said. She looked at Carl. "You never know what's in these children's minds," she said with a smile.

"Guess not," Carl said.

There was an awkward silence. Marsha wondered what was going on.

"Milk or lemon?" Edith asked, coming into the room and breaking the silence. She carried a tray into the living room and put it on the coffee table.

"Lemon," Marsha said. She took the cup from Edith and held it while Edith poured. Then she squeezed in a little lemon. When she was finished, she settled back. Then she noticed that the other three people were not joining her. They were just staring.

"No one else is having any tea?" Marsha asked, feeling progressively self-conscious.

"You enjoy it," Edith said.

Marsha took a sip. It was hot, so she placed it on the coffee table. She cleared her throat nervously. "I'm sorry to have barged in on you like this."

"Not at all," Edith said. "Being a rainy day and all, we've just been relaxing around the house."

"I've wanted to meet you for some time," Marsha said. "You've been awfully nice to VJ, I'd like to return the favor."

"What exactly do you mean?" Edith asked.

"Well, for one thing," Marsha said, "I'd like to have Richie come over to our home and spend the night. If he'd like to, of course. Would you like to do that, Richie?"

Richie shrugged his shoulders.

"Why exactly would you like Richie to spend the night?" Carl asked.

"To return the favor, of course," Marsha said. "Since VJ has spent so many nights over here, I thought it only natural that Richie come to our house once in a while."

Carl and Edith exchanged glances. Edith spoke: "Your son has never spent the night here. I'm afraid I don't know what you're talking about."

Marsha looked from one person to the other, her confusion mounting. "VJ has never stayed here overnight?" she asked incredulously.

"Never," Carl said.

Looking down at Richie, Marsha asked, "What about last Sunday. Did you and VJ spend time together?"

"No," Richie said, shaking his head.

"Well, then, I suppose I have to apologize for taking your time," Marsha said, embarrassed. She stood up. Edith and Carl did the same.

"We thought you'd come to talk about the fight," Carl said.

"What fight?" Marsha asked.

"Apparently VJ and our boy had a little disagreement," Carl said. "Richie had to spend the night in the infirmary with a broken nose."

"Oh, I'm terribly sorry," Marsha said. "I'll have to have a talk with VJ."

As quickly and as gracefully as she could, Marsha

left the Blakemore house. When she got into her car, she was furious. She sure would have a talk with VJ. He was even worse off than she'd thought. How could she have missed so much? It was as though her son had a separate life, one entirely different from the one he presented. Such cool, calm deceit was markedly abnormal! What was happening to her little boy?

# 11

Victor regained consciousness gradually. Through a haze, he heard muffled noises he couldn't make out. Then he realized the noises were voices. Finally he recognized VJ's voice, and the boy was angry, yelling at someone, telling them that Victor was his father.

"I'm sorry." The words carried a heavy Spanish accent. "How was I to know?"

Victor felt himself being shaken. The jostling made him aware that his head hurt. He felt dizzy. Reaching up, he felt a lump the size of a golf ball on the top of his forehead.

"Dad?" VJ called.

Victor opened his eyes groggily. For a moment the headache became intense, then waned. He was looking up into VJ's icy blue eyes. His son was holding his shoulders. Beyond VJ were other faces with swarthy complexions. Next to VJ was a particularly dark man with an almost sinister expression on his face, heightened by the effect of an eyelid that drooped over his left eye.

255

Closing his eyes again and gritting his teeth, Victor sat up. Dizziness made him totter for a moment, but VJ helped steady him. When the dizziness passed, Victor opened his eyes again. He also felt the bump again, only vaguely remembering how he'd gotten it.

"Are you all right, Dad?" VJ persisted.

"I think so," Victor said. He looked at the strangers. They were dressed in the typical Chimera security uniforms, but he didn't recognize any of them. Behind them stood Philip, looking sheepish and afraid.

Glancing around the room to orient himself, Victor first thought he was back in his lab because he was surrounded by the usual bevy of sophisticated scientific instrumentation. Right next to him he noticed one of the newest instruments available on the market: a fast protein liquid chromatography unit.

But he wasn't in his lab. The setting was an inappropriate combination of high-tech with a rustic background of exposed granite and hewn beams.

"Where am I?" Victor asked as he rubbed his eyes with the knuckles of his index fingers.

"You are where you aren't supposed to be," VJ said.

"What happened to me?" Victor asked as he tried to get his feet under him to stand.

"Why don't you just relax a minute," VJ said, restraining him. "You hit your head."

"That's an understatement," Victor was tempted to say. He reached up and felt the impressive lump once more, then examined his fingers to see if there was any blood. He was still confused but his head was beginning to clear. "What do you mean, 'I'm where I'm not supposed to be'?" he asked as if suddenly hearing VJ's comment for the first time.

"You weren't supposed to see this hidden lab of

mine for another month or so," VJ said. "At least not until we were in my new digs across the river."

Victor blinked. Suddenly his mind was clear. He remembered the dark figure who'd clobbered him. He looked at his son's smiling face, then let his eyes wander around the unlikely laboratory. It was as if he'd taken a step beyond reality where mass spectrometers competed with hand-chiseled granite. "Exactly where am I?" Victor asked.

"We are in the basement of the clock tower building," VJ said as he let go of Victor and stood up. VJ made a sweeping gesture with his hand and said, "But we've changed the decor to suit our needs. What do you think?"

Victor swallowed and licked his dry lips. He glanced at his son only to see him beaming proudly. He watched as Philip nervously wrung his hands. Victor looked at the three men in Chimera security guard uniforms—swarthy Hispanics with tanned faces and shiny black hair. Then his eyes slowly swept around the high-ceilinged room. It was one of the most astounding sights he'd ever seen. Directly in front of him was the yawning maw of the opening into the sluice. A slime of green mold oozed out of the lower lip with a trickle of moisture. Most of the opening was covered with a makeshift hatch made of heavy old lumber. The huge wooden trough that used to carry the water through the room had been dismantled to serve as raw materials for the hatch, the lab benches, and bookshelves.

The room appeared to be about sixty feet across and about a hundred feet in length. The largest of the old paddle wheels still stood in its vertical position in the center of the room like a piece of modern sculpture.

A number of the laboratory instruments were pushed up against its huge blades, forming a giant circle.

At both ends of the room were several heavy doors reinforced with metal rivets. The walls of the room on all four sides were constructed of the same gray granite. The ceiling consisted of open joists supporting heavy planking. In addition to the largest of the paddle wheels, most of the old mechanical apparatus of huge rods and gears that had transmitted the water-power were still in their original places, supported from the ceiling joists by metal sheaths.

Just behind Victor was a flight of wooden stairs that rose up to the ceiling, dead-ending into wooden planks.

"Well, Dad?" VJ questioned with anticipation. "Come on! What do you think?"

Victor rose to his feet unsteadily. "This is your lab?" he asked.

"That's right," VJ said. "Pretty cool, wouldn't you say?"

Wobbling, Victor made his way over to a DNA synthesizer and ran his hand along its top edge. It was the newest model available, better than the unit Victor had in his own lab.

"Where did all this equipment come from?" Victor asked, spotting a magnetic electron microscope on the other side of the paddle wheel.

"You could say it's on loan," said VJ. He followed his father and gazed lovingly at the synthesizer.

Victor turned to VJ, studying the boy's face. "Is this the equipment that was stolen from Chimera?"

"It was never stolen," VJ said with an impish grin. "Let's say it was merely rerouted. It belongs to Chimera, and it's still on Chimera grounds. I don't think you could consider it stolen unless it left the Chimera complex."

Walking on to the next laboratory appliance, an elaborate gas chromatography unit, Victor tried to pull himself together. His headache still bothered him, especially when he moved, and he felt quite dizzy. But he was starting to think the dizziness could be attributed as much to the revelation of this lab than the blow to his head. This was something out of a dream—a nightmare. Gently touching one of the chromatography columns, he assured himself it was real. Then he turned to VJ, who was right behind him.

"I think you had better explain this place from the beginning."

"Sure," VJ said. "But why don't we go into the living quarters where we'll be more comfortable."

VJ led the way around the large paddle wheel, passed the electron microscope, and headed for the end of the room. When he got there, he opened the door on the left. He pointed to the door on the right: "More lab spaces through there. We never seem to have enough."

As Victor followed VJ, he noticed over his shoulder that Philip was coming but the security guards paid them no heed. Two of them had already sat down on a makeshift bench and started playing cards.

VJ led Victor to the room that indeed looked like living quarters. Rugs in various sizes and shapes had been hung over the granite walls to provide a warmer atmosphere. About ten rollaway cots with bed linens cluttered the floor. Near the entrance door was a round table with six captain's chairs. VJ motioned for his father to have a seat.

Victor pulled out a chair and sat down. Philip silently sat down several chairs away.

"Want something to drink? Hot chocolate or tea?" VJ asked, playing host. "We have all the comforts of home here."

"I think you'd better tell me what this is all about," Victor said.

VJ nodded, then quietly began. "You know I've been interested in what was going on in your lab from the first days you brought me to Chimera. The problem was nobody let me touch anything."

"Of course not," Victor said. "You were an infant."

"I didn't feel like an infant," VJ said. "Needless to say, I decided early on I needed a lab of my own if I were to do anything at all. It started out small, but it had to get bigger since I kept needing more equipment."

"How old were you when you started?" Victor asked.

"It was about seven years ago," VJ said. "I was three. It was surprisingly easy to set the lab up with Philip around to lend the needed muscles." Philip smiled proudly. VJ went on: "At first, I was in the building next to the cafeteria. But then there was talk about it's being renovated, so we moved everything here to the clock tower. It's been my little secret ever since."

"For seven years?" Victor questioned.

VJ nodded. "About that."

"But why?" Victor asked.

"So I could do some serious work," VJ said. "Watching you and being around the lab I became fascinated with the potential of biology. It is the science of the future. I had some ideas of my own about how the research should have been conducted."

"But you could have worked in my lab," Victor said.

"Impossible," VJ said with a wave of his hand. "I'm too young. No one would have let me do what I've been doing. I needed freedom from restrictions, from rules, from helping hands. I needed my own space, and let me tell you, it has paid off beyond your wildest dreams. I've been dying to show you what I've been doing for at least a year. You're going to flip."

"You've had some successes?" Victor asked hesitantly, suddenly curious.

"Several astounding breakthroughs is a better description," VJ said. "Maybe you should try to guess."

"I couldn't," Victor said.

"I think you could," VJ said. "One of the projects is something that you yourself have been working on."

"I've been working on a lot of things," Victor said evasively.

"Listen," VJ said, "my idea is to let you have credit for the discoveries so that Chimera can patent them and prosper. We don't want anybody to know that I'm involved at all."

"Something like the swimming race?" Victor asked.

VJ laughed heartily. "Something like that, I suppose. I prefer not to draw attention to myself. I don't want anyone to pry, and people seem to get so curious when there's a prodigy in their midst. I'd prefer you to get the credit. Chimera will get the patent. We can say I'll offer you my results to compensate for space and equipment."

"Give me an idea of what you've turned up."

"For starters, I've solved the mystery of the implantation of a fertilized egg in a uterus," VJ said proudly. "As long as the zygote is normal, I can guarantee one hundred percent implantation."

"You're joking," said Victor.

"I'm not joking," VJ said somewhat crossly. "The answer turned out to be both simple and more complicated than expected. It involves the juxtaposition of the zygote and the surface cells of the uterus, initiating a kind of chemical communication which most people would probably call an antibody-antigen reaction. It is this reaction that releases a polypeptide vessel proliferation factor which results in the implantation. I've isolated this factor and have produced it in quantity with recombinant DNA techniques. A shot of it guarantees one hundred percent implantation of a healthy fertilized egg."

To emphasize his point, VJ pulled a vial out of his pocket and placed it on the table in front of his father. "It's for you," he said. "Who knows, maybe you'll win a Nobel Prize." VJ laughed and Philip joined in.

Victor picked up the vial and stared at the clear, viscous fluid within. "Something like this has to be tested," he said.

"It's been tested," VJ said. "Animals, humans, it's all the same. One hundred percent successful."

Victor looked at his son, then at Philip. Philip smiled hesitantly, unsure of Victor's reaction. Victor glanced at the vial again. He could immediately appreciate the academic and economic impact of such a discovery. It would be monumental, revolutionizing in-vitro fertilization techniques. With a product like this, Fertility, Inc., would dominate the field. It would have worldwide impact.

Victor took a deep breath. "Are you sure this works in humans?" he asked.

"Absolutely," VJ said. "As I said, it's been tested."

"In whom?" Victor asked.

"Volunteers, of course," VJ said. "But there will be plenty of time to give you the details later."

*Volunteers?* Victor's head reeled. Didn't VJ realize he couldn't blithely experiment with real people? There were laws to think of, ethics. But the possibilities were irresistible. And who was Victor to judge? Hadn't he engineered the conception of the extraordinary boy he had before him now?

"Let me look at your lab again," Victor said, pushing away from the table.

VJ ran ahead to open the door. Victor returned to the main room where the security men were still playing cards, talking loudly in Spanish.

Victor slowly walked around the circle, gazing at the instrumentation. Impressive was an understatement. He realized his headache seemed suddenly better. He felt a growing sense of elation. It was hard to believe that his ten-year-old son was responsible for all this.

"Who knows about this lab?" Victor asked, stopping to appreciate the electron microscope. He ran a hand over its curved surface.

"Philip and a handful of security people," said VJ. "And now you."

Victor shot VJ a quick glance. VJ smiled back.

All at once Victor laughed. "And to think this has been going on under our noses all this time!" Victor shook his head in disbelief, continuing around the circle of scientific appliances, tapping the tops of some of them with the tips of his fingers. "And are you sure about this implantation protein?" Victor asked, already considering likely trade names: Conceptol. Fertol.

"Completely," VJ said. "And that's just one of the

discoveries that I've made. There are many more. I've made some advances in understanding the process of cellular differentiation and development I believe will herald a new era of biology."

Victor stopped his wandering and turned back to VJ. "Does Marsha know anything about this?" he asked.

"Nothing!" VJ said with emphasis.

"She is going to be one happy lady," Victor said with a smile. "She's been worrying herself sick that something is wrong with you since you don't have time for kids your own age."

"I've been a little too busy for Cub Scouts," said VJ.

Victor laughed. "God, I'll say. She's going to love this. We'll have to tell her and bring her here."

"I'm not convinced that's such a good idea," VJ said.

"It is, believe me," Victor said. "It will relieve her enormously and I won't have to listen to another lecture on your psychological development."

"I don't want people knowing about this lab," VJ said. "It was an unexpected accident that you discovered it. I wasn't planning on telling you any of this until I'd moved the lab to the new location."

"Where is that?" Victor asked.

"Nearby," VJ said. "I'll show it to you on another day."

"But we have to tell Marsha," Victor insisted. "You have no idea how worried she's been about you. I'll take care of her. She won't tell anyone."

"It's a risk," VJ said. "I don't think she'll be as impressed as you by my accomplishments. She's not as enthusiastic about science as we are."

"She'll be ecstatic that you are such a genius. And

that you've put all this together. It's just extraordinary."

"Well, maybe . . ." VJ said, trying to decide.

"Trust me," Victor said enthusiastically.

"Perhaps on this one issue I'll have to bow to your better judgment," VJ said. "I guess you know her better than I do. All I can say is that I hope you're right. She could cause a lot of trouble."

"I'll get her right now," Victor said with obvious excitement.

"How will you get her over here to the building without people noticing?" VJ said.

"It's Saturday," Victor said. "Hardly anyone is around, especially so late in the day."

"Okay," VJ said with resignation.

Victor headed for the stairs, practically running. "I'll be back in thirty minutes. Forty-five, tops," he said. He charged up a half dozen steps, then came to a stop. As he noticed before, the stairs dead-ended into heavy planks.

"Is this the way out?" Victor asked.

"Just give it a shove," VJ said. "It's counterweighted."

Victor went up the rest of the stairs more slowly until his hand rested on the overhead planks. Tentatively, he pushed upward. To his surprise, a large trapdoor opened with amazing ease. Casting a last glance down at VJ, Victor winked, then climbed up the rest of the stairs. When he let go of the trapdoor, it sank silently into place, cutting off the light from below.

Victor ran from the building, his pulse up from sheer exhilaration. He hadn't felt so ecstatic in years.

\* \* \*

Having returned from her two upsetting visits, Marsha made herself a real cup of tea. She'd taken it into her study to try to calm down when she heard Victor's car start up the drive.

It wasn't long before his head popped through the door. He still had his coat on. "Ah, there you are, sweet thing!"

Sweet thing? Marsha thought disdainfully. He hasn't called me that for years. "Come in here!" she called to him.

But Victor was already on his way into the room. He grabbed her hand, trying to pull her from her couch. Marsha resisted and got her hand free. "What are you doing?" she questioned.

"I've got something to show you." There was a distinct twinkle in his eye.

"What's come over you?"

"Come on!" Victor urged, pulling her to her feet. "I've got a surprise for you that you are going to love."

"I've got a surprise for you that you are not going to love," Marsha said. "Sit down. I have something important to tell you."

"Later," Victor said. "What I've got is more important."

"I doubt that," Marsha said. "I've learned some more disturbing things about VJ."

"Isn't that appropriate?" Victor said with a smile. "Because what I've discovered is going to make you forget all VJ's traits you've been agonizing over."

Victor tried to drag Marsha from the room. "Victor!" she called out sharply. She pulled her arm free again. "You're acting like a child!"

"I'm immune to your worst epithet," Victor said

gaily. "Marsha, I'm not kidding—I have some great news for you."

Marsha put her hands on her hips and spread her legs for stability. "VJ has been lying to us about other things besides the school situation. I found out that he has never stayed at the Blakemore house. Never!"

"I'm not surprised," Victor said, thinking how much time VJ would need to spend in his lab to accomplish what he apparently had.

"You're not surprised?" Marsha said with exasperation, throwing her hands into the air. "Richie Blakemore and VJ are not even friends. In fact, they had a fight recently in which VJ broke the Blakemore boy's nose."

"Okay, okay!" Victor said, assuming a calm tone of voice. He gripped Marsha's upper arms and looked directly into her warm eyes. "Calm down and listen to me. What I have to show you will explain where VJ has been spending most of his time. Now will you just trust me and come?"

Marsha's eyes narrowed. At least he sounded sincere. "Where are you taking me?" she demanded suspiciously.

"Out to the car," Victor said enthusiastically. "Come on, get your coat."

"I hope you know what you're doing," Marsha said as she allowed herself to be led from her study. She got her coat and a few minutes later she was holding on to the dash to steady herself. "Do we have to drive this fast?" she asked.

"I can't wait for you to see this," Victor said. He banked sharply. "And to think I was proud of a secret tree house I built when I was twelve!"

Marsha wondered if he'd taken leave of his senses.

He'd been behaving so oddly lately, but she'd never seen him like this.

Victor thundered over the Merrimack River and eventually pulled into Chimera. The security shift had changed in the guardhouse. Fred wasn't the one manning the gate.

In deference to VJ's concern for secrecy, Victor parked in his usual spot in front of the administration building. "We have a little walk," he said to Marsha as they alighted from the car.

It was late afternoon as they approached the river. Long shadows had begun to creep across the alleyways. It was also quite cold. Marsha guessed it was in the thirties. Victor walked slightly ahead of her, glancing back over his shoulder as if he expected someone might be following them. Marsha glanced behind them out of curiosity, but no one was there. She pulled her coat around her more closely, and decided what was chilling her was more than the weather.

Victor took hold of her hand as her gait began to slow. She'd noticed they had moved from the occupied section of the complex to the part that was unrenovated. On either side of her were the dark hulks of abandoned buildings. They loomed ominously in the gathering dusk.

"Victor, where are you taking me?" she asked, threatening to stop.

"We're almost there," Victor said, urging her onward.

When they got to the gaping entranceway of the derelict clock tower building, Marsha stopped.

"You don't expect me to go in there?" she asked, incredulous. She leaned back and looked up at the soaring tower. Rapidly moving clouds made her momentarily dizzy. She had to look away.

"Please," Victor said. "VJ is here. You'll be wonderfully surprised. Trust me."

Marsha looked from Victor's excited face to the interior gloom of the building and back. Victor's eyes were bright with anticipation. "This is crazy," she said. Grudgingly, she moved forward. The gloom enveloped them.

Marsha let Victor lead as they stumbled over the rubble-strewn floor. "Just a little further," Victor said.

Marsha's eyes adjusted enough to see vague outlines on the floor. To her left were large window openings through which came the roar of the falls as well as reflected light from the surface of the millpond. Victor stopped in front of an empty corner. He let go of Marsha's hand and bent down. He knocked on the floor. To Marsha's surprise, a section of the floor lifted and incandescent light flooded up.

"Mother," VJ said. "Come in quickly."

Marsha gingerly climbed down the stairs. Victor followed and VJ let the trapdoor glide back into place.

Marsha looked around the room. To her, it looked like a scene out of a science fiction movie. The combination of the rusted gears, the huge paddle wheel, and the granite, along with the profusion of high-tech instrumentation, was disorienting. She nodded to Philip, who nodded back at her. She nodded to the Chimera security guards but they didn't return the gesture. She noticed the man with the droopy eyelid.

"Isn't it the most amazing thing you've ever seen?" Victor said as he came up alongside Marsha. She looked at him. He was beside himself with excitement.

"What is it?" Marsha questioned.

"It's VJ's lab." Victor said as he launched into a brief explanation of the setup, including how VJ had been able to build it without anyone having had the slightest suspicion. He even told Marsha about VJ's discovery of the implantation protein, and what that would mean to the infertility field.

"So now you have some idea why VJ hasn't been as social as you'd like," concluded Victor. "He's been here, working his butt off!" Victor chuckled as he let his own eyes roam around the room.

Marsha glanced at VJ, who was eyeing her cautiously, waiting for her reaction, no doubt. There was an enormous piece of equipment in front of her. She had no idea what it was. "Where did all this equipment come from?" she asked.

"That's the best part," Victor said. "It all belongs to Chimera."

"How did it get here?" Marsha asked.

"I guess . . ." Victor began, but then stopped. He looked at VJ. "How did you get this stuff here?"

"A number of people helped," VJ said vaguely. "Philip did most of the actual moving. Some of the things had to be disassembled, then put together again. We used the old tunnel system."

"Was Gephardt one of the people that helped?" Victor asked, suddenly suspicious.

"He helped," VJ admitted.

"Why was someone like Gephardt willing to help you get equipment?" Marsha asked.

"He decided it was the prudent thing to do," VJ said cryptically. "I'd spent some time with the Chimera computer, and I'd discovered a number of people who'd been embezzling the company. Once I had that information, I merely asked these people for help from their respective departments. Of course, no one knew that the others were involved, or what they were doing. So it all stayed nice and quiet. But the point is, all this equipment belongs to Chimera. Nothing has been stolen. It's all right here."

"I'd call it blackmail," Marsha said.

"I never once threatened anybody," VJ said. "I merely let them know what I knew, then asked for a favor."

"I'd say VJ was quite resourceful," Victor said. "But I'd like to have this list of embezzlers."

"Sorry," VJ said. "But I have an understanding with these people. Besides, the worst offender, Dr. Gephardt, was already exposed by the IRS. The ironic thing was that he thought that I'd been behind his exposure." VJ laughed.

Victor's face lit up with sudden comprehension. "I get it," he said. "Gephardt was directing the messages at you when he tossed the brick and killed poor Kissa."

VJ nodded. "The fool," he said.

"I want to get out of here!" Marsha said suddenly, surprising both Victor and VJ.

"But there's more to see," Victor said.

"I'm sure there is," Marsha said. "But for the moment I've seen enough. I want to leave." She looked from father to son, then glanced around the room. She felt distinctly uncomfortable. The place scared her.

"There are living quarters . . ." Victor said, pointing toward the west end of the room.

271

Marsha ignored his gesture. She walked back to the stairs and started up.

"I told you we shouldn't have told her," VJ whispered.

Victor put a hand on his shoulder and whispered back, "Don't worry, I'll take care of her." Then to Marsha he called, "Just a second, I'll come along."

Marsha went directly up to the trapdoor and pushed. Once out of the basement, she stumbled blindly across the wide expanse of rubble-filled floor space. When she reached the door and the fresh air, she felt a flood of relief.

"Marsha, for goodness sake," said Victor, catching up with her and turning her around. "Where are you going?"

"Home!" She walked on with determination. But Victor caught up to her again.

"Why are you acting this way?" Victor asked.

Marsha didn't answer. Instead she increased her pace. They were practically running. When they got to Victor's car, she opened her door and got in.

Victor got in on his side. "You won't talk to me?" he questioned with some irritation.

Setting her jaw, Marsha stared ahead. They drove home in strained silence.

Once they were home, Marsha poured herself a glass of white wine.

"Marsha," Victor began, breaking the veil of silence, "why are you acting like this? I thought you'd be as thrilled as I am, especially after all your worry about whether VJ's intelligence would drop again. Obviously the boy's just fine. He's as bright as ever."

"That's just the point," Marsha said sharply. "VJ's intelligence is fine, and it terrifies me. By the looks of that lab, he must still be in the genius range, wouldn't you say?"

"Clearly," said Victor. "Isn't that wonderful?"

"No," Marsha snapped. She put her wineglass on the table. "If he is still a genius, then the whole episode of his intelligence drop had to be a charade. He's been pretending all this time. He's been smart enough to outwit my psychological tests, except for that validity scale. Victor, his whole life with us is a sham. Just one big lie."

"Maybe there's another explanation," Victor said. "Maybe his intelligence dropped, then rebounded."

"I just did an IQ test this week," Marsha said. "He's tested around 130 since he was three and a half."

"Okay," Victor said with some irritation of his own. "The point is that VJ is okay and we don't have to worry about him. In fact, he is more than okay. He's put that lab together all by himself. His IQ has to be much higher than 130. And that means my NGF project is an unqualified success."

Marsha shook her head. She couldn't believe he could be so myopic. "What exactly do you think you have created with VJ and your mutations and gene manipulations?" she asked.

"I've created an essentially normal child with superior intelligence," Victor said without hesitation.

"What else?"

"What do you mean, what else?"

"What about this person's personality?" Marsha asked.

"This person?" Victor questioned. "You are talking about VJ, our son."

"What about his personality?" Marsha repeated.

"Oh, damn the personality," Victor snapped. "The

kid is a prodigy. He's already accomplished research breakthroughs. So what if he has a few hangups? We all do."

"You've created a monster," Marsha said softly, her voice breaking. She bit her lip. Why couldn't she control her tears? "You've created a monster and I'll never forgive you for it."

"Give me a break," Victor said, exasperated.

"VJ is an oddity," Marsha snapped. "His intelligence has set him apart, made him lonely. He apparently realized it when he was three. His intelligence is so far above everyone else's, he doesn't respond to the same social restraints. His intelligence has put him beyond everyone, everything."

"Are you finished?" Victor demanded.

"No, I'm not!" Marsha shouted, suddenly angry though tears streamed down her face. "What about the deaths of those children that had the same gene as VJ? Why did they die?"

"Why are you bringing that up again?"

"What about the deaths of David and Janice?" Marsha asked, lowering her voice, ignoring Victor's question. "I didn't have a chance to tell you before, but I visited the Fays today. They told me that Janice had been convinced that VJ had something to do with David's death. She told them he was evil."

"We heard that nonsense before her death," Victor said. "She became a religious psychotic. You said so yourself."

"Visiting her parents made me rethink what happened back then," Marsha said. "Janice had been convinced she'd been drugged and poisoned."

"Marsha," Victor said sharply. He grabbed her by her shoulders. "Get ahold of yourself. You're talking nonsense. David died of liver cancer, remember? Janice went a little crazy before she died. Remember that? She had some paranoia in addition to her other troubles. She probably had a brain metastasis, the poor woman. Besides, people don't get liver cancer because they're poisoned." But even as he said the words, doubts of his own sprang up. He recalled the troublesome bit of DNA that he'd found in both David's and Janice's tumor cells. "And about those children's deaths," Victor said as he sat down across from her. "I'm sure they had something to do with the internal politics of Chimera. Somebody has found out about the NGF experiment and wants to discredit me. That's why I want someone with VJ."

"When did you decide this?" Marsha asked, lowering her glass.

Victor shrugged. "I don't remember exactly," he said. "Sometime this week."

"That means even you think the deaths were really murders; that somebody deliberately killed those children," Marsha said with renewed alarm.

Victor had forgotten that he'd purposefully kept the information about the cephaloclor from her. He swallowed uncomfortably.

"Victor!" Marsha said with resentment. "What haven't you told me?"

Stalling, Victor took a sip from his drink. He tried to think of some smoke screen to cover the truth, but couldn't think of a thing. The day's revelations had made him careless. With a sigh he explained about the cephaloclor in the children's blood.

"My God!" Marsha whispered. "Are you sure it was someone at Chimera who gave the children the cephaloclor?"

"Absolutely," Victor said. "The only place the children's lives intersected was at the Chimera day-care center. That had to be where they were given the cephaloclor."

"But who would do such a terrible thing?" Marsha asked. She wanted to be reassured that VJ could not be involved.

"It had to be either Hurst or Ronald. If I had to pick one, I'd pick Hurst. But until I get harder evidence, all I can do is keep the security man with VJ to be sure no one tries to give him any cephaloclor."

Just then the back door burst open and VJ, Philip, and Pedro Gonzales came into the family room. Marsha stayed in her seat, but Victor jumped up. "Hello, everybody," Victor said, trying to sound cheerful. He started to introduce Pedro to Marsha but she interrupted him and said that they'd already met that morning.

"That's good," Victor said, rubbing his hands together. He obviously didn't know what to do.

Marsha looked at VJ. VJ stared back at her with his penetrating blue eyes. She had to avert her gaze. It was a terrifying feeling for her to harbor the thoughts she had about him, especially since she'd come to realize that she was afraid of him.

"Why don't you guys hit the pool?" Victor said to VJ and Philip.

"Sounds good to me," VJ said. He and Philip went up the back stairs.

"You'll be back in the morning?" Victor asked Pedro.

"Yes, sir," he said. "Six A.M., I'll be out in the courtyard in my car."

Victor saw the man off, then came back into the kitchen.

"I'll go have a talk with VJ," Victor announced. "I'll ask him directly about this intelligence question. Maybe whatever he says will make you feel better."

"I think I already know what he'll say," said Marsha, "but suit yourself."

Victor went up the stairs quickly and turned into VJ's room. VJ looked expectantly at his father as he entered. Victor realized how awed he felt by his own creation. The boy was beautiful and had a mind that must be boundless. Victor didn't know whether to be jealous or proud.

"Mother isn't as excited about the lab as you are," VJ said. "I can tell."

"It was a little overwhelming for her," Victor explained.

"I wish I hadn't agreed to let her see it," VJ said.

"Don't worry," Victor assured him. "I'll take care of her. But there is something that has been bothering her for years. Did you fake your loss of intelligence back when you were three and a half?"

"Of course," VJ said, slipping on his robe over his hairless body. "I had to. If I hadn't, I'd never have been able to work as I have. I needed anonymity which I couldn't have had as some superintelligent freak. I wanted to be treated normally, and for that to happen, I had to appear normal. Or close to it."

"You didn't think you could have talked to me about it?" Victor asked.

"Are you kidding?" VJ said. "You and Mom constantly had me on show. There was no way you would have been willing to let me quit."

"You're probably right," Victor admitted. "For a while there your abilities were the focus of our lives."

"Are you going to swim with us?" VJ asked with a smile. "I'll let you win."

Victor laughed in spite of himself. "Thanks, but I'd better go back and talk with Marsha. Get her to calm down. You have fun." Victor went to the door, but turned back toward the room. "Tomorrow I'd like to hear the details about the implantation project."

"I'll be excited to show you," VJ said.

Victor nodded, smiled, then went back downstairs. As he neared the kitchen he could smell garlic, onions, and peppers sauteeing for spaghetti sauce. A good sign, Marsha working on dinner.

Marsha had thrown herself into preparing the meal as a form of instant therapy. Her mind was such a jumble from the day's numerous revelations. Busy-work was a way of avoiding thinking about the implications. When Victor returned from talking to VJ, she studiously ignored him, instead focusing her attention on the tomato paste she was in the process of opening.

Victor didn't say anything for a time. Instead, he laid the table and opened a bottle of Chianti. When he ran out of things to do, he sat on one of the bar stools at the kitchen counter and said, "You were right about VJ feigning his loss of intelligence."

"I'm not surprised," Marsha said. She got out the lettuce, onions, and cucumbers for the salad.

"But he had a damn good reason." He gave her VJ's to-the-point explanation.

"I guess that's supposed to make me feel more comfortable," Marsha said when Victor was done.

Victor said nothing.

Marsha persisted. "Tell me, when you were upstairs

talking with VJ, did you ask him about the deaths of those children, and about David's and Janice's?"

"Of course not!" Victor said, horrified at the suggestion. "Why should I do that?"

"Why shouldn't you?"

"Because it's preposterous."

"I think you haven't asked VJ anything about them because you're afraid to," Marsha said.

"Oh, come on," Victor snapped. "You're talking nonsense again."

"I'm afraid to ask him," Marsha said flatly. But she could feel the tug in her throat.

"You're letting your imagination run wild. Now I know it's been an upsetting day for you. I'm sorry. I really thought you'd be thrilled. But someday I think you're going to look back on this day and laugh at yourself. If this implantation work is anything like he says it is, the sky's the limit for VJ's career."

"I hope so," Marsha said without conviction.

"But you have to promise that you won't tell anyone about VJ's lab," Victor said.

"Who would I tell?"

"Let me handle VJ for the time being," Victor said. "I'm sure we are going to be very proud of him."

Marsha shuddered involuntarily as a chill passed down her spine. "Is it cold in here?" she asked.

Victor checked the thermostat. "Nope. If anything, it's too warm."

# 12

## *Sunday Morning*

At four-thirty in the morning Marsha woke up with a start. She had no idea what had awakened her, and for a few minutes she breathed shallowly, and listened to the nighttime noises of the house. She heard nothing out of the ordinary. She rolled over and tried to go back to sleep but it was impossible. In her mind's eye, she kept seeing VJ's eerie lab with its juxtaposition of the old and the very new. Then she'd see the strange appearance of the man with the lidded eye.

Swinging her feet from beneath the covers, Marsha sat on the edge of the bed. So as not to bother Victor, she stood up, wiggled into her slippers, and pulled on her robe. As quietly as possible she eased open the door to the bedroom and equally as quietly, pulled it shut.

She stood in the hall for a moment, thinking about where she should go. As if pulled by some unseen force, she found herself walking the length of the hall, heading toward VJ's room. When she got there, she noticed the door was slightly ajar.

Marsha quietly pushed the door open wider. A gentle light was coming through the window from the post lamps lining the driveway. To her relief, VJ was fast asleep. He was lying on his side facing her. Sleeping, he looked like an angel of a boy. Could her darling baby really have had a hand in the dark events at Chimera? She couldn't bring herself to think of Janice and David, her beloved first son. But with horror, a vision of David in his last days, his skin yellowed from the disease, flashed upon her.

Marsha stifled a cry. All of a sudden her mind conjured up a horrid image of her taking a pillow and pushing it down on VJ's peaceful face, smothering him. Horrified, she recoiled from the thought and shook herself. Then she fled silently down the hall, running from herself.

Marsha stopped at the guest room door, which had temporarily become Philip's room. Pushing the door open, she could make out Philip's massive head silhouetted against the stark white of the bed linens. After a moment's thought, Marsha slipped into the room and stood next to the bed. The man was snoring deeply, his breath softly whistling on exhale. Bending down, Marsha gave his shoulder a gentle nudge. "Philip," she called softly. "Philip!"

Philip's closely set eyes blinked open. Abruptly, he sat up. A look of momentary fear flashed across his face before he recognized Marsha. Then he smiled, revealing his square, widely spaced teeth.

"Sorry to awaken you," she whispered. "But I need to talk to you for a moment."

"Okay," Philip said groggily. He leaned back on an elbow.

Marsha pulled a chair over to the bed, turned on the

light on the nightstand, and sat down. "I wanted to thank you for being such a good friend to VJ," she said.

Philip's face broke out in a wide smile as he squinted in the light. He nodded.

"You must have been a great help in setting up the lab," Marsha said.

Philip nodded again.

"Who else helped with the lab?"

Philip's smile waned. He looked around the room nervously. "I'm not supposed to say."

"I'm VJ's mother," Marsha reminded him. "It's all right to tell me."

Philip shifted his weight uneasily.

Marsha waited but Philip didn't say anything.

"Did Mr. Gephardt help?" Marsha asked.

Philip nodded.

"But then Mr. Gephardt got into trouble. Did he get angry at VJ?"

"Oh, yeah!" Philip said. "He got angry and then VJ got angry. But VJ talked with Mr. Martinez."

"What's Mr. Martinez's first name?"

"Orlando," Philip said.

"Does Mr. Martinez work at Chimera, too?"

Philip's agitation began to return. "No," he said. "He works in Mattapan."

"The town of Mattapan?" Marsha asked. "South of Boston?"

Philip nodded.

Marsha started to ask another question but she suddenly felt a presence that sent a shiver up her spine. She turned to the door. VJ was standing in the doorway with his hands on the jambs, his chin jutting forward.

"I think Philip needs his sleep," he said.

Marsha stood up abruptly. She started to say something but the words wouldn't come out. Instead she hurriedly brushed by VJ and ran down to her room.

For the next half hour, Marsha lay there, terrified that VJ would come into their bedroom. She jumped every time the wind blew the oak tree branches against the side of the house.

When he didn't appear, Marsha finally relaxed. She turned over and tried to sleep, but her mind would not stop. Her thoughts drifted to the mysterious Orlando Martinez. Then she began to think about Janice Fay. She thought about David, feeling the familiar sadness. She thought about Mr. Remington and the Pendleton Academy. Then she recalled the teacher who tried to befriend VJ and the fact that he died. She wondered what he'd died of.

The next thing she knew, Victor was waking her to tell her he was leaving with VJ.

"What time is it?" Marsha asked, looking at the clock herself. To her surprise, it was nine-thirty.

"You were sleeping so soundly I didn't have the heart to wake you," Victor said. "VJ and I are off to his lab. He's going to show me the details of the implantation work he's done. Why don't you come along? I have a feeling this is really going to be something."

Marsha shook her head. "I'll stay here," she said. "You can tell me about it."

"You sure?" Victor questioned. "If this is as good as I think it will be, maybe you'll feel better about the whole situation."

"I'm sure," Marsha said, but her tone was doubtful.

Victor planted a kiss on her forehead. "Try to relax,

okay? Everything is going to work out for the best. I'm sure of it."

Victor went down the back stairs, literally shivering with excitement. If the implantation was real, he could surprise the other board members with the news at the Wednesday board meeting.

"Mom's not coming?" VJ asked. He was near the back door with his coat already on. Philip was standing next to him.

"No, but she's calmer this morning," Victor said. "I can tell."

"She was pumping Philip for information in the middle of the night," VJ said. "That's the kind of behavior that disturbs me."

After the car pulled out of the drive, Marsha went to the upstairs study and got out the Boston phone book. She sat on the couch and looked up Martinez. Unfortunately, there were hordes of Martinezes, even Orlando Martinezes. But she found one Orlando Martinez in Mattapan. Taking the phone in her lap, she called the number. The phone was answered, and Marsha was about to start talking when she realized she was connected to an answering machine.

The message on the machine told her that the office of Martinez Enterprises was open Monday through Friday. She didn't leave a message. From the phone book she copied down the address.

Marsha took a shower, dressed, made herself some coffee and a poached egg. Then she donned her down coat and went out to her car. Fifteen minutes later, she was on the grounds of Pendleton Academy.

It was a blustery but sunny day with the wind

roughing the surface of the puddles left by the previous day's rain. Many of the students were in evidence,
most of them going to and from the obligatory attendance at chapel. Marsha pulled up as close as she could
to the tiny Gothic structure and waited. She was looking for Mr. Remington and was hoping to catch him
out and about.

Soon the bells in the bell tower tolled the eleven
o'clock hour. The doors to the chapel opened and rosy-
cheeked kids spilled out into the fresh air and sunshine. Among them were a number of adult staff members, including Mr. Remington. His heavily bearded
profile stood out among the crowds.

Marsha got out of the car and waited. Mr. Remington's path would take him right by her. He was walking with a deliberate step. When he got about ten feet
away, Marsha called his name. He stopped and looked
at her.

"Dr. Frank!" he said with some surprise.

"Good morning," Marsha said. "I hope I'm not in-
truding."

"Not at all," Remington said. "Something on your
mind?"

"There is," Marsha said. "I wanted to ask you a question which might sound a little strange. I hope you
will indulge me. You told me that the instructor who
tried so hard to befriend VJ died. What did he die of?"

"The poor man died of cancer," Mr. Remington
said.

"I was afraid of that," Marsha said.

"Excuse me?"

But Marsha didn't explain herself. "Do you know
what kind of cancer?" she asked.

285

"I'm afraid I don't, but I believe I mentioned that his wife is still on staff here. Her name is Stephanie. Stephanie Cavendish."

"Do you think I might speak with her today?" Marsha asked.

"I don't see why not," Mr. Remington said. "She lives in the cottage on the grounds of my headmaster's house. We both share the same lawn. I was on my way home and the cottage is just a stone's throw away. I'd be happy to introduce you to her."

Marsha fell in step with Mr. Remington and they walked the length of the quad. While they were walking, Marsha asked, "Was any staff member close to my late son, David?"

"Most of the instructors were fond of David," Mr. Remington said. "He was a popular boy. If I had to pick one, I'd say Joe Arnold. He's a very popular history teacher who I believe was close to your David."

The cottage Mr. Remington had spoken of looked like some cottage out of the Cotswold section of England. With whitewashed walls and a roof that was made to look thatched, it appeared as if it belonged in a fairy tale. Mr. Remington rang the bell himself. He introduced Marsha to Mrs. Cavendish, a slim, attractive woman Marsha guessed was about her own age. Marsha learned that she was the head of the school's physical education department.

Mr. Remington excused himself after Mrs. Cavendish invited Marsha inside.

Mrs. Cavendish led Marsha into her kitchen and offered her a cup of tea. "Please, call me Stephanie," she said as they sat down. "So you're VJ's mother! My husband was a big fan of your boy. He was convinced

VJ was extraordinarily bright. He really raved about him."

"That's what Mr. Remington said," Marsha said.

"He loved to relate the story of VJ solving an algebra problem to everyone who'd listen."

Marsha nodded and said that Mr. Remington had told the story to her.

"But Raymond thought your son was troubled," Stephanie said. That's why he tried so hard to get VJ to be less withdrawn. Ray really did try. He thought that VJ was alone too much and was afraid VJ might be suicidal. He worried about the boy—oh, never academically. But socially, I think."

Marsha nodded.

"How is he these days?" Stephanie asked. "I don't have much occasion to see him."

"I'm afraid he still doesn't have many friends. He's not very outgoing."

"I'm sorry to hear that," said Stephanie.

Marsha gathered her courage. "I hope you don't think me too forward, but I'd like to ask a personal question. Mr. Remington told me your late husband died of cancer. Would you mind if I asked what kind of cancer?"

"I don't mind," said Stephanie. There was a sudden tightening in her throat. "It was a while before I could talk about it," she allowed. "Ray died of a form of liver cancer. It was very rare. He was treated at Mass. General in Boston. The doctors there had only seen a couple of similar cases."

Although Marsha had expected as much, she still felt as though she'd been hit. This was exactly what she was afraid of hearing.

As tactfully as she could, Marsha ended the conversation, but not before enlisting Mrs. Cavendish's aid in getting an invitation over to Joe Arnold's house.

He wasn't the sort of stuffy history professor-type Marsha had expected. His warm brown eyes lit up when he opened the door to greet her. Like Stephanie Cavendish, he seemed about her own age. Between his swarthy good looks, empathic eyes, and somewhat disheveled clothing, Marsha could see he had a beguiling demeanor. He was no doubt an excellent teacher; he had the kind of enthusiasm students would find infectious. No wonder David had gravitated toward this man.

"It's a pleasure to meet you, Mrs. Frank. Come in, please come in." He held the door for her and led her into the book-lined study. She looked around the room admiringly. "David used to spend lots of afternoons right here."

Marsha felt unbidden tears threaten to appear. It saddened her a little to think how much of David's life she didn't know. She quickly composed herself.

After thanking Joe for seeing her on such short notice, Marsha got to the point of why she was interested in seeing him. She asked Joe if David had ever discussed his brother VJ.

"On a few occasions," Joe said. "David admitted to me that he'd had trouble with VJ from the first day that VJ had arrived home from the hospital. That's normal enough, but to tell you the truth, I got the feeling it went beyond the usual sibling rivalry. I tried to get him to talk about it, but David would never elaborate. We had a strong relationship, I think, but on this one subject he wouldn't open up."

"He never got more specific about his feelings or what the trouble was?"

"Well, David once told me that he was afraid of VJ."

"Did he say why?"

"I was under the impression that VJ threatened him," Joe said. "That was as much as he'd say. I know brothers' relationships can be tricky, especially at that age. But quite frankly, I had a funny feeling about David's trouble with VJ. David seemed genuinely spooked—almost too afraid to talk about it. In the end, I insisted he see the school psychologist."

"Did he?" Marsha questioned. She'd never heard about that, and it added to her guilt.

"You bet he did," Joe told her. "I wasn't about to let this thing drop. David was very special . . ." For a moment, Joe choked up. "Whew, sorry," he apologized after a pause. But Marsha was touched by such an obvious display of feeling. She nodded, moved herself.

"Is the psychologist still on staff?" Marsha asked.

"Madeline Zinnzer?" Joe asked. "Absolutely. She's an institution around here. She's been here longer than anybody else."

Marsha made use of Joe Arnold's hospitality to get herself invited over to Madeline Zinnzer's home. Marsha couldn't thank him enough.

"Anytime," said Joe, giving her hand an extra squeeze. "Really, anytime."

Madeline Zinnzer looked like an institution. She was a large woman, well over two hundred pounds. Her gray hair had been permed into tight curls. She took Marsha into a comfortable, spacious living room with a picture window looking out over the Pendleton Academy quad.

"One of the benefits of being on the staff so long," Madeline said, following Marsha's line of sight. "I finally got to move into the best of the faculty housing."

"I hope you don't mind my stopping by on a Sunday," Marsha began.

"Not at all," Madeline insisted.

"I have some questions about my children that maybe you can help me with."

"That's what Joe Arnold mentioned," Madeline said. "I'm afraid I don't have the memory he does of your boy, David. But I do have a file which I went over after Joe called. What's on your mind?"

"David told Joe that his younger brother, VJ, had threatened him, but he wouldn't tell Joe much more than that. Were you able to learn anything more?"

Madeline made a tent with her fingers and leaned back in her chair. Then she cleared her throat. "I saw David on a number of occasions," she began. "After talking with him at length, it was my opinion that David was using the defense mechanism of projection. It was my feeling that David projected his own feelings of competition and hostility onto VJ."

"Then the threat wasn't specific?" Marsha asked.

"I didn't say that," Madeline said. "Apparently there had been a specific threat."

"What was it about?"

"Boy stuff," Madeline said. "Something about a hiding place that VJ had that David found out about. Something innocuous like that."

"Could it have been a lab rather than a hiding place?" Marsha asked.

"Could have been," Madeline said. "David could have said lab, but I wrote hiding place in the file."

"Did you ever talk with VJ?" Marsha asked.

"Once," Madeline said. "I thought it would be helpful to get a feeling for the reality about the relationship. VJ was extremely straightforward. He told me that his brother David had been jealous of him from the day VJ had arrived home from the hospital." Then Madeline laughed. "VJ told me that he could remember arriving home after he was born. That tickled me at the time."

"Did David ever say what the threat was?" Marsha asked.

"Oh, yes," Madeline said. "David told me that VJ had threatened to kill him."

From the Pendleton Academy Marsha drove to Boston. Much as she resisted putting the pieces together, she felt utterly compelled to assemble them. She kept telling herself that everything she was learning was either circumstantial, coincidental, or innocuous. She had already lost one child. But even so, she knew she couldn't rest until she found the truth.

Marsha had taken her psychiatric residency at the Massachusetts General Hospital. Visiting there was like going home. But she didn't go to the psych unit. Instead, she went directly to Pathology and found a senior resident, Dr. Preston Gordon.

"Sure I can do that," Preston said. "Since you don't know the birthday, it will take a little searching, but nothing else is happening right now."

Marsha followed Preston into the center of the pathology department where they sat at one of the hospital computers. There were several Raymond Cavendishes listed in the system, but by knowing the approximate year of death, they were able to find the Raymond Cavendish of Boxford, Massachusetts.

"All right," Preston said. "Here comes the record." The screen filled with the man's hospital record. Preston scrolled through. "Here's the biopsy," he said. "And here's the diagnosis: liver cancer of Kupffer cell of reticuloendothelial origin." Preston whistled. "Now that's a zebra. I've never even heard of that one."

"Can you tell me if there have been any similar cases treated at the hospital?" Marsha asked.

Preston returned to the keyboard and began a search. It took him only a few minutes to get the answer. A name flashed on the screen. "There has only been one other case at this hospital," he said. "The name was Janice Fay."

Victor tuned his car radio to a station that played oldies but goodies and sang along happily to a group of songs from the late fifties, a time when he'd been in high school. He was in a great mood on his drive home, having spent the day totally engrossed and spellbound by VJ's prodigious output from his hidden basement laboratory. It had turned out to be exactly as VJ had said it would be: beyond his wildest dreams.

As Victor turned into the driveway, the songs had changed to the late sixties, and he belted out "Sweet Caroline" along with Neil Diamond. He drove the car around the house and waited for the garage door to open. After he pulled the car into the garage, he sang until the song was over before turning off the ignition, getting out and skirting Marsha's car, heading into the house.

"Marsha!" Victor yelled as soon as he got inside. He

knew she was home because her car was there, but the lights weren't on.

"Marsha!" he yelled again, but her name caught in his throat. She was sitting no more than ten feet from him in the relative darkness of the family room. "There you are," he said.

"Where's VJ?" she asked. She sounded tired.

"He insisted on going off on his bicycle," Victor said. "But have no fear. Pedro's with him."

"I'm not worried about VJ at this point," Marsha said. "Maybe we should worry about the security man."

Victor turned on a light. Marsha shielded her eyes. "Please," she said. "Keep it off for now."

Victor obliged. He'd hoped she'd be in a better mood by the time he got home, but it wasn't looking good. Undaunted, Victor sat down and launched into lavish praise of VJ's work and his astounding accomplishments. He told Marsha that the implantation protein really worked. The evidence was incontrovertible. Then he told her the *pièce de résistance:* solving the implantation problem unlocked the door to the mystery of the entire differentiation process.

"If VJ wasn't so intent on secrecy," Victor said, "he could be in contention for a Nobel Prize. I'm convinced of it. As it is, he wants me to take all the credit and Chimera to get all the economic benefit. What do you think? Does that sound like a personality disorder to you? To me it sounds pretty generous."

Without any response from Marsha, Victor ran out of things to say. After he was quiet for a moment, she said, "I hate to ruin your day, but I'm afraid I have learned more disturbing things about VJ."

Victor rolled his eyes as he ran his fingers through

his hair. This was not the response he was hoping for.

"The one teacher at the Pendleton Academy who made a big effort to get close to VJ died a few years ago."

"I'm sorry to hear that."

"He died of cancer."

"Okay, he died of cancer," Victor said. He could feel his pulse quicken.

"Liver cancer."

"Oh," Victor said. He did not like the drift of this conversation.

"It was the same rare type that both David and Janice died of," Marsha said.

A heavy silence settled over the family room. The refrigerator compressor started. Victor did not want to hear these things. He wanted to talk about the implantation technology and what it would do for all those infertile couples when the zygotes refused to implant.

"For an extremely rare cancer, a lot of people seem to be contracting it. People who cross VJ. I had a talk with Mr. Cavendish's wife. His widow. She's a very kind woman. She teaches at Pendleton too. And I spoke to a Mr. Arnold. It turns out he was close to David. Do you know that VJ threatened David?"

"For God's sakes, Marsha! Kids always threaten each other. I did it myself when my older brother wrecked a snow house I'd built."

"VJ threatened to kill David, Victor. And not in the heat of an argument." Marsha was near tears. "Wake up, Victor!"

"I don't want to talk about it anymore," Victor said angrily, "at least not now." He was still high from the day's tour of VJ's lab. Was there a darker side to his son's genius? At times in the past, he'd had his suspicions, but they were all too easy to dismiss. VJ seemed such a perfect child. But now Marsha was expressing the same kind of doubts and backing them up so that they made a kind of evil sense. Could the little boy who gave him a tour of the lab, the genius behind the new implantation process, also be behind unspeakable acts? The murder of those children, of Janice Fay, of his own son David? Victor couldn't consider the horror of it all. He banished such thoughts. It was impossible. Someone at the lab killed the kids. The other deaths had to have been coincidental. Marsha was really pushing this too far. But then, she'd been on the hysterical side ever since the Hobbs and Murray kids had died. But if her fears were in any way justified, what would he do? How could he blithely support VJ in his many scientific endeavors? And if it was true, if VJ was half prodigy, half monster, what did it say of him, his creator?

Marsha might have insisted more, but just then VJ arrived home. He came in just as he had a week ago Sunday night, with his saddlebags over his shoulder. It was as though he'd known what they'd been talking about. VJ glared at Marsha, his blue eyes more chilling than ever. Marsha shuddered. She could not return his stare. Her fear of him was escalating.

Victor paced his study, absently chewing on the end of a pen. The door was closed and the house was quiet. As far as he knew, everybody was long since tucked into bed. It had been a strained evening with Marsha closeting herself in the bedroom after Victor had refused to discuss VJ anymore.

Victor had planned to spend the night working on his presentation of the new implantation method for Wednesday's board meeting. But he just couldn't concentrate. Marsha's words nagged him. Try as he would, he couldn't put them out of his mind. So what if VJ threatened David? Boys would be boys.

But the idea of yet another case of the rare liver cancer ate at him, especially in light of the fact that both David's and Janice's tumors had that extra bit of DNA in them. That had yet to be explained. Victor had purposefully kept the discovery from Marsha. It was bad enough he had to think of it. If he couldn't spare her the pain of what might be the awful truth of the matter, at least he'd spare her each small revelation that pointed to it.

And then there was Marsha's question of what else VJ was doing behind his lab's closed doors. The boy was so resourceful, and he had all the equipment to do almost anything in experimental biology. Aside from the implantation method, just what was he up to? Even during the tour, extensive though it was, Victor couldn't help but feel VJ wasn't letting him in on everything.

"Maybe I ought to take a look," Victor said aloud as he tossed the pen onto his desk. It was quarter to two in the morning, but who cared!

Victor scribbled a short note in case Marsha or VJ came down to look for him. Then he got his coat and a flashlight, backed his car out of the garage, and lowered the door with his remote. When he got to the end of the driveway, he stopped and looked back at the house. No lights came on; no one had gotten up.

At Chimera, the security guard working the gate came out of the office and shined a light into Victor's face. "Excuse me, Dr. Frank," he said as he ran back inside to lift the gate.

Victor commended him for his diligence, then drove down to the building that housed his lab. He parked his car directly in front of it. When he was sure that he was not being observed, he jogged toward the river. He was tempted to use his flashlight, but he was afraid to do so. He didn't want others to know of the existence of VJ's lab.

As he approached the river, the roar of the falls seemed even more deafening at night. Gusts of wind whipped about the alleyways, kicking up dust and debris, forcing Victor to lower his head. At last he reached the entrance to the clock tower building.

Victor hesitated at the entranceway. He was not the type to be spooked, but the place was so desolate and dark that he felt a little bit afraid. Again, he would have liked to use the flashlight, but again it would have been a giveaway if anybody happened to see the glow.

Victor felt his way in the dark, tapping his foot ahead gingerly before taking a step. He was deep into the first floor level, close to the trapdoor, when he felt the flutter of wings right at his face. He cried out in surprise, then realized he'd only disturbed a bevy of pigeons that had made the deserted clock tower building their roost.

Victor took a deep breath and moved on. With relief, he reached the trapdoor, only to realize he didn't know how to raise it. He tried in various locations to get a grip on the floorboards with his fingernails, but he couldn't get it to lift.

In frustration, Victor turned on the flashlight to survey the area. He had no choice. On the floor among the other trash was a short metal rod. He picked it up and returned to the trapdoor. Without much trouble, he was able to pry it open about an inch. As soon as he did, it rose effortlessly.

Victor quickly eased himself down the stairs far enough to allow the trapdoor to close above him. It was dark in the lab save for the beam of his flashlight. Victor searched for the panel that would turn on the lights. He found it under the stairs and flipped the switches. As the room filled with fluorescent light, Victor breathed a sigh of relief.

He decided to examine a lab area VJ hadn't shown him, a room he'd been fairly dismissive of even when Victor questioned him.

But he never made it to the door. He was about fifteen feet away when the door to the living quarters burst open and an attack dog came snarling at him. Victor leaped back, throwing his arms up to guard his face. He closed his eyes and braced for the contact.

But there wasn't any. Victor opened his eyes cautiously. The vicious dog had been brought up short by a chain held by a Chimera security guard.

"Thank God!" Victor cried. "Am I glad to see you!"

"Who are you?" the man demanded, his heavy accent clearly Spanish.

"Victor Frank," Frank said. "I'm one of the officers of Chimera. I'm surprised you don't recognize me. I'm also VJ's father."

"Okay," the guard said. The dog growled.

"And your name?" Victor asked.

"Ramirez," the guard said.

"I've never met you," Victor said. "But I'm glad you were on the other end of that chain." Victor started for the door. Ramirez grabbed his arm to restrain him.

Surprised by this, Victor stared at the man's hand wrapped around his arm. Then he looked him in the eye and said, "I just told you who I am. Would you please let go of me?" Victor tried to sound stern, but he already felt Ramirez had the best of the situation.

The dog growled. His bared teeth were inches away from Victor.

"I'm sorry," said Ramirez, not sounding sorry at all. "No one is allowed through that door unless VJ specifically says it is okay."

Victor examined Ramirez's expression. There was no doubt the man meant what he said. Victor wondered what to do in this ridiculous situation. "Maybe we should call your supervisor, Mr. Ramirez," Victor said evenly.

"This is the graveyard shift," Ramirez said. "I'm the supervisor."

They stared at each other for another minute. Victor was convinced of the man's intransigence and of the dog's power of persuasion. "Okay!" he said. Ramirez relaxed his grip and pulled the dog away.

"In that case I'll be leaving," Victor said, keeping an eye on the dog. Victor decided that he would see to Ramirez in the morning. He'd take the matter up with VJ.

Victor left the way he'd come in. Stopping at the gate to exit, he called the guard over to his car. "How long has a Ramirez been on the guard staff?" he asked.

"Ramirez?" the guard questioned. "There isn't any Ramirez on the force."

# 13

The atmosphere at breakfast was anything but normal. Marsha had promised herself as she took her morning shower that she would act as if everything was fine, but she found it impossible. When VJ appeared for breakfast about fifteen minutes behind schedule, she told him he'd better hurry since it was a school day. She knew she was baiting him, but she couldn't help herself.

"Now that the secret is out," VJ said, "I think it is rather ridiculous for me to go to school and pretend to be interested and absorbed in fifth-grade work."

"But I thought it was important to maintain your anonymity," Marsha persisted.

VJ glanced toward his father for support, but Victor calmly drank his coffee. He was staying out of it.

"At this point, going to school or not going to school will in no way affect my anonymity," VJ said coldly.

"The law says you must go to school," said Marsha.

"There are higher laws," VJ retorted.

Marsha wasn't going to make a stand alone. "Whatever you and Victor decide is fine with me," she told them. She left for work before learning Victor's decision.

"She is going to be trouble," VJ warned once she was gone.

"She needs a little more time," Victor said. "But you might have to come to some compromise on the school issue."

"I don't see why. It's not going to help my work. If anything, it will slow things down. Aren't results more important?"

"They're important," said Victor, "but they're not everything. Now, how do you want to get to Chimera today? You want to ride with me?"

"Nope," said VJ. "I want to take my bike. Is it all right for Philip to use yours?"

"Sure," Victor said. "I'll see you in your lab about midmorning. I'll need the details on the implantation protein for the legal department to start the patent application. I also want to see the rest of your lab as well as the new lab." Victor didn't mention the episode with Ramirez earlier that morning.

"Fine," VJ said. "Just be careful about coming. I don't want any other visitors."

Fifteen minutes later, VJ was plunging down Stanhope Street with the wind whistling past his head. Philip was right behind him on Victor's bike, and behind Philip was Pedro in his Ford Taurus.

VJ told Philip and Pedro to wait for him outside when he went into the bank with his saddlebags. Luckily Mr. Scott was occupied with another customer, and VJ was able to use his safe deposit box for another large deposit without getting a lecture.

Victor's ride to work was not as carefree. Although

he tried to think of other things, his mind was haunted by Marsha's words: "For an extremely rare cancer, a lot of people seem to be contracting it. People who cross VJ." Victor was wondering just how he'd feel if Marsha contracted it. Just how was VJ prepared to handle trouble?

Despite his apprehensions, Victor was fueled by enthusiasm for the new implantation protein project. He tackled the laborious administrative details that had accumulated by Monday morning with a good deal more equanimity than usual. He welcomed the busy-work; it kept his mind from wandering. Colleen came in with her usual stack of messages and situations needing attention. Victor had her go through them rapidly before making any decisions, half hoping for some kind of communication that would suggest blackmail about the NGF project, but there was nothing.

The most satisfying decision involved the question of whether Victor wanted to press charges against Sharon Carver. He told Colleen to let the parties know that he was willing to drop charges if the groundless sex-discrimination suit was also dropped.

The final item that Victor requested Colleen to do was to schedule a meeting with Ronald so that he could confront the man about the problems associated with the NGF work. If that didn't turn up anything, which he didn't expect it would, he would schedule a meeting with Hurst. Hurst had to be the culprit; in fact, Victor prayed as much. More than anything else he wanted to uncover some hard evidence that he could lay in front of Marsha and say: "VJ had nothing to do with this."

\* \* \*

Marsha found work intolerable. As much as she tried, she couldn't maintain the degree of attention that was required for her therapy sessions. With no explanation, she suddenly told Jean to cancel the rest of the day's appointments. Jean agreed but was clearly not pleased.

As soon as Marsha finished with the patients already there, she slipped out the back entrance and went down to her car. She took 495 to 93 and turned toward Boston. But she didn't stop in Boston. She continued on the South East Expressway to Neponset, then on to Mattapan.

With the address slip unfolded on the seat next to her, Marsha searched for Martinez Enterprises. The neighborhood was not good. The buildings were mostly decaying wood-frame three-deckers with occasional burnt-out hulks.

The address for Martinez Enterprises turned out to be an old warehouse with no windows. Undaunted, Marsha pulled over to the curb and got out of her car. There was no bell of any kind. Marsha knocked, timidly at first, but when there was no response, she pounded harder. Still there was no response.

Marsha stepped back, eyeing the building's door, then the façade. She jumped when she realized that at the left-hand corner of the building a man in a dark suit and white tie was watching her. He was leaning against the building with a slightly amused expression. A cigarette was tucked between his first and second fingers. When he noticed that Marsha had spotted him, he spoke to her in Spanish.

"I don't speak Spanish," Marsha said.

"What do you want?" the man asked with a heavy accent.

"I want to talk with Orlando Martinez."

At first the man didn't respond. He smoked his cigarette, then tossed it into the gutter. "Come with me," he said and disappeared from sight.

Marsha walked to the edge of the building and glanced down a litter-filled alleyway. She hesitated while her better judgment told her to go back and get into her car, but she wanted to see this through. She followed the man. Halfway down the alley was another door. This one was ajar.

The inside of the building looked the same as the outside. The major difference was the interior had a damp, moldy smell. The walls were unpainted concrete. Bare light bulbs were held in ceramic ceiling fixtures. Near the back of the cavernous room was a desk surrounded by a group of mismatched, threadbare couches. There were about ten men in the room, all in various states of repose, all dressed in dark suits like the man who had brought Marsha inside. The only man dressed differently was the man at the desk. He had on a lacy white shirt that was worn outside his pants.

"What do you want?" asked the man at the desk. He also had a Spanish accent, but not nearly as heavy as the others'.

"I'm looking for Orlando Martinez," Marsha said. She walked directly up to the desk.

"What for?" the man asked.

"I'm concerned about my child," Marsha said. "His name is VJ, and I'd been told that he has some association with Orlando Martinez of Mattapan."

Marsha became aware of a stir of conversation among the men on the couches. She shot a look at them, then back to the man at the desk.

"Are you Orlando Martinez?" Marsha asked.

"I could be," the man said.

Marsha looked more closely at the man. He was in his forties, with dark skin, dark eyes, and almost black hair. He was festooned with all manner of gold jewelry and wore diamond cuff links. "I wanted to ask you what business you have with my son."

"Lady, I think I should give you some advice. If I were you, I'd go home and enjoy life. Don't interfere in what you don't understand. It will cause trouble for everyone." Then he raised his hand and pointed at one of the other men. "José, show this lady out before she gets herself hurt."

José came forward and gently pulled Marsha toward the door. She kept staring at Orlando, trying to think of what else she could say. But it seemed useless. Turning her head, she happened to catch a glimpse of a dark man on one of the couches with one eyelid drooping over his eye. Marsha recognized him. She'd seen him in VJ's lab when Victor took her there.

José didn't say anything. He accompanied Marsha to the door, then closed it in her face. Marsha stood facing the blank door, not sure if she should be thankful or irritated.

Returning to the street, she got into her car and started it up. She got halfway down the block when she saw a policeman. Pulling to the curb, Marsha rolled her window down.

"Excuse me," she said, then pointed back to the warehouse. "Do you have any idea what those people do in that building?"

The policeman stepped off the curb and bent down to see exactly where Marsha was pointing. "Oh, there," he said. He straightened. "I don't know for sure, but

I was told a group of Colombians are setting up some kind of furniture business."

As soon as Victor had the opportunity, he phoned Chad Newhouse, the director of security and safety. Victor asked the man about Ramirez.

"Sure, he's a member of the force," Chad said. "He's been on the payroll for a number of years. Is there a problem?"

"Was he hired through normal channels?" Victor inquired.

Chad laughed. "Are you trying to pull my leg, Dr. Frank? You hired Ramirez along with the rest of that special industrial espionage team. He's responsible directly to you."

Victor hung up the phone. He would have to talk with VJ about Ramirez.

After the administrative work was done and the meeting with Ronald scheduled for eleven-fifteen, Victor left for VJ's lab. Before he got to the clock tower building, he stepped into the shadow of one of the other deserted buildings and made certain he was not being observed. Only then did he run across the street into the clock tower building.

One knock brought up the trapdoor. Victor scampered down. Several of the guards in the Chimera uniforms were sitting around, entertaining themselves with cards and magazines. VJ came into the room through the door that Victor had tried to enter on his last visit, wiping his hands on a towel. His eyes had a more intense look than usual.

"Did you come here to the lab last night?" VJ demanded.

"I did—" Victor said.

"I don't want you to do that," VJ interrupted sternly. "Not unless I authorize it. Understand? I need a little respect and privacy."

Victor regarded his son. For a moment he was speechless. Victor had planned on being angry about the episode, but suddenly he was on the defensive. "I'm sorry," he said. "I didn't mean any harm. I was curious about what other facilities you had down here."

"You'll see them soon enough," VJ said, his voice softening. "First I want you to see the new lab."

"Fine," Victor said, relieved to have the ill feelings dissipate so quickly.

They used Victor's car, left Chimera, and crossed the bridge over the Merrimack. While Victor was driving he brought up the question of Ramirez.

"I inserted a number of security people into the Chimera payroll," VJ said. "If you are concerned about the expense, just remember the enormous benefit Chimera is about to accrue from such a small investment."

"I wasn't concerned about the payroll," Victor said. It was the ease with which VJ was able to do whatever he wanted that bothered him.

With VJ's directions, they soon pulled up to one of the old mills across the river from Chimera. VJ was out of the car first, eager to show Victor his creation.

The building was set right on the river. The clock tower building was in clear view on the other bank. But unlike VJ's previous quarters, the new lab was modern in every respect, including its decor. It had three floors and was the most impressive setup Victor had ever seen. In the basement were animal rooms, operating theaters, huge stainless-steel fermentors, and a cyclotron for making radioactive substances. On the first floor was an NMR scanner, a PET scanner, and a whole microbiology laboratory. The second floor had most of the general laboratory space and most of the sophisticated equipment necessary for gene manipulation and fabrication. The third and top floor was devoted to computer space, library, and administrative offices.

"What do you think?" VJ asked proudly as they stood in the hall on the third floor. They had to move frequently as there were workmen everywhere, installing the most recently delivered equipment, doing last-minute painting and carpentry.

"Like everything you've done, I'm simply astounded," Victor said. "But this has cost a fortune. Where did the money come from?"

"One of my side projects was to develop a marketable product from recombinant DNA technology," VJ said. "Obviously it succeeded."

"What's the product?" Victor asked eagerly.

VJ grinned. "It's a trade secret!"

VJ then went to a closed door, opened it a crack, glanced inside, then turned back to Victor. "I've got one more surprise for you. There's someone I'd like you to meet."

VJ threw the door open and gestured for Victor to go inside. A young woman bent over a desk straightened up, saying, "Dr. Frank! What a surprise!"

For a moment Victor didn't know what to say. He was looking at someone he'd never expected to see again: Mary Millman, the surrogate who'd carried VJ.

VJ reveled in his father's shock. "I needed a good secretary," he explained, "so I brought her in from

Detroit. I have to admit I was curious to meet the woman who gave birth to me."

Victor shook Mary's hand, which she'd put out to him. "Nice to see you again," he said, somewhat dazed.

"Likewise," Mary said.

"Well," VJ said with a laugh, "I really should get back to my lab."

Victor self-consciously looked at his watch. "I've got to go myself."

The meeting with Ronald Beekman was a waste of time. Victor had tried to be confrontational about the NGF project to find out whether Ronald knew anything about it. But Ronald had said neither yes nor no, cleverly sensing this was an issue that might provide him with some leverage. When Victor had reminded him that at their last meeting Ronald had threatened to get even and make Victor's life miserable, Ronald had just brushed it off as being a figure of speech. So Victor left the man's office not knowing any more than he had when he'd entered.

The only possible potential benefit of the meeting was that Ronald had indicated a sharp interest in the implantation project, and Victor had promised to put something together for him to read.

Leaving Ronald's office, Victor headed back to his own. He'd ask Colleen to arrange a meeting with Hurst. Victor wasn't looking forward to it.

"Robert Grimes called you from your lab," Colleen said as soon as Victor entered the office. "He said he has something very interesting for you. He wants you to call him immediately."

Victor sat down heavily at his desk. Under normal

circumstances such a message from his head technician would have made him tingle with anticipation. It
would have heralded some breakthrough on one of
the experiments. But now it had to be something else.
It had to involve the special work that Victor had
given Robert, and Victor wasn't sure he wanted to
hear "something very interesting."

Fortifying himself as best he could, Victor made the
call and waited for Robert to be located. While Victor
waited he thought about his own experiments and
realized that they now held very little interest for him.
After all, VJ had solved most of the questions involved. It was humbling for Victor to be so far behind
his ten-year-old son. But the good side was what they
would be able to accomplish together. That was thrill-
ing indeed.

"Dr. Frank!" Robert said suddenly into the phone,
waking Victor from his musings. "I'm glad I found
you. I've pretty well sequenced the DNA fragment in
the two tumors, and I wanted to make sure you
wanted me to go ahead and reproduce the sequence
with recombinant techniques. It will take me some
time to do, but it is the only way we'll be able to
ascertain exactly what it codes for."

"Do you have any idea what it codes for?" Victor
asked hesitantly.

"Oh, yeah," Robert said. "It's undoubtedly some
kind of unique polypeptide growth factor."

"So it's not some kind of retro virus," Victor said
with a ray of hope, thinking that a retro virus could
have been an infectious particle artificially dissemi-
nated.

"Nope, it's certainly not a retro virus," Robert said.

"In fact, it's some kind of artificially fabricated gene." Then with a laugh he added, "I'd have to call it a Chimera gene. Within the sequence is an internal promoter that I've used myself on a number of occasions—one taken from the SV40 simian virus. But the rest of the gene had to come from some other microorganism, either a bacterium or a virus."

There was a pause.

"Are you still there, Dr. Frank?" Robert asked, thinking the connection had broken.

"You're sure about all this?" Victor asked, his voice wavering. The implications were becoming all too clear.

"Absolutely," Robert said. "I was surprised myself. I've never heard of such a thing. My first guess was that these people picked up some kind of DNA vector and it got into their bloodstreams. That seemed so strange that I gave it a lot more thought. The only possible mechanism that I could come up with involves red-blood-cell bags filled with this infective gene. As soon as the Kupffer cells in the liver picked them up, the infective particles inserted themselves into the cell's genome. The new genes then turned proto-oncogenes into oncogenes, and bingo: liver cancer. But there's only one problem with this scenario. You know what it is?"

"No, what?"

"There's only one way that RBC membrane bags could get into somebody's bloodstream," Robert said, oblivious to the effect all this was having on Victor. "They would have to be injected. I know that—"

Robert never had a chance to finish his sentence. Victor had hung up.

The mounting evidence was incontrovertible. There was no denying it: David and Janice had died of liver cancer caused by a piece of foreign DNA inserting itself into their chromosomes. And on top of that, there was the instructor from Pendleton Marsha had told him about. All these people were intimately related to VJ. And VJ was a scientific genius with an ultramodern, sophisticated laboratory at his disposal.

Colleen poked her head in. "I was waiting for you to get off the phone," she said brightly. "Your wife is here. Can I send her in?"

Victor nodded. Suddenly he felt extremely tired.

Marsha came into the room and closed the door forcibly. The wind rustled the papers on Victor's desk. She walked directly over to Victor and leaned forward over his blotter, looking him directly in the eye.

"I know you would rather not do anything," she said. "I know you don't want to upset VJ, and I know you are excited about his accomplishments, but you are going to have to face the reality that the boy is not playing by the rules. Let me tell you about my latest discovery. VJ is involved with a group of Colombians who are supposedly opening a furniture import business in Mattapan. I met these men and let me tell you, they don't look like furniture merchants to me."

Marsha stopped abruptly. Victor wasn't reacting. "Victor?" Marsha said questioningly. His eyes had a dazed, unfocused look.

"Marsha, sit down," Victor said, shaking his head with sad, slow deliberation. He cradled his head in his hands and leaned forward, resting his elbows on his desk. Then he ran his fingers through his hair, rubbed his neck, and straightened up. Marsha sat down, studying her husband intently. Her pulse began to race.

"I've just learned something worse," Victor said. "A few days ago I got samples of David's and Janice's tumors. Robert has been working on them. He just called to tell me that their cancers had been artificially induced. A foreign cancer-causing gene was put into their bloodstreams."

Marsha cried out, bringing her hands to her mouth in dismay. Even though she had begun to suspect as much, the confirmation was as horrifying as if she'd been given the news cold. Coming from Victor, who'd fought her tooth and nail when it came to her fears and apprehensions, made it all the more damning. She bit her lower lip while she quivered with a combination of anger, sadness, and fear. "It had to be VJ!" she whispered.

Victor slammed his palm on top of his desk, sending papers flying. "We don't know that for sure!" he shouted.

"All these people knew VJ intimately," Marsha said, echoing Victor's own thoughts. "And he wanted them out of the way."

Victor shook his head in grim resignation. How much blame lay at his door, and how much lay at VJ's? He was the one who'd ensured the boy's brilliance. But did he stop for one second to think what might go hand in hand with that genius? If David and Janice and that teacher had died by VJ's hand, Victor wasn't sure he could live with his conscience.

Marsha began hesitantly, but her conviction made

her strong. "I think we have to know exactly what VJ is doing in the rest of that lab of his."

Victor let his arms fall limply to his side and stared out the window. He looked at the clock tower, knowing that VJ was working there right now. He turned to Marsha and said, "Let's go find out."

# 14

Marsha had to run to keep up with Victor as he made his way toward the river. The two soon left the reno-vated part of the complex behind. In broad daylight the abandoned buildings did not look quite so sinister.

Entering the building, Victor went straight to the trapdoor, bent down, and rapped sharply on the floor several times.

In a minute or two the trapdoor came up. A man in a Chimera security uniform eyed Victor and Marsha warily, then motioned for them to descend.

Victor went first. By the time Marsha was down the stairs, Victor had rounded the paddle wheel and was heading toward the intimidating metal door barring the entrance to the unexplored portion of VJ's lab. For Marsha, the lab itself was as forbidding as it had been the last time she'd been there. She knew that the fruits of scientific research could be put to good or evil use, but something about the eerie basement quarters gave Marsha the feeling that the research conducted here was for a darker purpose.

315

"Hey!" yelled one of the guards, seeing Victor approach the restricted door. He jumped up and sprinted across the room diagonally, and grabbed Victor by the arm. He pulled him around roughly. "Nobody's allowed in there," he snarled in his strong Spanish accent.

To Marsha's surprise, Victor put his hand squarely on the man's face and pushed him back. The gesture took the man by surprise, and he fell to one knee, but he maintained a hold on Victor's jacket sleeve. With a forcible yank, Victor shook free of the man's grasp and reached around to the door.

The security guard pulled a knife from his boot and flicked it open. A flash of light glinted off its razor surface.

"Victor!" Marsha screamed. Victor turned when he heard her scream. The guard came at him, holding the knife out in front of his body like a miniature rapier. Victor parried the thrust but the man got hold of his arm. The knife rose menacingly.

"Stop it!" VJ yelled as he burst through the door toward which Victor had been heading. The two other security men who were in the room got between the two combatants, one restraining Victor, the other dealing with the knife-wielding guard.

"Let my father go!" VJ commanded.

"He was going into the back lab," the guard with the knife cried.

"Let him go," VJ ordered even more sternly than before.

Victor was released with a shove. He staggered forward, trying to maintain his balance. Doing so, he made another move for the door. VJ reached out and grasped his arm just as Victor was about to push through to the other side.

"Are you sure you're ready for this?" VJ asked.

"I want to see it all," Victor said flatly.

"Remember the Tree of Knowledge?"

"Of Good and Evil," countered Victor. "You can't talk me out of this."

VJ pulled his hand back. "Suit yourself, but you may not appreciate the consequences."

Victor looked to Marsha, who nodded for him to go. Turning again to the door, he pulled it open. Pale blue light flooded out. Victor stepped over the threshold with Marsha right behind him. VJ followed, then pulled the door closed.

The room was about fifty feet long and rather narrow. On a long bench built of rough-hewn lumber sat four fifty-gallon glass tanks. The sides were fused with silicone. The tanks were illuminated by heat lamps and gave off the eerie blue light as it refracted through the contained fluid.

Marsha's jaw dropped in horror when she realized what was in the tanks. Inside each one and enveloped in transparent membranes were four fetuses, each perhaps eight months old, who were swimming about in their artificial wombs. They watched Marsha as she walked down the aisle, their blue eyes fully open. They gestured, smiled, and even yawned.

Casually, but with an air of arrogant pride, VJ gave a cursory explanation of the system. In each tank the placentas were plastered onto a plexiglass grid against a membrane bag connected to a sort of heart-lung machine. Each machine had its own computer, which was in turn attached to a protein synthesizer. The liquid surface of each tank was covered with plastic balls to retard evaporation.

Neither Marsha nor Victor could speak, so appalled were they by the sight of the gestating children. Although they had tried to prepare themselves for the unexpected, this was a shock too outrageous to behold.

"I'm sure you're wondering what this is all about," VJ said, moving up to one of the tanks and checking one of the many read-out devices. He hit it with his fist and a stuck needle indicator sprang into the green-painted normal zone. "My early work on implantation had me modeling wombs with tissue culture. Solving the implantation problem also solved the problems of why a uterus was needed at all."

"How old are these children?" Marsha asked.

"Eight and a half months," VJ said, confirming Marsha's impression. "I'll be keeping them gestating a lot longer than the usual nine months. They will be easier to raise the longer I keep them in their tanks."

"Where did you get the zygotes?" Victor asked, although he already knew the answer.

"I'm pleased to say that they are my brothers and sisters."

Marsha's incredulous gaze went from the fetuses in the tanks to VJ.

VJ laughed at her expression. "Come now, this can't be that much of a surprise. I got the zygotes from the freezer in Father's lab. No sense letting them go to waste or letting Dad implant them in other people."

"There were five," Victor said. "Where's the fifth?"

"Good memory," VJ said. "Unfortunately, I had to waste the fifth on an early test of the implantation protocol. But four is plenty for statistical extrapolation, at least for the first batch."

Marsha turned back to the gestating children. They were her own!

"Let's not be too surprised at all this," VJ said. "You knew this technology was on its way. I've just speeded it up."

Victor went up to one of the computers as it sprang to life and spewed out a half page of data. As soon as it was finished printing, the protein synthesizer turned on and began making a protein.

"The system is sensing the need for some kind of growth factor," VJ explained.

Victor looked at the print-out. It included the vital signs, chemistries, and blood count of the child. He was astounded at the sophistication of the setup. Victor knew that VJ had had to artificially duplicate the fantastically complicated interplay of forces necessary to take a fertilized egg to an entire organism. The feat represented a quantum leap in biotechnology. A radically new and successful implantation technology was one thing, but this was entirely another. Victor shuddered to consider the diabolic potential of what his creation had created.

Marsha timidly approached one of the tanks and peered in at a boy-child from closer range. The child looked back at her as if he wanted her; he put a tiny palm up against the glass. Marsha reached out with her own and laid her hand over the child's with just the thickness of the glass separating them. But then she drew her hand back, revolted. "Their heads!" she cried.

Victor came up beside her and leaned toward the child. "What's the matter with his head?"

"Look at the eyebrows. Their heads slant back without foreheads."

"They're mutated," VJ explained casually. "I removed Victor's added segment, then destroyed some of the normal NGF loci. I'm aiming at a level of intelligence similar to Philip's. Philip has been more helpful in aiding me in all my efforts than anyone else."

Marsha shuddered, gripping Victor's hand out of VJ's sight. Victor ignored her and pointed to the door at the end of the room. "What's beyond that door?"

"Haven't you seen enough?" VJ asked.

"I've got to see it all," Victor said. He left Marsha and walked down the length of the room. For a moment Marsha stared at the tiny boy-child with his prominent brow and flattened head. It was as if human evolution had stepped back five hundred thousand years. How could VJ deliberately make his own brothers and sisters—such as they were—retarded? His Machiavellian rationale made her shudder.

Marsha pulled herself away from the gestation tanks and followed Victor. She had to see everything too. Could there really be anything worse than what she had just seen?

The next room had huge stainless-steel containers lined in a row. They looked like giant kettles she'd seen at a brewery when she was a teenager. It was warmer and more humid in this room. Several men without shirts labored over one of the vats, adding ingredients to it. They stopped working and looked back at Victor and Marsha.

"What are these tanks?" Marsha asked.

Victor could answer. "They're fermentors for grow-

320

ing microorganisms like bacteria or yeast." Then he asked VJ, "What's growing inside?"

"E. coli bacteria," VJ said. "The workhorse of recombinant DNA technology."

"What are they making?" Victor said.

"I'd rather not say," VJ answered. "Don't you think the gestational units are enough for one day?"

"I want to know everything," Victor said. "I want it all out on the table."

"They are making money," VJ said with a smile.

"I'm not in the mood for riddles," Victor said.

VJ sighed. "I had the short-term need for a major capital infusion for the new lab. Obviously, going public wasn't an alternative for me. Instead, I imported some coca plants from South America and extracted the appropriate genes. I then inserted these genes into a lac operon of E. coli, and using a plasmid that carried a resistance to tetracycline, I put the whole thing back into the bacteria. The product is marvelous. Even the E. coli love it."

"What is he saying?" Marsha asked Victor.

"He's saying that these fermentors are making cocaine," Victor said.

"That explains Martinez Enterprises," Marsha said with a gasp.

"But this production line is purely temporary," VJ explained. "It is an expedient means of providing immediate capital. Shortly the new lab will be running on its own merit without the need for contraband. And yes, Martinez Enterprises is a temporary partner. In fact, we can field a small army on a moment's notice. For now, a number of them are on the Chimera payroll."

Victor walked down the line of fermentors. The degree of sophistication of these units also amazed him. He could tell at a glance they were far superior to what Chimera was using. Victor pulled away from them with a heavy sigh and rejoined Marsha and VJ.

"Now you've seen it all," said VJ. "But now that you have, we have to have a serious talk."

VJ turned and walked back toward the main room with Victor and Marsha following. As they passed through the gestation room, the fetuses again moved to the glass. It seemed they longed for human company. If VJ noticed, he didn't show it.

Without a word, VJ led them through the main room, back into the living quarters. Victor realized then that even here there was space he had not seen. There was a smaller room off the main area. Judging from the decor and journals, Victor guessed this was where VJ stayed. There was one bed, a card table with folding chairs, a large bookcase filled with periodicals, and a reading chair. VJ motioned toward the card table and sat down.

Victor and Marsha sat down as well. VJ had his elbows on the table with his hands clasped. He looked from Victor to Marsha, his piercingly blue eyes sparkling like sapphires. "I have to know what you are planning to do about all this. I've been honest with you, it's time you were honest with me."

Victor and Marsha exchanged glances. When Victor didn't speak, Marsha did: "I have to know the truth about David, Janice, and Mr. Cavendish."

"At the moment, I'm not interested in peripheral issues," VJ said. "I'm interested in discussing the magnitude of my projects. I hope you can appreciate the enormity of these experiments. Their value tran-

scends all other issues that otherwise might be perti-
nent."

"I'm afraid I have to know about these people before
I can judge," Marsha said calmly.

VJ glanced at Victor. "Is this your opinion also?"

Slowly, Victor nodded.

"I was afraid of this," VJ murmured. He eyed them
both severely, as though he was their parent and they
were his erring children. Finally he spoke. "All right,
I'll answer your questions. I'll tell you everything you
want to know. The three people you mentioned were
planning to expose me. At that point it would have
been devastating for my work. I tried to keep them
from finding out much about the lab and my experiments, but these three were relentless. I had to let
nature handle it."

"What does that mean?" Victor asked.

"Through my extensive research on growth factors
involved in solving the problem of the artificial womb,
I discovered certain proteins that acted as powerful
enhancers for proto-oncogenes. I packaged them in
RBC sacs, then let nature take over."

"You mean you injected them," Victor said.

"Of course I injected them!" VJ snapped. "That's not
the kind of thing you can take orally."

Marsha tried to remain calm. "You're telling me you
killed your brother. And you felt nothing?"

"I was only an intermediary. David died of cancer.
I pleaded with him to leave me alone. But instead he
followed me, thinking he could bring me down. It was
his jealousy that drove him."

"And what about the two babies?" Marsha asked.

"Can't we talk about the major issues?" VJ demanded, pounding the table with his fist.

"You asked what we were going to do about all this," Marsha said. "First we have to know all the facts. What about the children?"

VJ drummed his fingers on the surface of the card table. His patience was wearing thin. "They were getting too smart. They were beginning to realize their potential. I didn't want the competition. A little cephaloclor in the day-care center's milk was all it took. I'm sure it was good for most of the kids."

"And how did it make you feel when they died?" Marsha asked.

"Relieved," VJ said.

"Not sorry or sad in any way?" Marsha persisted.

"This isn't a therapy session, Mother," VJ snapped. "My feelings aren't at issue here. You now know all the dark secrets. It's your turn for some honesty. I need to know your intentions."

Marsha looked to Victor, hoping he would denounce VJ's demonic actions, but Victor only stared blankly at VJ, too stunned for speech.

Marsha interpreted his silence to mean acquiescence, possibly even approval. Could Victor be so caught up in VJ's achievements that he could dismiss five murders? The murder of their own little boy? Well, she wasn't going to take this silently. Victor be damned.

"Well?" VJ demanded.

Marsha turned to face him. His unblinking eyes looked to her in calm expectation. Their crystal blue color, so striking since birth, and his angelic blond hair, dissolved Marsha to tears. He was their baby, too, wasn't he? And if he had committed such horrors, was it really his fault? He was a freak of science. For whatever Victor had accomplished in terms of ensuring his brilliance, a conscience seemed to have been lost in the balance. If VJ were guilty, Victor was as culpable as he. Marsha felt a sudden wave of compassion for the boy. "VJ," she began. "I don't believe that Victor realized all the repercussions of his NGF experiment—"

But VJ cut her off. "Quite the contrary," he told her. "Victor knew precisely what he wanted to achieve. And now he can look at me and at what I've accomplished and know that he has been ultimately successful. I am exactly what Victor wanted and hoped for; I'm what he'd like to be himself. I am what science can be. I am the future." VJ smiled. "You'd better get used to me."

"Maybe you are what Victor intended in scientific respects," Marsha continued, undaunted. "But I don't think he foresaw the kind of personality he was creating. VJ, what I'm trying to say is, if you did commit those murders, if you are manufacturing cocaine . . . and can't see the moral objections to these actions, well, it's not all your fault."

"Mother," said VJ, exasperated, "you always get so sidetracked. Feelings, symptoms, personality. I reveal to you the greatest biological achievement of all time and you probably want me to take another Rorschach test. This is absurd."

"Science is not supreme," Marsha said. "Morality must be brought to bear. Can't you understand that?"

"That's where you're wrong," VJ said. "And Victor proved that he holds science above morality by the act of creating me. By conventional morality's dictates, he should not have gone through with the NGF experiment, but he did anyway. He is a hero."

"What Victor did in creating you was born out of

unthinking arrogance. He didn't stop to consider the possible outcome; he was so obsessed with the means and his singular goal. Science runs amok when it shakes loose from the bonds of morality and consequence."

VJ clucked his tongue in disagreement. Then he turned his fierce blue eyes on Marsha. "Morality cannot rule science because morality is relative and therefore variable. Science is not. Morality is based on man and his society, which changes over the years, from culture to culture. What's taboo for some is sacred for others. Such vagaries should have no bearing here. The only thing that is immutable in this world are the laws of nature that govern the present universe. Reason is the ultimate arbiter, not moralistic whims."

"VJ, it's not your fault," Marsha said softly, sadly shaking her head. There would be no reasoning with him. "Your superior intelligence has isolated you and made you a person who is missing the human qualities of compassion, empathy, even love. You feel you have no limits. But you do. You never developed a conscience. But you can't see it. It's like trying to explain the concept of color to someone blind since birth."

VJ leaped from his chair in disgust. "With all due respect," he said, "I don't have time for this sophistry. I've got work to do. I must know your intentions."

"Your father and I will have a talk," Marsha said, avoiding VJ's gaze.

"Go ahead, talk," VJ said, putting his hands on his narrow hips.

"We'll have a talk without children present," Marsha said.

VJ set his mouth petulantly. His breath had quick-

326

ened, his eyes were afire. Then he turned and left the room. The door slammed and clicked. VJ had locked them in.

Marsha turned to face Victor. Victor shook his head in helpless dismay.

"Is there any question in your mind at this point what we're dealing with?" Marsha asked.

Victor shook his head lamely.

"Good," said Marsha. "Now, what are you prepared to do about it?"

Victor only shook his head again. "I never thought it would come to this." He looked at his wife. "Marsha, you have to believe me. If I'd known . . ." His voice broke off. He needed Marsha's support, her understanding. But even he had trouble comprehending the magnitude of his error. If they ever got through this, he wasn't sure he could live with himself. How could he expect Marsha to?

Victor put his face in his hands.

Marsha touched his shoulder. For as awful as the situation was, at least Victor had finally come to his senses. "We have to decide what to do now," she said gently.

Victor pulled himself up out of his chair, suddenly emboldened. "I'm the one responsible. You're perfectly right about VJ. He wouldn't be the way he is if it weren't for me and my scientific meddling." He turned again to his wife. "First, we have to get out of here."

Marsha looked at him gravely. "You think VJ is about to let us waltz out of here? Be reasonable! Remember how he's handled trouble in the past? David, Janice, that poor teacher, those kids, and now his troublesome parents."

"You think he'll just keep us here indefinitely?" Victor asked.

"I haven't the slightest idea of what his intentions are. I just don't think it's going to be so easy to get out. He must have some feeling for us. Otherwise he wouldn't have even bothered explaining, and he wouldn't be interested in our opinions or plans. But he certainly isn't going to let us leave here until he's convinced we'll present no problem for him."

For a moment, the two were silent. Then Marsha said, "Maybe we could make some kind of bargain. Get him to let one of us go while the other stays here."

"So one of us becomes a hostage?"

Marsha nodded.

"If he'll agree, I think you should go," Victor told her.

"Uh-uh," Marsha said, shaking her head. "If it comes to that, then you go. You've got to figure out how to put a stop to him."

"I think you should go," Victor said. "I can handle VJ better than you can at this point."

"I don't think anybody can handle VJ," said Marsha. "He's in a world of his own, with no restraints and no conscience. But I'm confident he won't harm me, at least not until he's sure that I mean to cause him trouble. I do think he trusts you more than he trusts me. In that sense, you can deal with him better than I can. He seems to seek your approval. He wants to make you proud. In that respect he seems to be like any other child."

"But what to do?" said Victor, pacing. "I'm not sure the police would be a lot of help. The best route to go might be via the DEA. I suppose he's the most vulnerable with the drug stuff."

Marsha only nodded. Tears sprang to her eyes. She couldn't believe it had come to this. It was still hard to think of VJ as anything but her little boy. But there was no question: because of the nature of his genetic manipulation, he'd become a monster. There'd be no reining him in.

"Could we get him committed to a psychiatric hospital?" Victor asked.

"We'd be hard put to commit him without psychotic behavior, which he hasn't demonstrated, or without getting him acquitted of murder by reason of insanity. But I doubt we could even get him indicted. I'm sure he was careful not to leave any evidence, especially with such a high-tech crime. He has a personality disorder, but he's not crazy. You're going to have to come up with something better than that. I only wish I could say what."

"I'll think of something," Victor assured her. He smoothed out his coat and ran his fingers through his hair in an attempt to comb it. Taking a deep breath, he tried the door. It was locked. He banged on it with his fist four times.

After some delay the lock clicked and the door swung open. VJ appeared in the doorway with several of the South Americans backing him.

"I'm ready to talk," Victor said.

VJ looked from Victor to Marsha. She looked away to avoid his cold stare.

"Alone," Victor added.

VJ nodded and stepped aside while Victor crossed into the main living quarters. Victor walked directly out into the main lab as he heard VJ locking Marsha in. It was clear that he and Marsha really were prisoners, held by their own son.

"She's really upset," Victor said. "Killing David. That was inexcusable."

"I didn't have any choice," VJ said.

"A mother has a hard time dealing with that," Victor said. VJ's eyes didn't blink.

"I knew we shouldn't have told Marsha about the lab," said VJ. "She doesn't have the same regard for science as we do."

"You're right about that," Victor said. "She was appalled at the artificial wombs. I was astounded by them. I know what an achievement they represent scientifically. The impact they'll have on the scientific community will be stupendous. And their commercial potential is enormous."

"I'm counting on the commercial profits to enable me to dump the cocaine connection," VJ said.

"That's a good idea. You're putting your work in serious jeopardy dabbling in the drug business."

"I took that into consideration some time ago," VJ said. "I have several contingency plans if trouble starts."

"I bet you do."

VJ eyed Victor closely. "I think you'd better tell me what your intentions are about my lab and my work."

"My main goal is to deal with Marsha," Victor said. "But I think she'll come around, once the shock of everything wears off."

"How do you plan to deal with her?"

"I'll convince her of the importance of your work and your discoveries," Victor said. "She'll feel differently once she understands that you've done more than any other person in the history of biology, and you are only ten years old."

VJ seemed to swell with pride. Marsha had been right: like any other kid, he sought his father's praise. If only he really could be like any other kid, Victor thought ruefully. But he never will be, thanks to me.

Victor continued. "As soon as possible, I'd like to see a list of the protein growth factors that are involved with the artificial womb."

"There are over five hundred of them," VJ said. "I can give you a print-out, but of course it won't be for publication."

"I understand," Victor said. He glanced down at his son and smiled. "Well, I have to get back to work and I'm sure Marsha has patients to see. So I think we'll be leaving. We'll see you at home."

VJ shook his head. "I think it is too soon for you to leave. I think it will be better if you plan to stay for a few days. I have a phone hookup so you can do your business by phone. Mom will have to reschedule her patients. You'll find it quite comfortable here."

Victor laughed a hollow laugh at this suggestion. "But you're joking, of course. We can't stay here. Marsha may be able to reschedule her patients, but Chimera can't be put on hold. I have a lot of work to do. Besides, everyone knows I'm on the grounds. Sooner or later they'd start searching for me."

VJ considered the situation. "Okay," he said at last. "You can go. But Mom will have to stay here."

Victor was impressed that Marsha had been able to anticipate him so correctly. "I'd be with her every minute," Victor said, still trying to get them both out.

"One or the other," VJ said. "It's not up for discussion."

"All right, if you insist," said Victor. "I'll tell Marsha. Be right back."

Victor made his way back to the door to VJ's living quarters. One of the guards had to come and open it with a key. Victor went over to Marsha and whispered, "He's agreed to let one of us out. Are you sure you don't want to be the one to go?"

Marsha shook her head no. "Please just contact Jean and tell her I won't be available until further notice. Tell her to refer emergencies to Dr. Maddox."

Victor nodded. He kissed Marsha on the cheek, grateful she didn't recoil. Then he turned to go.

Back in the main lab room VJ was giving instructions to two of the guards.

"This is Jorge," VJ said, introducing Victor to a smiling South American. He was the same man who'd earlier tried to knife Victor. Apparently there were no hard feelings on his side, because along with the smile, he stuck out his hand for Victor to shake.

"Jorge has offered to accompany you," VJ said.

"I don't need a baby-sitter," Victor said, suppressing his anger.

With a grim smile, VJ said, "I don't think you understand. It's not your choice. Jorge is to stay with you to remind you not to be tempted to talk with anyone who might give me trouble. He will also remind you that Marsha is here with one of Jorge's friends." VJ let the threat hang unspoken.

"But I don't need a guard. And how will I explain him? Really, VJ, I didn't expect this of you."

"I have perfect confidence that you will think of a way to explain him," VJ said. "Jorge will make us all sleep just a little better. And let me warn you: trouble with the police or other authorities would only be a bother and slow the program, not stop it. Don't disappoint me, Father. Together we will revolutionize the biotechnology industry."

Victor swallowed with difficulty. His mouth had gone dry.

# 15

The day had turned cloudy and blustery by the time Victor emerged from the clock tower building and set off for his office. A few steps behind him was Jorge, who'd made a show of displaying the knife he kept hidden in his right boot. But the gesture had had the desired effect. Victor knew that he was in the presence of a man accustomed to killing.

Despite telling Marsha he'd think of something, Victor had no idea what to do. He was in a dazed frenzy by the time he reached his office. He traversed the pool of secretaries unsteadily, with Jorge one step behind him.

"Excuse me!" Colleen said as Victor cruised by her desk. She jumped up, snatching a pile of messages. Victor had reached the door to his office. He turned to the South American. "You'll have to wait out here," he said.

Jorge brushed past Victor as if Victor had not said anything. Colleen, who had witnessed this exchange, was appalled, especially since the South American was wearing a Chimera security uniform. "Should I call security?" she whispered to Victor.

Victor said it wouldn't be necessary. Colleen shrugged and got down to business. "I have a lot of messages," she said. "I've been trying to call you. I need—"

Victor placed his hand on her arm and eased her back so he could swing the door shut. "Later," he told her.

"But—" Colleen intoned as the door was shut in her face.

Victor locked the door as an added precaution. Jorge had already made himself comfortable on the couch in the rear of the room. The man was casually attending to his fingernails.

Victor went behind his desk and sat down. The phone rang immediately but he didn't answer. He knew it was Colleen. He looked over at Jorge, who waved with his nail clipper and smiled a toothy grin.

Victor let his head sink into his hands. What he needed was a plan. Jorge was an unwanted distraction. The man exuded a reckless, haughty confidence that said, "I'm a killer and I'm sitting in your office and you can't do a thing about it." It was difficult for Victor to concentrate with Jorge watching over him.

"You don't look like you're doing much work to me," Jorge said suddenly. "VJ said that you needed to leave because you had a lot of work to do. I suggest you get busy unless you want me to call VJ and tell him that you are just sitting around holding your head."

"I was just gathering my thoughts," Victor said. He leaned over and pressed his intercom. When Colleen responded, he said, "Bring in my messages and let's get to work."

For the first hour, Marsha occupied herself by looking through some of the hundreds of periodicals in the bookcase. But they were over her head; all were highly technical, devoted to theories and experiments on the cutting edge of biology, physics, and chemistry. She got up and paced the room and even tried the door, but, as expected, it was locked.

She sat down at the table again, wondering what course of action Victor would take. He would have to be very resourceful. VJ was an exceptional adversary. He'd also have to have an enormous amount of moral courage, and in light of his NGF experiments, she had no idea if he had it in him.

Just then the bolt of the lock was thrown and VJ stepped in. "I thought maybe you could use a little company," he said cheerfully. "There's someone I'd like you to meet." He stepped aside and Mary Millman walked in smiling, her hand outstretched.

Marsha stood up, searching for words.

"Mrs. Frank!" Mary said, shaking her hand with enthusiasm. "I've been looking forward to seeing you. I thought I'd have to wait for at least another year. How are you?"

"Fine, I guess," Marsha said.

"I thought you ladies would enjoy chatting," said VJ. "I'll be leaving this door ajar; if you're hungry or thirsty, just let one of Martinez's people know."

"Thank you," Mary said. "Isn't he wonderful?" she said to Marsha after he was gone.

"He's unique," Marsha said. "How did you get here?"

"It's a surprise, isn't it?" Mary said. "Well, it surprised me too, at the time. I'll tell you how it happened."

"What next?" Victor asked. Colleen was sitting in her usual spot, directly across from him. Jorge was still back on the couch, lounging comfortably. Colleen shuffled through her papers and messages. "I think that does it for now. Anything you want me to do?" She rotated her eyes toward Jorge meaningfully.

"Nope," Victor said as he handed over the last document he had signed. "I'll be heading home. If there are any problems, call me there."

After a quick glance at her watch, Colleen looked back at Victor. "Is everything all right?" He'd been acting strangely ever since he'd returned with the Chimera security guard in tow.

"Everything is just hunky-dory," he said, slipping his pen inside his top drawer.

Colleen looked at her boss of seven years. He'd never used that term before. She stood up, gave Jorge a dirty look, and left the room.

"Time to go," Victor said to Jorge.

Jorge pulled himself up from the couch. "We going back to the lab?" he asked in his heavy accent.

"I'm going home," Victor said, getting his coat. "I don't know where you're going."

"I'm with you, friend."

Victor was curious if there would be any trouble as he tried to drive off the site. But the guard at the gate saluted as usual. The fact that a Chimera guard was accompanying him drew no comment from the man stationed at the gate.

As they were crossing the Merrimack, Jorge reached over and turned on the radio. He searched for and found a Spanish station. Then he turned up the sound to nearly deafening levels, snapping his fingers to the beat.

It was clear to Victor that Jorge was his first hurdle. As he drove up the drive and rounded the house he began to think of his alternatives. There was a root cellar below the barn with a stout door Victor felt he could secure. The problem was luring the man into it.

As they got out of the car, Victor let the garage door down, wondering if he could sneak up on Jorge and bop him on the head just as he'd been hit when he'd first stumbled onto VJ's lab. Victor opened the door into the family room and left it open for Jorge, who insisted on walking behind.

Victor took off his coat and draped it over the couch. Being a realist, he decided he couldn't hit the man. He knew he'd hit him either too softly or too hard, and either would be a disaster. He'd have to try something else. But what?

Victor was at a loss until he used the downstairs bathroom. Spotting a bottle of aspirin in the medicine cabinet, he remembered the old doctor's bag he'd been given as a fourth-year medical student. He'd used it all the way through his training and, as far as he could remember, it was still filled with a variety of commonly prescribed drugs.

Emerging from the bathroom, Victor found Jorge in front of the family room TV, flipping the channels aimlessly. Victor went upstairs. Unfortunately, Jorge followed. But in the upstairs study, Victor again got him interested in the television. Victor went into the closet and found the black bag.

Taking a handful of Seconal, Valium, and Dalmane, Victor put the bag back, slipping the pills and capsules into his pocket. When he backed out into the room, he discovered that Jorge had found the Spanish cable station.

"I usually have a drink when I get home," Victor said. "Can I offer you anything?"

"What do you have?" Jorge asked without taking his eyes from the TV.

"Just about anything," Victor said. "How about I make up some margaritas?"

"What are margaritas?" Jorge asked.

The question surprised Victor; he had thought margaritas were a popular South American drink. Maybe they were more Mexican than South American. He told Jorge what was in them.

"I'll have whatever you have," Jorge said.

Victor went down to the kitchen. Jorge followed, going back to the TV in the family room. Victor got out all the ingredients, including the salt. He made the drinks in a small glass pitcher, and, making sure that Jorge wasn't paying attention, opened each of the capsules and poured the contents into the concoction. The Valium went in as is. There was still some sediment on the bottom even after Victor had vigorously stirred the mixture, so he put it on the blender for a moment. Then he held the pitcher up to the light. It looked fine. Victor estimated there was enough knockout power in the concoction to take someone through abdominal surgery without stirring.

Victor took a tiny sip. It had a bitter aftertaste, but if Jorge had never had a margarita, he wouldn't know the difference. Victor then put the salt around the rim of the glasses. He made his own drink out of pure lemon juice. When he was ready, he carried the two poured drinks and the pitcher over to the coffee table.

ROBIN COOK

Jorge took his drink without taking his eyes from
the TV. Victor sat back and watched it himself. Some
kind of soap opera was on the tube. Victor didn't understand Spanish, but he got the drift quickly enough.

Out of the corner of his eye, he watched Jorge swallow his drink, then lean forward and pour himself
some more. Victor was pleased he was enjoying it so
much. The first sign of an effect came quickly enough:
Jorge began to blink a lot. He couldn't focus on the TV.
Finally he looked over at Victor, trying to focus as best
he could. The alcohol must have carried the drugs into
his system efficiently enough. Jorge had barely
touched his second glass and he could barely keep his
eyes open.

All of a sudden, Jorge tried to get to his feet. He must
have realized what was happening because he threw
his glass across the room. Victor put his own glass
down and grabbed Jorge as he tried to dial the phone.
Jorge even attempted to pull out his knife, but his
movements were already too uncoordinated and
slow. Victor easily disarmed him. In another minute,
Jorge was out cold. Victor laid his limp body on the
couch. He got some parenteral Valium he kept upstairs and administered the man ten milligrams in-
tramuscularly as a backup. Then he dragged his body
across the courtyard and down alongside the barn. He
got him into the root cellar and covered him with old
blankets and rags to keep his body temperature
steady. Then he locked the door with an old padlock.

Returning to the house, Victor enjoyed his sense of
accomplishment, and he thought he had the luxury of
time to think of the next step. But as he came through
the door, the phone rang. Its ringing scared him into
wondering if someone were calling Jorge or if Jorge

was supposed to check in now and then. Victor didn't answer the phone. Instead, he put on his coat and went out to the car. Without coming up with another idea, he decided to go to the police.

The police station was in the corner of the municipal green. It was a two-story brick structure with a pair of ornate brass post lamps topped with blue glass spheres. Victor pulled up to the front and parked in the visitor parking area. When he'd left the house, he'd felt good about having finally made a decision. He was looking forward to dumping the whole mess into somebody else's lap. But as he climbed the front steps between the two spheres, he became less certain about going to the police.

Victor hesitated just outside the front door. His biggest worry was Marsha, but there were other worries as well. Just as VJ had said, the police probably couldn't do a whole lot, and VJ would be out on the street. The legal system couldn't even handle simple punks, what would it do with a ten-year-old with the intelligence of two Einsteins put together?

Victor was still debating with himself whether to go in or not when the door to the police station opened and Sergeant Cerullo came barging out, bumping into Victor.

Cerullo juggled his hat, which had been jarred from his head, then excused himself vehemently before he recognized Victor. "Dr. Frank!" he said. He apologized again, then asked, "What brings you into town?"

Victor tried to think of something that sounded reasonable but he couldn't. The truth was too much in his mind. "I have a problem. Can I talk to you?"

"Geez, I'm sorry," Cerullo said. "I'm on dinner break. We gotta eat when we can. But Murphy is in at

341

the desk. He'll help you. When I get back from supper, I'll make sure they treated you right. Take care."

Cerullo gave Victor's arm a friendly punch, then pulled the door open for him. Whether he wanted to or not, Victor found himself inside.

"Hey, Murphy!" Cerullo called. His foot held the door open. "This here is Dr. Frank. He's a friend of mine. You treat him good, understand?"

Murphy was a beefy, red-faced, freckled Irish cop whose father had been a cop and whose father's father had been a cop. He squinted at Victor through heavy bifocals. "I'll be with you in a minute," he said. "Take a seat." He pointed with his pencil to a stained and scarred oak bench, then went back to a form he was laboriously filling out.

Sitting where he was advised, Victor's mind went over the conversation he was about to have with Officer Murphy. He could see himself telling the policeman that he has a son who is an utter genius and who is growing a race of retarded workers in glass jars and who has killed people to protect a secret lab he built by blackmailing embezzlers in his father's company. The mere fact of putting the situation into words convinced Victor that no one would believe him. And even if someone did, what would happen? There would be no way to associate VJ with any of the deaths. It was all circumstantial. As far as the lab equipment was concerned, it wasn't stolen, at least not by VJ. As far as the cocaine was concerned, the poor kid was coerced by a foreign drug lord.

Victor bit his lower lip. Murphy was still struggling with the form, holding the pencil in his meaty hand, his tongue slightly protruding from his mouth. He didn't look up so Victor continued his daydream. He could see VJ shuffled through the legal system and out the back door. He'd have his fully modern lab up and running with a capability of almost anything. And VJ had already proven his willingness to eliminate those who dared to stand in his way. Victor wondered how long he and Marsha would live under those circumstances.

With a sense of depression that bordered on tears, Victor had to admit to himself that his experiment had been too successful. As Marsha had said, he hadn't considered the ramifications of success. He'd been too overwhelmed with the excitement of doing it to think of the result. VJ was more than he'd bargained for, and with the constitutional constraints of law enforcement, the social system was ill-equipped to deal with an alien like VJ. It was as if he were from another planet.

"Okay," Murphy said as he tossed his form into a wire mesh basket on the corner of his desk. "What can we do for you, Dr. Frank?" He cracked his knuckles after the strain of holding the pencil.

Without much confidence, Victor got up and walked over to the duty desk. Murphy regarded him with his blue eyes. His shirt collar appeared too tight and the skin of his neck hung over it.

"Well, watcha got, Doc?" Murphy asked, leaning back in his chair. He had large heavy arms, and he looked like just the kind of guy you'd like to have arrive if kids were stealing your hubcaps or removing your tape deck.

"I have a problem with my son," Victor began. "We found out that he'd been skipping school to—"

"Excuse me, Doc," Murphy said. "Shouldn't you be talking to a social worker, somebody like that?"

"I'm afraid the situation is beyond the ken of a social worker," Victor said. "My son has decided to associate with criminal elements and—"

"Excuse me for interrupting again, Doc," Murphy said. "Maybe I should have said psychologist. How old is your boy?"

"He's ten," Victor said. "But he is—"

"I have to tell you that we have never gotten a call about him. What's his name?"

"VJ," Victor said. "I know that—"

"Before you go any further," Murphy said, "I have to tell you that we have a lot of trouble dealing with juveniles. I'm trying to be helpful. If your son had done something really bad, like expose himself in the park or break into one of the widows' houses, maybe it would be worth involving us. Otherwise I think a psychologist and maybe some old-fashioned discipline would be best. You get my drift?"

"Yeah," Victor said. "I think you are entirely right. Thanks for your time."

"Not at all, Doc," Murphy said. "I'm being straight with you since you're a friend of Cerullo's."

"I appreciate it," Victor said as he backed away from the desk. Then he turned and fled to his car. Once inside his car, Victor felt a tremendous panic. All of a sudden he realized that he alone had to deal with VJ. It was to be father against son, creator against creature. The comprehension brought forth a feeling of nausea that rose up into Victor's throat. He opened the car door, but by shuddering he was able to dispel the nausea without vomiting. He closed the car door and leaned his forehead against the steering wheel. He was drenched in sudden sweat.

From Old Testament studies as a child, the plight of

Abraham came to Victor. But he knew there were two huge differences. God wasn't about to intervene in this instance, and Victor knew that he could not kill his son with his hands. But it was becoming progressively clear that it would be VJ or Victor.

Then, of course, there was the problem of Marsha. How was he to get her out of the lab? Another wave of panic settled over Victor. He knew that he had to act quickly before VJ's intelligence could become a factor. Besides, Victor knew that if he didn't act quickly, he might lose his nerve and commitment.

Victor started the car and drove home by reflex as his mind struggled with coming up with some kind of plan. When he arrived at home, he first went to the root cellar and checked Jorge. He was sleeping like a baby, comfy and cozy beneath his mound of blankets and rags. Victor filled an empty wine bottle with water and left it by the man's head.

Coming into the house, the phone again frightened Victor. Victor looked at it and debated. What if it were Marsha? As it started its fourth ring, Victor snatched up the receiver. He said hello timidly, and for good reason. The voice on the other end was a man's voice with a heavy Spanish accent. He asked for Jorge.

Victor's mind momentarily went blank. The voice asked for Jorge again, a bit more insistently.

"He's in the john," Victor managed.

Without understanding the Spanish, Victor could tell there was no comprehension. "Toilet!" Victor shouted. "He is in the toilet!"

"Okay," the man said.

Victor hung up the phone. Another wave of panic spread through his body like a bolt of electricity. Time was pressing in on Victor like a runaway train ap-

proaching a precipice. Jorge could only be in the john
for so long before an army would be sent out like the
one that visited Gephardt's home.

Victor pounded his hand repeatedly on the counter
top. He hoped that the violence of the act would shock
him into getting hold of himself so that he could think.
He had to come up with a plan.

Fire was Victor's first thought. After all, the clock
tower building was ancient and the timber dry. He
wanted to come up with some sort of cataclysmic
event that would get rid of the entire mess in one fell
swoop. But the problem with fire was that it could be
extinguished. Half a job would be worse than nothing
because then Victor would face VJ's wrath, backed up
by Martinez's muscle.

An explosion was a much better idea, Victor decided upon reflection. But how to pull it off? Victor
was certain he could rig a small explosive device, but
certainly not one capable of demolishing the entire
building.

He'd think of something, but first he had to get Marsha out. Going into his study, Victor took out the pho-
tocopies he'd made when he had been searching for a
way into the building's basement. He hoped he might
get Marsha out through one of the tunnels. But from
studying the floor plans, it immediately became clear
that none of the tunnels entered the clock tower building anywhere near the living quarters where she was
being held. He folded the plans and put them in his
pocket.

The phone rang again, further jangling Victor's
frayed nerves. Victor didn't answer a second time. He
knew he had to get out of the house. VJ or the Martinez gang were sure to get suspicious if Jorge re-

mained incommunicado for long. Who could tell when they might show up to check for themselves?

It was well past dark now, as Victor pulled out of the garage. He turned his lights on and headed for Chimera, praying to God he might come up with some sort of strategy for getting Marsha out and ridding the world of this Pandora's box of his own creation.

Victor suddenly jammed on his brakes, bringing his car to a screeching halt at the side of the road. Almost miraculously, a plan began to form in his mind. The details began to fall into place. "It might work," he said through clenched teeth. Taking his foot from the brake, he stomped on the accelerator and the car leaped ahead.

Victor could barely contain himself as he went through the rigmarole of gaining entry to Chimera. Once in, he drove directly to the building housing his lab and parked right in front of the door. Because of the late hour, the structure was deserted and locked. Victor fumbled with his keys and unlocked the door. When he got into his lab, he forced himself to stop for a moment to calm down. He sat down in a chair, closed his eyes, and tried to relax every muscle in his body. Gradually, his heart rate began to slow. Victor knew that to accomplish the first part of his plan he needed his wits about him. He needed a steady hand.

Victor had all the things he needed in the lab. He had plenty of glycerin and both sulfuric and nitric acids. He also had a closed vessel with cooling ports. For the first time in his life, all the hours he'd spent in chemistry lab in college paid off. With ease he set up a system for the nitrification of the glycerin. While that was in progress, he prepared the neutralization vat. By far the most critical stage was carried out with an electrical drying apparatus which he set up under a ventilation hood.

Before the drying was complete, Victor got one of the laboratory timing devices and a battery pack and hooked up a small ignition filament. The next step was the most trying. There was a very small amount of mercury fulminate in the lab. Victor carefully packed it gently into a small plastic container. Carefully, he pushed in the ignition filament and closed the cap.

By this time the nitroglycerin was dry enough to be packed into an empty soda can that he'd retrieved from the wastebasket. When it was about one quarter full, Victor gently lowered the container with the ignition filament into the can until it rested on the contents. He then added the rest of the nitroglycerin and sealed the can with paraffin wax.

Taking everything back to his lab office, Victor started a search for some appropriate container. Glancing into one of the technicians' offices, he spotted a vinyl briefcase. Victor opened the latches and unceremoniously dumped the contents onto the individual's desk. He carried the case back to his office.

With the empty briefcase on his desk, Victor wadded up paper towels to create a cushioned bed. Carefully he laid the soda can, the battery pack, and the timing device on the crumpled paper towels. He then wadded up additional paper towels to fill the briefcase to overflowing. With gentle pressure, he forcibly closed and latched the lid.

From the main part of the lab, Victor got a flashlight. He took out the plans that showed the tunnel network. He studied them carefully, noting that one of the main tunnels ran from the clock tower to the building housing the cafeteria. What was especially encouraging was that close to the clock tower, a tunnel led off in a westerly direction.

Carrying the briefcase as carefully as possible, Victor crossed to the cafeteria building. Access to the basement was in a central stairwell. Victor went down into the basement and opened the heavy door that sealed the tunnel to the clock tower.

Victor shined his flashlight into the tunnel. It was constructed of stone blocks. It reminded Victor of some ancient Egyptian tomb. He could only see about forty feet in front of him since the passageway turned sharply to the left after that. The floor was filled with rubble and trash. Water trickled in the direction of the river, forming black pools at intervals.

Taking a deep breath for courage, Victor stepped into the cold, damp tunnel and pulled the door shut behind him. The only light was the swath cut by his flashlight beam.

Victor set off, determined but cautious. Too much was at stake. He couldn't fail. In the distance he could hear the sound of water running. Within a few minutes he'd passed a half dozen tunnels that branched off the main alley he was in. As he got closer to the river he could feel the falls' throb as much as hear it.

Victor felt something brush by his legs. Forgetting himself, he leaped back in terror, flailing the briefcase precariously. Once he'd calmed himself, he flashed a beam of light behind him. A pair of eyes gleamed in the beam of the ray. Victor shuddered, realizing he was staring at a sewer rat the size of a small cat. Summoning his courage, he pressed on.

But only a few steps past the rat, Victor slid on the floor's suddenly slippery surface. Frantic to maintain his balance, he had the presence of mind to hug the briefcase tightly as he fell against the wall of the tunnel. Victor stayed on his feet; he did not fall to the ground. Luckily, his elbow had slammed into the stone, not the case. If the briefcase had hit instead, or if he had fallen, it would undoubtedly have detonated.

A second time, Victor began to make his nerve-racking way through the subterranean obstacle course. Finally, he came to the path that left the main tunnel at the proper angle; it had to be the tunnel that went west. With some confidence, Victor followed this tunnel until it entered the basement of the edifice immediately upriver from the clock tower building.

Victor turned his flashlight off after noting where the stairs were located. He could not take the risk of the glow from the beam being seen by someone in the clock tower.

The next forty feet were the worst of all. Victor moved a step at a time, advancing first his right foot, then bringing up his left. He skirted the debris as best he could, ever fearful of a fall.

Finally, he got to the stairs and started up. Once he reached the first floor, he went to the nearest window and glanced at the clock tower building. A sliver of moon had risen in the eastern sky almost directly in line with the Big Ben replica. Victor surveyed the darkened hulk for ten minutes, but saw no one.

He then looked toward the river. Lowering his gaze, he saw his goal. About forty feet from where he stood was the point where the old main sluice left the river, running toward the clock tower and into its tunnel.

After one last look at the clock tower building to make sure there were no guards about, Victor left the building he was in and hurried over to the sluice. He kept as low to the ground as possible, knowing he was at his most vulnerable.

When he got to the sluice he quickly went to the steep steps just behind the sluice gates. With no hesitation, he made his way down the steps, hugging the granite wall to stay as out of sight as possible. Reaching the floor, he was pleased to see that he could only make out a portion of the clock tower. That meant no one at the ground level could spot him.

Wasting no time, Victor walked directly to the two rusted metal gates that held back the water in the millpond. There was a slight amount of leakage; a small stream dribbled along the floor of the sluice. Otherwise, the old gates were watertight.

Bending down, Victor carefully laid the briefcase on the floor of the sluice. With equal care, he unsnapped the latches and raised the lid. The apparatus had survived the trip. Now he just had to set it to blow.

Too little time would be a disaster; but so would too much. Surprise was his main advantage. But there was no good way to guess how much time he'd need for his next task. Finally, and a bit arbitrarily, he settled on thirty minutes. As gently as possibly, Victor opened the face of the laboratory timing device. On his hands and knees, he shielded the flashlight with his body and turned it on. In the spare light, he moved the minute hand of the timer.

Victor killed the light and carefully closed the briefcase. Taking a deep breath, he carried it to the sluice gate and wedged it between the gate on the left and the steel rod that supported it. A single rusty bolt kept the steel rod in place. Victor felt that this bolt was the Achilles' heel of the mechanism; he pushed the briefcase as close to the bolt as he could. Then he headed up the steep granite steps.

Peering over the lip of the sluice, Victor looked for signs of life in the darkened clock tower building, but all was quiet. Keeping his head down low, he scampered back to the nearby building and descended into the tunnel system. He groped back to the cafeteria, already wishing he had given himself more than thirty minutes.

Once out in the open air, Victor ran toward the river, slowing as the clock tower came into view. In case someone was on watch, he wanted to appear calm in his approach, not anxious or stealthy.

Completely winded, Victor arrived at the front steps. He hesitated for a moment to catch his breath, but a glance at his watch horrified him. He only had sixteen minutes left. "My God," he whispered as he rushed inside.

Victor ran to the trapdoor and rapped on it three times. When no one came to open it, he rapped again with more force. Still no answer. Bending down, he felt around the floor for the metal rod he'd used on his last nighttime visit, but before he could find it, the trapdoor opened and light flooded up from below. One of Martinez's people was there.

Victor hopped down the stairs.

"Where's VJ?" he asked, trying to sound as calm as possible.

The guard pointed to the gestation room. Victor started in that direction, but VJ pushed the door open before he got there.

"Father?" VJ said with surprise. "I didn't expect you until tomorrow."

"Couldn't stay away," Victor said with a laugh. "I

finished up what I had to get done. Now it's your mother's turn. She has some patients who need her. She hasn't made her hospital rounds."

Victor's eyes wandered away from VJ and once again surveyed the room. What he needed to decide was where he should be at zero hour. He thought he'd have to be as close to the stairs as possible. The instrument that was the closest was the giant gas chromatography unit, and Victor decided that he'd allow it to occupy his attention when the time came.

Directly in the middle of the wall facing the river was the opening of the sluice with its makeshift hatch constructed of rough-hewn timbers. Victor made a mental calculation of the force that would hit that door when the sluice gate blew and the water rushed in. The preceding concussion wave would be like an explosion, and combined with the force of the water, it could loosen the foundation and topple the whole building. Victor figured there would be an approximate twenty-second delay from the explosion to the moment the tsunami struck.

"I think it might be too soon to let Marsha leave," VJ said. "And it would be awkward for Jorge to be constantly with her." VJ paused as his sharp eyes regarded his father. "Where is Jorge?"

"Topside," Victor said with a shiver of fear. VJ missed nothing. "He saw me down and stayed up there to smoke."

VJ glanced over at the two guards, who were reading magazines. "Juan! Go up and tell Jorge to come down here."

Victor swallowed uneasily. His throat was parched. "Marsha will not be a problem. I guarantee it."

"She hasn't changed her opinion," VJ said. "I've had

Mary Millman try talking with her, but her obstinate moralistic stance is unshakable. I'm afraid she'll make trouble."

Victor sneaked a look at his watch. Nine minutes! He should have allowed himself more time. "But Marsha is a realist," he blurted. "She's stubborn. That's nothing new to either of us. And, you'll have me. She wouldn't try anything knowing you had me here. Besides, she wouldn't know what to do even if she was tempted to do something."

"You're nervous," VJ said.

"Of course I'm nervous," Victor snapped. "Anybody would be nervous under the circumstances." He tried to smile and appear more at ease. "Mainly, I'm excited—about your accomplishments. I'd like to see that list of growth factors for the artificial womb tonight."

"I'd be delighted to show it to you," VJ admitted.

Victor walked over and opened the door to the living quarters. "Well, that's encouraging," he said, looking at VJ. "You don't feel you have to lock her in anymore. I'd say that was progress."

VJ rolled his eyes.

Victor hurriedly went into the smaller room where Marsha and Mary were sitting.

"Victor, look who's here," Marsha said, gesturing toward Mary.

"We've already met," Victor said, nodding at Mary.

VJ was standing in the doorway with a grin on his face.

"Not every kid has three legitimate biological parents," Victor said, attempting to ease the tension. He glanced at his watch: only six minutes to go.

"Mary has told me some interesting things about the

new lab," Marsha said with subtle sarcasm that only Victor could appreciate.

"Wonderful," said Victor, "That's wonderful. But, Marsha, it's your turn to leave. You have dozens of patients who are desperate for your attention. Jean is frantic. She's called me three times. Now that I've handled my pressing problems, it's your turn to go."

Marsha eyed VJ, then looked at Victor. "I thought that you were going to take care of things," she said with irritation. "Valerie Maddox can handle any emergencies. I think it's more important for you to do what you have to do."

Victor had to get her out of there. Why wouldn't she just leave? Did she really not trust him? Did she really think he was just going to let this go on? Sadly, Victor realized that for the past few years he hadn't given her much reason to expect better from him. Yet a solution was coming, and it was only a few frightening moments away.

"Marsha, I want you to go do your hospital rounds. Now!"

But Marsha wouldn't budge.

"I think she likes it here!" VJ joked. Then one of the security men called him from the main part of the lab and he left.

Half-crazed with mounting anxiety, Victor leaned over to Marsha and, forgetting Mary, hissed: "You have to get out of here this instant. Trust me."

Marsha looked in his eyes. Victor nodded. "Please!" he moaned. "Get out of here!"

"Is something going to happen?" Marsha asked him.

"Yes, for chrissake!" Victor forcibly whispered.

"What's going to happen?" Mary said nervously, looking back and forth between the Franks.

"What about you?" Marsha questioned, ignoring Mary.

"Don't worry about me," Victor snapped.

"You're not going to do something foolish?" Marsha asked.

Victor slapped his hands over his eyes. The tension was becoming unbearable. His watch said less than three minutes.

VJ reappeared at the doorway. "Jorge is not upstairs," he said to Victor.

Mary turned to VJ. "Something is going to happen!" she cried.

"What?" VJ demanded.

"He's doing something," Mary said anxiously. "He's got something planned."

Victor looked at his watch: two minutes.

VJ called over his shoulder for Security, then grabbed Victor's arm. Shaking him, he demanded, "What have you done?"

Victor lost control. The tension was too much and fear overflowed into emotion, bringing a sudden gush of tears. For a moment he couldn't talk. He knew that he had utterly failed. He'd not been up to the challenge.

"What have you done?" VJ repeated as he shouted into Victor's face, shaking him again. Victor did not resist.

"We all have to get out of the lab," Victor managed through his tears.

"Why?" VJ questioned.

"Because the sluice is going to open," Victor wailed.

There was a pause as VJ's mind processed this sudden information.

"When?" VJ demanded, shaking his father again.

Victor looked at his watch. There was less than a minute. "Now!" he said.

VJ's eyes blazed at his father. "I counted on you," he said with burning hatred. "I thought you were a true scientist. Well, now you are history."

Victor leaped up, knocking VJ to the side, where he tripped on the leg of a chair. Victor grabbed Marsha's wrist and yanked her to her feet. He ran her through the living quarters and out into the main lab.

VJ had regained his feet instantly and followed his parents, screaming for the security men to stop them.

From their bench it was easy for the two security men to catch Victor, grabbing him by both arms. Victor managed to give Marsha a push up the stairs. She ran partway up, then turned back to the room.

"Go!" Victor shouted at her. Then, to the two guards he urgently said, "This whole lab is about to disintegrate in seconds. Trust me."

Looking at Victor's face, the guards believed him. They let go of him and fled up the stairs, passing Marsha.

"Wait!" VJ cried from the middle of the lab floor. But the stampede had started. Even Mary brushed by him in her haste to get to the stairs.

Marsha got out, with Mary following on her heels.

VJ's eyes blazed at his father. "I counted on you," he raged. "I trusted you. I thought you were a man of science. I wanted to be like you. Guards!" he shouted. "Guards!" But the guards had fled along with the women.

VJ whirled around, looking at the main lab. Then he looked over at the gestational room.

Just then, the muffled roar of an explosion rocked the entire basement. A sound like thunder began to

build and vibrate the room. VJ sensed what was coming and started to run for the stairs, but Victor reached
out and grabbed him.

"What are you doing?" VJ cried. "Let me go. We've
got to get out of here."

"No," Victor said over the din. "No, we don't."

VJ struggled, but Victor's hold was firm. Wryly, he
realized for all his son's vast mental powers, he still
had the body—and strength—of a ten-year-old.

VJ squirmed and tried to kick, but Victor hooked his
free hand behind VJ's knees and swept the boy off his
feet.

"Help!" VJ cried. "Security!" he cried, but his voice
was lost in a low rumbling noise that steadily increased, rattling the laboratory glassware. It was like
the beginnings of an earthquake.

Victor stepped over to the crude door covering the
opening of the sluice tunnel. He stopped five feet from
it. He looked down into his son's unblinking ice-blue
eyes which stared back defiantly.

"I'm sorry, VJ." But the apology was not for what he
was doing that minute. For that he was not sorry. But
Victor felt he owed his son an apology for the experiment he'd carried out in a lab a little over ten years
ago. The experiment that had yielded his brilliant but
conscienceless son. "Good-bye, Isaac."

At that moment, one hundred tons of incompressi-
ble water burst through the sluice opening. The old
paddle wheel in the center of the room turned madly,
cranking the old rusted gears and rods for the first
time in years and, for a brief moment, the giant clock
in the top of the tower chimed haphazardly. But the
undirected and uncontrolled water quickly pulverized
everything in its path, undermining even the granite

foundation blocks within minutes. Several of the larger blocks shifted, and the beams supporting the first floor began to fall through to the basement. Ten minutes after the explosion, the clock tower itself began to wobble and then, seemingly in slow motion, it crumbled. In the end, all that was left of the building and secret basement lab was a soggy mass of rubble.

# Epilogue

*One Year Later*

"You have one more patient," Jean said, poking her head through the door, "then you're free."

"It's an add-on?" Marsha asked, slightly perturbed. She had planned on being free by four. With another patient she wouldn't be out until five. Under normal circumstances she wouldn't have cared, but today she was supposed to meet Joe Arnold, David's old history teacher, at six o'clock. He was taking her to the pet shop in the mall to pick up that golden retriever puppy he'd persuaded her to get. "It'll do you good," he told her. "Pet therapy. I'm telling you, dogs could put you psychiatrists out of business."

A few days after he'd read of the tragedy in the papers, he'd called Marsha to say how sorry he was and that he'd always regretted not contacting her to express his condolences after David's death. Gradually, the two were becoming friends. Joe seemed determined to break her willful isolation.

"The woman was insistent," Jean said. "If I didn't

360

squeeze her in today, we couldn't have seen her for a week. She says it's an emergency."

"Emergency!" Marsha grumbled. True psychiatric emergencies were luckily few and far between. "Okay," she said with a sigh.

"You're a dear," Jean said. She pulled the door shut.

Marsha went around her desk and sat down. She dictated her last session. When she was through, she whirled her chair around and gazed out the large picture window at the scenic landscape. Spring was coming. The grass had become a more vibrant green than its pale winter hue. The crocuses would be up soon. A few buds were already on the trees.

Marsha took a deep breath. She'd come a long way. It was just a little over a year now since that fateful night when she'd lost her husband and second son in what had been deemed a freak accident. The newspapers had even carried a picture of the rusty bolt that had apparently given way on an old sluice gate when the Merrimack had been at its spring thaw heights. Marsha had never tried to contradict the story, preferring the nightmare to end with a seemingly accidental tragedy. It was so much simpler than the truth.

Dealing with her grief had been exceedingly difficult. She'd sold the big house that she and Victor had shared, as well as her stock in Chimera. With some of the profits from these sales, she had bought herself a charming house on an ocean inlet in Ipswich. It was only a short walk to the beach with its glorious sand dunes. She'd spent many a weekend alone on the beach in pensive seclusion with no sounds to trouble her save the waves and an occasional squawk of a sea gull. Marsha had found solace in nature ever since she was a little girl.

Neither Victor's nor VJ's body had been recovered. Evidently the tremendous force of the rushing water had washed them God knows where. But the fact there were no bodies made Marsha's adjustment all the more difficult, though not for the reasons most psychiatrists would suspect. Jean had gently suggested to Marsha that she go in for some therapy herself, but Marsha resisted this encouragement. How could she explain that by not finding their remains, she was left with the uncomfortable sense that the horrid episode was not over yet. No remains of the four fetuses had been found either, not that anyone had known to look for them. But, for months after, Marsha had had disturbing nightmares in which she would come across a finger or a limb on the beach where she walked.

Marsha's biggest savior had been her work. After the initial shock and grief had abated, she'd really thrown herself into it, even volunteering for extra hours in various community organizations. And Valerie Maddox had also been of tremendous help, often staying with Marsha for weekends at Marsha's new beach house. Marsha knew she was indebted to the woman.

Marsha swung back to her desk. It was just about four o'clock. Time to see the last patient and then get to the pet store. Marsha buzzed Jean to indicate she was ready. Getting to her feet, she went to the door. Taking the new chart Jean handed her, Marsha caught sight of a woman who was about forty-five years old. She smiled at Marsha and Marsha smiled back. Marsha gestured for the woman to come into her office.

Turning around, Marsha left the door ajar and walked over to the chair she always used for her sessions. Next to it was a small table with a box of tissues for patients who couldn't contain their emotions. Two other chairs faced hers.

Hearing the woman enter the office, Marsha turned to greet her. The woman wasn't alone. A thin girl in her teens who looked sallow and drawn followed in behind her. The girl's sandy blond hair was stringy and badly in need of a wash. In her arms was a blond baby who looked to be about eighteen months old. The baby was clutching a magazine.

Marsha wondered who the patient was. Whichever one it was, she'd have to insist the other leave. For the moment, all she said was, "Please sit down." Marsha decided to let them present their reasons for coming. Over the years, she'd found that this technique yielded more information than any question-and-answer session could.

The woman held the child while the girl sat down in one of the chairs facing Marsha, then settled him in the girl's lap. He seemed quite preoccupied with the magazine's illustrations. Marsha casually wondered why they'd brought the child along. Surely it couldn't be that difficult to get a baby-sitter.

Marsha felt that the young girl was not in the best physical health. Her frail frame and extremely pale complexion indicated depression if not malnutrition.

"I'm Josephine Steinburger and this is my daughter, Judith," the woman began. "Thank you for seeing us. We're pretty desperate."

Marsha nodded encouragingly.

Mrs. Steinburger leaned forward confidentially, but spoke loudly enough for Judith to hear. "My daughter here is not too swift, if you know what I mean. She's been in a lot of trouble for a long time. Drugs, running away from home, fighting with her brother, no-good friends, those kinds of things."

Marsha nodded again. She looked at the daughter to see how she responded to this criticism, but the girl only stared blankly ahead.

"These kids are into everything these days," Josephine continued. "You know, sex and all that. What a difference when I was young. I didn't know what sex was until I was too old to enjoy it, you know what I mean?"

Marsha nodded again. She hoped the daughter would participate, but she remained silent. Marsha wondered if she might be on drugs right then.

"Anyway," Josephine continued, "Judith here tells me she never had sex, so obviously I was surprised when she delivered this little bundle of joy about a year and a half ago." She laughed sarcastically.

Marsha wasn't surprised. Of all the defense mechanisms, denial was the most common. A lot of teenagers initially tried to deny sexual contact even when the evidence was overwhelming.

"Judith says that the father was a young boy who gave her money to put his little tube in her," Josephine said, rolling her eyes for Marsha's benefit. "I've heard it called a lot of things but never a little tube. Anyway—"

Marsha rarely interrupted the people who came to see her, but in this case, the girl in question wasn't getting a word in. "Perhaps it would be better if the patient told me her story in her own words."

"What do you mean, her words?" Josephine asked, her brow furrowing in confusion.

"Exactly what I said," Marsha said. "I think the patient should tell the story, or at least participate."

Josephine laughed heartily, then got herself under control. "Sorry, it struck a funny bone. Judith is fine. She's even gotten a little more responsible now that she's a mother. It's the kid who's messed up. He's the patient."

"Oh, of course," said Marsha, somewhat baffled. She'd treated children before, but never so young.

"The kid is a terror," Josephine went on. "We can't control him."

Marsha had to get her to be more specific. Plenty of parents could call their toddlers terrors. She needed more specific symptoms. "In what way is he a problem?" she asked.

"Ah!" Josephine intoned. "You name it, he does it. I'm telling you, he's enough to drive you to drink." She turned to the child. "Look at the lady, Jason."

But Jason was absorbed in his magazine.

"Jason!" Josephine called. She reached across and yanked the magazine out of the infant's hands and tossed it on Marsha's desk. It was then that Marsha noticed it was the latest issue of the *Journal of Cell Biology*.

"The kid can already read better than his mother. Now he's asking for a chemistry set."

Marsha felt a jolt of fear as it grabbed her by the throat. Slowly she raised her eyes.

"Frankly, I'm afraid to get the kid a chemistry set at age one and a half," Josephine continued. "It ain't normal. He'll probably blow the whole house up."

Marsha looked at the boy in Judith's lap. The child

365

returned her stare with his own piercing, ice-blue eyes. There was an air of intelligence about him that far outstripped his cherubic baby face. Marsha was taken back in time. This boy was the spitting image of VJ at the same age.

Marsha knew instantly what was before her: the final zygote. The one VJ said he'd wasted on the implantation study. A child created from her own sixth ovum.

Marsha couldn't move. A small cry escaped her as she realized the chilling truth: the nightmare wasn't over.

Josephine got to her feet and stepped over to Marsha. "Dr. Frank?" she asked with some alarm. "Are you all right?"

"I . . . I'm fine," Marsha said feebly. "I'm sorry. Really, I'm okay." She couldn't take her eyes off the child.

"So like I was saying," continued Josephine, "this kid's beyond all of us. Why, just the other day—"

Marsha cut her off. Doing her best to keep a quiver out of her voice, she said, "Mrs. Steinburger, we'll have to set up an appointment for Jason himself. I really think it would be best if I saw him privately. But it has to be another day."

"Well, whatever," sighed Josephine. "You're the doctor. You're the one to know. I suppose we can wait a few days. I just hope you can help us."

Once they had gone, Marsha closed the door behind them and leaned heavily against it. She sighed and said aloud, "I hope so too."

She knew she had to do something about this child, this prodigy whose villainy might match or even surpass her son's. But what to do?

She picked up the phone to call Joe Arnold to say

she was running a little late. Just hearing his voice on the line helped calm her down.

"Well, I'm glad you're not trying to cancel on me, 'cause I'm not letting you off the hook." He laughed warmly. "I thought we might eat in tonight. Can't leave a dog alone his first night home. I hope you're up to braving my cooking. I make a mean chili. I'm working on it right now."

Marsha hoped she was up to braving quite a lot of things, starting with the truth. And of the people she felt closest to—Valerie, Joe, Jean—Joe might be the one to confide in, the one she could count on the most. "Chili sounds great," she told him. "And I'd just as soon eat in." It was on the tip of her tongue to tell him about Jason, but it would keep. She didn't want to say anything over the phone.

"Terrific. I was beginning to think I'd have to sign up as a patient to get to see you alone. Meet you at the pet shop at seven? I think they're open until eight."

"Seven will be fine. And, Joe . . . thanks."

She hung up the phone and got her coat.

Marsha drove to the mall, feeling better already just knowing she'd soon be telling someone the true story behind Victor's and VJ's deaths. She'd bottled the whole thing up for so long. It would be a relief to finally get it off her chest. She felt all the luckier for having Joe to talk to. Ever since he'd come into her life, he'd been a real godsend.

She drove into the mall parking lot and picked a spot near the entrance closest to the pet shop and turned the engine off. Gripping the steering wheel, she broke into soft sobs. Somehow, she would have to face this last demon-child, and with Joe's help, end forever the nightmare her husband had begun.